BENEATH MACKEREL SKIES

Elizabeth Egerton Wilder

Red Dobie
P R E S S

Exton, Pennsylvania

First Edition
Library of Congress Control Number: 2014946274
CreateSpace Independent Publishing Platform
North Charleston, South Carolina
ISBN: 0989387135
ISBN 978-0-9893871-3-2

Published by:
Red Dobie Press
an imprint of Alexemi Publishing
P.O. Box 1266
Exton, PA 19341

www.AlexemiPublishing.com
Cover Design by Bradley Wind, www.bradleywind.com

Please visit the author's website: www.eewilder.com

Other novels by the author include: *The Spruce Gum Box* and *Granite
Hearts*

Printed in the United States of America

Beneath Mackerel Skies, the story of a family,
is dedicated to my family.

ACKNOWLEDGEMENTS

I thank my husband Cal, and children Rob, Scott, and Cheryl for their continued support that held up my resolve to complete the story of the Ryan family as the final novel of the trilogy following *The Spruce Gum Box* and *Granite Hearts*.

Preparing for the addition of the town of Searsport to the "Maine at Heart" trilogy, my husband and I spent several days walking the waterfront of the small seaport town. We explored a cemetery, which even many of the townspeople did not know existed, but was pointed out to us by the owners of the Yardarm Motel on Route One, as it was tucked in the woods behind their establishment. It was on their land that we found the remains of the memorial tree planted for President Abraham Lincoln after his assassination. They helped us visualize the scene from their home, a stately ship builder's homestead, that once had a clear view of Searsport Harbor during its heyday of seventeen yards, where two hundred ships were built with the support of myriad small marine businesses. I appreciate their eye-opening input.

Thank you to the researchers at the Stephen Phillips Memorial Library found on the grounds of the Penobscot Marine Museum. I was allowed to view archived records including a scrapbook of a Captain's wife who sailed to China on his Searsport-built schooner. Her collection of ephemera from many ports during the 1800's was a trigger for my imagination. At that time, ten percent of all the nation's deep sea captains lived in Searsport.

My appreciation goes to the docents at the museum for their eagerness to tell their tales of homes and residents of the era. When I spotted an oil painting in the dining room of a sea captain's home, the guide took the time to field my questions about the scene as it depicted a clear view down the hill to the harbor. She then confirmed that the dirt carriage road running across the lower part of the painting became what is now Route One. It became my route from the Fort Knox area in Prospect Ferry, to Stockton, then to Searsport.

That same guide spent time with me walking around the grounds and pointed out that the Methodist Church was the only obstruction of the view down Church St. to the harbor so builders could keep their eyes on the shipyards. Thus the image of the harbor became clearer to me despite the current one-hundred-fifty-year growth of foliage.

Driving north on Route One in Maine, I recommend a visit to the Penobscot Maritime Museum in Searsport, especially if there is an interest in maritime history and/or touring the historic houses of the era that still stand as they stood.

Thank you to my beta and final readers for their edits and recommendations: Jennifer Wilder, Rob Wilder, Sabrina Wilder, Sara Carter, Cheryl Krass, and Randy Arner.

Thank you to my cover designer Bradley Wind, for finding just the right photo to manipulate into my vision of an angry mackerel sky.

Once again, my heartfelt thanks to my daughter Cheryl Krass, for not only her keen edits, but also for her guidance through the maze of indie publishing. Her knowledge astounds me as she assists authors towards the fruition of their dreams through her Alexemi Publishing, www. AlexemiPublishing.com.

FAMILY TREE—THE MAINE AT HEART TRILOGY 1825–1869

THE SPRUCE GUM BOX AND GRANITE HEARTS

Aroostook River 1825 - 1844

Cateline Croteau –Raised by her Micmac tribal leader grandfather and grandmother in New Brunswick, Canada. Married at age 17 to Pierre Croteau, a fur trader in the Territory of Maine. Known as Nuga, short for nou' gou' mitj (grandmother), she is the wise spiritual leader of her Micmac family along the Aroostook River. As grandmother of Jacob and Hanna, she raised them when their mother died at the birth of Hanna.

Jacob Buck–Known to the young in their settlement as Uncle Jacob. He becomes a strong leader (sagamore) who devotes his life to the care of his tribal family.

Frank Ryan–Marries Hanna. They raise three boys – Peter, Joe and Sean (who Uncle Jacob calls Trouble).

Jedediah Smythe–English walking boss in the forests of the Territory of Maine. He turns to Jacob for help when forced into the wilderness with his infant son Ben.

Ben Smythe–He marries his childhood sweetheart Nettie Thorpe. They have two children, JJ and Kate.

Penobscot River 1844-1865

Sean and Gert Ryan –Sean settles in Prospect Ferry with his bride to find work on the construction of Fort Knox. They have five children – Mike, Dan, Joey, Jack and little Comfort (Cece) who was born after her two big brothers went to war.
  Nana Hodge–Neighbor and benefactor of the Ryans who becomes a surrogate grandmother to the Ryan children.

Indian Island

Tomah–A leader in the Penobscot Indian Nation, he is married to Adele. They have one daughter, Annie.
  Joe and Annie Ryan–Joe and Annie married and have two children. Holly and Frankie are cousins to the Sean Ryan children.
Historical Characters
Joshua Chamberlain–Leader of the Maine 20th Voluntary Infantry including the Ryan boys and JJ.
Hannibal Hamlin–President Lincoln's first Vice President.
Molly Molasses–Powerful spiritual presence within the Penobscot Nation.

Beneath Mackerel Skies

1868–1869 The story continues.

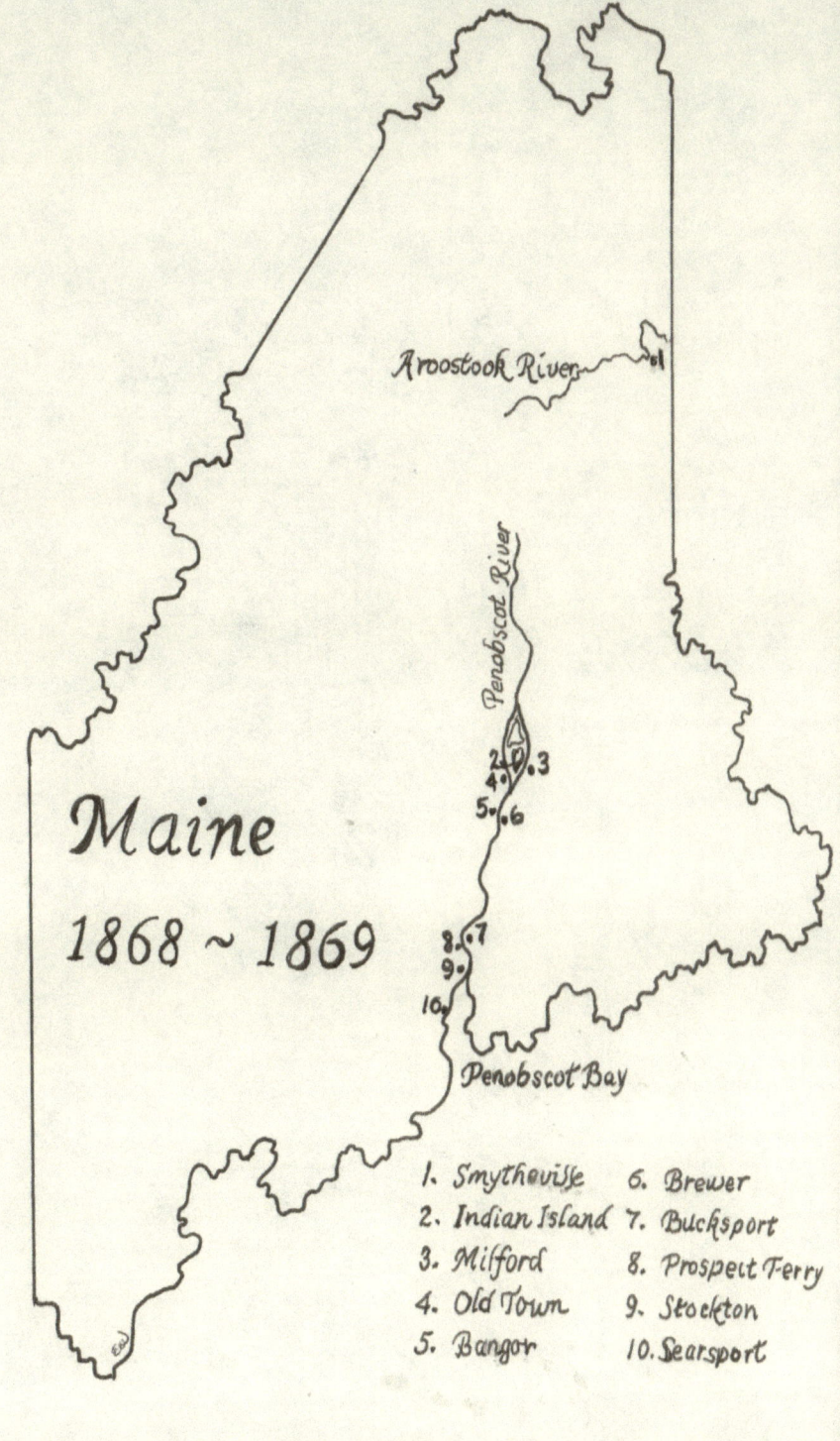

Aroostook River

Penobscot River

Maine

1868 ~ 1869

2. 1. .3
4. .
5. .6

8. .7
9.
10.

Penobscot Bay

1. Smytheville   6. Brewer
2. Indian Island 7. Bucksport
3. Milford   8. Prospect Ferry
4. Old Town   9. Stockton
5. Bangor   10. Searsport

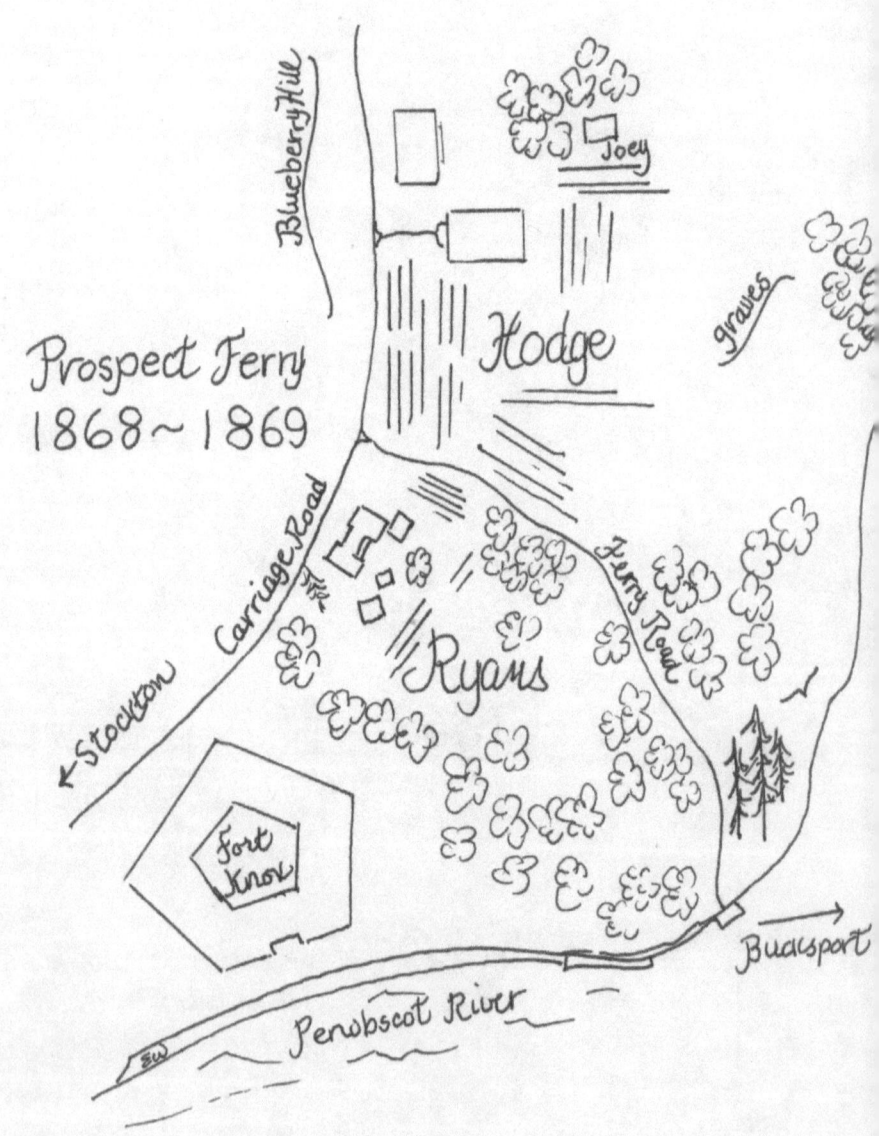

Prospect Ferry
1868~1869

I

Decoration Day

May 30, 1868

In a large nest atop an old forest pine, a bald eagle carefully rolled her clutch of three eggs to protect the growing embryos from sticking to the inside of the shell. Her mate scanned the surrounding terrain, his keen eyesight able to pick up any danger to his hatching eaglets. From his vantage, the Penobscot River ran like a shimmering artery flowing from the heart of the shipping docks in Bangor to the bay and sea beyond. Above the hustle and bustle of the city, dams sliced the river like great carving knives to provide power to saw mills. Just beyond, islands of the Penobscot Indian Reservation dotted the river, unaltered for generations. Hardly a twig had changed since Henry David Thoreau visited on his way into the Maine woods with his Penobscot guide Joe Polis, twenty years prior.

The motion that caught the large bird's attention was a small group of people laying lilac branches at grave markers on the slope by the river. The Ryan family and neighbor Nana Hodge were honoring the wishes of President Abraham Lincoln to decorate the graves of fallen soldiers from the Civil

War. This year, General Logan, commander and chief of the Grand Army of the Republic, had designated the date of May 30 for the tribute. Once the white and lilac blossoms were set, the group made their way down the Ferry Road to the river landing.

The Ryan twins, Joey and Jack were taking a steamer to Searsport for a schooner cruise to the Gulf of Maine. Nana Hodge still had a strong circle of friends in the ship-building community and managed to get the brothers aboard the ship for her maiden trip. Nana spent many years living onboard with Captain Hodge as he sailed up and down the east coast of America. Whenever they went up the Penobscot River to deliver cargo to Bangor, he always thought the land on the curve just past Verona Island was a little piece of heaven. Suddenly one day, he lowered the sails to leave the sea and bought the acreage where he and Nana developed the splendid Hodge Farm.

Standing on the landing, the brothers took turns looking upstream so they could flag down the Boston steamer while their father Sean went back to his office just down the river path to Fort Knox. Their mother Gert, Joey's wife Peg, and Nana enjoyed the fresh breeze making tiny ripples across the water while five-year-old Cece stood fascinated by the activity at the top of the pine above them.

The night before, a great horned owl had tried to get at the incubating eggs but was fought off by the protective father. The battle was difficult for the eagle, leaving one of his feathers lying precariously on the lip of the nest. This morning, when the great bald eagle stretched his wings to preen, the quill floated slowly towards Ferry Road. Cece watched as it dropped softly at her feet. She knew it should be taken to the leaders at Indian Island but secretly wrapped it in the folds of the handkerchief doll her big brother Dan brought home from the Civil War. She looked up at the eagle and whispered, "I'll see your feather is honored one day."

"Comfort, did you say something?"

"No Mumma. I was just telling Lacey there are three eggs in the nest."

Nana smiled with a twinkle in her eye. "Tell me Cece, just how do you know that?"

"I not know. There just is." The little girl stuffed her doll carefully in the sash around her waist.

"Here it comes Ma." Jack waved to the pilot and the boat began to slip over to the dock.

Joey gave Peg a quick kiss on her cheek and he and Jack jumped aboard the steamer as it slid slowly by.

Cece shouted, "I want to go too. I want to see the puffins."

Jack turned back. "Cece! You know you're too small to go on an ocean schooner. You'd slip through the railing and be carried away by a whale. I promise I'll tell you all about them."

And with that the twins were off to the docks of Searsport to begin their adventure.

The two-mast schooner rode the swells of Penobscot Bay heading for the Gulf of Maine to see the nesting birds near Matinicus Island, then back to port to inspect the new ship rigging. Matinicus was named for the Abenaki Indian word meaning "far out island" and so it was. Joey and Jack had never been that far off shore and soon realized why Nana and the Captain loved the Maine coast. The shoreline had been cleared of trees by farmers or harvested by lumbermen creating a strip of spring green punctuated by small villages, farmhouses, rocky cliffs and an occasional sparkling inlet. From the open seas it looked like an emerald green ribbon embellished by gems. As they approached the island the sea turned angry forcing the captain to turn back early to the safety of the port.

Joey stood at the rail enjoying the rush of growing swells with an occasional cold spray. He was fascinated by the coordination of the crew while turning the schooner back towards the shelter of Searsport Harbor. Jack on the other hand was leaning over the rail wishing he really could slip through and be carried away by a whale. He was tossing every bit of his mother's wonderful food into the sea. Doubled over in agony, he lost things he never knew he'd eaten.

"Dear God. Make it stop." Jack stood straight, took in a deep breath, wrapped his arms around his stomach, groaned in agony, bent over the rail and continued to retch. "I swear that damn dolphin is laughing at me."

Joey took a look in the rolling sea and agreed with his brother. "He's probably following us to see if you have anything interesting left in your belly."

Jack made his way across the deck to the bench along the cabin wall. "It's not funny."

"We've always been told we look like two peas in a pod but you are the only one who looks green."

"Cut it out." Jack stood and stumbled towards his identical sibling as if to take a swing but lurched on by to once more hug the rail. Joey grabbed hold of the back of his brother's pants just in case he leaned too far.

One of the crewmen came over. "Everything all right here?"

"My brother is just enjoying his introduction to sea sickness," Joey chuckled.

"The seas churned up faster than predicted and if you are so inclined, it wouldn't take long to churn up your stomach too. Sorry." The crewman offered his hand to Joey. "My name is Tim. If there is anything I can do, just holler."

Jack made the effort to pull himself upright. "Can you get this torturous ride over as fast as possible?"

Tim took one look at Jack, then back at Joey. "There are two of you! I bet when your complexions match, folks find it hard to tell you apart."

Joey laughed. "It's easy once we open our mouths. You're apt to find his foot in his."

"I'll get you for ..." Jack started to shout but was cut off when he slapped a hand over his mouth and bent back over the rail.

"I'm also a twin but you would be able to tell us apart at one look." Tim added, "Yes, indeed. You would have no problem figuring us out."

"Do you live in the Searsport area? I don't think I've seen you there."

"We relocated recently from England and are staying with our aunt just off the center of Searsport." Tim continued, "I won't be there often. I'll be working as a second mate on this craft servicing the east coast with plans to become captain one day soon."

Joey looked surprised. "You seem young for so much responsibility."

"I'm twenty-two and started sailing as a cabin boy for my father when I was eleven years old. We carried goods between London, Spain, France and Denmark so I am well trained in the ways of the sea and shipping." Tim appeared a little put out that his skills were doubted.

Jack looked a bit more interested in the conversation and sat on a box with his mop of curly red hair resting on the highly polished wood rail. What he really wanted to do was curl up in a ball underneath the bench by the cabin and never come out.

Joey slapped Tim on the back. "Sounds like you've done the work to reach for your dream. Good luck."

Tim relaxed, "Thank you."

"Years ago, when Jack and I visited Searsport, we would marvel at the big houses where the ship builders and captains lived. I would brag that someday I was going to be a famous shipbuilder and my brother would tell everyone he was going to be a captain of one of my ships and sail it to China." A voice then was heard from the other side of the deck, "Imagine, a seasick sea captain. Now wouldn't that be something. Yes something indeed."

That caught Jack's attention. He forced his eyes open even though he could once again see the rolling waves. Walking towards him was a tall young woman with long black curly hair that sparkled in the sunlight. He blinked to make sure he wasn't hallucinating. Then his stomach started to roll as violently as the sea again and he just made it to the railing to once again look down at the laughing dolphin.

He could hear the vision with the long tresses teasing, "Can you imagine a seasick ship captain? Captain Seasick, what are your orders, sir?"

He thought, *I will strangle her with my bare hands if she doesn't stop.*

Tim took her by the arm. "Behave yourself."

"It just struck me funny, Timmy."

Tim looked at Joey and rolled his eyes. "I'd like you to meet my twin sister, Marisol."

Joey laughed out loud. "You are right. One could tell right away which twin was which."

Jack took a deep breath. "Marisol. Is that a fancy parasol? Do you have bangles and beads stitched around the hem of your skirt?"

"Listen to him Timmy. Captain Seasick is trying to be funny. How quaint. And, by the way, I love my name. It is quite special, yes indeed."

Jack mocked, "Special, yes indeed."

Marisol stamped her dainty foot. "Toss the damn fool overboard, Timmy. He can swim back with the rest of the strange sea creatures."

"My," said Jack, "the one with the sweet mouth spits out vile words. Are you practicing to become a fish wife on the Billingsgate docks of London?"

Joey quickly moved between his ghostly brother and Tim. I think we should start over. He offered his hand to the young lady. "It is very nice to meet you, Marisol. That is an unusual but quite lovely name."

She replied with a slight blush. "Thank you, Joey. My father gave it to me."

Jack took this break in the tension to slip over to the bench and curled up in the fetal position.

Tim continued his sister's thoughts. "Father loved sailing our route but his favorite location was Spain. He would stand on deck and take such pleasure watching the sun light dance upon the sea. The water, azure and rich beneath a never-ending blue sky, made a perfect canvas for splashes of gold. He would put his arm around my shoulders and tell me I would never find more beauty in the finest art museum."

As she listened, Marisol quietly wiped a tear with a handkerchief edged with delicate tatting.

"The story goes, so we've been told, when our father first held us he thought his daughter so beautiful that he called her Marisol." Tim smiled. "My mother would not hear of it until he explained that the baby reminded him of the beauty of the coast of Spain. The sea and sun in Spanish is called 'mar y sol'."

Joey was intrigued. "What a lovely story."

Marisol giggled. "See, Tim. There is another way to tell them apart. One is a gentleman."

Jack just shook his head and then thought it a bad idea as the scenery around him began to spin.

Tim walked away. "I need to help the crew. We're nearing the inner harbor and by the looks of it, just in time. There is a mackerel sky forming so we're going to have a change in the weather."

Joey laughed and looked at the bands of clouds overhead that were lining up to resemble fish scales. "Mackerel sky, mackerel sky; never long wet, never long dry. Nana has a ditty for all kinds of weather. Her husband, the sea captain, taught her well and she in turn would have us watch the clouds change while working in the fields."

Soon the deck hands navigated the schooner to the town dock to be secured by longshoremen.

Marisol smiled sweetly. "How often do you come to Searsport Joey? I live with my aunt just off Main Street and we would enjoy having you stop by for a cup of good English tea."

Jack pulled himself upright. "I don't think Joey's wife Peg would like that idea. She's had him on tight reins since grammar school."

Marisol sighed. "Isn't that the way? The nice ones are always taken."

Jack took a few zigzag steps toward Marisol to the amusement of all on deck.

Joey reached out a balancing hand. "You're walking all katawonkis. You must be totally empty by now so let me help you to the gangplank."

Marisol showed no pity. "He's so full of himself, he'll never be empty."

"Hey, enough is enough. Aunt Daphne is waiting for you with the surrey." Tim pointed at a wisp of a lady waving vigorously at the land end of the long dock. She looked like a good wind could carry her away.

Joey reached out and shook Tim's hand. Perhaps we'll meet again. We're the Ryan twins, Joey and Jack Ryan.

The handshake tightened. Tim put his other hand on Joey's shoulder and with a smile answered, "We're the Hodge twins, Timothy and Marisol Hodge"

II

I Not Know

The front door at the Ryan house flipped open with a bang startling Gert who was looking for a pan under the sideboard. She brought her head up so fast she made a bang of her own. "For heaven's sake, what in the world is going on?"

Joey looked a bit sheepish. "Sorry Ma."

"I actually saw stars for a moment." Gert blinked her eyes, trying to grasp what was going on. "Wait a minute. Why are you two coming in from the street side? Your sister has been sitting in the apple tree most of the afternoon watching for you on the Ferry Road. Did you miss your steamer? You're later than we thought."

"Whoa, Ma." Jack held tight to the sides of head as if it might fall off if he let go. "You're making me dizzy."

"Jack Ryan, you look like something the cat dragged in. What have you been up to?"

Joey grabbed his brother and sat him on the bench at the kitchen table. "You better sit down before you fall down."

Gert walked over holding a wet towel on her throbbing head. "Take this Jack. You seem to need it more than I." She looked in her son's blood shot eyes that made his complexion look ghastly white. "What in the world happened? I have a pot of stew simmering. Is your stomach empty?"

Jack just groaned.

Joey laughed out loud. "It's empty all right." Then he filled their mother in on all the details of their trip.

"I'll make you some weak tea and dry toast. In the meantime, go and lie on your bed. This too will pass John."

"You must really be sick brother. Ma only uses our given names when we are about to get a lecture for doing something wrong, or we are really under the weather. And you have certainly have been done in by the weather."

Gert snapped, "Joseph, that's enough."

Joey laughed, "See what I mean?"

Jack smiled for the first time since the schooner had begun to dip over the swells.

"I'll put him to bed." Joey brought his twin to his feet. "Would you ask Cece to run over to the house and tell Peg we're back and I'll be home soon?"

"I forgot about Comfort," said Gert. "She's been sitting in that tree most of the day afraid she'd miss you when you came off the river. I had to take her a biscuit and jam for lunch." Gert opened the back door and left to find Cece adding, "she'll let Peg know but be prepared for many questions."

"Remember how that old tree held all four of us boys for hours at a time? We made so many plans and decisions up in those limbs; some of which got us into a lot of trouble." Joey whispered as he helped his brother to his bedroom, "Sometimes I think the spirit of Mike sits in that tree now."

Jack shivered as he pulled his quilt up to his chin. "I'm freezing. Do you think that's the end of it?"

"It could be. Your body is reacting to a stressful day." Jack put an extra pillow behind Joey's head. "It's been a while since

I was in our bedroom. The ships and boats Ma painted on the walls are getting a bit faded. Don't you think it's about time you and big brother Dan put a new coat of paint on them?"

"No way. I love the boats on the walls. I just don't like boats on the water."

"This will warm you up." Gert brought in a steaming cup of tea and a toasted slab of her sourdough bread.

"Thank you, Ma."

The back door slammed shut. "Now what?" Gert went out to the kitchen to find Peg and Cece running in all flustered.

"What happened Mrs. Ryan? Cece told me the twins were very, very sick. Where's Joey?" Peg was still out of breath from running across the fields.

"Comfort, why did you tell Peg that Joey was in trouble?"

"I not know, Mama. I guess my ears got mixed up when you told me." Cece's eyes started to tear up. "What happened to them?"

"Yes," said Peg "what happened and where are they?"

Gert put her arm around Peg's shoulders, "They are in the back bedroom, Joey is fine, but Jack had a battle with seasickness and it won. He's really miserable."

"How did they get here? I've been watching the Bucksport landing all afternoon and no steamers stopped." Peg started to weep a bit from relief.

"They just walked in the front door."

Peg asked Cece, "Do you know how they got here?"

The little girl just shrugged her shoulders. "I not know. Can I go into the bedroom? Can I. Can I?"

Gert took her little face in her hands and looked straight in the eyes. "You may. But, no loud talking. That's something Jack doesn't need."

The little sister shushed with her finger over her mouth and then skipped over the wood floor to Joey and Dan's room.

"Quietly Comfort, quietly." Gert spoke with a stage whisper to which the little rascal walked on her tiptoes making Peg giggle.

Joey nearly tripped over his sister as he came out to the kitchen. "What's she up to? I wager it's something that Jack won't appreciate." He gave Peg a hug. "Hi, Sweets. We've had quite a day. Ma, you got any tea left? Perhaps very hot and very strong."

"The kettle I made for Jack should be brewed to your taste by now." Gert took three of her china tea cups off the shelf over the sideboard. "Sit for a minute so I can get this story straight to tell your father when he gets home." She put down a plate of fresh baked hermit cookies.

"You must learn how to make these Peg," Joey said as he reached for another treat only to get a whack on his hand from his wife with her spoon.

"I roasted a chicken for supper, so don't spoil your appetite."

Gert laughed, "I never thought of using a spoon across the knuckles. You taught me something."

"Now I need you to teach me how to bake these." Peg's look went solemn. "I wish I had paid more attention before I lost my mum. I learned young that you never know when your life can change forever. Guess that's why I panicked a bit when I heard Joey and Jack were sick."

"Sorry you had a scare, Sweets. There is nothing to worry about." Joey rubbed her shoulder.

"Why did you turn up out front when we were looking for you to come up river? I know your father has been watching from his office at the fort and he'll want answers when he comes up the path." Gert refilled the tea cups.

Joey took a couple more sips and explained. "When we finished the long walk off the town dock, Jack was done in.

I told him we had about twenty minutes before the next coastal steamer would be leaving for Bangor and it would be a couple hours later for the next one. Jack was adamant that he was not going to get on another boat, never mind crossing the river to get to Prospect Ferry from the wharf at Bucksport. I yanked him up to force the walk to the other side of the waterfront and he fought me all the way. Told him I wanted to be home sooner rather than later. In the middle of the scuffle a familiar voice shouted from between two of the workshops that crowded the busy area from the town to the water's edge where just about everything needed for shipbuilding and repair could be found. I strained my eyes and eventually saw Thomas waving from his wagon."

"What in the world was he doing down there? As Nana's farm foreman, he was supposed to start laying out planting chores today."

"She sent him to Searsport to pick up an order of rope needed for the barn and I was mighty happy to see him. He took one look at Jack and offered us a ride home. He and I had a great visit on the way up the coach road and actually did a lot of planning for the second planting now that the lower fields are freshly plowed. The first seedlings are up and doing well."

Gert felt badly about her assumptions. She should have known Thomas would have everything in order.

Joey put his cup on the sideboard and started for the door. "Gee, I almost forgot. Jack and I met another set of twins on our cruise. I had an interesting talk with them while we were waiting for Thomas to bring over the wagon. Tim helped me load Jack in the back between the coils of hemp."

Gert smiled. "Were they also two peas in a pod?"

"Well, they did look a lot alike but more like brother and sister."

This intrigued Peg. "I never knew twins could be different sexes. I wish I'd seen them."

"You'll get your chance soon. I invited them here for Sunday dinner next weekend. You don't mind, right Ma?"

"Did you think to check with me first? What if your father and I had plans of our own?"

Joey hugged his mother. "When have you and Pa ever gone off together on a Sunday? You're always working around the house or on your paintings while he spends most of Sunday working in the workshop on his granite pieces. It never changes."

Gert put her hands on her hips. "Well then, let me ask why you would bring total strangers here for Sunday dinner?"

"I did it for Nana. They are taking the first steamer Sunday so they can meet her and then we all can have the afternoon to visit."

Gert looked confused. "Now you have me curious."

"Me too," chimed in Peg.

"We had a nice talk on the dock. They recently came to Searsport from London and their name is Hodge."

Gert turned and put the cups in the dishpan to soak in the bubbles. "Have you any idea how many Hodge families there must be in England? Why would you do that?"

"How many young seamen from England have generations of captains in his family including a great uncle who disappeared many years ago. Whispers have it he went to America where he captained a coastal schooner."

"You don't think?"

"It's a possibility Ma and we shouldn't let it slip by. I just don't know whether we should prepare Nana or just surprise her."

"I'll talk it over with your father. My Lord, I have so much to do."

"I'll help Mrs. Ryan. We'll make a lovely meal." Peg was all aflutter.

Gert took her daughter-in-law's hands. "Peg, my dear, don't you think it is about time you stopped calling me Mrs. Ryan? The only Mrs. Ryan I know is Sean's mother and she lives a hundred miles from here on the shore of the Aroostook River."

Peg blushed. "I'm not sure I could."

"I'm not your mum, dear. I could never take her place but I'm sure she would not mind if you thought of me as Ma, after all you are my newest daughter."

Suddenly a command was heard from the back bedroom. "Hey, Ma! Come and get Miss 'I Not Know' out of here. She's driving me crazy."

Joey grabbed Peg's hand and pulled her quickly towards the back door. "We're out of here Ma. He sounds a lot stronger and quite cantankerous. Good luck."

Gert just sighed, gave the young couple a wave and closed the door behind them. "Comfort Claire, come out here and leave Jack alone."

The pouting tiny strawberry blonde came slowly, dragging her feet. Her treasured handkerchief doll draped over her shoulder. "Yes, Mama."

"What have you been up to Comfort? Why is Jack upset with you?"

"I not know. Maybe he is just plain grumpy."

"I heard that." Jack made his way into the kitchen looking like the loser in a rooster fight.

Cece imitated her mother's pose when she was displeased of hands on hips. "You promised you would tell me all about the puffins. Do they really have bright colors on their beaks? Did you see any babies? Did you get really close to them?"

"How many times do I have to tell you the ship did not get to the nesting place? I did not see the puffins!"

"But you promised!"

Jack tossed his hands in the air and filled a cold cup of water from the pitcher pump at the sink. "Ma, explain what sea sickness is to your stubborn daughter."

Gert checked the kettle of venison stew on the back of the wood stove. She had cut back a bit on the potatoes and carrots as the root cellar was getting lean. They had shared some of their stored vegetables with Joey and Peg when they moved into their own little house. "I'll do my best."

"While you are doing your best, how about teaching her the correct way to say 'I do not know'."

Gert shook her head. "I think you should get your head straight before your father comes home from the fort. We'll let the school master teach Comfort when she starts classes in September."

Just then Sean walked in the back door. He looked around at his frowning family in the kitchen where tension could be cut with the knife Gert was using to slice bread. "Jack, you look like the devil. Comfort, what's going on here?"

"I not know."

Jack walked over to his little sister and looked into her green-blue eyes. "Now listen. I–do–not–know!"

Cece looked at her father. "Papa, Jack not know too."

III

CAPTAIN TIMOTHY HODGE

"What a lovely early June day." Gert stretched her arms over head to shake out the final remnants of sleep. She was standing on the porch overlooking the Penobscot where river traffic had come to life like a giant creature slowly snaking its way towards Bangor. It would slowly change direction by evening so the greatest bulk of the monster would be crawling towards the bay and open ocean.

Sean stood at the kitchen door appreciating the silhouette of his wife's body through the light cotton nightdress. "It certainly is lovely from my angle."

Gert realized what the early slant of the morning sun was doing. She pulled the flowered garment close to her. "Married nearly 24 years, there's nothing you haven't seen before."

"My dear, your body is as much a feast for my eyes as it was on our wedding night when we started out on our journey. Remember the first time we saw our humble house?"

"How could I forget? I felt like walking the hundred miles back to the Aroostook Valley." Gert smiled. "We turned it into such a lovely home that you could not drag me away now."

"But I can drag you in so I don't share you with the jolly sailors gliding by. Do you always walk outside that way?"

"Well, hardly ever mid-winter." Gert enjoyed her little joke but Sean did not. He tossed her over his shoulder and walked back in the kitchen. He set her down and kissed her until she giggled.

Jack wandered out and covered his eyes with his hands. "That's not something I want to see first thing in the morning." After a week he was fully recovered from his nightmare with the laughing dolphin. "Ma, don't you think you need a robe?"

"I have biscuits in the oven. You two keep an eye on them while I get dressed. I don't want to change again before our company arrives. The tea is hot and after all these years, you should know where the butter and jam is kept."

"Why is she in such a dither? Please don't tell me it is because the Hodge twins are coming up river today."

Sean folded a towel and took the pan of hot biscuits out of the oven and almost dropped them on the floor. "Damn! That's a lot hotter than I thought." He finally got them in the basket on the kitchen table. "Don't stand there Jack. Get the butter crock and jam jar out of the pantry."

"When did the storage room become a pantry?"

"When your mother saw the new pantry Nana had built out of her mud room."

Jack laughed. "So a couple extra shelves and a new cupboard magically adds a pantry to the old kitchen?"

"Stop laughing at Mama's pantry." Cece punctuated her demand with a stamp of her little foot.

"That's the second time a girl has done that to me in a week. There will be no more stamping sister." Jack took a deep breath. "Go get your milk jug."

"I can't reach it. Mama gets it for me."

Sean piped up. "Jack, if I remember correctly the milk jug is right next to the other things you need to get."

Cece crossed her arms and gave her brother a satisfied look.

Jack finished setting up the table and then looked at his little sister sucking jam off her fingers. "Wipe them off Cece and get that mess off your face"

She gave him a look that could have knocked him off his seat.

Sean smiled and kept his mouth shut.

Jack pointed his finger at his young sibling. "Straighten up little girl. I don't want you growing up to be like that Hodge girl."

"Who that?" asked Cece as she wiped the jam from her face on the sleeve of her nightgown.

"It's 'who is that'. Say it right!"

"That's right. Who that?"

Sean tapped his son on the shoulder. "Give it up. She'll learn some day. Now who is this girl that seems to have irritated you so?"

"She's half of the twin set we are taking over to meet Nana. Frankly, I think it is a wasted day. I can't believe Nana could have anyone connected to someone that is so, so, yes – irritating. Maybe she'll do us a favor and not show up. Perhaps she'll be afraid of getting her fancy shoes dirty."

"John!" Gert stood in the doorway with her arms crossed.

"Oh, oh!" Cece looked at Jack. "She is really mad."

"Come on Comfort. Let's go to your bedroom and get cleaned up." Sean picked her up and gave Gert a peck on the cheek on the way by and whispered, "You look very pretty in that dress. It's the same color as your eyes."

"The dress is red Sean."

"And so is the fire in your eyes."

Gert stood on tiptoes to make her point to her son. "Jack. I will not let you spoil this day for Nana. You will treat our guests with respect and then they will be on their way. Do you understand?"

He nodded. "Tim is a good guy but his sister is nothing but trouble. I don't even know why you are doing this. You said yourself there are many Hodge families in England."

"I took a walk over to the cemetery. Your father told me to check out the captain's stone. Remember he was the one who carved the name on the granite. I had never noticed that it was Captain T. Hodge."

"Does Nana know this? Did you tell her that the twins might be from the same family."

Gert relaxed a bit, poured herself a cup of tea and sat at the table. "No, we spent more time talking about your cruise."

"The whole story? Ma you didn't tell her about me."

Gert smiled. "She was quite sympathetic. That was her one problem with living on the sea as a captain's wife. When the swells turned rough, she had a tendency to get sick and knows how miserable you felt."

Jack grabbed the biscuit basket

Gert shot her hand out. "Pass me one. I haven't had any breakfast."

"She knows the twins are named Hodge?"

"Yes, but she was more interested in meeting them because of their aunt. She is Nana's favorite seamstress so she asked they bring her along. That is why we are eating at the larger dining room at the Hodge farm rather than here."

"I was wondering why you weren't running around here in a dither." Jack stretched. "Guess I better get ready. Will Dan be there?"

"Maybe. This weekend he's helping your Uncle Joe get the fields ready for planting on Indian Island. The soil on the Penobscot reservation needs a lot of care to bring in a big enough crop for the winter. Also, he's still working part time at the brick works in Brewer to earn as much money as he can before we need to have everyone in the Hodge fields."

"I'm beginning to think your eldest son has a sweetheart among the Indian maidens." Jack smiled.

Gert was taken back for a minute. "No. He would never get it past Annie. My sister-in-law would have my ear about it right away."

"Now you know how quiet and sneaky we natives can be." Jack laughed and left his mother looking perplexed. Cece bounced in with her favorite pale green hair ribbon dangling around her neck. "Papa doesn't know how to make a bow."

"Now, think about it Gert. I was raised with two brothers and then with our family of four boys, when would I have practiced tying a fancy knot?"

"I've seen you tie some pretty fancy fishing lures," noted Gert.

"Your mother always has a comeback, Comfort. Will you also have all the answers when you become a lovely lady?"

"I not know."

Sean turned to hide his grin. Gert giggled softly as she tied back the curly golden red hair with the ribbon that brightened Cece's Irish green eyes.

"Everyone ready to go so we can get this visit over?" Jack questioned. "I could see the morning steamboat pull into Bucksport so I imagine the Hodge's are getting on the ferry to come over."

"It's a bit early. I hope Joey and Peg are already at the ferry landing." Gert grabbed her basket of baked goods to take to Nana's and shawls for herself and Cece in case it was colder near the river. Sean, please take your daughter so we can walk faster.

The ferry was just pulling up to the landing as they arrived. Joey shouted, "It's about time you got here."

First off was Daphne. Gert recognized her as they had been at meetings together at the Methodist church in Searsport. Next off was a nice looking young man followed by a girl who seemed uncomfortable and quite shy. Gert wondered if she did not want to deal with Jack any more than he wanted anything to do with her.

The seamstress walked over to speak with Gert. "Ah, yes. Now I can put a face to the name. We sat near each other last month when Mrs. Pendleton spoke of sailing with Captain Pendleton and keeping a home on the sea."

"It's nice of you to join your niece and nephew, Mrs. Merrill." Gert extended her hand.

"Please, you must call be Daphne."

"And I answer better to Gert." The ladies laughed and got on with the formalities. "Gert, this is my nephew Timothy who went from Timmy to Tim once he began his quest to captain a schooner."

With a bit of an embarrassed blush, Tim bowed slightly to Gert and then presented his sister. "Mrs. Ryan this is Marisol."

"Marisol. What a beautiful name." Gert reached out and took the girl's hand. "You look a bit reticent, my dear. Be assured, I will not bite. And I pledge the same of my sons although I believe you have already had some words with Jack."

Marisol's eyes darted from side to side. Tim laughed. "Don't mind her. One of the men on the docks told her not to travel to this area for there could be an Indian behind every tree." To that he got an elbow to his side.

Sean smiled broadly as he walked over to Marisol. I see that the ladies of London also use their elbows to make a point. I've had many bruised ribs over the years. Please call me Sean for I'm not old enough to be Mr. Ryan."

Cece pouted and yanked the edge of her father's shirt. "You are my papa too."

"How could I forget? Miss Hodge, may I introduce my daughter Comfort Clair Ryan."

"No. My name is Cece Ryan."

"How do you do Cece? I am Marisol Hodge."

Cece smiled and held out her hand. "It is very nice to meet you, Mary."

Jack blurted out, "For Pete's sake Cece. It's Marisol, not Mary. Why don't you listen?"

Gert put her hands on her hips. "Jack!"

That really tickled Miss Hodge.

Joey cleared his throat. "May I butt in? This is my wife Peg."

Marisol took her hand. "So you are the lucky one that captured the nice twin."

Gert laughed out loud. "I think it is time to start up the hill before Nana thinks we forgot her."

On the way up Ferry Road they stopped to look over magnificent Fort Knox where Sean worked for the past twenty-four years. "Gert and I made our hundred mile journey straight from our wedding on the Aroostook River and moved into a tiny house here on the Penobscot. I started out on the ground crew that cleared the land for the fort and had hopes to be a master stonemason one day. That dream came to a sudden stop when an accident nearly took my life and hampered the use of my arm. But those are stories for another time. That tiny home grew as our family grew and it sits over there beyond the fruit trees."

"It is lovely." Marisol continued, "There must be a glorious view of the river from the porch."

Gert picked up the story. "We met Nana Hodge on our first day and she has become the closest friend I shall ever have. Also, Nana is a loved grandmother figure to the boys and Comfort. The fields prepared for planting over there belong to the Hodge farm and the beautiful large house in the distance is her home."

Tim turned around to see the view from this area. "This really is a little piece of heaven."

Jack wondered, "Why would you say that?"

"It's something I read once."

That peaked the curiosity of all the Ryans except Cece who was in her own little world of trying to find nests of baby birds in the branches along the road.

Joey added to the conversation. "That small house on the edge of the far field is where Peg and I are making our home. We work on it any spare hour we find."

The twins were quite impressed.

"We are going to have to pick up the pace as this field is still too muddy to take a shortcut. I'm sure Nana and her live-in help, Cara, are finishing up the meal."

"Mrs. Ryan–I mean Gert–what are those beautiful flowers?"

The unplowed areas and the land across the road as they turned toward the farmhouse looked like a pastel carpet from white to pink to lavender with a touch of yellow.

"Those are lupine. You have come in their season and this landscape appears each June. It helps the spirit recharge after a cold, stark winter."

"It looks like a painting by a man I met in Paris. I took some time there before we left England for I was afraid I might never get back. His name was Claude Monet and he painted landscapes with a softness that gave you an impression of movement within the scene. He painted and studied with a group of artists that played with light upon the canvas and I can see that field of lupine done in his style. One day, I know he and his friends, Renoir and Sisley will be well known."

Cece was suddenly interested. "My mama paints pictures. They are just as pretty as any artist with a funny name."

Gert flushed up a bit. "I'm in hopes we can talk more about your experience in Paris."

Little Daphne who had been silent but attentive all this time spoke up. "Gert, you must come to Searsport with Mrs. Hodge so we can all have tea and a good visit at my shop."

"That would be lovely."

When they reached the house, Marisol looked at the stunning window in the front door. "Look Tim, there are pieces of cobalt blue glass making up a border."

Before they could knock, Cara opened the door. "Do come in. Hello, Mrs. Merrill. Nana is eager to see you all. She just went out on the back porch."

Gert led the way through the parlor, music room and dining room to the kitchen.

The beautiful and unusual items found in every nook awed Marisol. She stopped in the sitting room to look at the painted triptych of Bucksport on the wall. Rather than hinged panels, each of the three scenes was in a matching hand carved frame. "That is truly beautiful."

Cece grabbed her arm. "Mama painted the pictures and my big brother Dan made the frames." She was obviously very proud.

Cara pushed the group along. "Come now. Sunday dinner will be cold if we don't move out to the porch."

When the visitors came out of the kitchen door Nana was standing at the porch rail looking at the new buds on her trailing roses.

Gert said, "Nana, you have company."

The short stout lady slowly turned with her wonderful smile. Suddenly all the color drained from her face, she put her hand over her heart and stumbled towards the rail.

"Nana what's wrong?" Gert panicked and ran over to help ease Nana into her favorite wicker rocker.

Nana stretched her arm out towards Tim. "You are his spitting image." She began to sob while Gert tried to comfort her. "Come closer son. I need to see you more closely."

Tim walked slowly over to the chair. "I'm so sorry ma'am if I startled you."

"You have his hair–black as the coals in Wales with silky waves that shine in the sunlight. It's as if his brilliant blue eyes are looking at me once again. What is your given name?"

He knelt down beside her and took her hand. "I am Timothy, ma'am. Timothy Hodge."

She placed her other hand over his as tears of shock turned to tears of joy.

Tim looked into her aging eyes and saw the wisdom of her years. "Ma'am. Would your name be Fiona?"

Gert gasped as she backed away for few knew her given name. Nana reached for Tim and hugged him close to the softness of her body.

IV

GETTING TO KNOW HER

The dining room table was adorned with a large bouquet of lupines and set with the best Wedgwood bone china. Nana took her place at the head flanked on either side by Tim and Marisol. She would occasionally reach out and touch Tim's cheek to assure herself that he was still there and not just a dream or a figment of her imagination.

Marisol dabbed her mouth daintily with a linen napkin causing Jack to look at Joey with an eye roll. "That was a lovely meal Mrs. Hodge."

"Thank you dear but please call me Nana. It seems we have a common family bond and if I had ever been blessed with a daughter, I feel she would have looked like you, favoring my captain with his beautiful hair, blue eyes and good nature."

Marisol blushed slightly and Jack nearly choked on this last bite of Irish soda bread.

Cara came in from the kitchen wiping her hands on her apron. She whispered to Nana who smiled broadly.

"Thomas just put the rest of the summer chairs on the porch. Since this beautiful day is so warm, I thought we would enjoy tea and dessert on the porch."

Cece threw up her hands with a "yippee!"

As the group walked through the kitchen, Marisol noticed the large dried arrangement in a pewter pitcher on the table under the oversized window. "Mrs. Hodge—sorry Nana— what are these berries? I've never seen anything like them before. They remind me of something in a delicate Chinese woodblock print."

"They are wild bittersweet vines that have taken root near the barn and climb with gusto. They grow a small round yellow fruit. In the fall, the husk breaks open to reveal a deep red orange berry."

Joey piped in. "They may be pretty but also a nuisance when the roots spread into the fields and we have to chop them out to till."

Nana laughed. "I guess that is the bitter with the sweet. Now let's get to dessert."

Cara arranged the baked treats on a pedestal opal glass cake plate. Then set out the hand-painted dessert plates and matching cups.

"Gert and Peg, I would say you two outdid yourselves. This assortment of cookies is wonderful." Nana bit into a buttery scotch cake. "Yes indeed, wonderful."

Gert leaned against the porch rail watching the midday sun beat down on bright green leaves casting shadows that danced on the ground at the will of the breeze from the river. "In the many years I have lived here, I can't remember another early June day as warm as this. I think we all need to top off that meal with a walk."

"You go ahead. I'm going to help Cara clean up." Peg turned to Marisol. "I hope it won't be too long before we see you again."

Tim answered for his sister. "We'll be back soon as I have some items to show Nana."

"I don't feel I could go too far but perhaps we could walk over to your place so Tim and Marisol can see the home you have made for your family." Nana grasped the rail to pull herself up and stood for a moment to get her balance.

Tim took Nana's hand and led her down the steps off the porch, then helped his aunt Daphne on the narrow boards. He took a good look at the side yard. "That is a big barn. Do you have a lot of animals?"

"We have one cow, a dozen or so laying hens with the obligatory rooster—although I could wring his neck at sunrise—and of course my horses: Argos to pull the wagons and Hector, now in pasture. We have a pair of mules that work well in the fields. I sold the oxen to the lumberman near the quarry as we didn't need them once the fields were finally cleared. A lot of the barn is used for storage. Come on, we'll take a peek before we start down the road."

Tim was quite impressed.

"Be careful where you step young lady," shouted a voice from one of the stalls. Thomas came out and pointed to a pile of fresh waste from one of the horses.

Jack pulled Marisol back a bit. "We wouldn't want to mess up those pretty little shoes."

She in turn pouted and stepped back to stand with her brother.

Tim waved at Thomas. "It's nice to see you again, sir. You were a great help in getting Jack off the town landing."

Frank tipped his hat. "You are just as lovely as ever Miss Marisol." He waved a figure out from a storage room. "This is T. He and his mother Cara live with Mrs. Hodge."

T nodded in his bashful way.

Jack nudged them all out of the barn. "We better finish this tour before your ride comes down river from Bangor. You wouldn't want to miss getting back to Searsport."

Gert gave her son a "be careful" look.

Marisol moved over next to Joey. "What was wrong with that young man? Was he really missing an arm?"

"They had to take it off at a battlefield surgery during the civil war."

"How dreadful." She seemed truly touched.

Cece skipped over. "Mary, see my necklace?"

"It's Marisol–not Mary!" Jack was quite put out.

Marisol turned around and put her hands on her hips. "Jack! Mary is just fine with me. Leave her alone!"

Gert tried to hide her glee but it was very apparent she really liked this young woman.

"Let me see your necklace Cece."

She smiled broadly and pulled up the thin silk ribbon that was around her neck. It held a shiny brass button. "This was on my brother Mike's coat and he gave it to me."

Marisol was puzzled as her little friend clapped and skipped away.

As they walked slowly over the carriage road to the Ryan home, Joey filled her in on the tragedy of his oldest brother at Gettysburg. "My brothers Mike and Dan joined the Maine Twentieth Infantry Regiment early as it was thought the Union would start conscripting young men for the regular army. Our Uncle Joe was friendly with one of their leaders, Joshua Chamberlain, and the family felt better that the boys would be with someone local. The battle at Little Round Top was brutal with the Twentieth trapped at the top while General Lee's forces were coming up to take the vital position. Mike, Dan and JJ, their best friend from Aroostook County, were running for cover behind a boulder when Mike spotted a sniper. He pushed Dan and JJ towards the large rock and stood in front of them. He was killed by a vicious minie ball that tore into his chest.

I've heard since that ninety percent of deaths during the terrible war were caused by rifles using minie balls."

Marisol grabbed his arm. "I'm so sorry.."

"No. Let me finish. I'd like you to know about their bravery. Dan got a nasty gash on his forehead when he hit the boulder and blood flowed into his eye making it hard to see. Chamberlain called for his men to fix bayonets as ammunition was nearly gone. They charged down the hill so surprising the rebels they retreated and were trapped at the bottom by hidden union soldiers who had arrived and fired from behind stone walls. That battle turned the war and stopped Lee's plans to go on to Philadelphia. But Dan was not jubilant at the victory. His brother was still at the top of the hill and he was afraid they would bury him in a shallow unmarked grave. Late that night, he and JJ climbed back with just enough moonlight and buried Mike in a deep grave at the base of the boulder. Mike never saw Cece but loved her dearly from our mother's letters. He had always planned to give the baby some of the shiny buttons from his uniform. I took them and gave one to Cece and one to Kate, Mike's sweetheart. She had given him a small stone shaped like a heart so I made sure it was in his pocket before we left his grave. My mother has the rest of the buttons in a glass dish next to the photograph of her boys on the mantle in the parlor."

Marisol wiped a tear at the corner of her eye. "Thank you. In England we heard stories about brother fighting brother in your war between the states. I never realized how tragic it must have been."

"The word at the fort is at least a half a million men died in the war. Joey just shook his head.

As the group led by Sean and Gert crossed over the top of Ferry Road, Cece was excited by what she saw and shouted, "Frankie, Frankie!"

Two figures were walking up from the landing. The man was quite tall and the boy about the size of Cece.

The boy, Frankie, ran up the hill. He was dressed in a buckskin tunic over his working pants. His hair was black and pulled back behind his neck and tied with a piece of rawhide. Cece gave him a hug and they walked up the rest of the way together, hand in hand.

Marisol was aghast. "You allow your little girl to play with savages?"

Tim left Nana's side and took his sister by the arm. "What is wrong with you?"

"It's true. What Matt said is true. There are Indians up here. He warned me to stay away." Then she whispered, "He said Joey and Jack were half-breeds and to keep away from them. He said the ladies in Searsport wouldn't have anything to do with me if they see me with them. They don't look like Indians, right?"

Daphne excused herself from Nana and walked over to her niece. "Marisol, what are you doing? You are embarrassing me. Now behave."

The man came into the group. He looked so much like Sean's Uncle Jacob in Aroostook County, one would think he was his son. His bronze chiseled face was framed with two black braids that hung on the shoulders of his work tunic. On his feet were handmade moccasins. He swung Cece up to sit on his shoulders as she giggled in glee.

Marisol gasped and hid behind her twin.

Joey brought the stranger over to Tim. "I'd like you to meet my brother Dan."

The two men shook hands as Marisol's heart began to race.

Dan said, "So you are one of the twins I've heard about. News travels up this valley like leaves on the winds."

"Very nice to meet you, Dan. I've heard a lot about you this afternoon but to tell the truth you are not quite what I expected."

Dan smiled broadly showing his beautiful white teeth. "I left the island on the spur of the moment as a friend was heading to Bucksport and had room in his wagon. Didn't have time to change out of my work clothes. I must look a fright."

Marisol took a peek around her brother, blanched and hid once again.

Jack walked behind her as quiet as one with Indian blood can. "He tapped her on the shoulder and whispered "Boo!" in her ear.

Marisol let out a piercing scream, turned quickly smacking the intruder across the chest with her arm, which put him off balance. Jack teetered backward, tripped over Cece's scooter that was lying on the front lawn and fell ass over teakettle into his mother's rose garden, prickly thorns and all.

Jack stood trying not to let anyone know just how much his body and pride was hurt. "Cece! How many times have I told you not to leave your scooter in the front yard?"

Cece ran to her mother while Frankie sprinted across the lawn, picked up the scooter and carried it away. All the men, Nana and Gert laughed while Daphne seemed confused. Marisol stomped out of her safe spot behind Tim, her face now red with a mixture of anger and embarrassment. Gert came to the rescue, took her hand and led her into the house. "Come, dear. I want to show you around our humble home and I suspect a nice cold glass of water would help."

Dan watched the young lady walk into the house. "So that's the other half of the Hodge twins. She's quite a treat for the eyes."

As Nana and Daphne entered the house, Sean took time to explain to Tim that the small section at the front door was their original home. Over the years he and Gert had added a dining area, three bedrooms to one side and a good-sized parlor with fireplace to the other side. Again their back porch was a perfect place to watch the river. Sean pointed out the two workshops where he worked on his granite pieces and Gert did her paintings.

Tim looked at the glow of the sun getting low in the west. "We really need to get to the ferry landing. It's much later than I thought. It looks like tomorrow is going to be another beauty."

"Indeed," said Nana. Red sky at night, sailor's delight."

Just then Gert's cat came out of the bushes, ignored the company and took his pleasure by rubbing against his human's leg. "Goodness Lady. Where have you been all day? I was beginning to worry about you."

"Is that one of Captain Coon's cats?" Tim got down on one knee and tried to stroke her long silky hair but was not received well. "I've heard how big they are but this is the first I've seen. If I ever get my own schooner to captain, I want one just like her to take care of the mice on board."

Sean laughed. "Young man, if you get your own command we'll scour the waterfront and find one for you. Now we better get you three down to the river."

Dan shook Tim's hand. "Thank you for seeking out Nana. I'm sure as you get to know her, you will come to love her as much as we do."

When Dan turned to Marisol and nodded, she began to tremble, then calmed when seeing the scar on his forehead and remembering his story. "It was nice to meet you."

Nana gave Marisol a hug then reached up and gave Tim a kiss on the cheek. She whispered, "How did you know my name?"

"I'll show you when we next meet."

"Gert and I will be driving my surrey down in a fortnight to visit Daphne. She said you would still be in Searsport."

"I should be there for up to two months while all the final work is done on the schooner. She'll be a strong, beautiful vessel when we start servicing the east coast. We'll try to fill in some of the blanks in the story at Aunt Daphne's shop."

Gert gathered the children. "Dan, how long is Frankie going to be with us?"

"Uncle Joe will pick him up before the end of the week. This will be a break for him and Annie while they are working on the sowing and I didn't think you would mind."

"Take Frankie and Cece and walk Nana home please. Your father and I will be back soon."

As Joey and the twins took the lead down the path Jack was leaning against the frame of the door to Sean's work area. He looked at Marisol and gave her a salute. She in turn did her best to ignore him.

Joey shouted up the hill, "I can hear the Boston Boat coming." With Gert on one side and Sean on the other, they hustled Daphne down to the docking side-wheeler.

V

FIONA HODGE

As the sun began to peep over the tall pines to the east, Nana waited impatiently for Gert to come out to the wagon. They were going to Searsport sooner than thought.

Sean's brother Joe sent a message he was coming to pick up Frankie and asked if he could borrow Nana's wagon to go to Searsport to pick up some supplies for the reservation. He was bringing his little girl Holly to visit Cece. She had been feeling left out because her brother had been here for nearly a week.

Hearing this, Nana jumped at the chance to ride to the coast with him and was able to make plans with Daphne to visit with the twins.

Nana was drumming her fingers on the side of the wagon seat when Gert trotted out the front door carrying a good-sized travel bag and a quilt for some comfort in the back of the wagon. She was just as excited to talk with Tim and Marisol and hoped they could help Nana with more of the mystery of the Captain's family. Next out were Jack and his Uncle Joe.

Nana looked puzzled. "Jack?"

Gert laughed as she climbed into the back. "It was a choice between helping his Uncle Joe load the supplies or staying to help Peg watch over the children until Joey finished chores in the fields. He jumped at the chance to go to Searsport."

The three children came running around to the front of the house waving.

Jack hopped in. "Quick, make our escape."

With a flick of the reins, they were off. Cece shouted into the trailing dust, "Tell Mary hello."

Going to Searsport by boat is much faster than by the carriage road but the wait for a Boston boat could be long while catching a Bangor cargo ship was hit or miss. When they reached the docks at Stockton, Joe pulled over to give the horse a break.

While Joe tended to Argos, the ladies walked a bit on the dock. The seagulls were squawking and fighting over bits and pieces tossed from fishing boats. The fresh morning breeze turned up ripples on the bay and Nana stretched filling her soul with memories of many mornings like this with her Captain when they were in port. The low slant of the sunrise reflected in the village windows turning them to nuggets of gold. Soon the beautiful sight would be gone for another twenty-four hours.

Joe whistled to get everyone's attention. "Time to move on. We have five more miles so we should be at Mrs. Merrill's shop in an hour and a half."

"That's perfect." Nana rubbed her hands in anticipation. "I told Daphne before noon."

Jack moaned at the fact he was riding in the back. "Ma, you should have brought me a quilt."

"I figured you would just curl up in a ball and lay on the floor like the last time you came home from Searsport." That brought chuckles from those on the wagon seat.

As they entered a more populated part of Searsport, Nana asked Joe to stop for a minute. She pointed to a lovely large house on the right, set on a slope up from the road. "That is the Packard home."

"It's lovely, Nana. I wish Dan could see the hand carved trim." Looking up, Gert shaded her eyes against the midday sun. "The house is quite large. Is he a sea captain?"

"Marlborough is a successful business man who manages more than a few important shipyards along the water. I imagine he set his home on higher ground to have a better view of the harbor. He and Mary's family of four energetic children keep her very busy."

"Thus the big house," grumbled Jack who was obviously getting impatient. "Can we get on with it?"

"Hold your horses, young man. I want you all to look at the young white cedar tree planted on the corner of the yard. When Abraham Lincoln was assassinated, Marlboro and his neighbor Captain Nickels were very upset as dedicated followers of the president. They planted that tree in the summer of 1865, soon after the tragedy. They wanted a living memorial to the man they so respected and I am happy to see how well it has taken and is showing new growth."

"There should be more memorial trees out there for my brother and all the volunteers from here that did not come back. I hated that war." Jack banged his fist against the rough boards on the side of the wagon. "Damn, another splinter."

Joe looked at his sister-in-law. Gert was sitting quietly, looking at the tree as a tear slipped down her cheek. "Jack, have some respect for your mother. Think before you speak."

Gert took a handkerchief from Nana. "It's fine. I think it is a beautiful idea and perhaps we should do the same next spring."

After a few moments of silence, Joe continued the last segment of the trip and soon stopped the wagon in front of Daphne's shop on Main Street in the Merithew Block, not far from the Searsport Bank. Tim came right out as if he had been watching for quite a while, helped the ladies to the sidewalk and took their travelling bags. Joe laughed, "Don't worry, they're not staying a week. We should be back in two to three hours so I have a chance to get the folks back to the Hodge Farm before dark."

As the wagon started to turn down the road to the busy harbor, Jack noticed Marisol peeking through the corner of the large window and waved at her. She quickly ducked out of the way. Soon Argos and his passengers disappeared among the canvas makers, foundries, blacksmiths, cabinet makers, carpenters and all the other workers needed to support ship building.

Gert was quite taken by the quaint shop. It was small but arranged cleverly to display some bolts of lovely fabric, cones of thread and spools of lace. On the polished oak counter was a display of sample single buttons that could be found in glass front drawers in a tall narrow cabinet against the wall. Behind the glass front beneath the counter, shelves held an array of unusual buckles, crocheted collars and hand decorated hatpins. Behind the counter was obviously Daphne's work area with a cutting table, several projects hanging on pegs and one partially made dress on a form.

"Perhaps you should cover your eyes at the mess as we go into the parlor." Daphne led her company through a beaded door curtain to a comfortable room with a round claw-foot table covered with a linen cloth finished with a deep tatted border. A lovely tea set surrounded a tiered silver plate holding an assortment of finger sandwiches.

Gert put her flowered tapestry bag on one of the chairs with needlepoint covers. "This is lovely Daphne."

"I spend so many hours in the shop, it made sense for me to use a bit of the floor space for a place to relax. Take a look out the back window."

Gert pulled the light curtain aside. "O my, this is such a beautiful view of the harbor. I didn't realize there were so many shipyards and everything is busy all the way to the high tide line.

Tim spoke up. "I haven't counted, but I hear eleven yards and that is why so many craftsmen have opened businesses to supply the needs. There is a new cooper to fill the need for barrels since so many are used for shipping. We seem to have moved here at the right time."

Daphne laughed. "It certainly helps my business. The captain's wives like to look their finest. Gert, is that the painting I wanted?"

Nana looked surprised. This was nothing she knew about.

Gert opened her bag and took out a parlor-sized scene in a carved frame with gold colored finish. The radiant lupines looked like you could pick them exposing the gently flowing river in the background.

"It's perfect Gert. I asked her to bring me one of her paintings to sell in the shop. It could work out well for both of us when it sells, and in the meantime, will decorate the room."

Marisol, who had been quiet, remarked on the delightful technique of the brush strokes.

The bell on the shop door rang. "Please have a bite to eat."

Tim settled in the chair next to Nana while Marisol poured the tea. Unlike the Ryan's who liked their tea strong and plain, Tim put 2 sugar cubes and cream in his. Gert thought this must be another difference between the city English and the country Irish.

Daphne hustled back in the parlor just a bit out of breath from rushing though a question from a customer. "Now, what did I miss?"

"Not a thing." Tim tugged a small bundle of letters out of his pocket and placed it on the table. Around it was a faded red velvet ribbon. "First I want to explore the pathway to our connection. I'm not sure what you may know about Captain Hodge's background."

"He never talked about his family. I didn't know if there were any brothers or sisters and he never once mentioned his father." Nana thought for a moment. "I feel he was quite close to his mother for once in awhile he would whisper to the wind, 'Mum would have loved to see this'. I learned very early in our marriage not to ask as it would put him in a dark place that we would have to work through. On occasion I would see him reading a letter in the moonlight in a quiet place. I think he would get these messages when we were docked in Boston but here again, I respected his privacy."

Tim stood and took a look through the back window at the busy harbor as high tide was beginning to turn. "Most of what I could put together is from bits of stories passed down to my father, Reginald Hodge, Jr. His mother heard talk of the missing captain through the chitchat among the help. It almost seemed taboo to speak of him in the family, including mentioning his name. My father was intrigued and would try to pry information from his father, Reginald Senior, who finally confirmed he remembered an uncle who would come to the house with little bags of sweets and once brought him a small rowboat he had carved including a pair of tiny oars. His name was Timothy and his younger brother was Richard. My grandfather worked with his Uncle Richard in the shipping offices and on the sea. He never saw or heard about his Uncle Timothy again."

Tim sat back down and sipped his tea, which was now cold. Marisol took the cup and filled it with a fresh brew.

Nana squinted her eyes and stared at the ceiling as if trying to make out the intricate patterns hammered into the tin. You could almost hear her mind spinning to grasp the information and make sense of it.

Gert stood behind her and put her hands on the shoulders of her dearest friend. "Nana, are you alright? Would you like a glass of water?"

Nana reached up and squeezed Gert's hand. "I'll be fine, dear." She turned and looked Tim in the eyes. "If I have this right, you are saying that my Captain is your great uncle. How can you be sure and why on earth did he leave his family behind? Why did your father name you after him? Marisol's name is so special to him so what did he see special in your name? How did you know my name if he cut himself off from his family? Was it through his mother?" Nana took a deep breath. "I'll take that drink of water now to calm my insides."

"I'll get it." Marisol got up and reached for the porcelain pitcher. "I've lived with this story since before we left England but did not know the answer would be in Aunt Daphne's neighborhood. Tim was in hopes to find some Hodge families while he sailed the eastern seacoast." She opened the window a bit to let in some refreshing sea air. Nana seemed to be getting red in the face from anticipation.

Tim stood and began to pace. "I need to take you back a bit further in the family history. Timothy Hodge was the apple of his father's eye. He groomed him to be the next head of the family and pinned the future of his shipping business on him. The company served the European coast such as my father and I had. That is until Mr. Hodge began to see the profits being made by the ship owners in Liverpool who were well into the slave trade."

Gert gasped, "Good heavens, no." She had been involved with the underground railway that went through Bangor towards Canada.

"I'll try to make this short. Mr. Hodge had a grand idea to become one of the wealthiest ship owners in London. Plans were set to have one of his larger ships refitted to carry human cargo. Not as big as the slave ship Brookes that could pack in six to seven-hundred men, women and children, but he did redesign one to carry three-hundred-fifty to four-hundred depending on how they were shackled. Either on their backs or spoon-style on their sides. He could also squeeze in several more if boys and girls."

Nana's fists were clenched. "Did my Captain know about this?"

Tim sat back down next to her and took her hands in his. "No. He was a brilliant navigator and had been taught well how to captain a ship knowing every chore on board. When Captain Timothy returned from a run to Portugal, his father took him to see the newly rigged ship and with pride turned it over to him to run the triangle from England to Africa to the Americas and then back to Britain."

"No, he never could." Nana was getting upset.

"The story that came down from some of the crew was that he refused and told his father he had seen the ways of the slave trade as Portugal had been a central location for the ships for many years. He wanted no part of it even if it would bring huge profits to the family."

"There has to be more to the story." Nana slammed her hand on the table. Gert, Daphne and Marisol sat silently, not even wanting to take a breath.

"Mr. Hodge would not take no for an answer. He grabbed his son by the collar daring him to refuse his order. The captain pushed him away causing his father to trip over a coil of rope and slide on the newly finished deck."

Marisol had not heard that part and gasped. She knew at that time, no one spoke up against the head of the family especially one as important as Mr. Hodge.

Tim took a deep breath and continued. "Captain Timothy shouted at his father who was sprawled on the wide boards. 'Have you ever watched slave traders on the African coast? Ever seen a line of men loaded under the whip or at the barrel of the gun to be strapped down in stifling lower decks with barely any room between each other? Have you choked on the stench of suffering as the ship stayed at anchor until they had a full load? Have you watched Africans selling Africans from other tribes? I have and I won't be part of it.' He then turned to go down the gangplank."

Tim swatted away a fly that found its way through the blowing thin lace curtains at the open window.

"And?" asked Nana staring at him with eyes aged with wisdom that knew there had to be more.

"From anecdotal reports, Mr. Hodge screamed that Timothy was a bloody ungrateful traitor to his family and he would not be able to stop this ship from sailing its course on the golden triangle as Richard would be his captain. A townsman heard Timothy shout, 'I will not let you pull our family into this filthy trade.' It is said that his father shouted, 'For God's sake. They are goods to be traded.' Everything seemed frozen for a moment in time."

A tear fell down Nana's cheek, dropped on Tim's hand and slid silently to the linen cloth.

"The few crewmen on board reported that Tim turned and ran back on deck nearly tripping over his father. He spread out on his stomach, reached in the open hatch and grabbed a lantern hanging on a nail to light the floor below. Then he swung the lantern with all his strength and let it fly. It skidded along the stowage area until becoming wedged between two forged brackets made to lock down the chains of the human chattel. When it tipped, oil spread and the flames quickly engulfed one end of the lower interior. Mr. Hodge yelled at the crew to form a bucket line. In the frantic commotion Timothy ran down the gangplank and caught his father's eye as he ran away. He yelled, 'I hope Richard's ship settles at the bottom of the Thames' to which Mr. Hodge threw his bucket in his direction and answered. 'I have but one son and I'll see that you never again get work on these trade routes.' That was the last time they saw each other.

Gert stood and went over and wrapped her arms around Nana who was sobbing, "Dear God. Oh, my dear God."

Daphne looked at Gert. "I think we need a break. Do we have time?"

Gert nodded yes. "We'll make time."

Marisol brought Nana a soft cloth made damp with cold water. "Thank you, my dear." She held it over her blood shot eyes and then relaxed with a shudder.

Daphne broke the spell by bringing a tray of dessert dishes holding squares of applesauce spice cake topped with a warm rum sauce. Marisol followed with a freshly brewed pot of tea.

The group sat silent as they enjoyed the tasty treat. Gert sat back in her chair and smiled. "I must have that recipe Daphne."

Their hostess grinned. "It is a wonderful way to use up the tail end of last year's apple crop."

Nana looked at Tim. "I still have some questions for you to answer."

"Are you ready Mrs. Hodge?"

"I have never been more ready for anything. I do understand now why he was so upset with me at one of the southern ports. He would let me wander some of the docks if there were shops where I might find a new book to add to my library. On the way back to the ship, I got twisted around and found myself in the center of town where they were having an outside sale. I went closer and saw some men dragging a young negro boy away while his mother was being held back screaming. It was a slave auction. I was upset when I boarded and told him what I had seen. He forbade me to go ashore again in any of the southern ports. I thought it was because of me but I see now it was to protect me from what he hated."

Tim picked up the package of letters. "When Tim ran off the docks he never went home again. He went straight to the bank and closed his account, taking his savings in gold coins. You will find that story and how he got to Boston in these few envelopes. He knew he had to see his mother. She had one true friend that she trusted and it was not any of the social-climbing wives that surrounded her. It was her seamstress."

Everyone looked at Daphne and laughed. That eased the rest of the tension. "I'd say that was pretty ironic." Marisol gave her aunt a wink.

"When Timothy went through the alleyway to her back door, Miss Ellis was afraid to open it until he convinced her it was important to see his mother. Hearing the story, she knew her friend needed to have this chance to say goodbye. He hid in her upstairs apartment and she sent her assistant to the Hodge home with a note. Mrs. Hodge was busy planning dinner with the cook and was surprised to see her seamstress needed to see her for a special fitting so late in the day but it piqued her curiosity. Obviously, Mr. Hodge had not been home."

Gert agreed. "He never would have let her leave the house after what happened."

Tim picked up the letters and untied the ribbon. "Imagine her surprise when she saw Timothy and how shocked she must have been realizing it would be for the last time. I imagine tears were shed and hugs shared for she and Timothy were close. They enjoyed the same interests especially in literature and the arts. I can imagine her also wishing the ship would find a place on the bottom of the river. She could not stay long as Mr. Hodge would be expecting dinner some time soon. When they parted, he promised to send a note to Miss Ellis when he had a better idea where he would be. He only knew if he succeeded it would be somewhere along the coast of North America"

Questions came from all directions. Did the ship sink? How did you get the letters? Why is your name Timothy?

"We are running out of time, so here goes. I would not be here as a seaman if the ship sank. It was badly damaged and held up the start of the trading but Richard, my great grand-father joined the rest sailing the golden triangle. Before you ask, ships would go to Africa and trade manufactured goods for slaves, trade them at the English colonies in the Caribbean for sugar, tobacco and coffee, then back to England with these raw materials for the manufacturers in England and then start the triangle again. When the rice, cotton and tobacco plantations grew larger in the southern states, the slave shippers would take a large part of their human cargo there taking more raw materials back to England where prosperity was growing from the jobs at mills for workers and more profits for the owners. The shippers, slave traders and plantation owners became wealthy including the Hodge family."

"The letters?" Gert knew they were running out of time.

"When the old Hodge home was sold in London, my father was part of the extended family that helped clean it out. When he opened one of the trunks hidden well in a corner of the attic, he found this package of letters. Reading them only added to the respect he held for Timothy and that is where I got my name for it meant as much to him as Marisol. Captain Timothy was ahead of the times for in 1807, Great Britain abolished the slave trade. Still Mr. Hodge became wealthy and his shipping business prospered."

"Wow." Gert's head spun trying to absorb all this new information.

Marisol peeked out the window. "I think I see the wagon just making its way through the buildings to the road up from the docks."

"Well, I must answer one more question." Tim took the letter on top. "I'm going to read this one and then you take them and let Gert read them to you in order. You will get many more answers." He opened the letter.

June 30, 1801

Dearest Mother,

My hope is that I find you well. When I last heard, you were fighting some type of illness leaving you feeling weak. That was some time ago for that note came just after I left Boston and since then I have traveled to the southern ports and back.

I have some news that I feel will pick up your spirits. The last few times I anchored in Boston Harbor I saw this little sprite of a lass on the docks. She has locks of red spun gold and fairly skips through her chores. I have only seen her quiet when totally engrossed in her reading.

Early this spring on an unusually warm day, she was sitting on a crate with her nose in a book and did not see my mate toss a mooring rope. It hit her on the head knocking her to the dock. I got to her as quickly as possible and as she was dazed, carried her home to a crowded tenement. I thought this is not a place for a girl with such fire. Not even the freshest breezes at sea could clear her from my mind. When I returned I went back to the tenement and asked her father if I could have her hand in marriage. Her parents (as Irish as an Irishman can be) were shocked but left it up to the girl. Her beautiful green eyes sparkled with glee and my heart fluttered in anticipation. I told her to gather her family and be at the dock in one month and I would make all the arrangements.

This is the day mother. We will wed on deck. The harbor is sparkling like diamonds this morning. It is as if the sun and sea know something special is about to happen. By this afternoon I shall be a married man and set out with my wife to live in the captain's cabin and begin our journey together.

I know you will be happy for me mother for I shall not be alone. Somehow I wish we could tell father that I am marrying an Irish girl from the tenements of Boston Harbor. He would certainly have a stroke.

I must go and gather flowers and make final plans with the justice of the peace. I'm sure this will not please her parents with their daughter marrying without a priest and to an Englishman. But I know in my heart it is the right thing.

Sending you my undying love, Timothy

Post Script - I forgot to say her name is Fiona.

Nana and Gert clapped their hands in glee.

"Thank you. Thank you my dear Timothy Hodge. My dear nephew." Nana reached for her travel bag and Gert picked it up for her.

"What in the world do you have in there? It feels as heavy as one of Sean's pieces of granite."

Nana finally laughed out loud. She opened her bag and pulled out a long brass spyglass and compass. "Even before I knew the story, I wanted you to have these. They belonged to my Captain."

"Mrs. Hodge, I mean Nana. I simply couldn't take these from you."

"You must Tim, for it would please me to have you be able to see your way ahead at sea but even more important, be able to find your way back to us."

Gert looked out the window. "Joe and Jack are about half way up the hill."

"I have a question Gert." Tim seemed confused. "Why is there a Joe and a Joey?"

Gert smiled broadly. "Sean's brother Joe was very generous to us when we were married. As we travelled down from the Aroostook Valley after our wedding, he made arrangements for us to stay at a beautiful inn at Houlton. It is something we will never forget. And then when he met our stagecoach in Brewer, he surprised us with a night at a very expensive hotel overlooking the river. When we asked how could we ever repay him, he laughed and told us to just name our second son after him. We did, not thinking about future confusion."

Daphne went out to the shop and opened the front door. "They should be turning the corner at any minute."

Tim helped Nana up from her chair and took her hand. Gert picked up the empty travel bags.

Tim looked at Nana. "I have something I want you to take."

He put an object in her hand. She looked and there laid a small hand carved boat with two oars, one broken but bound together by butcher twine. She had no words.

VI

GATHERING CLOUDS

Marisol walked out on the brick sidewalk, looked right and left and seemed befuddled. She shrugged her shoulders and shouted, "They're not here."

Gert came out and put the travel bags against the wall. "I watched them come up the hill. They certainly couldn't have disappeared into thin air."

Daphne went back to the parlor, checked out the window and yelled to Tim. "They pulled in behind the building and something doesn't look right."

"Marisol, take Nana to a chair. I'll be right back."

Gert whispered, "Now what has Jack been up to?" She followed Tim around the corner and ran to the common area behind the business block.

"I hope it's no problem to pull the wagon in. I was afraid I would block Main Street if I left it out front while I got a little help to clean up Jack and make him more comfortable for the long ride home." Joe himself looked as though he would also be in need of some care as his bloody nose was still dripping on his work shirt.

Gert looked in the wagon bed. "Good God, Jack! Who did this to you?" The area around his eyes was already turning a dark purple and the color was travelling down his checks giving him the appearance of an owl.

Daphne called out the window. "Bring them in to get some cool water on those bruises and give them something to drink."

"Are you sure?"

"By all means. Marisol, you go help your brother."

She frowned slightly at her aunt but was soon helping Tim get Jack out of the wagon and up to the front door. A pair of ladies of the community crossed to the other side of the street whispering their disapproval of Daphne for bringing what they considered riff-raff into her shop.

When Nana saw Joe and his nephew, she murmured, "Not again. When is this foolishness going to stop?"

Jack could not hold back his groan as Tim lowered him in a straight back chair in the parlor. Daphne placed a porcelain bowl on the table and Marisol followed with the matching pitcher of new drawn water to help cool the injuries.

Gert cleaned Joe's face with a damp soft rag. "I suspect you were not the target but got in the way of a fist meant for Jack. I hope you gave back some of what you got."

"I did manage to connect with the chin of the finely dressed brute that appeared to be the leader." Joe chuckled but then wished he had kept his smile to himself as it crinkled his nose, reminding him of his bloody injury, but then saw his own skinned knuckles he laughed. "I suspect he won't find eating comfortable for awhile."

"When Annie gets a look she will keep you on the reservation with the so called savages." Gert sighed, "You would be much safer there."

Marisol held a damp towel over Jack's eyes. There was nothing she could do for the obvious pain he was hugging around his ribs.

Nana came into the parlor and gently hugged her dear Joe. It has been twenty plus years since she first met him at the seminary library in Bangor. She was very impressed by this intelligent young man; his devotion to the Penobscot reservation on Indian Island and teaching at the little schoolhouse in North Brewer. Her Captain still held anger at the tribe for what he saw as past grievances with the English but soon warmed to Joe and started to take the island ferryboat to tell stories of the sea to the children. How they looked forward to his sharing tales of places they had never seen. "Have you any idea who did this to you?"

"As Gert said, I was not the target. Three young men jumped Jack as we were leaving the cooper with new rain barrels. Two were obviously dockworkers but one looked more like he belonged at a desk. I bet he did not have one callous on his hands."

This caught Marisol's attention. "What did he look like?"

"He seemed about my height with curly light brown hair and was a bit husky. I'd say he never had a day when he missed a meal."

"He most likely belongs to one of the well-off families in town. Perhaps a ship builder for if related to a sea captain, he would be working on board learning the trade as Tim did." Nana sat down next to Jack and looked closely at the ever-expanding bruises on his face and suspected his ribs looked about the same. "What I don't understand is I have seen Jack take on men twice his size and he never looked like this when it was over."

Joe took a look at his swelling nose in the ornate round mirror above the marble-top buffet against the wall. "Before today he had a fighting chance. The other two men stood on either side of Jack holding his arms to pin him through the spokes of the wagon wheel. I noticed one of them was missing a finger so he may be a worker in the sawmill. They kept shouting 'give it to him Matt' and 'show the half breed he needs to remember his place' as the bully kept punching."

Tim slapped the top of the table and looked at his sister.

Marisol was ashen. "Not Matthew. He wouldn't do that."

Jack opened his eyes and mimicked in a falsetto voice. "No, he wouldn't do that."

Marisol wouldn't believe it. "Why in the world would he do such a thing?"

Joe laughed. "I won't be able to repeat the colorful harbor language they used but near as I can make out, he wants Jack to stay away from you. He was not happy to see the two of you talking when you came in to tie up from the schooner cruise."

Jack moaned. "Cruise? That was a trip from hell and I can't remember us talking. It was more like knocking heads."

"I'm afraid that was not what it looked like from the dock. I would say Mr. Matthew has his eye on Miss Marisol and doesn't want any competition, especially from a bloody no-good like Jack."

Marisol was obviously irritated with Jack's Uncle Joe. "Hogwash. It could not be Matthew Roberts. He is a gentleman from a fine Boston family who is working in the office of one of Mr. Merithew's yards to sharpen his business skills. In a few months, he will be going back to work at his uncle's ship yard on the Charles River."

"Hogwash," whispered Jack.

"Gert, we need to start up the river road." Joe turned to Daphne. "May I have another drink of water? I think Jack could also use one."

"Marisol, see to it. Then run over to the house and pick up the two old quilts I have stored under your bed. And make it snappy." Daphne sounded a bit put out with her niece.

Tim made his way through the bead curtain. "Let me go. I can run much faster."

Daphne gave him a wave and Marisol shot him a look of thanks.

Gert looked surprised. "You don't live upstairs?"

"Oh, I thought you knew. I have a small two-bedroom home off Mount Ephraim Road behind the Smart Building. The second floor here has offices for some of the shipping companies. They have a wonderful view of the ships arriving in the harbor. Not quite like the grand view Mr. Merithew has from his office on the third floor of his home up the hill on Church Street. He misses nothing and sometimes the work-men on the docks wave up at him just to have some fun."

Gert took a look at her son who was looking worse by the minute. She coaxed him into drinking from the cut glass goblet while Marisol filled a water jug and packed a basket with the rest of the pastries and finger sandwiches.

Daphne picked up the refreshments and started for the door. "We need to start moving Jack to the sidewalk."

Joe reached up to see if his nose was still there. It felt like a new-dug potato housing a headache that had slipped to the middle of his face. "I'll go bring up the wagon."

As Tim ran up Main Street he nearly bumped into the group of Searsport ladies gathered to take a look at the scene in front of Daphne's store. He crossed over with his bundle of quilts just as Joe brought Argos to a halt.

Emerging from the shop, Nana used her hand to shade her eyes against the sun beginning its trip towards the west. "What in the world is going on across the way?"

Tim shook his head. "It is just a gaggle of biddies putting their noses in where they don't belong. Too bad they didn't have more productive things to do with their time."

Marisol and Gert led Jack slowly out the door. The town ladies pretended not to notice and ended up looking like a pod of harbor seals with their heads popping up and down in the swells.

"Shall we?" Joe took the hint from Tim and as if choreographed they smiled broadly and they waved at the spectators.

Marisol did not take kindly to the demonstration. "Timothy Alfred Hodge, behave yourself. You are embarrassing me."

"Just as soon as they behave, dear sister."

The ladies put their heads down and rapidly broke away in two directions. Two of the youngest peeked back at the handsome sailor and giggled.

Jumping into the back of the wagon, Tim folded the quilts lengthwise one on the other to make a thick mat in the middle between the row of barrels and boxed supplies. "Auntie, I brought one of the extra feather pillows. Hope you don't mind."

"Wish I had thought of it myself. Now let's get him into the back and settled."

To make him more comfortable, Gert unbuttoned Jack's shirt and gasped when she saw all the bruising. Marisol also saw, covered her mouth and quickly jumped back to the sidewalk.

After the friends exchanged promises of meeting again soon, Gert covered her son with her comfort quilt. "I've made a seat for myself on the coil of rope. Let's go home."

VII

Now What?

The sun was slipping lower in the western sky when Argos pulled to a stop in front of the Ryan house. Three little urchins tumbled out of the front door, stumbling over each other to get to the wagon first.

"Mama, how come you're so late? Papa is really mad about something and won't tell me why. Then he got more mad that you weren't home to make supper and then he was mad that Uncle Joe didn't get you home on time and then he got madder about...."

"Hold it, Comfort. Not now." Gert looked at Nana. "What else could go wrong with this day that started out so lovely?"

Holly folded her arms in front of her and started in on her father. "Da, it's getting dark and you promised you would put up the swing when you got back. Uncle Joey had to do it."

Joe forgot he brought a left over piece of rope and a notched board to put a swing on a limb of the apple tree.

"I can go up to the sky." Cece swooped her arms way over her head.

Frankie clapped his hands. "I can go higher Da."

Gert hopped out of the back of the wagon. "Great. As if I didn't have enough children with bruises. Comfort, go and get your father. I need his help."

"Papa's in his workshop. He locked us out."

Gert looked anxiously over at Nana. She was working hard to hold the tears back.

Nana took the reins. "Joe, help Jack into the house. Then we'll take the children over to my place for the evening."

Peg opened the front door. "Everything all right out there? I was just doing up the dishes."

"Where's Joey? We could use another hand." Gert pulled her bag and basket out of the wagon and tossed them on the ground.

"He went over to help Thomas in the barn. The calf decided to join us tonight and there was a problem with the surprise delivery."

Gert just threw up her hands. She knew enough not to shout what else could happen.

Peg walked to the wagon and gasped when she saw her husband's twin. "My God, who did this to you?"

Jack mumbled, "One of Marisol's delightful friends."

With his Uncle Joe on one side and mother on the other, they moved him to the edge of the tailgate.

"Wait just a second," shouted Peg. She was back in no time with an empty wooden crate from the storage pantry and placed it upside down so Jack had a step to the ground. "I'll go turn down his bedding. Holly, come and hold the door open."

Cece came skipping around to the back of the wagon, saw Jack and ran to hug him. Gert put her arm out to stop her. "Who did this to my big brother?" She started to cry and put up her fists. "I'll beat him up. Who was it?"

Frankie copied his cousin by punching the air. "Yeah, I'll beat him up too."

As soon as they settled Jack on his bed, Joe left to take the three children to the Hodge farm. "I'll be right back and see about getting my stubborn jackass of a brother out of hiding. He needs to be in here helping you.

"You needn't bother. From what I hear, he would find the situation my fault and have something else to be madder about, as Comfort would say."

Within minutes Joey ran into the bedroom. "The children came sprinting into the barn and told me Jack doesn't look like me anymore. Cece was crying, 'he's all beat up' and Frankie was fired up to go 'punch on someone' himself."

Gert was wringing cold water out a piece of flannel to sooth the bruises on Jack's face. "Have they settled down or should I go over to explain he is going to heal?"

"There's nothing to worry about. As soon as they saw the new calf, all thoughts of Jack disappeared." Joey took a closer look at his brother. "Whoa, what does the other guy look like?"

"From what I can make out, he barely had a scratch. Two of his associates pinned Jack's arms through the spokes of the wagon wheel while the bully beat him. Your Uncle Joe tried to step in and ended up with a bloodied nose." Gert opened Jack's shirt to expose his bruised ribs.

Joey let out a long quiet whistle. "Do we know why?"

"Apparently he has his eye on Marisol and got quite jealous when she was talking with Jack at the rail of the schooner when they were docking."

"Apparently he was out of earshot. They were most likely arguing. I've never seen a couple take such an instant dislike for each other." Joe helped take his twin's work shoes off. "There has to be more to the story."

"Also, this refined so-called gentleman was not pleased to see a half breed daring to chat with Marisol."

"Damn!" Joey slapped his hand sharply on the mattress bringing a spontaneous yelp from Jack. "Sorry buddy. Have they no clue? With our Micmac, French and Irish heritage along with red hair and fair skin, can they not understand we are at most less than an eighth native American. A smidgeon does not equal what is considered a half breed."

Gert smiled. "I guess it is your beautiful dark brown eyes that give you away. Right now Jack's are a bit dulled by the fringe of purple."

"Of all of us, Danny got the largest share of Micmac. When we were younger I used to be jealous of his darker complexion and black hair. I wanted to be the one that looked like Uncle Jacob. I wanted to be the leader of our tribe on the shore of the Aroostook River when I grew up." Joey looked at his mother. "Sorry Ma, you are the perfect Irish lassie and I love your red curls."

"Nice recovery, sweetheart." Peg giggled at her husband's bumbling catch. She brought in a fresh pitcher of cold water and some more flannels.

"Tell me. Do you mind being married to a 'half breed'?"

Peg winked at him. "Not at all, my dear. Especially when you let out a sudden war whoop."

From the bed came, "Watch it brother. Even with a slit for an eye I can see you are blushing."

Peg looked at her mother-in-law and they both laughed out loud. "Think I'd better change the subject. I saw Joe pounding on Pa's workshop. He didn't look happy."

Gert sighed. "If there is anyone that can talk some sense to Sean, it will be his brother."

As if on cue, Sean could be heard coming in the back door loudly disputing his need to go inside. "Look, I've had an unsettling day and don't need to deal with the turmoil that bounces off the walls in the house when the family finally decides to show up. It must be nice to gallivant to the coast, drink tea and relax with friends while I'm pulling my hair out at the fort. And then, not bothering to get home on time to fix the evening meal for the family. There's absolutely no excuse. And who the hell put that swing in the apple tree. I've said no to that since the boys were small."

Joe had just about had it. "For God's sake, Sean Ryan, get your self-righteous rear end into Jack's bedroom and open your eyes long enough to see what is going on with your family."

When Sean got to his son's bedside, Peg had just lit a lantern as dusk was settling. He seemed speechless for a moment but then let loose. "Now what! Jack, what kind of trouble did you get yourself into today?"

That tore at Gert's last nerve. She stood, put her hands on her hips and glared at her husband.

The first to speak was Peg. "Let's get the stove stoked so I can make a kettle of fresh tea and a basin of warm water to clean up Jack and get him into his sleeping clothes."

The men gratefully took the invitation to get out of that room. Peg closed the door behind them and whispered, "It's a hands-on-the-hips moment."

Joe whispered back, "He deserves it."

"Say something Gert or am I suppose to guess how this happened. Why was Jack in Searsport? I thought he was going to work the fields with Joey. Nana will never finish getting the crops in if all he does is look for trouble at the docks."

Gert stood still, staring at her husband. Her arms were now folded in front of her as if protecting her heart from breaking. She stared into Sean's dark brown eyes trying to peek into his soul.

"What's going on?" Sean's tone began to soften. "What is it Gert?"

A single tear began its trip down her cheek, then settled on her chin before dropping on her arms. She spoke softly but firmly. "Sean, you've been drinking."

"What are you talking about Gert? Are you trying to find a way to get around talking about what mischief Jack has been in?" His voice began to rise. "You are always making excuses for the boys, especially this one."

"I got a lot of experience by making excuses for you and I thought that was over. You've been drinking." She kept her voice soft, steady and direct.

Sean put his arms out and began to walk towards his wife. She put one hand up. "Stop right there. I can smell it from here."

"Please don't fight," came the strained voice from the bed. "I'm sorry Pa. I was in the wrong place at the right time to meet a jerk that doesn't seem to like me."

Gert went over and straightened the lightweight quilt over Jack and turned the lantern down low. "Shh sweetheart, try to get some rest. It will be the best for you." Then she turned to Sean. "You, out."

Sean walked into the kitchen and Gert followed. Keeping herself steady she told Peg to make the tea stronger and then give her father-in-law a cup. She pointed at the bench at the table and motioned Sean to sit. Then she turned to Joe. "You knew didn't you?

Joe nodded. "I told him he shouldn't go in right away but my stubborn brother thought you'd never notice."

"I would know if he got into alcohol if he stood a mile away." As Sean sipped his tea, Gert asked Joe to explain what happened by the harbor so that Joey and Peg could hear the whole story at the same time. Predictably the men had the same reaction of anger. Peg, however knew what her mother-in-law needed and held her in her arms.

Finally Sean spoke up. "Today has not been a bed of roses for me either. I may not have the visible bruises but my insides have taken a beaten."

Nobody said a word.

He continued. "The military bigwigs have decided that work at the fort will cease next year. So, within months I will be without a job."

To this news, Gert looked up as if looking for some help from the great Wabanaki spirits. She walked to the back door and let wandering Lady in. "What have you been up to you naughty girl?" That broke the tension a bit. "Sean, the fort is not complete. What about the Rodman cannons they have installed and all the others that have not been delivered? And you told me they have just started the officer's quarters."

"Gert, I have twenty-four years of labor at the fort. What in the world am I going to do now? My crippled arm isn't strong enough to work the clay at the brick works and my small granite work will always be rough. How will I support my family and the home we've built?"

If she wasn't so mad at his slip with the drinking, Gert would have tried to comfort her husband. Instead, she picked up the hefty coon cat and cradled her in her arms. Swaying back and forth, she dared to say it. "What's next?"

To this Joey and Peg stood on either side of his mother and whispered in her ears. "You are going to be a grandmother."

VIII

FAIR WEATHER CLOUDS

Nothing picks up the spirits of a family then to hear there is a baby coming. Long stored knitting supplies were pulled from the trunks along with yards of soft flannel and squares of cotton. Out came the embroidery hoops, crochet needles, collected little buttons and bits of trim. Whenever chores allowed, the ladies gathered to cut, stitch and share stories of other births. It had been over five years since Cece was born and Frankie one week later.

And the men in the fields were just as busy planning. Jack designed a cradle that would be suitable for the baby past infancy. Every once in a while he would stop, pick up a stick and alter his plan in the soil, look it over and usually rubbed out the drawing with his foot. If he liked the changes he'd call for Dan to take a look so he could imagine how he would carve designs in the cradle for their first niece or nephew.

Dan had decided to leave the brick factory earlier than planned so he could take up some of the slack in the sowing. Jack was still having problems with his ribs and could not work the hours needed. Nana stood supported by the rail on the back porch and looked over her vast fields. She could see that the seeding was going slower than usual. The plots that had sprouted were battling for space with the weeds. She used to be as energetic as any man and could do the work of two if need be. And Thomas, dear faithful Thomas had been losing his sight due mostly to labor in the sun as he helped the Hodge Farm grow to success. T worked dawn to dusk but he was hampered in his chores by the loss of his arm to battle. Her dear Captain had searched the banks of the Penobscot to find the best piece of tillable land among the rocks and ledge. He chose well but now she was seeing it being lost to neglect. A tear fell on the railing then slipped onto a soft petal of one of the roses creeping along the fancy latticework that enclosed the base of the veranda.

"Nana, what can I do to help?" Gert sat in a chair beside the dear lady that guided her and Sean through their first tumultuous twenty-four years. They were always able to store enough root vegetables and fruit to carry them over the winter months, but never expanded their land such as she had. Mrs. Hodge supported her beautiful home and land with the toil of her harvests. Now Joey and Peg were begin-ning their life journey with her generous gift of a piece of land to sustain them and soon their growing family. "The day is turning very warm, Nana. Please go inside and have Cara make you some tea and then put your feet up for a while. I'll check things out in the fields. I want to go out with water and see how Jack is holding up."

It was easy to tell Nana was not up to the task for without any question she went inside. Gert couldn't help but think she had never seen her friend so resigned to her age. The view from her vegetable garden did not show just how far behind schedule things were in the Hodge fields. The problem was easier to see as she walked into the gardens from Nana's porch. Gert checked on Jack and ordered him home for a rest promising Dan she'd have him back in an hour. Then she made some plans of her own including working on the Ryan vegetable plots earlier in the mornings so she had time to help Joey supervise the fields for the rest of the day. Yes, indeed. Things could be done with a bit of help.

After checking out Jack's injuries and leaving him to rest with some cold compresses, Gert pulled out her writing desk and began to work on her new strategy.

Needing to catch the mid-morning mail boat she jogged out the back door. On her way past the apple tree she gave a push to Cece on the swing where she had been pouting since her Uncle Joe left early that morning with her two playmate cousins.

"Where you going, Mama?"

"I have some messages to send up to Bangor and while I'm gone, I want you to change into your garden work clothes."

"Why?"

"Because, that is what you are going to do. Work in Nana's garden."

"But."

"Don't pout. You have no choice." As she ran down the Ferry Road, she shouted back. "Make sure you are ready and don't bother Jack. He needs to rest for a bit."

Nana intertwined her fingers and stretched them in front of her to wake the sleep in her arms. "My goodness, I dozed off." She spoke to no one in the empty sitting room. She was most comfortable in her Boston rocker on the cushion of crushed velvet that followed the curves of the solid seat. The color matched the vine of trailing roses Gert had painted on the top tail. "Cara, are you baking ginger snaps?"

"I wanted to use up the bit of molasses in the jug so I could have it filled when I go to market in the morning. I'm going to take a basket of the snaps over to Peg for the worker's lunch." Cara walked in wiping her hands on her long cotton apron that was stained by the memories of many memorable meals. "I have your lunch out on the porch. It would be a shame to waste another minute of this beautiful day."

Settling in her white wicker chair, Nana basked in the sunshine that was playing hide and seek with the fluffy fair weather clouds. She delayed the slice of fresh baked bread with cold chicken and went straight for the ginger cookies that were crisp enough to make a perfect snap when she bit into them. Looking over her fields she was surprised by what she saw. "Cara. Is that Cece working in the pumpkin patch?"

"Yes, indeed and Gert is looking after the pole beans. You can just see her between the new plants making sure the position of the stakes is okay. She came running into the fields a half hour ago, grabbed Joey and started barking orders like one of the officers at the fort."

"But, Cece?"

Cara laughed. "Miss Cece was promised the biggest and best pumpkin she could find to carve into her jack-o-lantern. Her duties include keeping the patch weeded and helping Joe and Peg in any way they ask."

"But Gert has her own garden to tend and a house to keep with a family that pops in and out more frequently than guests at the local inn."

"I don't know her plan but I know she has one to make sure your acres are planted and tended." Cara cleared Nana's lunch dishes and left her with a fresh cup of tea. "However, I do know that once she gets her jaw set with determination, no one is going to change her mind so I suggest you don't even try."

The sound of a small school bell rang out across the fields. "What in the world is that?" Nana stood and tried to see the nexus of the sound.

"Gert has decided that it would make more sense to feed the workers together rather than stagger the times. Peg is going to make a picnic meal each noon to serve in the pine grove next to her house. This way, time will be saved by getting the full crew back to the planting and weeding faster."

"Crew? What crew? I haven't been able to get a crew together since the war ended. We lost our Mike and so many other local boys. Some field workers have found higher paying jobs in the growing brick works in Brewer or loading the lumber schooners at the Bangor docks. Once I could do the work of more than one farmhand. Now I just sit here like one of the coal clunkers in the parlor stove. Good for nothing."

"Have you lost your cooking skills?" Cara smiled as she knew Nana loved her kitchen with the latest in stoves complete with a thermostat for the oven.

"You have so spoiled me that I haven't used them as much. What's going on?"

"Frankly, I don't know but Gert has something cooking and not the type of thing that uses a stove. I do know that her plans include feeding a few extra mystery guests. She is keeping that pretty close. She would like us to take up some of the cooking to ease the load on Peg."

"Just how big a meal is she planning?"

"It is not the size but the number. She said to plan on three to four meals a day for at least a week for twelve to fourteen."

Nana laughed and tossed her arms in the air. "Twelve to fourteen what? Where in the world would she find that many workers? All the farms around here are in the middle of planting. I can't think of any that could release a single worker or family member, never mind a dozen or more."

Cara shrugged her shoulders. "As Miss Cece would say, 'I not know'. Speaking of our little sprite, here she comes bouncing over one row to another of squash seedlings."

Nana smiled, "I'm sure her mother has promised her more than first choice out of the pumpkin patch. She would make quite a horse trader, that one."

"She' going to be a force to contend with for some fellow some day." Cara giggled as she picked up lunch dishes.

Nana took a closer look in the fields. "Cara, please fetch my opera glasses." She had recently treated herself to a pair of lovely Lemaire binoculars decorated with mother of pearl. "These are not anywhere near the strength of the looking glass I gave Tim, but they do help me see the workers. It seems that Cece is having quite a conversation with Thomas. Poor man probably just walked by to see how she was doing."

Cara shaded her eyes with her hand. "What do suppose that is all about? It looks like she has her hands on her hips." She brushed the stray long graying red hair out of her eyes and tucked it behind her ear. "Just like Gert when she gets out of sorts."

"Now she is waving her finger at him. I'd say Thomas had better run to the other side of the potato field." Nana shook her head and smiled. "I feel my spirits rising up from the depths. Yes indeed, let's bake up some gingerbread for the crew for supper. See if we have some top cream in the pantry to whip."

Cara opened the kitchen window wide to let the river breeze blow through the crocheted curtains. "We are so late in getting in all the crops. Do you think we have a chance to get everything in long enough to beat any frost before harvest?"

"We have always dealt with a short growing season starting the very end of May but if Gert can get everything planted in the next week or two, we'll make it." Nana tried to ease her own doubts by beating the dickens out of the batter in her stoneware mixing bowl.

Cara took the bowl out of the crook in Nana's arm. "We better pour the mix in the baking tin before you shatter that wooden spoon. We don't want to serve the workers splinters in their dessert. You can get rid of more frustration by whipping the cream later."

Nana walked into her front parlor and opened the front door to get some cross ventilation. The lupine along the road and up the hill across the way was fading for another year. Yet the beauty of the softer color was still a delight for her aging eyes. She walked over to the small fireplace and took a highly decorated clay pipe off its stand on the mantle. Sitting in the plush velvet chair by the window, she smiled at the carved designs that brought back sweet memories. There was still a light odor of the Virginia tobacco Captain Hodge liked so much. It was shipped in the barrels used for carrying rum from the islands so the faint flavor in the wood was transferred to the tobacco leaves. *Dear Captain, am I destroying your dream of this farm along the river? Is my age going to destroy all our work? I seem to be losing my way as to what to do next. Without Gert and her family I never could have kept it going this long. Am I a complete failure in your eyes? I still feel your presence and at times swear I can smell your pipe as I move through the house.* She began to stand to put the pipe back when there was a loud commotion on the back porch that startled her and she almost dropped the precious pipe. "What in the world is going on?"

Cece came stomping into the room. "Nana, come see."

"Just give me a minute." The pipe was carefully placed back on its stand.

Cece nearly dragged Nana to the porch and pointed west. "See. There is going to be a change."

"Well, so there is. It looks like we are going to lose the sun but I'm sure we can still keep working in the fields."

"I know that!" With a pout, Cece folded her arms in front of her. "Mr. Thomas told me that was a buttermilk sky coming and I told him no sir. It was a mackerel sky heading our way and that is why the weather is going to change. Then he told me no, it was a buttermilk sky showing us the weather may change. Then he just walked away." She stamped her foot scaring a pair of rabbits out of their hiding place under the porch.

Nana took her hand and they sat together in the wicker rocker. "Well, little girl, both of you are right."

"Well that's not what you told me. You said a mackerel sky meant there was going to be a change. Don't you remember? 'Mackerel Sky, Mackerel Sky - never long wet - never long dry.' That's what you said."

"You see, I was taught that rhyme by Captain Hodge when we were living on his ship and the seamen thought that type of cloud formation looked like the scales on a mackerel. Now, Mr. Thomas always worked on the land and to a farmer those clouds remind them of the curds on top of the buttermilk."

Cece's eyes lit up. "Oh, but I think I'll still call it what Captain Hodge taught you."

"I know he would have liked that. Now Cece, you should go back to work and if you see Mr. Thomas, tell him he was right too."

After a hug, she started to run back to the fields then turned around. "Nana, things keep changing at my house. I had three big brothers then Joey left with Peg, Dan comes and goes, Papa is fun then he is mad because his job is going away, Mama is happy and then she is sad, Jack is nice and then he is mean, Lady acts funny and doesn't purr much when I love her, now I'm going to be an auntie and I'm only five years old. Change. Change. Change. Are we a mackerel sky family?"

IX

What's Next?

The last rumbles of thunder echoed down the valley towards the sea. Gert was grumbling about the surprise heavy rain to no one in particular. Lady strolled by and rubbed against her legs as if to say that she was also not happy about the sloppy conditions outside. Her morning meanderings down to the riverside would be very muddy and there will be a fuss about her dirty paws.

Gert picked up the longhaired cat and took her to the kitchen rocker. "My goodness, Lady, how much weight have you gained? I swear you are turning into the largest Maine coon I have ever seen." Lady stretched full length up her human mother's body and laid her head on Gert's shoulder, her purr louder than ever. "Oh my goodness. No wonder! Lady, you are going to have kittens! Why didn't I check you before this? I should have known, you've been acting so strange."

"Kittens. Did I hear kittens?" Cece came hopping out of her room on one foot while trying to pull a sock on the other.

"There certainly is no problem with your ears little girl. Funny, you can never hear me when I call you in for chores. Now hop back into your room, get dressed and straighten up your bed."

"But Mama." Her plea did not help as Gert pointed to the back bedroom.

Suddenly the backdoor open and in tromped Sean doing his best not to drag in mud on the kitchen floor. Gert tossed him a towel to clean off his feet.

"What in the world is going on? You never leave the job in the morning. Are you ill?" Gert walked over and placed the back of her hand on Sean's forehead.

He brushed her hand away. "What in the world is going on is the question I planned to ask."

Gert cocked her head with a puzzled looked.

"Three telegraph messages were just forwarded to the fort addressed to you in care of me."

Now Gert started to get excited. "What did they say?" She was practically jumping up and down.

"From Smytheville, '2 to 3 Saturday.' From Searsport, '2 Saturday.' From Indian Island, '2 Saturday.' Gertrude Ryan, what are you up to now?"

"Yes, yes! I knew I could count on them."

Sean tossed his hands in the air. "Who and for what?"

"Nana's crew, that's who. If they all get here Saturday, we should have the rest of the planting done in a few days. I think there is still time to have a good crop by the harvest."

"You're a dreamer Gert. How are we going to get our crop to harvest if all your time is taken up by the Hodge farm?"

"For God's sake, Sean, what has happened to you? You're turning into a selfish bastard. Certainly you haven't forgotten Nana's generosity when we came to the Penobscot River as newlyweds."

Sean tossed the muddy towel towards the dry sink but missed as it landed it on the sideboard.

Gert quickly retrieved it. "You'll be the first to be upset if you find dirt in the supper biscuits. What's your problem?"

"I don't like you going behind my back to make plans for us over the next few weeks." Gert started to rebut but he stopped her. "Yes, I do remember how Nana helped us get started and deeded us this property. And I know she is more like a grandmother to our children. But I also know I have my own labor in this land and have provided for our own family and I don't deserve you leaving me out."

"If I had talked this over with you, would you have gone along with my idea?"

"Would I have had a choice? No!" Sean's Irish short fuse was starting to smolder.

"Take it easy Sean. This is exactly why I didn't get you involved. Now-a-days it's easier for me to make plans and deal with your disapproval later than have to go through this every time I want to take on a problem. I'll make sure our garden produces what we need. I always have."

"Tell me. How did you get the message out this fast?"

Gert slowly walked over to the sink and began to draw water from the pitcher pump. She answered just above a whisper. "I sent them all a telegram."

"What did you say?" Sean was definitely not speaking softly.

"You heard me. I sent out telegrams."

"And just how did you do that. I know that the line at the fort has not been active for a few days and was shocked when the first messages to come through were for you." Now it was Sean with his hands on his hips.

"As soon as I saw the need, I wrote notes and took them down to the mail boat. I gave the mate enough money to send the messages and a tip for himself for taking them to the Bangor telegraph office."

"And just how did you know those lines would not be down?" Sean was glaring at his wife.

"Just think about it. Bangor is now considered the lumber capital of the world so the businessmen would do everything possible to keep the telegrams flowing. Also Dan told me most buildings in the new Back Bay of Boston are being constructed with Brewer brick. They are very busy shipping along the Penobscot River to the ocean ports so I knew my messages would go."

Still obviously angry, Sean was not letting up. "And, just how did you pay for all this?"

Gert's face turned a bit red as she grabbed the kettle off the stove set a new pot of tea to seep.

"Gert! Don't ignore me."

"I used the egg money."

"We've been saving that for shoes for Comfort when she starts school this fall." Sean slammed his fist on the sideboard. "We promised her new shoes. How are you going to replace that?"

"I'll get it in time."

"How? Do you plan to whip those old hens into laying twice as many eggs to sell?"

"Please Sean, I will find a way to replace the money from the egg fund." Gert was having a hard time controlling a tear that wanted to escape Cece came running out of her bedroom. "The egg money's gone? What about my new shoes for school?"

Sean picked up his pride and joy. "Don't worry sweetie, Mama is going to get the money back. Right, Gert?"

Gert walked over and gave her daughter a kiss on the cheek. "You'll have new shoes, I promise."

Cece's smile seemed to go from ear to ear. She gave her father a big hug around his neck and then wiggled out of his arms. As she started to go out to the swing she stopped short. "Papa, did you know we are a family that is always changing?"

Sean cocked his head and gave Gert a quizzical glance. She shrugged.

"Yep and now Lady is going to have kittens. I hope there's lots and lots."

As Cece bounced out the door, Sean turned to Gert and rolled his eyes. "What's next?"

Gert wrapped her arms around Sean's neck and whispered in his ear. "Remember. We never ask – what's next."

X

THE CREW

S aturday at dawn, Gert was humming a tune as she poured the batter for the second batch of corn bread into the well-worn baking tin. The first was cooling on the back porch, ready to be wrapped in gingham for the picnic basket along with a small stoneware crock of molasses.

"Well, it's about time you got up, you lazy bum." Lady stretched and then rubbed against her mistress' leg, taking her first comfort of the day, saying thanks with a loud purr. Gert reached down and stroked the longhaired feline under her chin. She loved that and stretched her neck up for more loving. "I wish I had been more attentive so we had an idea when your babies will arrive." Gert tested the bread with a bit of straw off the broom. "Perfect! Come on Lady, let's set this out to cool and then do some weeding in the garden before our family wants breakfast." Not wanting to disturb Sean, Gert pulled on her leather garden boots and put on Jack's red wool work shirt over her nightgown. To keep her long red hair from falling in her eyes while bending over, she grabbed one of boy's stocking caps from the box in the storage room.

Waking up alone in the feather bed that had held up well over the past twenty-four years, Sean went to see where Gert may be. As he filled the water pitcher from the pump in the kitchen, something caught his eye out the window. The early morning sun was playing peek-a-boo through the limbs of the stately stand of pines at the crest of the slope from the river's edge. Sean was looking at what he thought was a scarecrow standing in the center of their potato plot. *It seems to me that Gert should have placed him between the rows of yellow eye beans. That area has just been seeded and would make a feast for some sharp-eyed crows.* Suddenly he tried to stifle a laugh that would wake the rest of the house as the raggedly pole man began to jump around.

Gert had been very still midst the sprouting potato plants as she watched the activity atop what Cece called the eagle tree. The slanting early sun appeared to give a pinkish tint to the white feathers on the eagles. Gert found this most beautiful as they flew back and forth to the nest. Then to her delight, two tiny balls of white fluff could be seen bopping up and down as their parents came close. *Comfort is going to be so excited that the eaglets have hatched. According to whisperings from her great-great-grandmother Nuga, she told us there were eggs nestled in fresh straw in the giant nest. Perhaps there is something to her spirits.* Suddenly something cold and wet pressed against the back of Gert's leg just below the hem of her nightgown and she let out a scream and turned around flapping her arms to fend off whatever had attacked.

Sean ran out and calmed his wife assuring her there were no wild animals, snakes or other creatures that crawl in the night. "Besides, the way you are dressed you would be the one to scare them all away."

Suddenly Cece came running into the garden with her red braids unraveling around her face as she jumped the potato plants. "Mama, I heard you scream. And why are you in a nightdress outside. You look pretty silly. Right Papa?"

"I've told her not to wear it outdoors but you know how much your mother listens to me."

"I'm just fine, sweetheart. I was just startled when something cold pressed against my leg."

Cece giggled. "It was just Lady. See, she is sitting in the next row and I think she's laughing at you."

Not sure it was still dark enough to hide her red face, Gert put her head in her hands.

Sean put his arm around her shoulders. "Think of it this way Gert, we know Lady must be healthy with that wet cold nose."

Confident she had yanked out any new weeds between the potato foliage, she headed towards the porch. "Come on you two. Get cleaned up for breakfast. We have a busy day ahead."

Sean picked up his little girl and tossed her over his shoulder. "We should finally find out who is part of Mama's field crew."

The next couple of hours flew by faster than eagles diving for a fish spied from a great height. Gert changed the bedding on Cece's bed and the spare bed. Next she freshened up the beds in Dan and Jack's room in the front of the house and put all the linens on the porch in the tub Sean filled with hot water. "Comfort, get the washing stick and start making suds with the flakes I shaved off the soap. I'll get the rinse tub ready in a minute." She took another look around then opened the front window wide to allow fresh air to eliminate the staleness of the boy's room.

Sean finished cleaning the ashes from the parlor fireplace and laid fresh logs in case of a chilly night. "What next General?"

Gert walked in and smacked him across the behind with her dusting rag. "If you are looking for orders, how about getting those ashes in the bin so I can make some soap in the next few weeks. Then help me fill the rinse tub with hot and cold water so we can get the linens out on the line in this wonderfully warm wind. They should dry in no time in case we need to make up more beds."

"Yes, Ma'am! Where are the boys and how come they aren't in the cleaning up brigade?"

"They had to help Frank clean out some stalls in the barn so we better keep the left over rinse water to toss over them. Remember many moons ago when the boys decided to go sliding on the wet barn floor and came home smelling like a stockyard? It took a lot of scrubbing before I'd let them in the house."

"And I thought you had just seasoned the garden with more cow manure." Sean shook his head and snickered. "Where has the time gone Gert?"

"Time disappears like the geese flying south each year. Here, then gone. Just the way the hours have vanished this morning. Help me hang the laundry and then I'll make lunch before our mysterious company arrives."

Soon the hurry-up-pace in the Ryan household came to a crawl. Resting in the porch rocker, Gert took a deep breath and listened to the river traffic punctuated by the staccato of the flapping sheets and Sean chipping away at granite in his workshop. Her reverie was broken when Dan leaned over her chair and kissed her on the cheek.

"Sorry, Ma. I didn't mean to startle you. You were miles away in thought."

"My mind is going in so many different directions it is hard to untangle my ideas to make a reasonable plan."

"Don't over think it Ma. Just let us know what needs to be done and let us find the way to do it."

"Danny, for me, that is easier to say than to do. I didn't hear you come back and you're all cleaned up."

"Nana wouldn't let us leave before we washed ourselves down and then sent us to change our clothes. When Jack saw our room he knew we were not going to use it and wanted to rest up before our so-called crew arrives. So, he's asleep on the sofa." Dan saw the alarm in his mother's eyes. "Not to worry, he took his shoes off and put down the quilt first."

Gert stood, stretched and then took another look up and down the river. There were no signs of traffic stopping at Bucksport or at the Prospect Ferry landing. "Maybe nobody's coming."

Dan gave his mother a hug. "I'm anxious to see who our farm hands are going to be."

"So am I." Gert took a deep breath and tried to let her body relax. She listened to the hypnotic squeaking of the ropes as Comfort swayed on the swing while watching the river.

A voice from the kitchen door broke her daydreams. "Can anyone get a cup of hot strong tea in this place?"

Jumping up, Gert caught her shoe in the hem of her skirt and she staggered into the arms of Tim. Behind him was Marisol doubled over in laughter. "Gert, I'd say you were into last year's hard cider if I didn't know better."

"No! Say it's not so. How could I miss that laugh? Please tell me you are only here to drop off your brother. You'd never take a chance on getting your shoes dirty or worse – you might break a fingernail." Jack had pulled himself off the sofa and was coming into the kitchen when he heard that telltale giggle. His hair resembled a matted dust mop, shirt was unbuttoned, and the hole in his right sock was big enough to expose three toes. "And furthermore, Master Pudgy Bigshot would not approve."

Marisol turned and snapped at Jack. "I'll have you know that Matthew thought it was wonderful for me to help Mrs.

Hodge. It seems many years ago when his uncle was a young apprentice he knew Captain Hodge. He has never forgotten how the captain helped him learn a great deal about ship construction by taking him on board whenever he docked in Boston Harbor."

"I'm impressed, at least for the time being." Jack stretched his arms over head with a big yawn. "Just trying to wake up enough to tackle that list my mother has ready."

Gert moved past her guests to put the kettle on. "How'd you two get here?"

"We borrowed Aunt Daphne's surrey for a week with Sweet Thing, her filly. We'll start back early Saturday morning. I hope that's enough time. I felt the wagon gave us a bit more flexibility than dealing with paddle boat schedules." Tim looked around. "Is Sean home or at the fort?"

Gert poured the boiling water over the tealeaves. "He's in his work shop. Go talk him into taking a break. Jack, change those embarrassing socks and then tend to Sweet Thing and the buggy. I'm sure Thomas has a stall you can use. Dan, put Marisol's bags in Comfort's room."

"See how good she is at orders?" Jack left with a salute.

Gert put out the butter crock, the tail end of the blueberry preserves and a fresh loaf of sourdough bread. "Help yourselves. We will have our main meal in the picnic grove next to Joey's house and by then all our planting volunteers should be here". *I hope.*

"Mama, someone's coming!" Cece was skipping across the back yard after doing a flip off her perch on the swing. "I saw them put a wagon on the ferry."

"Them? How many were there?" Gert was trying not to get too excited."

Cece shrugged. "I not know. I need one of those spy glasses like Tim got from Nana." She jumped on the porch, ran into the kitchen and saw her friend. "Mary! Look Mama, Mary's here." She was already hugging her newest friend.

Gert was hanging over the rail straining her eyes. Now that the leaves were filling out it was hard to see the bottom of Ferry Road. "I can't wait. I'm going to the landing to greet whoever is on that boat."

"And what if they turn out to be strangers?" Dan quickly finished his tea and popped a piece of bread in his mouth. "I'm going with you."

"No bother. I'll just pretend I was out for a walk when the ferry comes."

"You never know who could be coming to the fort. You're not going alone. There are some pretty rough characters looking for day work on closing things down. There's only one government military man staying there now. Everyone else has been pulled out. No, being at the ferry landing is not as safe as it used to be.

"Comfort, you stay with Marisol."

"Can I have a cookie?"

"Just one." Gert started down the stairs and turned back. "I mean it. Those are for supper."

As she ran towards the shortcut to the Ferry Road, Sean came out of the granite workshop. "Where in the world are you two going in such a hurry?"

"We may have more folks arriving at the landing. There's some food for you in the kitchen." She never missed a step in her race to keep up with Dan.

Tim shaded his eyes against the early afternoon sun to watch Gert running out of sight. "Does she always move like a whirling dervish?"

Sean nodded. "Guess that comes from raising four boys and a girl while her lame-brained husband devotes himself to building a useless fort."

At the ferry landing, Dan grabbed his mother around the waist as she sped to the bottom of the road fearful she wouldn't stop and toss herself into the Penobscot River. "Whoa there, Ma. The ferry is only half way across. Give it a couple more minutes."

Breathless, Gert stood on her tiptoes but at her stature it really didn't help. Dan lifted her up on a large rock where she steadied herself by leaning on his shoulder. She waved so hard he had to be careful they both would not land in the water. "I can see both Joe and Annie holding the horse steady but I'm not sure if the other people I see are with them."

"Are Holly and Frankie on board?"

"Can't see any children."

Dan took a deep sigh of thanks. "I'm not sure we would get much done if we had all the cousins together."

"Put me down. Put me down. I swear I saw JJ at the railing."

Lifting his "Ma" safely to the ground, he took a closer look and had to agree. "How in the world could he get away from the family potato farm during sowing time? Who is that beautiful woman standing next to him and waving at us?"

"Dear God, can it be?" A spontaneous tear dribbled down her check. "It's Kate."

Dan whistled softly. "She certainly has blossomed into one fine lady."

Gert wiped away tears with her apron. "I haven't seen her since Mike's memorial service on the hill three years ago. They were so in love."

The next few minutes were a flurry of activity. Ropes tied. An unhappy horse was lead off still pulling his load. Finally Kate was in Gert's arms with so many questions to be asked and answered when the dust settled. Next came a hug from JJ. He still had a noticeable limp from the war. Gert then greeted brother-in-law Joe and dear Annie. More questions. How were they able to leave Indian Island, especially at this time? And where were the children?

Dan soothed the jittery beast of burden and calmed him down before jumping up on the seat of the wagon. "JJ asked me to take the wagon up the hill so everyone could stretch their legs. The folks from Aroostook County have been cooped up in a stagecoach for a couple days. I'll see Willy is well stabled with Argos and Hector." With a flick of the reigns, Dan was off with the belongings and orders from Gert not to tell anyone who was here. She loved surprises.

The ferry began the trip back across the river as the group started walking. Within a few steps, a voice boomed out behind them. "And what about me? Do you think I'm too old to help?"

Gert knew that voice. She turned and ran back to the landing squealing. "Uncle Jacob! Uncle Jacob!" She flew into the arms of the tall, stately Micmac leader, wrapped her arms around his neck and would not let go. He was the same pillar of strength that led his tribe through so many years of uncertainty. The only sign of his age was his braids hanging over his shoulders were now snow white. "You're the mysterious number three. Sean is going to be beside himself."

"Probably because my nephew Trouble knows I am going to make him mind. Been doing that since he was small enough to ride around on my boot."

Gert loved to hear stories about the three young Ryan brothers in the woods along the Aroostook River. They could be quite a handful but not to their sagamore. His authority was never challenged.

There was so much chattering among the group walking through the shortcut, you could see all the birds lining up on the limbs to listen to the human songs.

As they reached the apple tree, Sean came out on the porch. "Glory be, are my eyes playing games? Jack, come and see if you remember any of these folks."

"Wahoo! Jack took one look and forgetting his damaged ribs, jumped over the railing. He recalled as soon as his feet hit the ground. Wrapping his arms around the mid-cage, he kept hobbling forward to greet his Uncle Jacob."

"What have you been up to now, Jack?"

"Why is that the first question everyone asks? It happens this time, I was innocent and the one unfairly injured."

Jacob looked at Gert and Sean. They nodded in the affirmative. "I must hear the whole story."

"You will, sir." Jack shook his uncle's hand with an unspoken, *please don't hug me.*

With hellos exchanged, the group walked towards the porch. JJ remarked, "That's quite a striking woman up there. Is she anyone in whom you have an interest?"

Jack chuckled. "Who, Marisol? She may be lovely but can knock you down with a word. No, I'd rather wrestle a bear. If you are up for a challenge, be my guest."

"Somehow I can't see her among the Micmac on the Aroostook. Beaded moccasins would not go well with that dress. I believe it is silk and it certainly drapes her body so as not to hide any curves."

Jack just smiled and looked to the sky. "Really, I hadn't noticed. Some English dolt who is interning at the ship building docks in Searsport is courting her. And believe me he can be jealous." Jack hugged his ribs.

"Aha, I'm beginning to get the picture."

Gert waved everyone to the porch. Tim leaned over and whispered in her ear. "Who is the lovely lady that just joined us."

"That is the daughter of Sean's childhood friend Ben Smythe. Her name is Kate and her brother JJ is with Jack.

Coming up the stairs, Kate noticed Cece peeking around Marisol. "My goodness, is that Miss Comfort Claire Ryan hiding back there?"

The answer, barely audible, was, "No! It's Cece." She was hugging her handkerchief doll.

"We were trying to find a name for that doll the last time we played. Did you find one?"

A brief flash of recognition twinkled in Cece's eyes yet she was still too shy to speak above a whisper. "She is Lacey."

Kate fingered the lace edge of the handmade toy, "Why Cece, that's perfect."

Sean took her by the hand and kissed her on both cheeks. "You look lovely Kate. I really am tongue-tied that you would come and I thank you."

"It's been three years Sean and about time. We want to help Mrs. Hodge and I want to look at some personal opportunities in this area.

The Smythe and Hodge siblings chattered in the parlor with Cece sitting cross-legged on the floor stroking Lady. The little girl seemed transfixed on the two young women, listening to every word. She noticed Tim never said a word but just stared at Kate.

JJ couldn't help but take a peek when Marisol leaned over to pat Lady. The lacey décolletage around the scoop neck of her blouse nicely set off her ample bosom. He thought, *lovely*. But the look he got from sister Kate sent a message he would get a talking to later. He thought, *worth it*.

In the kitchen, Gert was all agog. She was collecting extra tin cups and fairly dancing from the cabinets to the carrying basket.

Joey came running through the door breathless. "Peg is fairly beside herself hoping she has enough food. I don't want her to hurt the baby with excitement. Using your numbers she came up with fifteen places. Is that right?"

"I went through this same game in my head. Tell her to add two so she and Cara can join us."

Joey laughed. "She never thought of herself."

"And how about Nana? Do you suppose she might want to be part of this supper meal, at least for the first one? So if my brain is still working, we should set for eighteen.

"You can be amazing, Ma. Nana will find it hard to believe. And when can we expect them? Peg wants me to walk Nana to our house in about an hour. That would give us time to see each other before suppertime." Gert gave her son a hug around the neck and whispered in his ear. "They're already here. Take a look in the parlor."

"JJ! How in the world could you leave that huge potato farm this time of year? Dear Kate, you are a sight for sore eyes. And, the Hodge twins. Peg will be so excited."

Unfazed by the commotion, Cece and Lady never moved from the floor. Joey reached down and picked up his sister. "You'll be trampled by this famous farm crew if you are not careful."

Being up that high, Cece saw the narrow black velvet ribbon around Kate's neck and pointed at it. Kate pulled the ribbon up from inside her bodice. It was threaded through a perfect small granite heart and a brass button. Cece pulled out the ribbon from around her neck. It was threaded through an identical brass button. Then a sense of recognition fell over the child and she reached out into the arms of Kate. Cece smiled in the lap of the lady surrounded by a familiar light scent of rose water.

Tim looked at the tender scene. *How could I have been so stupid? Kate is the sweetheart of Michael Ryan; the son killed at Gettysburg.*

Gert called from the kitchen. "Joey, you better start home so you can get Nana. Take this basket with you and make sure you stop at your father's workshop." Watching her son enter Sean's inner sanctum, she waited. "Wahoo!" She bent with glee.

All Joey could see when he went from the bright sun to the haze of the shop were his father and brothers. "What is this, a meeting of Ryan and Sons?"

From the corner behind the scrap bin came a booming voice. "How about Ryan and Sons and Uncle?"

Joey spun around so fast he tripped over the top of a birdbath Sean was fashioning for Gert's flower garden. Jacob's reflexes were none the worse for age for he balanced the stumbling brother before he could do major damage to himself.

"Wahoo!" He gave the strong figure a bear hug. "Thank you for catching me. If I had turned an ankle or worse, broke something, my mother would make us all pay."

Jacob brushed the stone dust off Joey's shoulders. "Run along. Tell your lovely Peg that Mrs. Hodge's planting crew is on the way over. We'll have lots of time to tell tales about each other."

Jacob stood straight with his arms crossed and watched Joey fairly skipping across the fields to his home. He shook his head and looked back at Sean. "You know, I don't know which is worse for an old scout like me. The idea of one of your sons becoming a father, or the fact that my little Trouble is going to be a grandfather."

XI

Now it Begins

Joey noticed Nana's steps were becoming more unsteady. Somehow he thought she would always be their strong life force. In this season of newness within his family he was finding it hard to accept the changes in his neighbor. *We must find ways to hold her spirits high.*

As they entered the lovely grove of young pines scattered with birch trees, the afternoon sun shone in rays of light that appeared like ribbons as it sliced through the canopy of new leaves. Layers of pine needles formed a natural soft carpet on the ground. Joey and Peg were slowly building their home with the grove as a back yard, the fields of the Hodge farm on the eastern side, and the front facing the life on the river. Someday, they would have a porch of their own.

"This is marvelous." Nana whispered to the tops of the trees and the creatures within.

"Did you say something, Nana?" Peg was carrying out one of their chairs with a back and arms. Nana had called it a captain's chair when she gave it to them as she was cleaning the attic. It was one of many pieces of furniture they were grateful to receive.

"This is the very spot that my captain and I first cut the old growth pines. I had not realized how well the plot recovered over these many years. It's beautiful."

Peg helped Nana settle in at the long rough tables and benches. "Cece calls this her fairyland."

"That young child carries the wisdom of the ancients. I sometimes believe the spirit of her great-great-grandmother Nuga, rests in her heart. Jacob has told me so many stories about that strong lady."

"Did I hear someone mention my name?"

Nana twisted in her chair to catch Jacob towering above her and tried to stand up.

Jacob came down on one knee beside her chair. "I didn't mean to startle you. I just wanted to let you know your planting crew is here and ready to start work. At least by morning."

"Jacob, dear Jacob." Nana wanted to stand up and her dear friend helped her do so. She grabbed both his hands and looked straight into his eyes with disbelief and gratitude.

"My dear Mrs. Hodge, everything is going to be fine. Just take a look about me and you will know you are far from alone."

Hanging on tight to Jacob's arm, Nana held her hand over her mouth as if to hold back mixed screams of surprise and joy when seeing her 'farm hands'. Nana hung tighter to Jacob. That is until she saw Kate. Both her arms flung in the air and she reached out to be held by her, the both of them being steadied by JJ.

Suddenly the ringing of the schoolhouse bell brought all to attention. Gert told everyone to take a place on the benches so the meal could be served on the two long tables. Like a well-oiled wheel on the garden cart, the food appeared with no effort (though Nana, of course, knew the amount of time and planning needed to pull this together). Cara at one table and Peg at the other soon scooped out thick chicken and root vegetable stew on cream of tartar biscuits. Stoneware bowls on the tables held fresh fiddlehead fern greens and there were extra biscuits with small crocks of freshly churned butter.

Shared stories became jewels threaded on a ribbon of laughter. Joe and Annie explained that the children were staying with their grandparents who planned to spoil them each and every minute they had them alone on Indian Island.

Soon platters of cookies centered the tables, the cups were passed, and hot kettles of black tea followed. For Cece, her own special cup of cold milk from Nana's pantry. Then a strange pot with an attached wooden handle was added to the mix.

Nana smiled. "That's smells a lot like a fresh pot of coffee. Who brought this special treat to the table? I for one am going to enjoy a cup."

"I brought some grounds with me. My friends go to coffee houses in Boston and I found I like the brew." Marisol sipped on the hot black liquid. "I hope you like it."

"I knew you were trying some new foods but I never knew you were drinking coffee." Tim reached over and poured a half-cup. "Cece, may I have a drop of your milk for that's the way I like it best. I've known seamen that brew it very strong and add a lot of sugar as they do in Arabia."

"I think I'll stay with my tea until I feel more adventurous." Kate filled her tin adding delight to a sugar cookie. "Marisol, what other type of new food have you been trying?"

"Lately I have enjoyed lobster with drawn butter."

Cece fairly jumped out of her seat. "You eat those ugly things? Papa told me how the Indians would use them when they planted. You really eat fertilizer?"

Marisol was feeling the pink start to grow up her cheeks. "I would never eat fertilizer. These lobsters were collected in traps at sea and we received them fresh for the pot."

This got a laugh out of Uncle Jacob. "They actually take boats out to collect them? You do know they are bottom feeders that scavenge garbage?"

Sean piped up as he reached for another cookie only to have his hand slapped by Gert, to the amusement of her boys. "To be fair. Many have eaten lobsters to survive. At one time they were the only food available to the unfortunate. They would cover the beaches after a storm and residents would gather them in corn baskets to take to the poor houses."

Nana jumped into this exchange. "I heard that Massachusetts passed a law about lobsters. It seems they were being fed to prison inmates every day. To some this seemed so cruel that rules were written to protect the prisoners from this terrible punishment. They could not be served more than four times a week. Also the captain told me that many English indentured servants had it written in their contracts that they would not be fed lobster more than three times a week."

Thomas, who usually was never heard, laughed and added his two cents. "When I first started farming, my father would have me take a wagon to Sandy Point after a storm to collect the critters from the shoreline to be added to the potato rows."

Taking pity on Marisol, JJ added some words of support. "I think it is wonderful that you're not afraid to try something new and if you enjoy it, so be it. Perhaps you can challenge me to try a taste some day."

"Life would be terribly dull if you didn't find a change of pace." Nana wiped the bits of cookie crumbs from her place at the table. "I tried snails once and found them quite different but palatable."

Cece covered her mouth to stop a gag. "Nana, you didn't!"

Jack caught Marisol's eye. "Is this one of your Searsport fishermen who is using his boat to harvest the spiders of the sea? He'll soon be penniless for no one in his right mind would buy lobster to eat. Remember my word, this will be a fool's venture." He enjoyed his proclamation and Marisol's embarrassment. "Now, dear mother, what is next on your list?"

"I would say your uncle will take over the task and direct the men in the building of a wigwam out by our apple tree. That should be an ample shelter for you and he, Tim, JJ, and Dan."

Joey looked a bit left out. "What about me?"

The ladies around the table giggled while Peg gave her husband a sharp elbow to the ribs. Jack feigned bending over in pain "I'm sure glad that wasn't me."

Joey still had not figured out what happened. Then Uncle Jacob laid his hand on his nephew's shoulder and clarified. "Young man. You have made your bed now you need to sleep in it."

Red faced, Peg piled the dessert cups on the kitchen tray and made for her back door.

Tim leaned over to JJ. "Just what is a wigwam?"

"Have you ever heard of a teepee?"

"I read about them in some Western chapbooks. Does that mean we are going to sleep on the ground like the Indians do?"

JJ pointed at the Ryan men and Uncle Jacob. "In case you haven't noticed or no one told you, they are Indians. There was a time when British officers paid good money for the scalps of Micmac and Penobscot men. Since you and I are the only English men I see, perhaps we'd better do our best to work hard and please them."

Marisol looked a bit alarmed and took Kate's hand. "Does that mean we are the only British women here?"

Kate laughed. "Let me tell you my dear. There is no safer place for us then in the hands of these men. Pay no attention to any of the terrible untruths you may hear along the waterfront. Those who are ignorant and will never learn better spread that type of talk. I'm afraid it will take many years for their twisted views of the native tribes to change. The newly freed slaves will find the same."

"Marisol, my captain felt much the same about the four Wabanaki tribes when we first settled here and was unhappy when I brought Joe home to visit. Eventually he became like a son and Captain Hodge would go to Indian Island to tell stories of the sea and worlds far from here. The children loved him. And I know you will also grow to respect the native people."

Jack looked over at Marisol, picked his hair up with one hand and pretended to cut it off with the other hand.

Nana laughed out loud. "Except for that one. He may be a throw-back to the aborigines."

"We need that shelter up before dark. Sean has the saplings cut and there are several pieces of canvas under the porch. I'm sure we have enough granite scraps for the fire pit

"I saw all those canvas pieces from the sail maker, Ma. I just thought you were really getting back to painting." Joey pushed the benches under the tables for the night.

"Who knows, that might be the next project for the scraps."

In no time the eating grove was left to the creatures of the night. The horned owl sat patiently watching the small rodents feasting on scraps under the table. His turn would come once the moon rose.

After Nana was safely home, exhausted but more positive about the summer, Gert went through her cedar chests to collect extra quilts for the wigwam. Cara promised to get her lady to bed early.

Gert sat on the back steps of the porch with Cece in her arms while the lady houseguests leaned on the rail. They were mesmerized by the performance playing out before them as Jacob directed the construction. It was choreographed like a fine ballet with the symphony of the river as background music punctuated by brief directions from the leader. The many hands quickly set the tall saplings in holes equidistant along the large circular pattern scratched in the dirt with a sturdy stick. Then the tops of the "ribs" were bent and lashed together to form a dome. Jacob was heard to explain to Tim that this style shelter was a wigwam while lashing straight poles to make a cone formed the frame of a teepee. Next Sean dug a small fire pit in the center filling it partially with sand then set pieces of granite and small stones around the edge.

Marisol spoke just above a whisper as the pieces of canvas were being lashed together with strands of sinew from Nana's storage. "I can't believe what I'm seeing. Did the natives do this often."

Gert thought it was nice to hear her speak of natives rather than savages. "Very often. Not that long ago the tribes moved with the seasons to find food."

"Hey, Gert. Where's the door flap." Sean was securing the sides to the bottom of the poles while the boys were placing a layer of fresh pine boughs on the floor to be topped with quilts.

Gert shouted back, "You'll find it rolled up under the table in my painting shed." Then much quieter to the girls, "Men, they would have a hard time finding their heads if they weren't attached."

Once sleeping places were assigned, everyone settled in. Joe and Annie were in the front bedroom, Marisol and Kate in

Cece's room where Gert made up a sleeping palette under the window for her daughter and Lady.

Tim came running into the kitchen and grabbed his sister by the arm before she got away. "Marisol, you must see this." He pulled her over to the wigwam and pulled the heavy rawhide flap aside. He went in but she refused to go farther. Peeking through the opening she was surprised by the size of the room and how cozy it felt with the small fire in the pit that would be just enough to take off any late spring chill.

"It's very nice, Tim, but I have a real bed." She gave her twin's hand a squeeze then went to close the heavy flap. "Just what is this?"

She was startled by the voice of Jacob who stood beside her in the dark. "That is a rawhide. He was a large buck and we managed to save most of his skin in one piece." Just then the hide brushed against Marisol's arm causing her to stumble backwards in revulsion before Jacob could steady her and aim her towards the porch. She fairly flew over the grass not caring one wit about any creepy crawlies that may be under her feet.

As Sean dimmed the oil lamp to its lowest, he leaned over to kiss his wife to find her asleep as her head hit the pillow. "Sleep well little firefly. You have certainly earned your rest."

Out on the Ferry Road however, there was someone not asleep. A shadowy figure was straining to see any more movement around the savage's shelter. There were occasional voices and laughter after the last time the flap closed but nothing that could be heard clearly. The figure melted into the foliage near the fort.

XII

CECE'S SECRET

As dawn began to creep silently up river from the east, Gert was out in her own patch of carrots. She purposely made sure she tossed on a skirt and left the nightdress in the bedroom. She wanted no guests to be afraid of what they might see. She placed her lantern in between two rows of the delicate fern type tops that were popping up. Weeding carrots was her most disliked job so she made sure she did them first thing Sunday mornings to start the week. She just kept repeating, "you will be so tasty in a stew come midwinter."

"Do you always talk to your vegetables, Gert?"

"Jacob, how do you manage to walk up to folks without being heard? You nearly scared the life out of me."

"It's so dark out here, anyone could sneak up on you. Sean doesn't mind you out here before sunrise?" Jacob bent over and tried to distinguish between a new carrot frond and a wayward piece of sprouting thistle weed. "Do you have magical eyes?"

"We women have ways to see the unseen. Didn't your grandmother Nuga teach you that?"

"I guess I used to question how they decorated our clothes with porcupine needles and tiny beads by the light of fire pits in the dead of winter."

"We are just mysterious creatures, Jacob. By the way, do you ever sleep?"

"Funny, I was about to ask you the same thing."

"Sean would not let me take on this project for Nana if I neglected our own garden. The only time I have is before everyone is up."

"Then I'll meet you here each morning but no carrots for me. I'm much better at corn and pole beans."

"I just have two more rows to do and then I'll have the fun of waking up the crew."

As he turned, Gert grabbed his hand. "Thank you, Jacob." With a nod he was gone. *I swear he is a wizard.*

Carrots behind her for now, Gert grabbed the metal cover of her largest skillet and a forged spoon. She could hear the sounds of deep sleep from the wigwam. As *a mother, perhaps I shouldn't enjoy this so much*, she thought. Then with a devilish giggle, Gert started pounding on the cover with the spoon. It made a wonderful sound, at least to her. "From the words I'm hearing, I'd say we have at least one sailor in that shelter. Rise and shine crew. No decent potato was ever planted by lazy hands."

Cece was hanging precariously out the window. "What's going on Mama?"

"We need to get everyone up and ready for breakfast at the grove. The mist is lifting and overhead clouds are breaking. It should be a perfect day to work."

"Can I wake them up Mama?"

"Go to it baby girl!"

"Wahoo!"

That should do it.

Not even Jacob's flapjacks could manage to put some zip into the strange assortment of field hands. Gert had her chore list ready and barked off the assignments like a proper drill sergeant. When Marisol asked about the gray sky and possibly being caught in a rain, Gert took a good look at the sky. "There is more than enough coming from the west to mend a Dutchman's good-sized pair of pants. Not to worry."

Marisol looked at her brother who just shrugged and then followed JJ into the potato field.

Cece grabbed hold of Marisol's cotton skirt borrowed from Gert. Apparently none of her wardrobe was appropriate for farm work. "Come on Mary, we need to go to the barn to cut the seed potatoes.

In the barn they sat on two empty crates with two buckets between them and a corn basket of potatoes on the other. As she sat down, Marisol asked Cece what her Mama meant about the Dutchman's pants.

Cece laughed. "You don't know?"

Marisol shook her head.

"Nana says if you can see a patch of blue big enough to mend a Dutchman's pants then the sky is going to clear. Captain Hodge would always say that when they were living on the ocean and it works on land too." Cece picked up a potato and looked for the best eye growing out of it; cut a good size block of potato around it and tossed it in the seed pail. Then she tossed the rest of the potato in the other pail.

"You grow potatoes from potatoes?" Marisol had never heard of such a thing.

"You're funny Mary. You cut one."

Marisol sliced through a potato and tossed a piece in the seed pail.

"Mary, Mary. There is no eye on that piece. You have to have an eye to make a baby plant."

Marisol wondered how she ever got into a situation where a small child was teaching her about baby potatoes. She giggled.

"Watch me." Picking up a potato, Cece showed her friend that this one had two good eyes. "See this growing out? That is the beginning of a new plant. We can cut this to get two seeds."

Suddenly Marisol caught on and kept up with her little teacher. "Where does the pail of extra pieces go? Are they cooked up?"

"No, silly, those are for Frank to take home to his pigs."

Marisol decided not to ask any more silly questions and the pails started filling.

Mid morning, Jack came in to get the seed bucket and left an empty one. He turned and gave Marisol the once over. "Those look like my old work boots. Glad they fit but did you wear a pair of my toeless socks with them?" He ducked as a piece of potato flew past his ear.

The lunch bell rang just in time. The pungent odor of the various animals in the barn was beginning to upset Marisol's stomach and she quickly ran out the door to get some fresh air. She wondered if she would ever be able to eat a potato again.

Kettles of tea centered the tables surrounded by baskets of hot biscuits, tubs of butter and crocks of molasses. Everyone stopped at the outside pitcher pump to wash up and cool off as the noon sun was beating down. The squirrels were chattering more than the workers. Gert had her nose buried in her notes figuring where she should send everyone after lunch. Sean, Jacob and Dan were having their own quiet meeting while sitting on Joey's woodpile.

Jacob was curious about the Ferry Road. "Sean, do many walk the road up from the river at night?"

"Rarely. Frank usually walks home over the fields and a few neighbors walk to the ferry landing during daylight. The workers left at the fort walk out to the main road on the other side of the grounds. I can't see why anyone would have any business up here at night. Is there a problem?"

"I thought I heard some rustling in the trees last night so took a look this morning. There was a set of prints that were not like the farm boots you wear in the fields."

"Don't tell Ma. She'd end up sitting on a rock all night to see who it might be." Dan smiled. He knew his mother.

"Being only one, I'd say someone was snooping. I'm going to sweep the area with a branch before I go to bed and then we should have a better idea in the morning."

"I have to go to work early. You want me to check it?"

"You do your regular routine Sean. Dan and I will take care of any intruder."

Sean laughed out loud at the thought of someone bumping into that duo unexpectedly. "We better get a bite to eat before Gert sends us back into the fields with that damn bell."

Tim and JJ were deep in a discussion of spring planting. Tim was most interested in potatoes and confessed he never gave much thought to where his food came from and wanted to learn as much as he could over the few days.

Cece was getting bored as five year olds do around adults. Suddenly she hopped off her bench and motioned to Marisol and Kate to follow her. "I want to show you my secret place."

"Are you sure? Then it would not be secret anymore." Kate took her little friend's hand.

"Would it be anywhere that someone might see me dressed like this?"

"Silly Mary. Everyone looks like you when we work in the fields." She reached out with her other hand and the three of them slipped further into the grove. Just out of sight of Joey's house, Cece pointed to a fairly large rock that seemed to be out of place among the pines. "That's my magic castle. Come see."

She pulled her friends to the other side where the rock had a natural deep concave opening with a flat lip at the bottom. Marisol was far from thrilled. "Aren't you afraid there would be bugs in there? Or maybe snakes."

"The snakes are in the garden, not out here in the pine needles. Have you ever seen a garden snake in pine needles?"

"I'm afraid I've never even seen pine needles. I lived in the city of London. This is all new to me Cece."

"Then you've never seen a lady's slipper." Cece jumped up and sat on the top of the rock. "This is where I can watch over my secret place. Look there by the baby birch trees. See the pink flowers?"

Both young ladies squinted.

"My goodness, come with me." She led them to a group of seven lovely blossoms. "Nana calls them wild orchids."

Marisol was enthralled. "I've never seen anything like them. Beautiful."

"I come cross them this time of year along the Aroostook River but this grove is ideal. They love the acidic soil from the decaying needles." Kate looked around and saw another group.

"I can show you a very special bunch but remember this is my secret place and I don't want anyone to walk on them."

She led them behind a fairly large pine and nestled at the base were a bunch of lady's slippers that were yellow. Both ladies squealed with excitement until Cece pulled them away. "Let me show you my hideaway." She crawled into the small shallow cave and stretched out. "Look, I can see into the trees and if I stay still as can be, the birds and animals play for me. I love it when the sun comes through the leaves because it makes pretty shapes. And when I'm here, no one can see me and it is a space that I don't have to share with my brothers.

And when I'm sad, like when Papa yells at Mama or Jack teases and tickles me, I can come here with Lacey. Sometimes Lady comes too and hides with me."

Just then the school bell rang and Cece jumped out and ran towards Joey and Peg's house. Her friends just looked at each other for there were no words.

The afternoon passed quickly except for Marisol who was afraid she was going to see a garden snake slither by as she dropped seed corn into the prepared rows.

Nana joined them for venison stew with dumplings topped off with apple cake. She asked Tim to walk her home to read some of Captain Hodge's letters. Gert had been through all of them but she loved to hear the stories on how and why her captain left England and when he told his mother about their marriage. Kate asked if she could go along as she had not heard the tales.

Everyone looked as tired as Gert felt. Even the always-in-motion Cece was yawning. Sean nodded at Jacob and Dan as they wandered off towards the Ferry Road. This exchange was not lost on Gert but she knew well enough not to ask.

Jack stretched to test his ribs and found them not as sore. He swooped his sister up on his shoulders. "Come on little one. I'll save you the walk home."

"I'll go along and get her ready for bed." Actually Marisol was anxious to get there herself.

By the time Kate and Tim left the Hodge house, darkness had started to settle but a nearly full moon tempered it. Young Mr. Hodge stood at the top of the Ferry Road and took a deep breath. "At first I could not imagine why Captain Hodge would leave the sea to work the land. He called this his piece of heaven and now I understand why."

"Would you ever leave the sea for the land?"

"Right now I could not think of anything that would take me off the schooner but I imagine at one time he felt the same."

So intrigued by watching the moonlight sparkle on the river, Kate stepped into a rut and tripped. After three stuttering steps, Tim was able to grab her around the waist and set her straight. "No, just what I need. I think I twisted my ankle."

With no effort at all, Tim swept her up in his arms and headed towards the Ryan's front yard. "I better watch that I don't trip or we'll be in quite a stew with Gert."

Kate nestled her head on his shoulder and enjoyed the scent of the sea from his sun-bronzed skin. The aroma of her sweet rose water in turn captured him. As they stumbled in the front door, Kate was laughing out loud.

Gert whispered to Sean, "I never thought I'd ever hear her laugh again."

"Sorry, Gert. I may have hurt my ankle. Tim was kind enough to carry me back before I made it worse."

"Let me take a look." Kate grimaced a bit as Gert checked the ankle for swelling. "Sean grab me some of the old sheet strips. I don't think it is too bad but I want to bind it just in case."

When Sean came back with the material, he confessed to being plum tired out. "I need to get to bed so I can be at my office at the fort early. There are some bigwigs arriving from Washington to make decisions on when we will close construction. I don't think they will even complete the officer's quarters. Most that have the authority to end building at the fort have never spent one day working here. I'll make arrangements for tomorrow evening so Jack can show you the tunnels and the Rodman cannons that were forged in Pittsburg, Pennsylvania. All this planning for a fear the Brits would try to take Bangor again. Such a waste."

With that the household quickly settled. With a nod to Dan, Jacob tossed a bit of wood on the fire pit and closed the flap to capture the sounds of sleep.

XIII

Fog Delay

The second day of planting started the same. There was a chill in the morning air so Gert tossed her old shawl over her shoulders. She rubbed the softness against her cheek and remembered Nana bringing it to her when she was carrying Danny. It was so cold in their partially finished little house that winter she would never have survived the harshness without the love that went into crocheting that shawl.

After lighting the lantern she took a tin cup of hot tea off the warming stove. Gert wanted to get her poles up for the beans before tackling the weeds between the beets. To her surprise the poles were done and she nearly tripped over Jacob as he bent over to guide the young plants to start their climb. "Good God, don't you know that someone your age is supposed to get several hours sleep?"

"What I know Gert is that at my age I don't know how many spring seasons I have left and I don't plan to waste my time by sleeping the hours away. By the way, your potato plants are big enough to bury."

"I plan to send JJ and Tim over later this morning to do that. I'm amazed at how much our seaman wants to learn about gardening."

"He would find anything interesting that interested Kate. I think our young Mr. Hodge is quite smitten." Jacob looked up to the golden sunrise silhouetting the treetop eagles nest. He smiled broadly as he watched one of the adults stretching its wings for a new day of hunting and fishing. "How many eaglets?"

"I've only seen two little white heads popping up but Comfort swears there are three."

Jacob laughed as he pulled some errant weeds from between the poles. "If I were a betting man, I'd wager on the little one with the heart of ancients. Dan may look the most like a Micmac but she has the intuition of my grandmother Nuga."

The sun broke through to illuminate the Ryan's kitchen garden as Gert blew out her lantern.

"I need to leave a bit early, Gert. I'll see you at breakfast."

"What are you and Dan up to?"

"You don't miss a thing. Not a thing."

"I can't. I raised four boys, remember? Anything I should worry about?"

"Not at all dear girl. Your plate is full. Let us take care of those things that could be nothing."

As Jacob began his inspection of Ferry Road, he shook his head and grinned when the kettle top clanged to wake up Nana's farm crew.

In no time Sean was beside him on his way to the fort. "Find anything?"

"Looks like someone is really interested in what is going on in your backyard. The bottoms of his boots are smooth and I'd say this person is of a good size."

Sean took just a minute to make his own inspection. "The right sole has a funny crack on it that goes half way across from right to left. Other than that it seems a common walking boot. Definitely not a work boot. Do you plan to do something about this tonight?"

"It depends on the weather. I heard the bell clanging at the lighthouse down river this morning so it could be foggy tonight. We may have to wait a day and I think all the Ryan men should be included."

As he scooted down over the hill, Sean shouted back, "The more the merrier."

Breakfast was a bit more animated as platters of ham steaks and hot biscuits disappeared as if the French magician, Robert-Houdin, was plying his craft. Added was a pot of hot coffee for those who were beginning to like its aroma and flavor. Nana sent down one of her final jars of blueberry preserves from last summer.

Everyone was going to be working on planting the last of the yellow eye beans.

"Should I know what these are?" Tim was still working on his farming skills.

Jacob explained they were a staple in the diet of lumber-men when he was a camp cook. "Before you head back to the coast, I'll have you help me bury a kettle of them in the ground for a feast of bean-hole beans."

Everyone got a chuckle out of Tim's look that became even more perplexed after Gert told him he was going to bury her potato plants later that morning. He soon learned that if you mound the young plants with soil they become stronger and increase the yield.

At the supper meal, Sean announced he, Joe and the 'boys' were meeting with Jacob to go over some plans while Gert was at Nana's to sew for the baby. Jack would take Tim, Marisol, JJ and Kate to the fort for a tour.

Cece grabbed Jack's leg. "I want to go to the fort and see the cannons."

"I don't think our company needs to have you buzzing around." Jack was hoping that his mother would intercede but both the young ladies thought it would be lovely to have Cece as a guide.

"Look Mary!" Cece pointed in the direction of her secret place as three hen turkeys with their broods walked among the pines in a straight military line.

"What in the world? They are so big."

JJ got a big laugh out of Marisol's expression when she saw the birds. "Have you never seen a turkey?"

Tim laughed, "She's only seen them dressed and on the dining room table." This was answered by an embarrassed glare from his sister.

Walking down the Ferry Road, Jack spoke to no one in particular. "Did you know our respected statesman Benjamin Franklin thought the turkey should be the national bird? Can you imagine that turkey in place of that regal bird? He pointed to the male perched on the side of the nest.

Cece skipped along at the head of the procession. Occasionally she lifted Lacey in the air and spun around in circles.

Jack shook his head and shouted to his little sister. "Why did you bring that doll with you?"

"Lacey's not a doll. She's my very best friend and she likes to sit on the cannons."

Jack's guests were most impressed by the size of the magnificent granite fortification. As they walked the grounds Jack told them his father's story of total dedication to construction. They walked by the cannons in the two batteries at the riverside and inspected the Rodman cannons inside the fort that had been designed with special barrels to shoot downward at enemy ships as they passed through the narrows.

Cece laid Lacey near the mouth of the barrel. "Aren't you afraid she will fall out the window?" Kate went to pick up the doll.

"No. Lacey likes to watch the boats go by."

Jack lit an oil lantern. "If you want to see some of the tunnels we need to go before dusk. It's very dark down there." He led the group down narrow stairs to a series of brick-lined passages built to protect defensive positions of soldiers.

"My Papa got hurt real bad when he was building the tunnels." Cece ran her hands along the pattern of bricks.

Jack explained to the Hodge twins that Sean was trapped by a cave-in when supervising the construction. He was saved but his arm was crushed and the last several years have been difficult, especially for Gert. He started coming to his senses watching T work so hard on the farm with one arm.

Marisol looking ahead, and then behind, in the poorly lit tunnel began to tighten up in panic. She grabbed her brother's hand in dread that she might be buried alive in that dank place.

To this Jack put the lantern close to his back, which dimmed the light further in the passageway. "Don't worry Miss Hodge. The bricks and granite have been placed to stay in place long after we would be walking through them. The only thing I don't like is the occasional story of ghosts who like to float through." Jack let out a deep maniacal laugh.

Marisol screamed and turned with her hand clenched. "Jack Ryan, how did you sneak into your lovely family? You are just plain malicious. Mean–mean–mean!"

Cece hugged her Mary. "He's just a teaser that's all. Mama says ignore him then he won't have any fun and leave you alone."

Jack checked out the oil in the lantern and decided they better find a set of steps to take them out to the parade grounds.

Cece ran out first. "Wow. It is really misty out here and I can hear the fog bell."

Kate waved her hand in front of her face as if to push the vapor out of the way.

Jack grabbed two fresh lanterns from a supply room and gave one to JJ. This bank is coming in quickly so we better start for the house. JJ, lead the way. I need to lock up the equipment."

The first lantern could be seen heading towards the gate. Kate turned back. "Come on Cece".

As the little girl ran ahead, Marisol noticed that one of the ties was loose on her shoe. Jack knelt down and made it secure. "Navigating this pea soup fog will be hard enough without you tripping yourself up."

They all met again at the top of the hill near the path to the apple tree. The fog was not nearly as thick. When they spotted Lady her hair was drooping like a wet floor mop and they all laughed.

Jack glanced around for his sister. "Cece, doesn't she look funny? Cece? Cece!"

Marisol grabbed her brother. "I thought she was with you."

"She was but then she said something about Lacey and ran back to you. We could still see your lantern so didn't think much about it."

Kate was obviously very upset. "Did she leave the doll on the cannon?"

"It is getting dark and with this fog, how could she find it?" Marisol started the dash down the foggy Ferry Road followed by the rest of the group.

Jack took the lead at the bottom. "She knows her way around like the back of her hand. I'm sure we'll meet up with her." Cece! Cece! Where are you?"

They all took turns calling her name. "Cece." "Comfort." "Cece, call back to us!"

Jack bellowed, "Comfort Clair Ryan, answer me!"

"I want to go back inside where she left Lacey." Marisol spun around but was totally lost as to the direction.

Jack took control of the anxious friends. "I'll lead Marisol to the Rodman. You go along the riverside and walk around the batteries in case she got herself turned around. Stay close enough to see the lantern so we won't be looking for each other too.

The reverberation of the calls was dulled within the thick vapor. Jack and Marisol groped their way up stairs to the first cannon casement where Lacey was left but the doll was not there. Jack took Marisol's hand and led her to the next casement where he leaned out the cannon window and shouted to the group below, "Anything?" He could barely make out the glow of JJ's lantern.

"Nothing."

"Take the pathway to the fort landing. She sometimes walks that way. Be careful, it takes you close to the water." Jack took Marisol's hand. "She's been forbidden to walk the tops of any walls but she may have been disoriented."

Marisol snagged her dress on one of the metal hooks that held chains on the chamber openings but didn't care a bit about the tear. "Cece, it's Mary! Answer me!"

Now Jack was beginning to feel panic. "Cece it's Jack. Call out to me. I'm not mad at you. I just want to find you. Cece, answer me–please!"

Along the river path, the three decided to call out a couple times each and then remain silent for a while to listen carefully in hopes of hearing an answer. But all they could hear was the lapping of the water against the granite wall as the river was at high tide. They swung the lantern from one side to another in hopes of seeing better. The thick fog was relentless and didn't show any sign of lifting.

"What's that?" Kate pointed to something floating in the water. "Over there. It's white so probably a piece of paper."

Tim tried but could not reach it. He picked up a branch lying next to the path and told JJ to hold on to the back of his pants as he reached out. Kate brought the lantern as close as she could to the water so he could snag the object and picked it out. Kate gasped and nearly dropped the light. It was Lacey.

Atop the wall that dropped to the parade grounds below, Jack crept along an inch at a time. He told Marisol that the ground sloped down gradually to her left but the drop to the right was deep. He held the lantern so she could plant each step safely. They stopped and listened but the murkiness muffled any sounds.

"Cece it's Mary. Help me find you and take you home. Talk to me."

Nothing.

"Cece, I need to get you home to Lady. Who is the cat going to sleep with tonight? Answer me. Where are you?"

Nothing.

They inched further out on the top of the wall. "Be careful Marisol. It looks like they are landscaping the grassy slope. It could be tricky where the soil is uneven. Damn, this is tricky."

A tiny voice called out. "Jack, you said a bad word."

Marisol got so excited Jack had to grab her so she didn't topple of the wall. "Cece tell us where you are."

The little voice was muffled. "Mary. Mary, I'm in a hole and can't get out. Help me."

Jack pulled Marisol onto the grassy area and told her not to move. He moved out of the area and called to JJ. "We found her. Come up to the grounds that lead to the granite wall over the officer's quarters."

"The left?" JJ shouted as loud as he could.

"Yes. Be careful. They are landscaping and some areas are rough." He went back and took Marisol by the hand and they inched slowly along the soil side of the wall. "Tell us where you are Cece."

"I'm in here and it's scary. I think there are worms." Her voice was a little clearer but no clue where it was coming from.

Marisol tried to keep it light even though she was scared herself. "You're not afraid of snakes. Why would you be frightened by a silly old worm?"

"I not know."

That definitely was clearer and Marisol pointed to a pile of soil that was barely visible through the relentless mist. They brought the lantern closer and a narrow hole was revealed.

Jack shouted into the hole. "Cece are you in there?"

"You don't have to shout. I'm right here."

He carefully lowered the light over the lip and could make out his sister wedged between the outer side of the wall and some lose dirt. "We'll get you little one."

The rest of the group came up the hill from the river as fast as they dared. Jack stopped them before they came any closer. "Where is she?"

Marisol explained she fell in the hole and is trapped. "We need to be careful not to make the soil slide into the opening."

JJ came over carefully to peek in. "We're too big to reach her without disturbing the ground."

"Am I going to be caved in like Papa?" The lantern reflected on the rivulets of tears cutting their way through her dirt-caked little face.

Marisol came up behind Jack. "Let me by. I'm small enough to reach in there."

"But are you strong enough?"

Cece answered her brother. "Girls are very strong."

"Please let me try. I'll be very careful."

Marisol lay on her stomach and slowly moved over the edge of the hole. "Hang on to me so I won't fall in too."

Jack lay behind her and wrapped his arms around her waist. Tim lay behind him and hung on to his waist. JJ and Kate each held the lanterns as close as they dared.

Marisol slowly went into the opening. It was hard for her to see as her body blocked out most of the lantern glow. When she reached Cece, one of the her arms was up but the other was pinned behind her back. "I've got to get my hands under your arms so I can pull you out safely. Pulling on one arm won't do."

"I'm glad your arms are long Mary." She was sobbing a bit now as she realized what a pickle she was in.

"Don't let me fall. I've nearly got her."

To this JJ got on the ground behind Tim to help Jack pull.

"I have her but there is no extra room. You need to pull quick and steady. The soil is falling around us."

Jack remembered how they had to pull his father out from under the granite slab with no time to spare. Now he was working strictly on adrenalin. On three. One – two – three – now!

Marisol held on as tight as she could and the men pulled as if they had the life of both in the hole in their hands. They did. For just as Cece cleared the lip, the sides of the hole caved in.

Tim lifted his sister her feet. "Are you hurt?"

"No, but I need to sit for a minute to catch my breath." She sat back on the ground and laid her head in her hands.

Jack picked up Cece and cradled her as he did when she was much younger. She was covered in dirt but looked wonderful to him. "Do you hurt anywhere little sister?"

"My arm hurts and I feel like I've been eating mud pies. Don't hold me like a baby."

He turned her over to JJ and Kate. "Take her home to get her cleaned up. Tim, please go along so you have both lanterns. The mist is thinning so I'll bring along your sister as soon as she is ready."

Jack watched the group go carefully along the river path and once they turned up the Ferry Road, he allowed himself to relax. He sat on the ground next to Marisol. She was sobbing quietly so he put his arm around her shoulders until she shuddered with relief. "Ready?" He helped Marisol up, reached out and pushed her hair behind her ears. "You were wonderful. How can I ever thank you?"

She looked over at the hole that was now half filled with soil and began to shiver. He pulled her to him and held her tightly until he could feel her body start to relax. Slowly she lifted her eyes still glistening from tears. He kissed her on the forehead, then one cheek, and then the other. She put her arms around his neck and he gently brushed his lips against hers whispering "thank you". She in turn, kissed him with a passion she never knew she had.

When the hazy moon allowed enough light the rest of Nana's field hands walked home from the Hodge property. They were chatting about their enjoyable evening until the front door opened and they looked into the kitchen. They were dumbstruck by the bedraggled group waiting for them. Kate sat in the rocking chair with a freshly bathed Cece bundled in a blanket on her lap. Lady was draped over Cece's lap. The rest sat at the table sipping tea. Hands and faces were clean but the same could not be said of their clothes. And why was Lacey hanging on the towel rack above the sink?

Jack stood and faced his parents. "It's a long story but all worked out well. You see, we nearly lost Cece."

From Kate's lap came a giggle. "Nobody can lose Cece."

XIV

The Snoop

Day three of planting was quiet. Gert decided she would go up to the main house and have a private talk with Nana about last night. She didn't want her dearest friend to be upset by hearsay. After, she planned to go home and work on her frayed nerves by washing the pile of muddy clothes on the back porch. She had few orders. Most everyone would work on rows of feed corn around the perimeter of the gardens. This would not take valuable produce space and eventually make a privacy barrier around the acres. Tim was sent to the earlier planting of Nana's potatoes as they were ready to bury. He was pleased that he knew just what to do. Jack was sent to see if the blossoming fruit trees needed trimming and then to the same for the few in the Ryan gardens. His mother knew he was not ready for chitchat after last night.

Cece skipped her way into the fields. Kate looked at JJ and they both shook their heads in amazement. Marisol stood straight in her borrowed working clothes and Jack's boots, once hated, they were now a source of security. T and Frank said they would join the corn rows once the animals were taken care of.

It was hard to believe the sky could be so clear and sun so warm after such a night. The fog did leave the soil damp but it soon would dry.

Sean went to work very early and passed Gert and Jacob weeding the squash. He was not happy. Gert whispered, "I would not want to be the worker that left that hole open."

The day passed quickly with each in their own thoughts. At one point Cece picked up an earthworm the size of a baby snake. "Look Mary, I'm really not afraid of a silly old worm." Marisol waved back at her and tried hard to swallow the lump in her throat.

At supper, it was no surprise to those who knew, most of Cece's favorites were served. Bowls of boiled potatoes, fresh churned butter, carrots, sliced roasted chicken and maple cornbread with two desserts. The applesauce cake was warm and sugar cookies huge. Cece nudged Kate and giggled when Marisol took the tiniest potato she could find.

Sean stretched. "We all need a more relaxed evening. Come on over to our house so we can visit and enjoy this lovely breeze coming up from the river. Joey, make sure you bring Peg over as soon as you can." Knowing that Sean is never up for company after a busy day, she looked over at Jacob. He just smiled broadly. Since he hardly does that, Gert knew for sure something was up.

Nana appeared to be more unsteady on her feet that evening. Tim and Marisol offered to walk her back to the house while Gert helped Cara carry the extra food. They were going to pack up the leftover sweets to take to the Ryan house. Nana looked at her new niece and nephew with pride. "Marisol, dear, don't ever grow old. Keep yourself strong in body and mind for as long as you can. Look at me. I can't even walk a straight line."

"Listen to you Nana. Your legs may be giving you fits but your brain is as fresh as ever. And you have never let your years stop you from doing what is important." Gert walked just behind the Hodge siblings. "Did you know your aunt is going to be honored at a women's charity luncheon meeting in Bangor next September?"

"I hope I can be there to hear it." Marisol had always wanted to be part of a group focusing on women's issues.

Tim rolled his eyes. "Oh, oh–now it begins."

Nana showed some spark and beamed at her niece. "That's my girl."

Coming into the kitchen, Nana told Cara she was quite tired and would like to go up to the sitting room next to her bedroom. To which Cara went out on the porch and shouted for T.

Tim went over to the back stairs. "I can help take her up."

"That's nice of you but T and I have worked out a way to take her up securely and we do it every night.

T secured Nana's back with the stub of his arm and grasped the banister with his hand.

Nana grabbed the other banister with her hand and Cara walked close behind for more help if needed.

Marisol helped Gert pack the treat basket to take home. "Cara and her son are deeply devoted to Aunt Fiona."

Tim thought the same.

Gert shouted up the stairs. "We are leaving Nana. Have a pleasant night."

"I shall, dear. Please give Mistress Cece an especially big hug."

"Consider it done."

On the way back to the Ryan's, Gert decided to tell the young Hodges the rest of T's story. "His father was killed in the same cave in that nearly took Sean. The authorities in

Prospect decided that since Cara had no assets of her own and no place to live, they would take her young son away and make him a ward of the state. When Nana heard this, she and I went to Bangor to see a friend of Captain Hodge who was a professor at the seminary. The Hodges had earned the respect of many due to their charitable and community work. At that time, a woman was not entitled to any of her husband's property should he die. To make things worse, T's father had no tangible assets so would have nothing to leave her no matter what. They found a law where if the woman had work of her own and a place to live, she stood a better chance to keep her children. So Nana drew up a contract for Cara to be her housekeeper where she and her child would live at the farm. The town father's backed away. When T was young and a classmate of Mike and Dan, he was influenced by his father as to the place half-breeds should be kept. But through Nana's influence, Mike and Dan became close to T and stayed with him in the army field hospital while they took off his arm. Determined not to let his mother down, he worked hard to overcome his disability and now farms as well as any."

"Wow, no wonder they are so devoted to her." Marisol looked at her brother. "I hope someday I can live up to my aunt's ways."

Cece came running out of the front door. "Do you have my cookies?"

Tim picked her up. "Who said they are your cookies? I like them too."

She giggled and hugged him. "Not to worry. I'll share."

Soon the Ryan's back yard was abuzz with storytelling, joking and laughter. When Peg arrived she carried a special treat in a covered tin. Marisol and Tim never had maple sugar candy before and it was love at first taste.

Sean made a little fire pit halfway between the porch and the wigwam and everyone sat on blankets on the ground, passing the tea and cookies. The sun put on a spectacular show as it set in glorious hues of red and orange.

"Look Mama. Tomorrow is going to be a wonderful day." Cece turned to Tim. "Did you know that a red sky at night is a sailor's delight."

"I do. And now I would say that the same can be said for a farmer."

JJ stood and stretched. "Marisol, have you ever been inside the wigwam?" She showed no interest.

Tim picked up the conversation. "Kate, see if you can get my sister to come in for a visit. I think she will be surprised how pleasant it is."

"Go ahead Marisol. That will give you something very different to talk about in Searsport." Gert started to pick up the picnic basket but found not a crumb of cookies to put away. Neither did she find a single Ryan man around. She shook her head at how they had all wandered away without notice. *Sneaky little Indian boys.*

"Mama, I want to go the wigwam."

Gert looked over at JJ and he gave Cece a wave in. Gert started the dishes in the kitchen sink looking out left and right wondering what her family was doing.

At the same time, a shadowy figure slipped from tree to tree making his way closer from the Ferry Road. He made a mental note of Miss Marisol going into that savage hovel.

In the wigwam, the young lady began to relax around the center fire. "I must admit this is much nicer than I thought with perhaps the exception of that terrible door covering."

Kate explained the respect the Indian hunter had for his prey. How nothing was wasted for each and every portion of the animal is used. The hunter thanked this massive buck for the protection from the elements.

Marisol peeked over at the rawhide. "Mr. Stag, I truly do appreciate your sacrifice but for me, I prefer a door with a handle."

This brought a round of laughter that could be heard outside the wigwam, which brought the mysterious figure closer.

The evening's bright moon was now laying shafts of light between the trees. There was the sound of whoosh and then thud next to the phantom figure. He turned and found a hatchet freshly buried in the pine next to his head. The dark figure's face turned white and he turned to run out to the road but blocking his way was Jacob resplendent in his tunic with Micmac ceremonial sash. He stood straight and tall as his tribe's sagamore, never moving or blinking. The stranger turned to the right to run and there in front of him was Jack in his beaded tunic and mud smeared under his eyes.

"It seems I have seen you before. I believe your hulking body and nine fingered friend held my arms jammed through a wagon wheel while a pasty faced coward gave me a beating."

"No. No. You have me confused with someone else. I did not do that to you!"

"Then perhaps to me?"

The man turned to his left to see Joey dressed the same as his twin. The man took looks back and forth but the brothers were as they were at birth, still two identical peas in a pod. At birth Gert could separate them because Joey has a small birthmark on the back of his neck but in time their personalities did the trick.

"No, no. Not me."

Just then Dan joined the circle dressed like his Uncle Jacob only carrying a hatchet.

Joe bumped the visitor from the back. When he turned around, the shaking unwanted guest blanched further. "Remember me? I was on the wrong end of your fist while it smashed my jaw and bloodied my nose."

"Please, it wasn't my idea."

Then Sean walked into the group carrying his hunting rifle. "Was it your idea to spy on my family and guests?" He aimed the rifle at the hapless intruder who at that moment thoroughly wet his pants.

He whimpered, "No, sir."

"Then get off my property and don't show your face around here again. Tell whoever you work for, that goes for him too."

The man stood frozen for a few seconds and then the twins jumped at him, with a war whoop. He ran out to the road and started down the hill with Joey and Jack on his tail for good measure.

When the boys came back, they could not help but laugh. "He sure ran funny with wet britches. We hope he had a boat tied up at the landing for if not, he is in the river."

From there the group went into the Nana's barn, took off their tunics and washed the mud off at the rain barrel. Jack would pick up the clothes in the morning.

As they separated to work their way back to the house, Jacob had a concern for Sean. "When you took aim, I was afraid the rifle might go off."

"No worry. It wasn't loaded. Do you think I would waste the cost of a bullet on that bugger?"

XV

Job Well Done

Days four and five went smoothly. Even the mid afternoon rain shower on Thursday could not dampen the spirits of Nana's field hands. As soon as the sun reappeared, everyone was back finishing the remaining planting or weeding the patches of seedlings.

Marisol stood between rows of sprouting carrots and spoke to no one in particular. "Why do the weeds grow so much faster and stronger than the vegetable seeds?"

"If you figure that out Miss Hodge, we farmers would be most appreciative." Thomas smiled and tipped his old fedora to the young lady as he passed by.

"Yes indeed Miss Hodge, I agree with Thomas." Marisol had not realized Jack was working just a few rows behind her. She turned with red cheeks not caused by the sun for they had not spoken since Cece was found. "Just think, one more day and you can be rid of my old work shoes."

"They have become quite comfortable. Actually, I've grown to like these boots." She gave him a quick smile that crinkled the corners of her azure blue eyes.

Now Jack felt warmth having nothing to do the sun.

The supper signal rang out. Marisol tossed her last handful of weeds in the basket and walked towards the grove. Passing Jack, she tapped him on the shoulder. "Saved by the bell Mr. Ryan."

The group seemed more jovial than usual as they washed up at the pump. It could be that the week of labor was nearly up or they had become more at ease with the task at hand.

As the gingerbread was being devoured, Jacob reminded Tim he had a hole to dig.

"You mean we are really going to cook some beans in the ground?"

"I don't make up stories about such things." Jacob put on his stern look until everyone started to laugh.

On the edge of the field not far from the grove, Tim dug to the perfect depth and width to hold a large baled kettle. Then Jacob had him cover the bottom with several large rocks and place split logs on ends around the sides inside the hole with kindling on top of the rocks. "Now, you meet me here at dawn so we can get this started for supper tomorrow."

"Dawn?"

"Yes, before Gert does her crazy wakeup clanging. I'll give you a nudge when I get up."

That evening everyone visited in Nana's parlor. Tomorrow would be the last full day her field hands would be together for the near future. Stories were shared that gave Mrs. Hodge great pleasure from Marisol cutting a seed potato with no eye to Tim trying to understand why anyone would bury perfectly healthy potato plants.

Gert thought her neighbor was quite quiet. "A penny for your thoughts, Nana."

"I was just wondering how a widow with no children of her own could be surrounded by such a large family."

Sean reached out and took her hand. "It was just the luck of the Irish that you opened your heart to a pair of newlyweds from Aroostook County."

Gert tossed up her arms. "Luck! I bet there were times when she wished she had never offered us that wonderful little house."

"Never my dear. Never."

Cece suddenly brought up the subject everyone else had skirted. "Papa, why was there a hole in the ground at the fort?"

You could hear one of Nana's darning needles fall in the quiet. "Well, it seems one of the workers dug the hole to put small stones along the wall to help the rain water drain away. He was not quite finished when one of his friends offered him a ride home in his wagon if he came right away. So he quickly put his shovel away and went off leaving that piece unmarked."

"Were you angry with him Papa?"

"He left just as quickly when I fired him."

"Good. I wish I could have waved goodbye." Cece jumped up on Nana's lap and hugged Lacey.

JJ announced he would stay on awhile with Kate at Indian Island. He was going to meet with faculty of the newly formed State College of Agriculture and the Mechanic Arts in Old Town. The school was signed off by President Lincoln in 1862 and would open in the fall. He was interested in applying in the future. For the time being he would help his father bring in the crop at the Thorpe potato farm. Their crew will leave in September to find themselves jobs in the lumber camps.

"I'd say my friend Ben has done great things with the farm." Sean was quite proud of his childhood buddy.

Gert added her view. "Don't forget to mention Nettie. It takes a strong woman to back a successful man."

Jack caught the confusion on Marisol's face. "JJ is the son of my father's best childhood friend Ben Smythe. His mother is Nettie Thorp, my mother's best friend." He realized that bit of information did nothing to help.

Kate broke in to the conversation. "I have news. I'm not leaving right away as I'm going to be working to prepare a teaching plan for the school at Indian Island. The children are going to be taught in English. Some are afraid they will lose their language and traditions of the Penobscot but I will do my best to combine the two"

Nana got very excited. "You will be living that much closer to us?"

"That's the plan." Kate smiled broadly and could not help notice Tim's attention pick up.

Marisol saw an opening. "Kate, if you are staying will you come and spend a few days with me in Searsport. I have so many things to show you. On Tuesday afternoon, Governor Joshua Chamberlain will be in town. He will be speaking with former vice president Hannibal Hamlin under President Lincoln. Then Wednesday we can see Tim off on the schooner for his first lumber run to New York. On Thursday the wife of one of the captains will be speaking at the Methodist Church about her life on the sea. You'll love meeting my Aunt Daphne and visiting her fabric store.

"I'd enjoy that but since you're leaving Saturday morning and I have plans to go over school supplies, I would not be free until Sunday."

Marisol looked at Tim. "Can we stay until Sunday? You don't have to be on the schooner until the middle of the week."

With the prospect of seeing Kate a bit longer, Tim saw no problem with the plan.

Marisol looked at her new friend. "What do you think?"

"Searsport it is on Sunday."

On the walk back to the Ryan house, Jack turned to Marisol. "What about dear Matt? Will he not be upset if you stay with we lower class for another day?"

She gave him a vicious look. Not taking any chances, he ran ahead as fast as possible.

Taking in the scene, Kate whispered to Tim. "I've heard a lot about this Matthew in scuttlebutt from the family as well as tidbits from Marisol. What in the world does she see in him? To me, he sounds like a self-important jackass."

"I certainly agree. We may have shared a womb at one time but now she doesn't give a wit about my opinion. Sometimes I think she visions herself in Boston high society."

"Yes, but at what cost?" She shivered from the thought.

Thinking she was cold, Tim put his arm around her shoulders and pulled her closer. Close enough to kiss her lightly on the cheek.

Early Friday morning, the shake by Uncle Jacob came as an abrupt shock to Tim. He blinked his eyes several times to come to his senses in the dim light left from dying embers in the fire pit. Jacob pointed at the flap and left.

Tim nearly tripped over Gert as she pulled weeds. She smiled and waved while he dragged his still tired body over the fields to the grove. Jacob was waiting with two steaming cups of strong black tea on the table. The fire in the hole was already lit.

Tim took a look at the blazing logs. "I thought I was supposed to strike that match."

"If you were my cookee in the lumber camps, I'd have to kick you out. The rocks have to be heating by dawn for the beans to bake by evening."

Tim still did not know what he was suppose to do but was amazed at how much heat was coming from the hole.

"Come on, we have work to do."

Inside the door of Peg's kitchen was a large kettle three quarter full of beans with the distinctive yellow eye. Peg had washed and soaked them a bit. Jacob picked up a heavy metal pole and put it through the bale. He got Tim on one side and he took the other to carry the beans out to one of the eating tables. Jacob showed him the size to cut the many chunks of salt pork, then mixed them with the beans and a good-sized jug of molasses. Jacob finished off with a handful of ground mustard seed. He gave Tim a paddle to combine the mixture while he checked the rocks. Tim watched as Jacob secured the lid and brought up the bale.

"Now we'll see just how strong a seaman can be."

The men got on each side of the kettle and lifted, Tim with a loud groan. After another check of the hot rocks, they slowly lowered the beans into the ground. Then Jacob had Tim shovel dirt to bury the metal pot leaving just the bale showing above ground.

Tim sat heavily on a bench. "Just how often did you do that in the lumber camps?"

"Every day. Every single day for the six or more months spent harvesting in the winter. That was one staple that kept the men going. Now sit there and sip your tea while I work on a batch of flapjacks and slab bacon to start your final day of farming."

He finally was fully awake by the time everyone arrived for breakfast. He was hard pressed to explain to his sister why their supper was buried in the ground.

After lunch, the work of Nana's field hands was complete and everyone went their separate ways until supper. Gert took a break to visit Nana who was sitting in her wicker rocker on the porch. She was looking over the fields with her binoculars and was amazed at what had been accomplished. She handed the glasses to Gert. "Take a look at the top of the slope."

It took a minute for her to focus but once done, Gert began to weep. Cece was standing by Mike's memorial next to Captain Hodge's grave. Both Tim and Kate had bouquets of wild flowers. He knelt down, pulled a few weeds and then placed the flowers in front of the Captain's stone. Kate bent and placed her flowers on Mike's marker then laid her head on Tim's shoulder. Cece did the same for her big brother with a single rose off her mother's bush and then clung to Kate.

Nana reached for Gert's hand and gave it a strong squeeze. "Job well done my dearest friend. Job well done."

XVI

SINISTER SKY

Saturday

Saturday morning was relaxed at the Ryan home. There was no clanging wake-up call so one could sleep in, but most were up bright and early. Gert set a breakfast table so everyone could take what they wanted whenever they wanted. Most found they were still full to the gills from the meal last night of hole baked beans and Jacob's reflector oven biscuits. Marisol was fascinated when her brother dug off the dirt to raise the kettle.

Kate, Annie and Joe settled at the dining room table going through a plethora of notes to help the tribe plan for the coming year. Joe wanted to get an idea of supplies he might need to pick up on the coast. Kate took up Marisol's invitation to stay in Searsport for a few days but was finding it hard to convince her new friend to come back with her to Indian Island. The city girl could not wrap her head around being surrounded by Indians on a reservation.

Jack was one that did sleep in and once out of the wigwam, passed Marisol sitting on the porch pulling on his work boots. "You've finished your field-hand duties so why are you dealing with those nasty things?"

"Everyone is busy so I thought I'd enjoy the fresh air of this lovely morning and help your mother with some weeding in her garden."

Jack thought anyone who would weed when she didn't have to must be crazy but handed Marisol one of Gert's baskets. "I say, to each his or her own, have fun."

At this time in the town of Searsport, Matthew Roberts was sitting in a booth enjoying a pastry and a cup of coffee with Lucky, one of his associates.

"You seem quite jovial this morning, Matt." The man with a missing finger stirred his tea and ordered a sweet roll for himself.

"This is the night those half breeds at Prospect Ferry are going to get their comeuppance. They'll get enough of a warning not to mess with me or my buddies."

"What did they ever do to any of your cohorts? It seems to me, we had the upper hand with the two that came for supplies three weeks back. As for you, you need to cool your obvious jealousy or you'll risk losing a chance to court Miss Hodge."

Matt bristled at the suggestion that he would not win the hand of Marisol. "I'll keep that idiot savage away from her and teach his family that they can't mess with one of my group."

"I still don't understand. What happened?"

"Your accomplice at the wagon wheel went up the Penobscot to keep an eye on Marisol."

"Good glory, Matt, won't you ever learn? Did she catch him watching her?"

"No. During the day he walked in the woods above the fields and saw she kept very busy working in the gardens, which was hard for me to imagine. She must really love that old lady up there or thinks she may be able to come into some money if she gets in her graces."

"Frankly, knowing Miss Hodge I'd say the first scenario. But for you, the second would be a better fit."

Matt shouted at the waitress and waved his coffee cup. When she didn't jump immediately, he shouted across the room. "Hey, are you stupid or something? I want another cup of the swill you call coffee."

"And you call yourself a sophisticated gentleman? I'm amazed Miss Hodge has not seen through the veneer. Either that or she is a gold digger playing your games."

"Watch your mouth or you may be on your way out of town like your bully partner."

"What happened? I thought she didn't see him."

"She was unaware but that big Indian who is helping out thought he saw someone after dark and set a trap. When our friend saw Marisol go inside one of those rag tag Indian shelters, he tried to get a closer look at the men with her."

"Why in the world would she crawl into one of those? It's probably full of bugs. What happened?"

"Someone threw a hatchet at him, barely missing his head as it sliced into a nearby tree. He tried to escape but several men dressed in Indian garb and painted faces circled him. One of them was our punching bag who seems to have recovered. Then Sean Ryan himself joined them with gun waving and warned him not to come anywhere near his family again. He was sure the gun would go off so ran through the group with two on his tail to the ferry landing where the rowboat was moored. He stopped by here with the story and I gave him enough money to get to Boston to look for dock work at my uncle's yard."

"How do you know Sean Ryan?"

"I've only heard he's not well liked by many of the day laborers working on landscaping the fort. Not long ago he fired one of them on the spot for not filling in a hole. Asshole! Good for me though for I have a ready group eager to get even."

"Are they going to take part in the revenge plot?"

"Yes, indeed. At least two."

A very large, unkempt man walked into the pastry shop. Matt pointed for him to sit in the booth and gave a slight wave to the waitress. The girl came over right away with a cup of coffee and a sweet roll. With a smirk he whispered to Lucky, "Did you learn anything? By the way, this is Tub from the Fort Knox crew."

Lucky gave a slight wave towards the counter and quickly he had a fresh cup of tea. He shook his head and smiled at his obnoxious teacher then turned his attention to the stranger. "Are you one of the Sean Ryan haters?"

Tub nearly spit on the floor but sucked it up after a glare from Matt. "I paid off a couple low-lives to go up to the farm after sunset to give them a scare. I'm sure they'll get your point across."

Matt seemed pleased. "Good. I'm making sure I'm well seen in town tonight. I'm going to surprise Marisol by taking her to a fancy charity dinner to raise money for the families of men lost at sea. She and her stuffed shirt brother should be back by noon with her aunt's surrey."

"She's not coming today."

"What are you talking about?

"I heard say she is waiting an extra day so her new friend can come back for a visit. They are planning to leave after breakfast and will do some sightseeing on the way back. I wouldn't expect her until Sunday evening."

Matthew's face turned red as he banged the table with his fist, causing all the customers to stare at him. "I told her to be back Saturday by mid-day so we can do something special for dinner. I told her!" He picked up his coffee cup and smashed it on the floor.

The baker came out of the kitchen and put his hand on Matt's shoulder. "Sir, I want you to leave and kindly do not come back."

"Do you know who I work for? Mr. Merithew might even own this building."

"I really don't care. It is you that I'm asking to take your leave."

To that Matt swept his arm across the table and sent the remaining tableware and half eaten pastries to the floor. "I would never come back for this garbage."

Lucky and Tub had to drag the irate blowhard to the street where he pulled away and went mumbling down the brick sidewalk. "I did not want her there tonight. When she hauls her skinny little ass back here, I'll let her know just where her future lies."

Meanwhile, back amongst Gert's squash plants, Marisol felt an unexpected cold chill, yet the breeze from the river was quite warm.

Jack loped across the rows with his long legs. Marisol caught him out of the corner of her eye so was prepared for any tomfoolery. Instead, he reached out and took her hand. "I have orders to make sure your surrey is clean and ready for your departure in the morning with Tim and Kate. Thought you might like to visit the filly and see if she's ready to go back to the shore."

Marisol's first and only time in the barn was when she was cutting potatoes. She saw no need to ever go back, but now that she had a minute to look around, she saw it differently. "I hadn't noticed how big it was inside and so well organized."

"Frank and T do a great job in here. Many times T sleeps in their little office so he doesn't wake up his mother and Nana if he needs to start some chores early. Here's the filly's stall next to Argos."

"Hello Sweet Thing. It looks like T has done a good job getting you ready to go home. Your mane just shines."

Argos put his head out of the stall and looked at his neighbor who put her head next to his. Old faithful Hector was in the stall on the other side.

Jack laughed. "Looks like Argos has his eye on Sweet Thing."

Marisol laughed as she dug Jack in the side with her elbow. "Only you would think of that."

"On the other side is Bessie and her calf next to Pete and Pansy." The pair of mules turned their heads in unison, looked at Jack and were disappointed that he did not have a carrot for them so turned back and ignored him.

"They look different than the donkeys I've seen on the docks in London."

"Ah, my dear, they are mules, offspring of a male donkey and a female horse."

"My goodness, that's quite a couple."

Jack took Marisol's hand, quickly pulled her into the adjoining empty stall, wrapped his arms around her tiny waist and pushed her against the rough boards. "I know two other animals that would make quite a couple." He prepared for sharp slap in the face but instead she wrapped her arms around his neck and pulled him even closer. He teased her lips with his. "I've been thinking about this since the night in the fog."

She did more than just tease his lips, locking her own on his as if she never wanted to part.

When they took a breath, Jack could not speak above a husky whisper. "You can be a mystery, Miss Hodge."

"I think that is the best thing to be." When Jack lifted a wisp of her hair and kissed her neck, Marisol heard a moan and with a blush, realized that it had escaped from her own lips and was not the sound of the cow across the way. She trembled at the way she was discovering feelings never felt before. Not wanting the moment to end, she offered no resistance when Jack unbuttoned the top of her blouse. When he slipped his hand into her blouse and gently caressed her breast, she knew without a doubt the moan now heard again was definitely not from Bessie. Then in a flash, the fire igniting between the couple was quickly doused by a small voice calling their names from the barn door.

Cece could not see her brother nor Mary when she looked around, but Kate had told her that she saw them walk in through the side door. "Jack! Mary! Mama wants you to come for some lunch so she can clean up the kitchen."

Jack whispered into Marisol's ear and then nibbled the lobe. "I'm only hungry for one thing."

"Jack and Mary are you hiding?" Cece started walking further into the barn.

Marisol put her hands on Jack's chest, gave him another soft warm kiss, then sighed deeply and pushed him away. "I'm coming Cece. I've been checking on Sweet Thing." She quickly buttoned the top of her blouse and tried to make her hair stay in place. Jack and I will be right there. Tell your mother we are on the way.

Cece took a look at the couple, smiled and ran away.

Jack splashed a bit of water on his face from the trough. Marisol reached out and took his hand. "Come on Sweet Thing." She grinned from ear to ear.

Cece was out of breath when she ran into the kitchen and took a seat next to Kate. "Yum, honey. Who found a bee hive?"

"Thomas found it just under the eaves near the hay loft door and divided the honey among the three houses. Glad he got rid of it before any of you started to store the new crop. Talking about finding, where are your brother and Marisol?"

Cece took a bite of her biscuit and then licked some of the honey off the top. "They were in the barn canoodling."

That got the attention of all the adults. Sean laughed and slapped his knee. "Never. Those two are like oil and water."

Their peers were dumbstruck. Kate wiped some extraneous honey off the little girl's chin with her handkerchief. "Cece, what do you know about canoodling?"

Everyone went quiet and waited for an answer. Cece licked honey off each one of her fingers. "I may be small but I'm a farm girl. I know a lot about canoodling. What would you like to know?"

Just as Marisol came in the front door, Jack opened the back. They stood there watching everyone laughing themselves silly. Jack looked from one to another and they laughed even harder. "What's going on in here?"

"You missed it. You should have been here on time." Gert was still giggling while plopping the tea mugs in the dishpan.

The afternoon sped by getting all bags packed and placed by the door. Kate checked the supply list one more time and added a bit more.

As evening began to settle, Jack pushed Marisol gently on the swing while the setting sun put on a brilliant show.

Pulling the seat close, he whispered in her ear. "You do know we have some unfinished business? That is unless your Matthew Roberts is waiting near the sea to sweep you off your feet."

Marisol spun the swing around and looked at the orange gold sun reflecting in Jack's deep brown eyes. "Matthew who?"

Turning her back to swing again, only the big tom turkey settled in a nearby pine could see the joy on Jack's face.

Finally relaxing with her guests on the back porch, Gert watched the two at the apple tree and spoke in general. "You don't suppose Comfort was right?"

Joe put his arm around Annie's shoulder. "You never know when cupid is going to strike." Joe kissed his wife on her cheek. "Bows and arrows abound on Indian Island."

Standing on the porch sipping a tin of cold water, JJ looked from one to another. "Has any one seen my sister?"

"Kate enjoys watching the color reflections on the river." Gert stretched her arms in front of her, hiding a bit of a knowing smile. "Tim walked her to the ferry landing."

Faking alarm, JJ clutched his chest. "That sailor man needs to shove off to sea as quickly as possible."

Ever present Cece put her doll to her ear. "Lacey thinks they might be doing a little bit of canoodling too."

To which JJ's alarm was a little more real.

The perfect evening was made more so by the refreshing breeze bathing the quiet landing. Standing behind Kate, Tim hugged her around the waist as a passing schooner sailed by to reach the bay before dark. Its wake washed against the granite wall causing a spray to turn into tiny chips of gold. "I don't think I'll ever again look at a glorious sunset without thinking of you."

She hugged his arms and snuggled a bit closer.

"Kate Smythe, you have captured my heart."

"Is that such a terrible thing?"

"I'm afraid if I'm too forward, I'll drive you away. But if I don't confess my feelings, you may forget me as soon as I sail off. I'm also fearful of encroaching on your memory of Mike and your devotion to his family."

Kate turned and pushed a black curl off his forehead. "Mike and I were young but very much in love. He gave me this perfect little granite heart." Kate touched the tiny stone that hung around her neck and then touched Tim's cheek. "I know he'd want me to be happy." She leaned up and gave her new sweetheart a gentle kiss.

"Kate, are you all right? You're shivering."

"I just felt a sudden chill."

"Perhaps there's a change coming in the weather. Look at that black cloud beginning to cross the moon."

"The Micmacs raised my father as one of their own. He was immersed in their culture and I can hear him say there is a happening coming our way."

"You don't really believe all those folklore premonitions do you? If I trusted all the stories from the old salts, I'd never come above deck but just hover among the storage fearing the worst."

At the Ryan's Jacob walked off the porch and stood looking at the moon. He never moved, just stared.

Dan stood beside him. "What do you think Uncle Jacob?"

"It's a bad cloud. There is blackness coming." He put his hand on Dan's shoulder. "Say nothing. I'll take the watch."

XVII

TRAGIC GLOW

Saturday Night

Jacob was nearly invisible the way he stood against the pine beside the Ferry Road. He was of no worry to the creatures of the night for they acted on their survival skills as usual. The final lamp had been extinguished in the Ryan house and the wigwam was closed to the world. Dan came by with such stealth that he took his uncle by surprise.

"I must say you have perfected the use of what Indian blood runs through your veins." Jacob had the sparkle of pride in his eyes. "But, just what are you doing here?"

"I'd feel better if I watched over the waterfront while you keep an eye on the fields and Ferry Road. I'll let out a warning whistle if I see any danger."

With a nod from his sagamore, Dan silently disappeared towards the still, night waters of the river.

At the same time two other figures were making their way down the hill opposite the Hodge farm. Apparently their boss warned them to stay away from the waterfront and Ferry Road so they came up the carriage road from Stockton. Nearing the fort they adjusted the long packs on their backs and made their way into the wooded hill. They certainly were not silent, cursing through the underbrush, stumbling over logs, ducking low limbs and battling fresh-hatched hordes of mosquitoes. Once down to the edge of the road in front of Nana's, the two hires didn't know which way to go.

"He said there were fields of new crops, a big house with a smaller one beyond and a big barn. We need to make sure they get a good scare."

The partner was sputtering about more money for the tears in his clothes and the miserable bug bites. "Look. There's a good sized pile of hay between the big house and the barn."

"I think Sean Ryan's house is the smaller one."

"But that one is closer to the Ferry Road. And who cares, they all take care of the crops."

The two nearly crawled across the road like the snakes they were. Passing the side of Nana's house and nearing the hay, they each pulled a torch from their packs. One struck a match.

"Ready?" With a nod the torches were lit and they moved quickly towards the hay.

Suddenly T came running out of the office in the barn. "What the hell are you doing?" He rushed towards the van-dals with a large pitchfork under his stub, his other arm hold-ing it straight and steady.

"Run. That cripple is crazy!" When the leading hooli-gan caught his foot in the rose trellis, the torch flew out of his hand and rolled under Nana's back porch.

T screamed, "No!"

A pair of raccoons pushed four young cubs out from under the covered shelter as flames fed by accumulated dried leaves started to lick up through the floorboards under Nana's wicker chair.

The two thugs ran towards the woods with one yelling to the other to get rid of the other torch. The man spun and let it fly. The sickening sound of shattering glass echoed across the fields as the flaming stick went through the dining room window.

Uncle Jacob heard the sound and saw the glow across the fields and let out the distress whistle he had taught the Ryan boys when they were young. Then he ran towards the commotion.

Dan heard the call for help and ran up the road from the water and repeated the whistle as he passed the wigwam and Ryan house.

T tried to get to the back door but the growing fire blocked access. He ran towards the front. When he saw fire through the smashed dining room he started to holler for his mother.

Jack, JJ and a bewildered Tim came out of the wigwam, took one look at the growing glow across the field and started running with shoes in hand. Jack stopped long enough to pound on his father's door and whistled as he sped away.

Nothing springs the Ryan family into action as fast as that family signal for help. The front door flew open, Sean took one look, ran back to grab his work boots with Joe right behind him. As they ran down the front to the carriage road he shouted back at Gert and Annie. "Grab some buckets and go ring the school house bell."

"Mama, mama," cried Cece.

Marisol picked her up. "I have her."

The last time Gert had taken part of ringing the large bell was when the tunnel collapsed at the fort trapping Sean. Her face was distorted in fear. The bell had been used over the years to summon help from families when a child was lost in the woods, for a tree fire after a hit by lightning, a chimney fire at the Svenson's and the like. "Dear God, not Nana's home."

When the first of the neighbors could be seen, Gert turned the bell over to Annie and ran with Kate to the farmhouse.

The men had already started a bucket line from Nana's dug well and the pitcher pump near the barn. Joey had another line going from his well and pitcher pump, which was a distance away, but as more men came, it became possible. Peg promised she would not come near the fire, especially the smoke but began to fill buckets as quickly as possible. Gert handed her pails over to some men then screamed when she saw the fire glow through the window of Nana's upstairs sitting room. Kate looked in panic at all the men until she spotted JJ directing one of the bucket brigades. "Where's Tim!" She spun in circles but could not see him. "Timothy!"

The pantry, kitchen and dining room areas in the back of the house were fully engulfed. Gert and Kate ran to the front lawn being careful not to hinder the men working with the buckets. Sparks had started to catch some of the grass and foliage so others were using blankets and shovels to snuff the small patches of flames. It was noticeable the men were focusing on wetting down the front parlor and staircase.

"Gert, where's Tim? Kate, have you seen him?" Marisol was calling from the other side of the carriage road clutching a frightened Cece."

Gert worked her way to the front of the line where Sean and Uncle Jacob were shouting orders. She wasn't able to get their attention in the cacophony.

Suddenly JJ pulled his sister back to the road and shouted to Gert. "Don't get in the way! T and Tim have gone up stairs to find Nana and Cara."

Both Kate and Marisol screamed while trying to get closer. JJ kept a tight hold on his sister as a sudden gust of wind drove sparks their way from a break in the roof. Gert took Cece from the arms of Marisol as she frantically fought her way to find her twin. Another shower of sparks fell on the group. Jack ran out of the line and picked up Marisol, carrying her back to the other side of the road. JJ did the same with his sister while Gert sheltered Cece with her body and followed.

In the parlor, the oil paint began to bubble on Gert's paintings of Bucksport and the river. The frames lovingly carved by Dan began to char. On the little table, the arrangement of dried bittersweet burst into flames and its dainty vase exploded with a loud pop "Hurry, more water!" Jacob fed the bucket as fast as possible to Sean who tossed the liquid on the back wall. Two of the men tore the front door off the hinges to make more room. Sean ran into the parlor so he could aim more water on the stairwell.

Gert screamed, "No Sean!" Cece sobbed.

As fingers of fire began to spread on the ceiling, Gert's paintings burst into flames and fell to the floor. "Water!" T was carrying his mother down the stairs. Sean tossed a bucket of water directly on them. Jacob reached to guide them through the thickening smoke and out to waiting arms. Sean could just make out Tim guiding Nana. He had a quilt over her head and talked her down each step. Sean tossed water at them as the banister began to buckle causing Tim to nearly lose his balance. All were choking. Sean reached up, took Nana's hand and led the couple to the floor.

"This way," Jacob shouted as a guide. He threw another bucket of water into thin air aiming in their direction. Just then fire broke through and ate at the stairwell while flaming ceiling pieces dropped like hot snowflakes."

"Take her out." It was hard for Tim to talk between coughing spasms. "I'm right behind you."

When Jacob and Sean led Nana out of the door and uncovered her head, a cheer went up. Joe, Joey and Dan carried

Nana to the edge of the road where Gert and the girls comforted her.

Just as Sean leaned in to grab Tim's arm a larger chunk of flaming ceiling fell, throwing Tim to the floor, trapping him.

Jacob grabbed the quilt and began to beat back the flames. "Quick. More water!"

Tim began to scream in pain as Sean, Jacob and two other men grabbed his legs and pulled him free. His right arm was on fire as they dragged him through the doorway.

This was seen by Marisol and Kate, who somehow found the strength of men twice their size, to twist from their protectors and push through the crowd as Sean smothered the arm on fire with Nana's quilt. Tim was obviously unconscious when Jacob picked him up and moved towards the road. The ladies were unceremoniously tossed kicking and yelling over the shoulders of JJ & Jack to follow Tim to safety.

The sight of her nephew so seriously injured jolted Nana from her state of shock. She stood straight with just a bit of support from Gert and started barking orders. "Have Thomas bring around the garden wagon with one of the mules. We must get Timothy to the Ryan house to clean his wounds." She then opened her fist and handed a small-carved rowboat and oars to Gert who put it in the deep pocket of her sweater.

As soon as he saw the flames, Thomas came across the fields and led the animals out to the back corral. He was careful to cover the horses' eyes so they would not panic.

Jack hollered over the din. "Thomas, Mrs. Hodge needs the garden wagon and one of the mules."

"I'll grab the harness and then you need to help me roll out the wagon. Was the lady injured?"

"No bodily harm. If it were not for T and Tim, both she and Cara would have perished."

"We'll use Pete. He's stronger. You can handle the wagon. I want to stay here, settle the animals and get them back in the barn."

As soon as the small wagon stopped, Marisol jumped in the back so she could cradle her brother for the short trip down the road. Dan and JJ helped get Nana up on the seat next to Jack. Gert and Annie ran ahead to prepare him a bed while Cece squeezed in next to Marisol. JJ and a very distressed Kate walked beside the wagon. Neighbors yelled up to Nana that she should use pig fat on the burns. Others suggested making a salve with butter but Nana knew what needed to be done.

The rest of the men were beginning to quell the flames. Concentrating the water on the parlor to aid the rescue of Nana and Cara, helped save a bit of the front of the house but overall the loss was near totality.

At the Ryan house, they quickly put Tim in Joe's bed. Marisol demanded that she sleep in the other bed.

Nana directed Gert to cut away the sleeve material from Tim's burned flesh. Kate felt a bit faint so took Cece to the other bedroom and got her cleaned up for bed. Then she rocked her in her arms and sang a sweet bedtime song. "Hush-a-bye, don't you cry–go to sleep now pretty baby. "So hush-a-bye, don't you cry–go to sleep now pretty Cece."

XVIII

Decisions

Sunday

Saturday night was difficult. Tim floated painfully in and out of consciousness. Once Nana and Gert removed his shirt they could see that the arm was injured, but not nearly as severely as his hand. Obviously Uncle Jacob's immediate smothering of the fire protected the upper arm and minimized the lower. Nana's concern was how deep the burns appeared on the hand and his fingers. Over many years at sea, she had picked up experience with injuries to the crew with cuts, broken bones and burns from tipped oil lamps.

Sunday morning Sean was sent to Stockton to fetch the new doctor. They had heard he was young but many spoke well of him as a physician as he was partnering with an older surgeon. Sean peeked in on Tim before he left. A pale, fatigued Nana grabbed his arm. "Make sure he brings some type of painkiller."

Sean leaned down and gave her a kiss on her cheek. He had never seen her appear this old. "I'll be back as quick as possible."

Gert brought in two cups of tea and some corn bread in hopes to get the two ladies to take some nourishment. Nana was redressing the lower arm with more wet cloths and drying a few of the small surface burns on the upper. Marisol had not said a word all night while she sat holding her brother's hand.

"These two spots just above his elbow are drying. We need to keep them soft. Have Jack run over and get my aloe vera plant on the windowsill over the kitchen sink."

Marisol and Gert looked at each other not knowing what to say.

Nana looked up and was not happy. "Someone must get the plant quickly or I'll have to wet these again. It's on the sill." Suddenly she looked like someone just punched her in the stomach and began to sob. "There is no sill, is there?" Her body now racked with spasms of grief.

Kate came in and wrapped her arms around her dear Nana Hodge. "Come with me. I've put fresh blankets on Marisol's bed and I insist you rest a bit. I'll sit with Tim."

Gert helped Nana up and out. They were all amazed she didn't put up a fight. Marisol and Kate looked at each other as tears fell. In the silence of the room, they heard the screams of each other's heartfelt pain.

"Nana thinks the juice from the aloe leaf can help soothe the minor burns. My aunt Daphne has two plants that were sent from a nursery in Boston. Somehow, I'm going to Searsport to bring them here."

Kate once again changed the wet compresses on the arm and used water to soak the hand with Marisol's help.

Annie and Peg walked in to see how they could help. They had placed a good amount of cold meat, bread and sweets on the tables in the grove so the men could take a break whenever needed. Small hot spots were still being found and drowned in the rubble. Apparently by focusing on the front parlor with extra buckets of water saved some items in the closed cabinets under the bookcases near the fireplace. Once sure it was safe from flaming, Sean would carefully remove what could be salvaged.

An apparently rattled Gert walked into Tim's room. "Nana fell into a deep sleep as soon as I covered her but I can't find Cece. She was going to stay close in case Nana needed help. I've looked everywhere, especially her hiding places when she didn't like what was going on in the house. She would sit in the chicken coop and tell stories to the hens or sit high in the apple tree like her brothers did when they were troubled. She would never go back to the fort alone after the foggy night. I even looked behind the barrels in the root cellar. Frankly I am at my wits end. I can't think of another place she would go for comfort. Lacey is gone and I can't find Lady which is another worry with all the confusion and fire last night." Gert sighed deeply and leaned against the wall decorated with paintings of schooners on the river. "Where could she be?"

Suddenly Kate and Marisol were hit with the same thought. Each took one of Gert's hands. "Come with us."

Marisol asked Peg to sit with Tim in case he woke to assure him they were safe and would be right back.

Annie had stretched some pieces of white cotton fabric under the sun for a good bleaching. She would stay with Peg while ripping and cutting new bandages and soaking cloths for Tim.

The girls nearly dragged Gert out the back door. The sky was a brilliant blue but the air carried the acrid odor of a smoldering lifetime. As the trio followed rows of sprouting plants towards Joey's house, they tried not to look at the pile of charred remains of the Hodge house and belongings. The tears that flowed were not completely from the bitter smell that at times caused uncontrollable coughs.

"Where in the world are you taking me? Cece would never hide in Joey's house. She loves Peg but would not hang around with her brother if she was upset."

"We're nearly there." Marisol led her past the house following Kate down the nearly undetectable path towards the large boulder.

Gert was quite taken by the lovely grove of pines, birches and lady's slippers that were nearing their prime. It was like a wall to hide the ugliness that lay just outside its boundary.

Kate went around the boulder then turned holding her finger to her lips in a hush. Marisol led Gert to her daughter's hidden secret place. There curled up in the concave was a sleeping Cece still in her nightdress. She was hugging Lacey while Lady stretched her full length against her side. The cat slowly opened her bright yellow green eyes, looked curiously at the intruders and then closed them again.

Gert reached down and picked up her exhausted little girl cuddling her so her head faced the river. Kate and Marisol walked between mother, daughter and the destruction just in case Cece woke up. She only mumbled, where's Lacey. Kate said she had her doll safely in her own arms. Gert peeked back at Lady waddling behind them. "Come on you little tramp."

It was obvious from the garden that many of the bucket brigade were back to help clean up the rubble.

They could see Argos and Nana's travel wagon tied at the front of the house. Behind him was the doctor's surrey and impatient filly. Kate took Cece from Gert to go in the back door. "You two go in with Tim. I hope the doctor can find a way to help."

Kate tiptoed into the back bedroom in hopes of not disturbing Nana and laid the little girl on the other bed. She thought if

Peg has no room for her to sleep at their house, she could bed down in the wigwam with JJ until they make new plans. It would not be the first time. She covered Cece with her patch-work quilt with appliquéd bunnies and went to the front bed-room to see what the doctor's plan was for Tim. Her heart was aching to help him.

Marisol was wiping her brother's forehead. He had picked up a slight fever but seemed a bit more comfortable. He opened his eyes slightly to the delight of the ladies.

The doctor examined the burns and was impressed with the way the minor ones on the arm were losing the redness. "I'm glad you did not use grease of any kind for it seals the wound and holds in the heat. That usually leads to blisters that can become infected."

Gert and Kate looked at each other with a nod and a smile.

The doctor lifted the badly injured hand from the ever-freshened clear water. He closely examined the depth of the burns but gave no opinion. This touching and movement by the doctor caused Tim distress and he cried out in pain. Marisol held his other hand and spoke softly for him to be brave.

"You have quelled the heat with the constant cool water. Now loosely cover the hand with clean dressings."

Gert wasn't sure of the orders from the doctor. "The cool water had been keeping his pain in check. Won't that increase his pain?"

"I brought a prepared laudanum solution. Give him a spoonful when necessary and he should rest with comfort. I'll be back in the morning with my partner, the surgeon, so he can give you his opinion on the damage to the hand. I'm afraid there will be infection, possibly gangrene could set in."

Jacob came into the room just as the doctor was leaving and heard his words. Gert caught his eye and they shared great concern.

Nana slowly came through the door. Gert ran and got her a walking stick to help with balance.

"Did he bring some morphine?"

Gert picked up the bottle of laudanum. "I'm getting a spoon."

Nana waved her hand dismissively. "Posh, he would get more help from the needle." She touched his forehead with the back of her hand. "His fever is growing. We need to keep a cool cloth on his head."

Jacob took a good look at the hand and saw the anger in the deep burns for the first time. "After we hear the plan from the doctors, we will need to make a quick decision."

Nana nodded in agreement. "We should prepare now just in case."

The girls looked at Gert but all she could do was shrug since she had no idea of their thinking.

Nana's complexion was gray and her body very frail but she was still quick of mind. "Marisol, make sure Tim gets a good spoonful of the medicine and he needs to drink some water."

Jacob put his hand on her shoulder. "Come with me. I have some boxes for you to see." He gave this arm to Nana to give her support while she fought for her strength to return.

Gert settled her neighbor in the kitchen rocking chair and placed the old shawl around her shoulders. There was moisture in the air and dark clouds rising from the west. The last thing Nana needed was a chill.

Jacob explained that some things in the corner of the parlor were saved but may have been water soaked. He opened a small wood crate and took off several pieces of protective cotton flannel.

Gert gasped seeing Nana's precious handmade ornaments from the first Christmas tree. she decorated nearly twenty years ago and the glass and tin baubles collected each year since.

"Dear Jacob, you've given me such a glorious gift but I can't deal with the memories right now." She began to choke up.

"I'll put everything in Gert's pantry until you are ready. But there is one thing I want you to have now." He unrolled an old towel and exposed Captain Hodges pipe he pulled off the fireplace mantel before the fire broke through.

Nana was speechless. She held the carved pipe to her nose. "He's still there." She then hugged the pipe to her breast and looked into the eyes of her dear friend and whispered. "Thank you. Thank you. Thank you." The only sound in the kitchen became the slight squeak of the rocker.

Sean came in the back door and could plainly feel the great sadness. Gert finally allowed herself to let go and fell into her husband's arms.

Even though it was late afternoon, the flash of lightning could be seen illuminating the window pane and the thunder took its time rolling down the valley to the sea.

"Mama! Mama!" Cece ran out of the bedroom and got behind her mother. "Mama, there's lightning boomers."

"Gert got down on her knees and hugged her. "Don't be frightened Comfort. Remember, you need to stay away from the window. This sounds like heat lightning so it shouldn't last long."

"Can I go into your bedroom and close the shutters?"

"Come on Miss Comfort, I'm hungry and I bet you are too. If you ask nicely, I bet your Mama would bring us some milk and cookies in our room." Sean put Cece up on his shoulders.

She was fine until the next crack of thunder, then started shaking.

"I'll bring you some real supper. I don't think either one of you has eaten all day. Now scoot."

"Now what was that about? I've never seen that little girl afraid of anything." Jacob sat at the kitchen table. "I also haven't had a bite. Peg put out a nice table but I didn't get around to it."

"There's chicken and potatoes in the stew pot. It won't take long to bake up some biscuits." While she was cutting in the lard, Gert explained her daughter's scare. "We had a bad storm that followed the river last summer. Before that night, Comfort loved to watch out the window to count the seconds from the lightning to thunder. At about five seconds per mile, she would figure out the distance to the storm. Well, suddenly the flash came at the same time as the bang and she saw the bolt jump from the top of the pine to the side of the house to the ground. She has hated thunder storms ever since."

Jack walked in the back door covered from head to foot in ash from the fire cleanup "We thought we might have instant roasted tom turkey but he must have been smart enough not to roost with lightning in the air."

Jacob stretched so his tired muscles wouldn't get stiff. "When the hit is that close, it's called a thunder crack."

"Well, there is something worse. You could see the flash but never hear the clap."

"Jack, don't let your sister hear that!" Gert swung around and took a look at her filthy son, grabbed the straw broom and chased him out on the porch. "I'll get you some clean clothes and toss them out. Don't you come in here to eat until you look more human."

"But Ma, it is starting to rain."

"Good, that will help you wash up."

Jacob took a look out the window and watched the rain turn heavy. "This is good. It will drown any missed hotspots and lay down the dust."

Nana looked at Jacob through red-rimmed eyes. "Is that what my home is now? Just ashes?"

"The only section still standing is a small corner of the parlor. Once we make sure we have any belongings out that can be saved, the remaining wall will need to come down so it won't become a hazard during the clean up."

"What about the front door? I barely remember it lying on the ground when you carried me to the road."

Jacob thought for a moment. "The last I saw, it was leaning against the office wall in the barn."

Nana suddenly looked alarmed. "Dear God, I forgot about T. Where did he take his mother?"

Gert tossed a bit of flour on the rolled out dough to make it less sticky for her tin biscuit cutter. "Sorry Nana, I forgot to mention Thomas opened up his boy's bedroom for Cara and T has been sharing his room. The neighbors have been wonderful with their donations of clothes for Cara and if I may add, for you." She pointed to a basket of clothes for Nana.

Nana shook her head at the unthinkable that suddenly become real. "Gert, you have always loved that door. I want you and Sean to make it your new front door."

"Nana, we'll think of that later." Gert pulled the biscuits out of the oven and then went to check on Tim. The room was so quiet that the caregivers were startled when she opened the door.

She whispered, "You both need to eat." Marisol started to dig in her heels. "Sweet girl, if you don't keep up your strength, you'll be of no help to your brother." Kate came around the bed and took her new friend's hand. Reluctantly, they left.

The room was so quiet Gert could hear her heart beating in her ears. Wringing a fresh wet cloth for Tim's fore head, she felt she was also wringing her stomach into a knot. "Dear boy, you are burning up from a fire within." She closed her eyes. *Lord, I know I don't talk to you as often as I did as a young girl. You were my strength in that lonely period of my life. We humans tend to be selfish with our time with you. Many times we don't say thank you yet are quick to ask your help. You have never left my heart so it is my fault that our conversations have become fewer. I'm the one who closed the door especially at the death of our Mike. Right now, I am watching this wonderful young man struggling with an inner fire that most certainly was set by the Devil himself. I'm not sure any of us, including the trained doctors, have the know-how to stop the poison that I fear is rushing through his frail body. Nana and Jacob are forming a plan and we will need to make a decision as to his care or at least his comfort. Please give us the wisdom to recognize the way we need to go. I place Timothy in your hands with us as your servants.*

Nana stood silently until Gert sighed and squeezed out a new cloth. "It looks like you were where I found myself many times this afternoon," Nana consoled Gert and continued, "At first with angry words as to 'why You did you do this to me? How could You destroy my dear Captain's dream?' But it didn't take me long to accept the fact that it was unthinking human cruelty that caused where I find myself and spilled the Hodge blood of this brave young man. Then I gave thanks that Timothy came into my life and asked for the strength and wisdom to find a way to save him." Nana kissed her closest friend on the cheek and asked to sit in the chair to freshen the coolness on Tim's face and neck.

Jacob had come in silently, as Jacob is wont to do. "This hand is not ready to be exposed to the air."

"I agree." Nana tried to turn the clammy pillow under Tim's head but needed Gert's help. "We'll keep it covered with fresh water to cool it, at least until morning. Then we'll hear what the learned doctors have to say for the next treatment."

Jacob agreed. "Sean and I will give Tim a good bath and change the bedding while the girls are gone."

"Where did you say Marisol and Kate went?" Gert brought in some towels, clean sheets, and a lightweight summer quilt.

"They are walking Annie over to Joey's. Peg is setting up a place for her to sleep. Marisol is staying in here, Kate with Nana with Cece on the floor."

"I forgot you are a Micmac Sagamore who knows how to put a plan in motion."

"Gert, I have many years of practice herding the Ryan boys around."

Tim began to whimper. "I'll put some water on to heat and send in Sean. Nana and I will make up a list in case we need to make a quick decision."

XIX

The Sign

Monday

Monday morning you could feel the heavy apprehension in the Ryan home. Even Cece was not her energetic self as she sat quietly in the parlor stroking Lady while looking at pictures in the fairy tale book from England that Nana gave her for Christmas. It didn't help that the sky was dull gray and a slight drizzle made things appear even gloomier.

Sean took a quick walk to the fort and told his boss the details of what happened and that he would not be in the office that day. He was offered men from the site if they were needed to clean up the rubble.

Gert pulled out her writing desk and put it on the table. It was important she made the morning post.

My Dear Nettie ~

I know how bad news travels quickly through the old Indian paths and river ways. Just in case you heard of the tragic fire that destroyed Nana's home, I wanted you to be assured that your two children are not hurt. Kate and JJ did everything they could to help. You should be very proud of them as I am of my boys. As usual Uncle Jacob took charge. I am so grateful they were here. Captain Hodge's nephew Tim was seriously injured and I fear for him. Even though they have not known each other for long, Kate is quite taken by him and he of her. Tim saved Nana from certain death as he led her from the fire. Our dear T led his mother to safety. I am not sure what will become of them as Cara was devoted to helping Nana and T is a hard working farm hand but it will be hard to find other work with one arm. This will be short as I want to make the post before the doctors arrive. We are busy making plans for several ways to face the future.

Sean and I send our very best to you and Ben. It must seem odd to have both your children away but they have been so supportive. Kate will be such a help with the school on Indian Island. I know Joe and Annie are thrilled.

As ever,

Your devoted friend Gert

The doctors arrived mid morning and made haste to Tim's room. Marisol refused to leave his bedside during the examination and Gert stood ground as her support. When the two physicians looked at Sean to take the women away, he could only explain they obviously were not budging. The doctors were far from pleased at such insolence.

Wrapping her arms around Marisol's shoulders, Gert was proud of the young woman's brave front for she could feel her trembling, especially when exposed to the severity of her brother's wounds. While probing the damaged tissue, the practitioners spoke in whispers and obscure medical language, which irritated Gert. *Do they think I can't hear or am not intelligent enough to catch the meaning?* By the way Marisol's body reacted Gert was sure she could understand some of the diagnosis but hoped not all.

Every head pivoted in unison as the door to Tim's room opened. The eyes of all those waiting in the kitchen were fixed on the doctors. Kate took Marisol by the hand and held it tightly while Sean wrapped his arms around Gert. The only sound for a moment was Nana rocking in the chair.

"Well, I can see that Timothy has a lot of support." The surgeon handed his bag to his partner. "You must know the young man is seriously ill. The burns on the upper arm will not be a problem but the tissue on his hand is infected and the burns have reduced the blood supply to his fingers. The best treatment to give him a chance for survival is to amputate his arm at the elbow."

Marisol fainted. Jack was at her side in an instant and carried her to the sofa in the parlor. JJ comforted Kate. He had never seen his sister so distraught.

"We'll make arrangements to have him taken to my surgery right away."

"No!" Nana used her walking stick to quickly get up to confront the doctor.

"Pardon me, Madam. Just who are you to speak for my patient?"

"I am Timothy Hodge's aunt and you need to wait until my niece has a chance to review all options before she agrees."

"We need to get that damaged limb off quickly or your nephew will die. Can you face that consequence of your tardiness?"

That set Sean on fire. "In all due respect doctor, you have no need to lecture us on this difficult decision. A family member will come by your office before the day is done."

"One of us will be at our workplace until six. After that you will need to leave written instructions through the mail slot on the office door." The only thing missing in that dramatic statement was a "harrumph" as he stomped out.

Jack was stroking Marisol's hair away from her face when she began to regain her senses. She inhaled raggedly while reaching to put her arms around her 'secret' sweetheart. "What am I ever going to do?"

"You need to pull yourself together and come out with the family so you can hear all options."

"What options?" Marisol flared with anger. "He loses his arm and still might die."

Hearing Marisol, Kate came into the parlor where the two friends fell into each other's arms. "Come with me, Tim is depending on us."

Chairs and benches were pulled into the kitchen so everyone could sit in a circle. "Sean, where is Comfort?"

"Dan took her over to the barn to help T feed and groom the horses in case they need to be used today. You know she'll do anything for T and he'll keep her safe."

"Thanks. She didn't need to see the initial reaction to Tim's condition." Gert settled between Nana and Sean while trying to keep her nerves in check. JJ sat close to his sister who was clenching Marisol's hand so tight it was red. Jack was next, then Joe. Jacob stood as usual, straight, tall and confident. In came Joey and Peg taking the last two chairs followed by Cece and her big brother Dan. They were steps ahead of a steady rain.

Cece looked around the circle. "Not to worry, you got me out of here for a while and now I'll take my book and go in the bedroom. If you need me, just holler."

That was just the relief the group needed. Emotionally, they were ready for decisions.

Kate was the first to notice. "Joe, where's Annie."

"She took the earliest ferry to meet the mail boat in Bucksport. We have many friends in Brewer to take her up to the Indian Island Ferry."

Marisol wondered why Annie had left and looked around for an answer.

It was Jacob that broke the silence. "I asked her to get a head start so her parents and others could prepare for our needs."

"Why would her parents need to prepare for us?" Marisol, getting agitated, pushed Jack's hand away and started pacing.

Jacob gave Nana a hand up so she could talk with the girl. "This is one of the plans we had in mind for Tim if the diagnosis was as bad as we feared."

"Do they have better doctors on Indian Island?"

Nana shook her head. "I'm afraid not a lot of doctors bother with the plight of the Penobscot but there are quite a few in the city of Bangor that would give more advice for the plight of an Englishman."

"If the doctor's in Stockton took Tim's arm, would that be that? Would he be rid of the infection?"

"It would in a perfect world." Nana sat again and started rocking as she thought of what to say. "We're getting closer to having medicine that could fight infection and the ravages of possible gangrene but now the offending limb is just hacked off rather than treating the whole body."

"You actually think treating Tim at an Indian reservation makes more sense than modern medicine?"

Nana placed her hand on Marisol's shoulder and looked deeply into her eyes. "There are times when the wisdom of the ancients works the best."

"Never! Tim is not going to be turned over to witch doctors."

"The blood of my Captain Hodge runs through the body of that young man. I would never do anything to harm him." Nana sat back into the rocker.

Marisol fell to her knees in front of her newfound aunt and laid her head in Nana's lap. "What am I suppose to do?" She sighed deeply. "If they take off the lower arm and it doesn't help, what would be next?"

"They would most likely take off the upper arm."

At that, Kate gasped. "His dreams of going to sea would be crushed."

Marisol turned and shouted, "But he would be alive!"

"Do you know that? Do you know that chopping him apart piece by piece will work?"

Marisol stood defiantly in the circle. "All of you! Have you all been planning behind my back? And just what is this master plan?"

All eyes turned to Jacob. "We want Tim to have the best chance possible. Many of the injuries seen in the Micmac and Penobscot settlements were burns. Open fires were the center of our survival. I've watched terrible wounds respond to the herbs and salves prepared by the elders. Yes, there was scarring and difficulty learning skills again, but many burns similar to Tim's were healed and fevers were driven out."

"I'm going to be on the reservation for the summer. We could help take care of Tim and take him into Bangor if special medical care is needed. On Indian Island he would have more than one method to save his life and hopefully save his arm." Kate's eyes were pleading with Marisol.

"You want me to live with Indians? In wigwams, or teepees or whatever?"

"I'm staying with Annie's parents," Kate explained. "You would share my bedroom in their lovely home."

"What about my belongings at Aunt Daphne's?"

"You and I will leave right away to take Sweet Thing and the surrey back to Searsport. Jack will hold the reins. Joe, Dan and Uncle Jacob will follow to pick up the school supplies and your luggage. Jack will join the men outside of town to camp for the night while you and I will go to spend the night with

Daphne and explain what is happening. The men will come to the suppliers in the morning, load the wagon, and pick us up at Daphne's house. We'll come back here for the night and leave for the reservation Wednesday morning." Kate rattled that off without a breath, then took a deep one and just waited for some reaction.

Uncle Jacob picked up the dialogue. "I have one meeting I need to make before we leave Searsport. It won't take long but should prove very satisfying."

"What about Tim? He needs care right away."

Gert continued with the plans. "As soon as you leave, JJ, Joey and Sean will harness Argos and move Tim into the Hodge wagon with Nana, Cece and me, supplies for his care and whatever food we can fit in. JJ will drive the wagon up to Milford where Joe has a friend with a fairly large flat bottom craft for moving supplies to the island. Tim will be ferried in that." Gert asked, "Did I leave anything out?"

Sean picked up the plans. "I'm staying here to watch over the house and work on the cleanup when I get home from the fort. Cara is going to help Peg while Joey, Frank and T work the fields. I'll look after our gardens before I go to work but I won't do it in my nightshirt." Sean gave Gert a squeeze while she rolled her eyes.

"We have a problem. We hadn't planned for the weather." Dan opened the back door letting in some needed fresh air but it was raw from the steady but gentle rain. "We may not make Searsport before dark with this dreariness."

"We certainly don't want Tim to get a chill but can't wait much longer before he gets treatment of some kind." Hope was draining from Nana's face.

Marisol went into the front bedroom and held her brother's good hand. Kate and Gert leaned against the doorframe.

"What do I do? If I only had a sign. Do I have the surgeon come and take him? Do I risk him getting sicker from the dampness? What if we fail at the reservation? Timmy, you've always made our decisions."

Just then a ray of sunshine burst through the window-pane. It pierced the dreariness of the sickroom and came to rest on Tim's face.

Running in from the kitchen, Cece nearly knocked over her mother. "Mary, Mary, the clouds are pulling apart and there is enough blue to mend pants for lots of Dutchmen.

Marisol looked at Kate and Gert. "Let's go."

XX

COMEUPPANCE

Just before sunset, Marisol guided Sweet Thing into the large doorway of the Searsport Livery. The stable hand watered the horse before settling the filly into a stall with fresh grains and hay. Then he insisted on walking the ladies up the hill to Daphne's house as the sun was getting low. When the girls entered the kitchen, Daphne nearly dropped her favorite Wedgwood teacup when she saw her niece. She rocked her in her arms in sheer relief. "There were rumors there was a fire at the Hodge farm but every story was different so I didn't know what to believe. Thank goodness you are here."

Marisol took her handkerchief and dabbed the tears off her aunt's cheeks. "This is my friend Kate Smythe. She and her brother JJ travelled from Aroostook County to work with us on Nana's planting."

"I am very pleased to meet you dear. I'm not surprised you would journey that far to help Mrs. Hodge. She is quite a remarkable lady. I just made a fresh pot of tea, join me?"

Marisol pulled out the oak kitchen chair with the lovely pressed floral design at the top and nodded to Kate to also sit. "I would say a cup of hot tea is just what we need while telling you what happened at the farm."

Daphne set out three more china cups and saucers. "Where is Timothy? Is he still tending to Sweet Thing?"

The next hour was emotional. Daphne had a terrible time with the news. Kate was worried about the amount of stress on both and did her best to console them while her heart was also breaking with fear that she may lose another love in her life.

"An Indian reservation? How could you choose putting Tim's life in the hands of the untrained and turn away from an experienced surgeon? Have you lost your mind?"

Frantically, Marisol looked to Kate for help as she was beginning to doubt herself. "What have I done?"

"You have given Tim a chance to heal while saving his arm. Do you truly believe that Nana Hodge would do anything to harm Tim now that she's found him? Never!"

That calmed the situation a bit. Just an occasional sob punctuated the sips of tea.

Marisol took a deep breath and tightly held her aunt's hand. "I'm going to spend the summer at Indian Island with Kate to be with Tim while he is healing."

Daphne pulled away, stood and stomped over to the kitchen sink where she stared out the window. The sunset was blood red as was her face. "What are you thinking?"

"I'm thinking that with that sunset, tomorrow should be a perfect day to travel. We will be spending the night at the Ryan's and then up to the island the next day. I'm anxious to see how they have settled Tim."

"I'm speaking about you girls living on an Indian reservation. Will you be sleeping in those teepee things?"

"They are wigwams, Aunt Daphne."

Kate had to smile at that. Her friend has turned a leaf just a bit. There will be a lot of culture shock to come. "We will be staying with Adele and Tomah. They have a lovely home overlooking the Penobscot River. Tomah is a leader in the tribe."

"Now dear Auntie, could we put some water on to take a nice hot bath. Neither one of us had a chance to have more than a quick wash up for over a week and then the ash from the fire really did us in." Marisol brushed off the top of her shoulder to make the point.

Daphne tossed up her hands in surrender and filled the kettles while the girls pulled out the copper tub. They were actually giddy while taking turns to soak in the bubbles, then washing each other's hair. Two light cotton nightshirts were pulled out of the cedar chest to the delight of the friends. While they brushed their long hair dry to a shine, the chocolate set was pulled from the china closet for the rich hot brew served in matching miniature cups.

Marisol's travel trunk was nearly hidden under bolts of fabric in the storage closet under the stairwell and was impossible for Daphne to move. She went to Marisol's room to tell her it would take two to pull it free but found both girls sound asleep.

Tuesday

Morning came much too soon for the young ladies. There was a lot of mumbling and grumbling coming from the bedroom at the top of the stairs. Marisol opened and banged the doors on the mahogany armoire, pulling a pile of clothes onto the bed to separate out things too dressy or not suitable for the wilds of the Penobscot Valley. She and Kate laughed at how small the assortment of skirts and blouses became under that criteria. She had two riding outfits that Kate thought perfect for exploring the string of islands that made up the reservation and hoped to use one.

The girls wiggled the small travel trunk out of the closet and Daphne found it quite funny there weren't many clothes to take so sent along several pieces of cotton prints from the end of bolts. "This will give you a few sets of skirts and blouses. That is as soon as you learn how to sew."

"That will be no problem with Gert and Nana there. Perhaps you can take a few days and spend some time with us to help replace Nana and Cara's wardrobe and the clothes they had made for Peg's baby."

Daphne turned the color of her new white enamel dish-pan. "My dear Kate, I can't imagine me visiting a reservation but that won't stop me from putting some items together right here in Searsport." Daphne folded a lovely crocheted shawl into the trunk. It was the color of Marisol's eyes. "I had worked this for Christmas but I think you'll need it before that. Also you should pack one social outfit, just in case. And put in your side laced high tops. I noticed your well-worn work shoes."

Marisol couldn't help but smile at the story of her boots. "We've left our dirty clothes. Do you mind? I don't see where we will have time to wash them before going to Indian Island."

"I already have them soaking. Now you have something to eat before your ride comes."

Aunt Daphne had set a lovely table. She made coddled eggs, scones and breakfast tea. In a dainty side dish was fresh lemon curd.

Kate picked up the coddler. "My Grandma Thorpe used something like this only she called it a pipkin. My uncles liked their eggs scrambled so I got a special egg when she and I were alone. I'd almost forgot that special memory."

"Thank you Auntie. You must teach me how to make the lemon curd."

"Goodness, Marisol. You are learning to cook? Is there someone special in your life that I don't know about? I hope not that loudmouth Matthew Roberts. I lost all respect for that young man after he beat on Gert's son."

"We believe he may have had something to do with the fire that destroyed Nana's house."

"That beautiful home was such a treasure to see. How could he do that?"

"He would never dirty his hands." Marisol was quite irritated when she piled the dirty dishes on the sideboard. "But I'm sure he paid some of his pals to take care of it.

He was responsible for hurting Tim and I'll never forgive him."

Daphne put her hands on her niece's shoulders. "That's not the story he is spreading around the harbor. He says when you come back to your senses he'll win your heart."

"That's a joke. I plan to tear his heart out if I bump into him."

The tapping at the kitchen door had to be repeated before any of the ladies heard.

"Goodness, I'm sorry. Come in, come in." Daphne opened the door and didn't know what to say.

Apparently the men in the group had also found a place to bathe and scrub up. Jack went over and put his arm around Marisol's waist. "I'd say you girls do clean up very nicely." He ran his hand through her hair. "Yes, nicely indeed."

Daphne looked at her niece who just grinned widely.

Marisol fixed the collar on Jack's red and black checked work shirt. "I'd say you all did a great clean up job yourselves. Daphne, you remember Jack Ryan and his uncle Joe."

"You both look much better today."

"This is Jack's brother Dan and their Uncle Jacob who also came down from the Aroostook River."

The sight of these two men set Daphne back on her heels. They were both dressed in soft near white deerskin tunics embellished with porcupine quills and glass beads around the neck and wrists. Jacob was wearing a red wool sash across one shoulder and held on the other side of his waist with a silver medallion. Both had their long hair set in braids that hung loosely over their shoulders.

"Uncle Jacob, would you like a cup of good strong tea?" Marisol held the kettle up.

"No thank you. We want to be in place to hear Hannibal and Joshua speak so we'll need to pack up our passengers quickly. Are you ready ladies?"

"Just one minute." Daphne opened her dainty writing desk and took out a good-sized envelope. "Marisol, please give this to Gert and tell her I'll be anxious for a reply."

With a few more hugs, a few more tears, and many waves, the wagon moved down the hill from Daphne's home, made a left on Main Street, then left on Church Street to climb the hill past the vestry to Mr. Merithew's home, then turned right into the yard of the carriage house where they secured the wagon near a water trough for Willy. Dan, Jacob and Joe turned many heads while walking up to the front of the Town Hall where a platform stood for the campaign speakers. Marisol took her chance to point out some of the homes of ship captains as they continued their walk up the hill and then had the group turn around to see a wonderful view of the working harbor and the schooners at dock.

"Well, look who is finally back where she belongs." A boisterous Matthew Roberts swept Marisol off her feet. Kate put out her arm to stop Jack from making a move.

"Matt, you put me down right this very minute. You are embarrassing me."

"Me, embarrassing you? You should be ashamed being seen in the company of the Ryans and Indian riff-raff." Matthew took a look at Kate. "And who is your lovely friend?"

"My name is Kate Smythe. The Ryans and what you call riff-raff are my parent's best friends."

"Marisol Hodge, you have a social position to protect and having this type of so called friend only drags you down to their level."

Jack tried to stop her but Kate was quick and got into Matt's face. "You arrogant ass! You will never reach the level of intelligence and caring found in Uncle Jacob. He is a great leader within the Wabanaki tribes."

"I would never get so low as to lead a bunch of dirty savages." Matt puffed himself up and got right back into Kate's face. That was a bad move as even Jack could not prevent the smack across Matt's cheek that could be heard as far up as the podium.

Matt clenched his fist as his face nearly turned purple.

"Matthew, don't you dare." Marisol was at her wits end and obviously at the end of any type of relationship with Mr. Roberts. "Jack, please walk Kate up to Jacob. I have a few things to say to Matt."

"You have nothing to say to me Missy but I have plenty to say to you. Go home and change out of those hideous farm girl clothes. Put on something befitting meeting the governor and vice president. Also my uncle is here from Boston visiting Mr. Merithew and will be on the platform with the dignitaries. Remember, you do represent me and my position at the ship yard."

"You lost any tie with me the minute one of your hoodlums struck the match at the Hodge farm."

"No one can tie me to any vandalism that may have occurred at that farm.

Jack came up behind Matthew. "You call that fire vandalism?"

"Don't come any closer Ryan or our first meeting will seem like a Sunday school picnic compared to the next one on the docks."

"If I were you, I'd be more concerned about the destruction of Mrs. Hodge's home."

"What do you mean her home? I heard someone set a pile of hay on fire."

"Saturday night when your goons were creeping up on the hay pile, Mrs. Hodge's farm hand surprised them. Frightened, one dropped his torch and watched it roll under the back porch. Flustered, the other idiot flung his, sending it through the dining room window." Jack's face was getting red while Matthew's was suddenly pale.

"Saturday night, I was in Searsport at a special dinner so had nothing to do with that unfortunate act."

Jack wrapped his arm around Marisol's waist to keep her from scratching Matthew's eyes out. "Better be careful Mr. Roberts. I heard those inept thugs found their way up river to Hell's Half Acre in Bangor where they drank and blabbed their way through the pubs before jumping the first Boston-bound schooner. You know how rumors start."

"Huh! Who in the world is going to believe scum over me? Marisol Hodge, get away from that insolent half breed while you still have a shred of respectability left."

Marisol lurched ahead so hard that Jack had to hold her back with both of his arms. "You bastard! Did you know that Mrs. Hodge was trapped upstairs and Tim led her out just in time?"

"Sounds like things worked out just fine. Now I want to get closer to the podium."

Marisol kept to his side like glue with Jack hanging on for dear life. "You! You!" She was hunting for the words that were flaming in her heart. "My brother Timothy nearly died in that fire. He is still fighting for his life and may lose his arm."

This caught the attention of the gathering crowd. Jack gave her a little nudge and nodded to the steps of the platform. "Shush little lady. Give our family a chance."

Matt's friend Lucky passed close by. "Be thankful that looks can't kill or I'd be tripping over your corpse right now."

Just above, Uncle Jacob, Joe and Dan approached the platform. A hush came over the large crowd when they saw the three. Matthew was almost apoplectic. "What the hell are they doing? Someone should be tossing the likes of them out on their asses."

Jack grinned and gave Marisol a gentler hug. "Watch and listen my dear. There may be some tales told about a certain young socialite."

Matthew puffed up his ego. "Who in their right mind would take their word over mine?"

Governor Joshua Chamberlain was about to speak when he saw the small band of visitors and stopped abruptly. He waved them up on the staging and softly introduced the group to the rest of the dignitaries.

"What in the world!" That was all Matt could get out as he was nearly speechless.

Jack explained quietly to a very confused self-important viewer. "Perhaps you didn't know that Joshua Chamberlain has been a friend of my Uncle Joe since meeting at the Bangor Theological Seminary as young men. Joe was a welcome dinner guest at the family home in Brewer and would travel with Joshua to hear guests speak at Bowdoin College."

"Why in the world is he shaking hands with the younger Indian? How could he do that?"

Jack smiled broadly. "That, sir, is my brother Dan. He went to war with Chamberlain's Maine 20th Infantry and fought bravely on Little Round Top in Gettysburg. It was there that my brother Mike was killed."

Matthew was finding this information hard to digest. "Good Lord, that big Indian is shaking hands with Vice President Hamlin. How dare he?"

"That big Indian is my Uncle Jacob. He was one of the Wabanaki tribal leaders that went to Boston to rally for the Lincoln/Hamlin ticket. You see, Captain and Mrs. Hodge were friendly with the vice president when he had his law practice just outside Brewer. As a matter of fact, my Nana Hodge was a quite close friend with his first wife Sarah before she died. Since she and the captain did so much to help the Penobscots who were relegated to Indian Island, they in turn wanted to help Attorney Hamlin."

It was obvious Matt was getting nervous as he began to rock back and forth in place when most of the public figures turned to find him in the crowd.

Jack picked up a softly crying Marisol in his arms and began to carry her out of the confusion. He turned back a bit. "Say there Matthew, if I remember correctly, your uncle considered Captain Hodge very important to his training as a ship builder and was grateful for his guidance. Have you figured out the home destroyed in the fire was built by Captain Hodge?"

Once Jack carried Marisol away to the carriage yard Lucky rushed by on his way out of town. He made one stop next to his former boss. "Tell me Matty me boy, is this what you meant by a comeuppance?"

XXI

Indian Island

Wednesday

The group from Prospect Ferry made a hasty departure from Searsport. The wagon left a cloud of dust as Joe drove Willy as quickly as possible with his load of passengers, reservation supplies and two good-sized aloe plants. In their wake, a red faced Mathew Roberts was getting a what for from his uncle and orders to get his things in order for a trip back to the docks of the Charles River.

The group made a short stop in Stockton and ate a quick lunch put together by Daphne. They found a grassy spot beneath an old growth tree to enjoy the cool shade while watching the energetic activity in the harbor.

Marisol shaded her eyes with her straw hat and pointed at one of the ship-building platforms. "Look Kate, there is a black headed sea gull perched on the top of that piling."

"We see them occasionally in the summer. Why is he so special?"

"It's a European gull. I used to watch them along the docks in London. My father said in the summer, the adventurous of their kind would go to the American northeast coast. I never thought I'd see one again."

Jack gave her a wink. "Nice to see you excited again." He smiled at her slight blush.

After a quick stop at the surgeon's to slip a payment for his services through the mail slot, Joe kept Willy at a slow but steady pace to Prospect Ferry. It was still daylight when they pulled the wagon into the Hodge barn. The sight of the rubble of Nana's once beautiful home set a pall over the group.

T was there in an instant to take care of the steed.

"Leave all the supplies in the wagon. We'll be rearranging to add trunks for the ladies after we fix something to eat."

Joe helped the girls to the ground. T settled Willy in with fresh water and grain, then came back to get a horse blanket from his office. "I nearly forgot. Miss Peg said for you all to come down to her house to freshen up. She has a meal already for you."

That made the group put a hustle on. What a wonderful treat. The ladies freshened up in Peg and Joey's bedroom where they found a basin of warm water touched with the scent of lavender. The men relished the coolness of the water from the pitcher pump.

It was going to be tight for eight around the handmade table but no one thought a thing about it. Peg had it covered with blue gingham. A flow blue pottery pitcher held an assortment of wildflowers in the center. The young ladies found it delightful.

"Something smells delicious, Peg." Uncle Jacob went over to take a peek but he dropped the lid back down as soon as he grabbed the handle on the kettle. "Ouch! That's hot!"

Joey laughed as his uncle jumped around pretending to be mortally wounded. "You know what happened to the curious cat. I say it holds for old nosey Indians too."

"That looks like turkey stew. How did you manage that as we mostly see hens with their new broods this time of year? Looks like it would take a large tom to fill that kettle."

'That's what happens when you mess with a planting by the Ryan family. He wandered out of the deep woods to fill up on the seed corn and my Pa made him pay."

Peg went out to the summer kitchen to pull a sheet of biscuits from the oven in the old woodstove. They and a tub of butter were put on the table as Peg picked up the turkey story. "When Sean started his walk to the fort he saw the bird meandering down the row scratching and pecking. He made a turn back to the house for his hunting rifle. The tom was so into his banquet that he never saw his adversary."

Joe picked up the story. "You know how stingy Pa is with his bullets. He got him with one clean shot and lugged him over here, dumped him on the table and went on his way." Once the bowls of turkey stew were served, all conversation stopped through the ending of ginger cake with cream.

It was then that Marisol was ready to ask some questions. "Has there been any word from Indian Island?"

"One of the message carriers from Bangor to Fort Knox said he heard that there was some trouble keeping the flat boat stable that was carrying Tim. But Tomah and a few others paddled their canoes on either side to keep the boat steady. Tim is very sick but travelled well and has started treatment." Joey placed his hands on her shoulders as she sat on the bench. "Don't worry. Nana is going to do everything in her power to get him help. I understand the doctor from Bangor has already examined him and approved of the move."

With Marisol relaxed, the group did the same. With thanks to Joey and Peg, they went to the Ryan home thinking they could never rest, but the trauma of the day in Searsport and the long ride straight back, quickly brought on sleep. Before they knew it, the rise of the sun was peeking behind the eagles exploring the river for breakfast for their hungry three.

When the group wandered into the kitchen by dawn's light Jacob was putting together a substantial breakfast to hold the voyagers and a basket of biscuits with jugs of water to take in the wagon. He and Dan were staying behind with Sean to keep the farm going and work on the clean up. Joe would drive the wagon with Jack on the bench leaving Marisol and Kate to find space between the supplies.

Once the wagon and travelers finished a fairly bumpy ferry ride over to Bucksport, Marisol was quite intrigued by the hustle and bustle along the Brewer Road. Expecting to be surrounded by wilderness, she was surprised by the brick-yards, saw mills and ship yards. She admired the beautiful Victorian and Greek Revival homes built by lumber barons and ship builders, was amazed by the congestion in the river between Brewer and Bangor, and found the connecting covered bridge remarkable at nearly 800 feet long.

"Jack, where are all those schooners going?" Marisol pointed to the ships of all sizes that sat so close you could barely see the water.

"Most carry goods to the cities on the east coast but some cargo will be shipped to ports around the world. It has been said most of Boston and much of New York and Philadelphia were built with Bangor lumber and Brewer brick."

As they continued towards the Indian Island ferry, the surroundings kept Marisol's head spinning. Her enthusiastic chatter with Kate momentarily took her mind off Tim's injuries.

At a lovely bend in the river, Joe pulled the wagon to the right into a grassy area shaded by a stand of birch trees. Setting back was a small building that was slowly losing a battle to the elements.

Jack hopped to the ground and stood hands on hips. "Wow, Uncle Joe. Look what time can do."

"Afraid it also does a job on us humans. Nothing lasts forever."

A curious Marisol used the wagon wheel to climb to the ground. "Just what is this place Joe?

"At one time, this is where I taught school. There was a small room in the back that I called home. I have great memories of the children of North Brewer and once in awhile I will meet one of them in Bangor, sometimes with a child or two in tow. That is when I feel my age."

"What happened to cause damage to the building?"

"About twenty-two years ago, an unexpected spring freshet rushed towards Bangor causing the river to jump the bank and flood to the eaves of the school. I barely made it out by running up the slope behind and made my way to Bucksport through the deep woods."

"Why didn't they rebuild?"

"Eventually they built a larger school nearer Bangor as the area was growing rapidly with the new mills opening."

"Were you the schoolmaster in that one?"

Joe looked wistfully at the ruins of his sweet memories. "No, it was no longer a one-room school and obviously there were several teachers."

Marisol stood straight and cocked her head. "Well, certainly you were one of them."

Jack put his hand on Joe's shoulder. "Go on, open her eyes to how a growing population ignorant of local history can spread their own beliefs.

"I was not offered a teaching position. Apparently some citizens heard about my mixed blood and took offense at the idea of their children being taught by an Indian. After all, they were certain I could not possibly be qualified and many did not want their children anywhere near savages."

Marisol could not find the words to continue as Jack put her back in the wagon. "Time to move on Miss Hodge."

The remaining ride to Milford was quite subdued with Marisol lost in her own thoughts. Kate held her hand knowing her friend must be worried about the condition of her brother for she was also deeply concerned about the man who quickly stole her heart.

At the stable where Willy was boarded and the wagon stored, everyone took their essential personal belongings and began the short trek to the dock. A long narrow boat used to carry passengers to the reservation was tied to a piling but no boatmen were in sight. Joe put two fingers to his lips and let out a piercing whistle, which nearly caused the girls to trip into the river.

"We're coming Joe. Just hold your horses."

Two rather portly townsmen shuffled their way along a river path from places unknown. One tipped his hat to the ladies and winked at Jack. The other just smiled showing the missing teeth that were most likely the result of a scuffle one evening on the town.

Marisol was wary of stepping into the rocking craft. She was not used to going out on the water in something that small. "There's a bridge over there. Why can't we use that?"

Joe smiled as he had heard that question many times. "That is the bridge over to Old Town. It is not connected to Indian Island."

"You mean there is no bridge to the reservation?"

"The prevailing feeling around here is that Indians have canoes, why would they need a bridge?"

One of the boatmen rowed while the other manned a small tiller in the back. It was a quick trip but not one that Marisol liked. She could see some of the rapids a bit further down river and could feel the strong currents so made most of the trip with her eyes closed.

As the ferry pulled up to the island dock with a jolt, a cacophony of excited young voices could be heard. Marisol opened her eyes to see a cluster of children bouncing up and down as they docked.

"Mary! Mary!" In the middle of the group she saw one mass of golden red hair and two little arms waving enthusiastically.

Jack jumped out of the boat, lifted bewildered Marisol out and plunked her back on her feet. "Your welcoming party awaits, Missy. You better go meet them so we all don't end up being bumped into the Penobscot."

The rest of the ferry passengers grinned at the sight as they unloaded their bags. As for Marisol, she did not quite know how to react to the gaggle of urchins. Their bare feet sent puffs of dry soil into the air as they danced around Cece's friend. Bright smiles punctuated little round faces framed by gleaming black braids, some with beads or tiny feathers. Their inquisitive brown/black eyes struck Marisol. Suddenly the little lady herself was up in her arms hugging with all her might. It would seem they were separated for weeks rather than only three days."

Joe finally came to the rescue. "That's enough. Off now to the central lodge. I'm sure it is time for stories." In a flash, Marisol was free from all but Cece. "You too. There will be plenty of time when we meet at Grandma Adele's later."

With a pout, Cece stomped her way up the path. Her bare feet sending up little dust puffs as she passed her mother coming down the slope.

Gert gave both girls a hug and took each by the hand. "He's been asking for both of you. Joe, will you take care of getting their bags to Adele's?"

"Jack will take care of them. I need to gather some of the men to go back to Milford to unload the wagon and bring the supplies over in their canoes."

Marisol was anxious to go. "Do you mean he is conscious and mending?"

"His condition hasn't really changed but he does float in and out of awareness and definitely knows you two are not here. The trip was difficult for him but he is a fighter. Try not to show your concern over his appearance."

Marisol looked around and was relieved to see a well-kept little village of humble homes. She was afraid it would be more like one of the tribes she read about in stories about the American Wild West. "Gert, where is the medical building?"

"Dear girl, there is no such thing as a hospital on the reservation. There is hope for one someday. They have constructed Tim his own wigwam where he will not be disturbed."

"Wigwam? You put my brother in a wigwam?"

"That's what is done here to care for the seriously ill. That way, only the people caring for him can be near." Kate tried to reassure Marisol. "Believe me, it is best for Tim."

"Just follow me and see for yourself." Gert led the two off the beaten trail away from the common hall and through a meadow with soft grasses and many multicolored wildflowers. In a pleasant grove of birch trees was a new shelter that Marisol thought must be Tim's. The flap was held wide open to catch freshening breezes from the river. The two young ladies stepped inside with nary a sound but then covered hushed gasps with their hands when they saw a frail Tim laying atop alternating layers of soft spruce branches and quilts with a lightweight cotton sheet as a cover. Nana was sitting next to him wiping his forehead with a damp cloth.

Marisol went over and gave her great auntie a kiss on the cheek. "May I? I'm here Tim. Kate and I are going to help you find the courage to fight this evil that is sapping your strength."

Gert helped Nana up and walked her outside while Marisol sat twisting out another cloth.

Kate followed them and took great relish in the fresh air. "What was the scent in there?"

Nana settled on a bench made of two split logs and took a deep breath of the cool breeze following the river. "They call it sweet flag. The Penobscot and Micmac believe steaming a small piece releases great power from spirits on the other side to drive away disease."

"And what do you believe?"

"Over the years, I have seen mysterious relief from many illnesses. The Shaman has ways to use herbs and roots in healing rituals, but flag root seems a panacea and the soothing effect of the aroma does keep the patient calm.

Gert stretched her arms to work out kinks in her body from sitting with Tim. "Kate, you must have seen some of this with the Micmacs. I know Uncle Jacob carries a dried rhizome in his medicine pouch and it only takes a tiny piece to make most compounds. He and Tomah are working on a salve for the smaller burns and a poultice for Tim's hand."

Nana looked at Gert and leaned her head in the direction of the path. "You have company coming, again."

Skipping through the meadow were Cece, Holly and Frankie. They were intercepted before getting too close to the wigwam. "Comfort, how many times have I told you that you need to stay away from this area while Tim is sick."

"But Mama, I want to see him."

"You must be quiet and stay away. You all should know better."

Cece stomped her foot, frightening up a cloud of grasshoppers bringing squeals of delight as Holly and her brother chased them. Gert tried to shush them with a finger to her lips and then just shook her head."

"He's always sleeping! I want to see him!"

Using her root walking stick, Nana came out of the wig-wam. "What's so important?"

Cece pointed to the sky. "See? Those clouds look just like a schooner with three sails moving through the clear blue sky like it was sailing the waves of the ocean. I want Tim to see it."

Nana just smiled and shooed Cece away. "He'll see a schooner like that someday when he goes to sea."

Cece skipped her way back through the meadow most likely disturbing more than grasshoppers. She turned back with a wave. "I don't want him to go to sea!"

Kate came out, shaded her eyes to watch the cloud ship sail slowly above the river towards the bay. *Neither do I.*

XXII

SALMON RINGS

Thursday

By Thursday a routine had set in. Gert and Nana were settled in a downstairs bedroom in Adele's home with Marisol and Kate in a small room upstairs. Cece was having a great time at Uncle Joe's sharing Holly's room while JJ, Jacob and Jack stayed in a wigwam nearby. Tim was never alone. The salve prepared for the superficial burns on the upper arm was showing positive results but the poultice for his hand was disappointing.

Tim would call out for Marisol and Kate but it was obvious he did not know they were with him. Nana would send them home to rest. His fever would show relief but then soar again to rack his fragile body. His caregivers could see him growing weaker.

Doctor Hingham was good about coming to observe the results of the treatment, making the thirteen-mile trip from Bangor to the Indian Island Ferry at Old Town twice. He supplied Nana with morphine to ease Tim's pain but was stumped as how to stop the infection that was eating at his flesh

He nodded as he watched Gert working to keep the fever at bay with cool water.

"I want to talk with those close to him. Could you two gather them at Tomah's house?

"Yes sir."

"I'll stay with Timothy until you send up two of the village women. I'd like you and Mrs. Hodge to be with the sister while we discuss an extreme remedy."

When Gert walked into the bedroom Marisol shared with Kate, there was a gentle breeze blowing the lace curtains at the open window. The bright sun created designs through the billowing material that danced along the walls. "This room is lovely. I'm sorry I had not stopped by earlier."

Marisol was alarmed to see Gert and jumped up to meet her. "Has something happened to Tim? Kate is reading to the children. Should I get her?"

"No, the doctor is coming soon to talk with us." Gert pushed back the lace curtains to enjoy the clear fresh air. "I had not realized you could see Old Town from this angle. Nana and I have the room that looks out on the Milford side of the water. I must bring her up to see the other view."

"This is truly a lovely home. When I first heard we were staying on the reservation, I feared the unknown. Tomah and Adele have been wonderful hosts. Tomorrow Annie is having us to their home for afternoon refreshments. She calls it a never-ending-work-in-process but I can imagine it is also lovely."

"Goodness Marisol, are you sewing?" Gert was quite surprised.

"I wish my Auntie Daphne could see me. She would say the same thing. I gave up on knitting. Those needles can be dangerous weapons. If Baby Ryan waited for a sweater until I was finished, I would have to start making an adult pullover now. But I think some of Daphne runs through my blood as hand stitching seems to come naturally. Right now I am doing night shirts and bibs but in time I want to try a real outfit."

"I never really knew your connection to Daphne. Is she also a Hodge?"

"She is my mother's sister who spent a lot of time with us in London after Mother died. I missed her greatly when she and her shipbuilding husband moved to Searsport to be part of the boom. Did you know that right now ten percent of the country's deep water captains live in that little town?"

"I had no idea. How did you come to live there?"

"Our father told us if anything should happen to him, we should go to America and find Daphne. Her husband was killed in a freak accident when part of the scaffolding collapsed at a building site. By then she felt Searsport was her home." Marisol took a packet off her bed stand. "I'm sorry Gert, I forgot to give you this from my auntie."

Sitting on the side of the bed, Gert opened the envelope, read the note and laughed in glee. "I sold the painting displayed in her shop and she would like two more. And the manager at the bank would like to see me about a larger painting for the lobby." She gave Marisol a bear hug. "Comfort will be so excited. This replaces all I used from the egg money. Now we can shop for her school shoes plus a bit extra."

Adele tapped lightly on the doorframe. "The doctor would like to see the two of you in the parlor."

The cousins had been sent to find Jack and send him to Gramma Adele's house. Then they were to go to Kate's story hour. When they passed on the message, Cece wondered if that meant Mary was going to faint again.

Jack laughed out loud but in his mind wondered the same thing.

Entering the parlor, Marisol gasped at the subdued atmosphere. Dr. Hingham pointed to an extra chair but she refused. "I'd rather stand, sir. I think it is due time to lay out your plans."

The doctor looked around the room then focused on Marisol. "I'm sure all accept the fact that Timothy is a critically injured young man. Frankly, I'm amazed he has survived this long but would not have if not for the diligent care from all of you. But we have come to a point where we must take drastic action or take off the arm. My fear is that he is so weak he won't survive the surgery."

Jack walked closer to Marisol.

Doctor Hingham paced a bit before clearing his throat. "The wound on the back of his hand has developed dead tissue that is preventing blood flow needed to grow healthy flesh. We absolutely need to remove the skin that is turning gangrenous. Looking for advice, I telegraphed an old friend at the Harvard Medical School. He answered an ancient technique is gaining favor by showing noticeable success in allowing new capillaries to grow. I believe this is Tim's best chance."

Realizing what the doctor was proposing, Nana kept a close eye on her niece.

"Before I leave this afternoon, I am going to attach several leeches to the wound."

Jack saw Marisol shudder.

"If circulation increases he could fight the infection and save the arm. If nothing else he will gain strength should we still need to amputate."

Marisol found her trembling voice. "Bloodsuckers?" She fainted dead away.

Jack had her up in his arms before she hit the floor. "Cece told me I was needed in case Mary fainted." That lightened the mood in the room for a moment.

"Take her out for a walk by the river for some fresh air. Don't let her come anywhere near the wigwam. You'll need to find JJ so he can help you tell Kate."

JJ split the log on end with one good whack of the ax. Then he did the same with the two halves and tossed the four pieces on the pile. When he saw Jack with Marisol in his arms, he ran to meet them. "What in the world?"

"We have some news on Tim's treatment."

"Obviously it was not easy to take. Take her to the sitting bench near the river and I'll get a cup of water."

"If Kate has finished today's story hour, bring her with you."

JJ took another look at Marisol and thought of his sister. "Perhaps I better bring two cups."

Kate's reaction to the extreme therapy was much the same and soon the two friends were holding each other while watching the river in hopes the lovely scene would replace what they were visualizing in their minds. The men stood nearby but left them room for their private thoughts.

Adele prepared a light meal for supper that night, with Tomah off at a council meeting she knew the ladies would not feel like eating much. In fact, no one felt like talking that much either. Nana had gone with the doctor to set the leeches and stayed the rest of the afternoon until Gert came to get her.

Her brilliant blue eyes dulled by a mist of worry and fatigue, Marisol finally gathered the nerve to ask Nana some questions. "Was it terrible to watch? Did they hurt Tim? Is the doctor reliable? What will ...?"

"Take a breath, dear. I'll answer all that I can but most answers will have to wait to see the results. Doctor Hingham uses leeches grown for medicinal purposes."

"People grow those ugly things?"

Gert cleared the table. "As Comfort would say, 'not to worry', they did not hunt the pond and swamps for them."

Nana patted Marisol's hand to comfort her. "The doctor placed them just where he felt they would help most to clear the dead skin and one produced just a tiny bit of blood which was a sign not all the circulation was destroyed. Tim never felt any pain. The doctor will return early Sunday morning to remove them."

Kate shuddered as she took her last sip of tea. "My brain doesn't want to accept Tim has those parasites on any part of him. I hope he doesn't open his eyes while they are attached."

"I want him to wake as quickly as possible!" Marisol stomped towards the door.

"I didn't mean to upset you." She followed her friend. "I'm coming too."

"Wait just a minute. I'm going to walk you both up, then stay for the evening." Gert finished putting the dishes on the kitchen sideboard.

The ever-present steaming flag root caused Marisol to sneeze several times. "Oh, dear. I don't think I'll ever like it, but if there is a chance it can help Tim I'll get used to it."

Gert sent the afternoon volunteers on their way with gratitude that they had managed to give him a few sips of a healing herbal tea. She noticed that Kate did everything to keep from looking at the lightly bandaged hand. "They won't escape."

Marisol kissed her brother on the forehead. She seemed calm. "It's fine Kate. It looks like the type of dressing they used before the poultice." She stroked Tim's coal black hair. One stubborn piece was always falling over his eyes. She got on her knees, laid her head next to his on the pillow and whispered in his ear. "Please Timmy. Use all your Hodge stubborn streak to deny more harm to your body. Please Timmy come back to us."

Kate sat behind her friend and took Tim's hand. "It's Kate. We're both here." She gently held his hand up to her cheek and kissed it. *I'm not letting go. Hang on Tim.* Kate still could not make herself look at the injured hand. *If I see something wiggle, I'll faint.*

Gert placed a fresh cool piece of fabric on his forehead. "He doesn't seem quite as warm."

Marisol spoke sharply with her demanding sister voice. "Timothy Hodge, listen to me. You need to take some nourishment. I've never known you to refuse a meal, so don't start now."

Kate tried not to get too excited. "He grasped my hand. I swear, I felt a gentle squeeze." Everyone went silent and stared to see some motion. "Yell at him again."

"Tim, Tim. We are here for you, now you need to help us."

This time Kate knew she felt something as she heard a slight moan.

"Is he in pain? Should we give him a bit of morphine?"

Gert looked at his eyelids as they began to flutter. "No. One of the problems is he needs to start fighting his way out of the pain killer sleep even if it does cause discomfort."

Slowly Tim's eyes opened and took some time to focus. He spoke with a weak raspy voice. "I must be in heaven for you two are surely angels."

The girls were speechless. Marisol was finally able to whisper. "Is your hand in pain?"

"I can't feel it." His eyes began to close.

"Stay awake Tim." Gert handed Marisol a cup of Adele's herbal broth. "You must eat."

He took several spoonful, then open his eyes wider. "You trying to poison me?"

"That's my brother. Always complaining about my cooking. Eat!"

With a great bit of cajoling, his three caregivers managed to feed him half the cup with several sips of water before he fell back into a deep sleep.

Peeking out of the wigwam, Gert could see faithful Jack sitting on a rock making some poor creature miserable by teasing it in the grass with a stick. When he finally looked up, she waved him over. "The girls are spent. Take them for a walk to watch the sun set over the river."

"What about you Ma?"

"They did the exhausting work of getting him to take some broth. He's sound asleep so I'm going to do some handwork before Adele and Tomah come up. They are going to bath him."

"Bet you are stitching up something for your first grandbaby."

"You just made me feel old."

"You are too full of grit and vinegar to ever be old. Now where are my sunset companions?"

Not wanting to, Gert had to assure Marisol someone would come get her if there was any big change.

As they started down the path, Kate excused herself. "I need to write my mother and let her know what is happening down here."

Jack took Marisol's hand. "Come with me to a very special place where Joey and I used to hide when we were dodging story time. Ma would bring us here to volunteer once in a while in the summer. Mike and Dan enjoyed working in the gardens and learning the ways of the Penobscot and Micmac. Frankly, I wish I had paid more attention."

"I bet you paid attention to the Indian maidens."

"Whenever I could get by their brothers." Holding Marisol's hand, he led her over some loose rocks then down natural steps of ledge to a flat rock just above the water. The sun was getting low and beginning to form a gold path on the river. "I used to pretend I could walk on that shining trail and it led to all kinds of adventures."

"Please don't tell me you were a pirate because I've seen your reaction to the open sea."

"You'll pay for that." He picked her up and sat on the rock with her in his lap. "Are you ticklish?"

"Don't you dare or I'll push you into your golden path and watch you float away to your dream world."

"My dream world is right here." He lifted her long hair and kissed her on the back of the neck. "Umm, lavender."

Suddenly there was a large splash about twenty feet out. "What was that?"

"Watch."

A circular ripple formed and spread on the surface.

"They're back right on time. Keep watching and the setting sun will soon make them easier to see."

Marisol scanned the river. "Look, there is another."

"The salmon are coming up the river to spawn. At one time there were many more and they were a staple of the reservation."

"What happened to them?"

"About thirty years ago, a dam was built across the rapids to provide power for a saw mill. Each year fewer make the journey past the obstruction and these wonderful creatures are decreasing. Have you never heard about a feast of Penobscot salmon and peas for Independence Day?"

"Jack, you idiot, I'm British so never have feasted on Independence Day. There's another!"

"The sun is just about right. Watch what happens to the salmon rings."

After what seemed like an eternity, a salmon that must have been a big fellow leapt at a hapless fly making the biggest ring so far. The sun caught the top and turned it into gold.

"I've never seen anything like it."

"There's so much beauty in the world, Marisol. So many never take time to look. Your father understood this and thus your name. This won't last long so feast your eyes."

And that she did. Over the next several minutes the rings came and went. Some interlocked as if the salmon were communicating with each other. They disappeared from human view as the sun slipped away once again only to let its presence known in the clouds with colors of purple, rose and pink.

"That was stunning and now the sky is breathtaking."

"Not nearly as breathtaking as you." With a gentle kiss, he turned her in his arms so he could gaze into the azure blue of her eyes.

She returned in kind. Her body began to shudder as the difficulties of the past five days came to the surface and she broke down with uncontrollable crying. Jack could do nothing but rock her gently.

"Tim could die! I may never be able to show him purple sky reflections in the Penobscot River or floating golden rings or listen to the water rushing at the dam. I would not be able to tell him about Cece's secret magical place or show him how I can stitch." She shivered but not from the cold.

Jack held her closer for he was at a loss as how to comfort her. She reached up and kissed him with desperate passion and pulled him down with her on the flat rock.

"Make love with me Jack. Please. Please. I need to feel part of you."

Jack looked into her eyes and saw her pain. He kissed her on the forehead. "No, sweet girl, not tonight. When the time is right it will be a want not a need. When we make love it will fill you with joy, not fill an emptiness of despair."

XXIII

THE WAIT

Friday

The next day became one of routine. Everyone knew their schedule to be with Tim, which gave time for the rest to do other chores.

Cece and her cousins came to Adele's kitchen for breakfast Friday morning as Annie needed to help Joe clean the weeds in their own vegetable garden. Adele certainly didn't mind, as nothing gave her more pleasure than having Holly and Frankie spend time with their Grammie.

It had been a while since Cece sat with her mother and Nana. This morning Adele made a treat for the children of milk tea. Usually they couldn't have tea but just a bit was placed in the cups with some maple syrup and lots of milk. Having tea with Nana made Cece feel very grown up.

Marisol had stayed late at the wigwam after her walk with Jack. She was back with him at dawn and finally allowed herself to come to the house to eat a bit. The aroma of her favorite coffee lifted her spirits the second she walked in, and she let Adele know with a long hug. "Do you have any more of those nice thick bread slices for toast?'

"I'm sure I can find some in the pantry." Adele returned with a loaf and the butter crock only to be immediately surrounded by three little ones begging for a slice of their own.

"I'm so sorry to start something."

"Not to worry Mary, Grammie Adele always likes to make toast for us." Cece sat back down next to her mother and sipped on her tea just as the ladies did.

The kettle was taken off the warming end of the wood stove and four pieces of thick sliced bread was laid on the hot metal cover. Then Adele brought out the jam jar before she flipped the bread to brown the other side.

For a few minutes there was no sound at the table while every morsel was devoured right down to the few straggle crumbs picked up with wet forefingers.

Gert relaxed while sitting in the ladder-back chair. "I never thought I'd miss Molly Molasses. Somehow I'd feel better with her presence in the wigwam no matter how grim her appearance.

Marisol got up to refill her coffee cup. "Who is she and how could she help?"

"The Penobscot considered her a shaman or me'toulin with great healing powers. She used to frighten me when we first met for I felt her looking right through me with those dark menacing eyes. She was close to John Neptune, also a strong shaman who governed the reservation for fifty years. Their shared magical powers kept the tribe in order.

Nana smiled for she knew what Gert meant. "Some believed that if she wanted you dead, she only had to give you a dark look. But over the many years when she floated in and out of the reservation or met me in the streets of Bangor, we developed a very unusual friendship."

For a moment Marisol felt hope even if it was with what she considered a witch doctor. "Would she come and use her powers to help Tim?"

Cece put down her cup and spoke directly. "She's dead."

Adele finally got off her feet for a few minutes. "Molly began to slip away after John Neptune died in 1865, living a full ninety seven years. People found her wandering the streets and alleys of Bangor speaking gibberish while selling her trinkets to visitors. She bore four children that most believed were fathered by John and without him her spirit slowly faded. She died last year at ninety-two.

"Well, her spirit is still with us. We only have to reach out to the other side for her help." Cece grinned. "Everyone knows that."

Both Holly and Frankie agreed. "Yah, we know she would always be with us to help."

Adele was stunned by what her grandchildren had to say. "Who told you that?"

All three children spoke at once. "Molly."

Gert noticed that Nana didn't show any reaction and made eye contact with her neighbor. "You knew about this?"

"Cece came to the island with me last spring while you were cleaning the root cellar."

"I remember."

"I was telling a story about one of my ocean trips to Georgia during the reading hour. I'd say most of the mothers were doing spring-cleaning of one sort of another. Three older ladies were preparing to make baskets at the tables."

Little Frankie remembered it well. "That was when the big waves nearly tipped your schooner over in a hurricane."

Nana grinned for sometimes she thought reading time was not heard over all the giggling. "Molly Molasses silently slipped past the group then turned and sat in the circle with the children."

Marisol gasped and Cece patted her hand. "Not to worry, Mary. Molly would never hurt us. Only stupid grown-ups think that."

Nana continued her story. "Molly gave me one of her looks and I felt what was coming. I think all these years with the natives on the island have sharpened my own intuition. She told the children she was going on a trip too."

Cece was getting excited about the story now and fidgeted in her chair. "She told us that no matter where she was, in this or the spirit world, she would always be with us. If we ever need help, we can call on her."

All three children hopped up and began to run out.

Gert grabbed Cece by the back of the collar. "Wait a minute, just where are you going?"

"We have to practice the spirit dance so Molly can hear us."

"Let them go, Gert. Anything might help at this moment." Nana stood with the aid of her stick. "It's my time with Tim and for you Miss Marisol, I don't want to see you for a few hours. I know the waiting is hard, but find a way to keep your mind free from the wigwam."

Not knowing what to do, Marisol wandered toward the river. She nearly jumped a foot when Jack blew on the back of her neck. "Jack Ryan, why would you do that?"

"Sorry, pretty lady. I've never seen your hair pulled up and couldn't resist that lovely neckline. What are you doing down here? The salmon rings are out there but very hard to see in the sunlight. Tomah is out at the bend doing his best to catch us a beauty. It was easier before the river was dammed. He told us he and his father could use a forked spear to harvest only what the family needed. Whether Penobscot or Micmac, we were taught to honor the wildlife that became our food. We learned never to waste a bit. It is obvious with the hides of the deer used for our tunics and moccasins. At one time in the Penobscot Reservation, without the smoked salmon, a family could starve during the winter. The heads were used to make fish oil and some of the bones became sewing needles. Others were big enough to use as combs for the hair. Perhaps we can find a comb to hold up your beautiful black tresses."

"Fish bones in my hair? You must be daft."

"Do you have some free time?"

"Nana sent me out to find some relief from the worry."

Jack put up his hand in a wait here gesture and walked to the wharf. After a moment of discussion with one of the residents, he waved her over.

"What type of mischief are you up to Jack Ryan?"

"I just want to acquaint you with the reservation. Your carriage awaits, madam." He was untying a canoe from its mooring.

Marisol was not quite sure what to do, run away or step into the small craft made of birch bark. But Jack smiled the smile that melted her heart and next thing she was in, hanging on to both sides for dear life when it started to rock.

"Sit still little lady or you'll roll us over."

She was about to yell, "let me out", but with two strong swipes of the paddle, they were off shore heading up river.

"Jack, are you sure you know what you are doing?"

"Miss Doubtful, I was raised on this river."

"That's not what I asked."

"Relax. Open your eyes to the world of the Penobscot."

The sound of the canoe gliding through the water with the even repetitions of the paddle was nearly hypnotic as Marisol began to relax and take in the rocky shoreline. The lush green background looked like a crowd of trees lining a parade route to cheer them on. "What is that lovely foliage around the edge of that little cove?"

"Those are ostrich ferns. Remember those coiled greens Peg served for supper when you came to sow the gardens? Those were fiddleheads picked from the tops of immature ferns soon after they broke through in the spring. Eventually they would mature and open into the fronds you see now."

"What would posses people to eat the top of ferns?" Marisol wrinkled her nose at the thought."

"Our ancestors spent the winter living on what was stored in the summer. After cold dreary months of dried berries, nuts, smoked game and fish, the fiddleheads were the first greens found in the spring. They still are an anticipated staple."

Shafts of sunlight that broke through the verdant canopy to illuminate the forest ground fascinated Marisol. *Beautiful.* "I haven't seen other villages."

"There are a few homes scattered throughout, but most of the population lives in the settlement we just left."

"Why are these people on a reservation? And is this all there is to it?"

"My, do I hear a bit of interest in the ways of the savages?"

Marisol crossed her arms in front of her and pouted in silence.

"See that bit of sand? That's the little beach we would sneak off to on hot summer days when Ma wasn't looking. The best place in Prospect Ferry was a couple old quarry holes we were forbidden to use."

"So that's where you learned your sneaky ways." Marisol smiled to herself. "Why were you on Indian Island so much when you were children?"

"My mother tried to spend a couple days, every other week helping with seasonal work. Nana would go with her to be with the children. We were always with Pa on the weekends." Jack pointed upstream. "Look straight ahead. What do you see?"

"More of the same."

"There are over 500 islands above us which make up the rest of the Penobscot Reservation."

"You mean the Penobscot people only live on islands?"

"Guess I can't get anything by you. It wasn't always so. The great Penobscot Nation used to run on both sides of the river from the bay up river to sacred Mount Katahdin. By 1803 the population of the tribe fell from 10,000 to 347 due to wars with Britain, battles with encroaching settlers, and small pox carried by Europeans. A treaty was signed with the Commonwealth of Massachusetts promising a band of land along the river so the people could trap and hunt. When Maine became a state in 1820, they reneged on the treaty and the Penobscot Nation was forced to the islands in the river. White settlers moved into the rich fertile land to farm or harvest the trees. Some felt it benevolent to grant the islands while others thought it would make the citizens nothing but lazy wards of the government.

"That's terrible but like Tim and I, the only thing we knew about Indians was their brutal nature we read about in story books. How do we get people to understand and accept those that are different than us?"

"As Cece would say, I not know. We better turn back before they send out a scouting party for us."

Jack deftly turned the canoe around and let it float for a while in the current. Marisol relaxed and leaned back against Jack's knees to catch the sun while enjoying the lovely breeze. She wished she had worn her straw hat but who could know when Jack was about to pull a surprise. She began to drift off.

"Wake up Miss Hodge. We can see the wharf so sit up like a lady."

On the waterfront the cousins spotted them coming and began to wave wildly.

Marisol waved back. "I wish I could bottle some of their energy so I could take a swig when mine begins to flag."

The three ran along the shoreline and started to run out on the wharf. The girls stopped short but Frankie kept running. The girls were hollering for him to come back.

Marisol sat even straighter. "What's that about?"

"They've been told never to go on the wharf unless an adult is with them."

Suddenly Frankie stopped short and began to turn around but tripped over a coil of rope and fell over the edge.

"Dear God, Jack. Paddle quickly!"

The girls began to scream. Holly ran out to the wharf, but her brother was already out of reach with the current pulling him farther away. Cece ran to find her Uncle Joe while hollering to anyone she saw.

Jack began to close the gap between the canoe and the struggling boy. Frankie was a good swimmer but had never been in the force of the river heading downstream "We've got to get him closer to shore."

Marisol could see Frankie's head bobbing ahead. "He's starting to go under. Hurry!"

Maneuvering the canoe to block off Frankie from slipping farther away from the lower end of the island, he swung the nose of the craft in the direction of the boy. "Can you see him?"

"You are nearly there. I'll try to grab him," she hollered as loud as she could. "Frankie, hold up your arm."

The little boy sank under the water then suddenly one limb popped through the surface and Marisol grabbed on nearly losing her grip on the slippery skin. She had to get her hands on his shirt so bent as far as she could over the side of the canoe. Jack worked to counterbalance her weight while paddling as hard as possible toward the shore.

Trying her best to keep Frankie's head above water, Marisol leaned dangerously low over the bound edge of the canoe. "No farther or I'll have you both in the river." Jack's voice echoed the panic that was raging through his body.

Marisol's right hand now had a death grip on the youngster's shirt, and her left hand cupped under his chin to keep his head above water. To her relief he coughed, but then started fighting against her grip and she had to use all the strength she could muster not to lose him again. Jack could see the line of people running along the shoreline towards the tip of the island. Joe was in the lead with Annie on his heels, followed by Kate and Gert. In his mind, Jack could not help but thinking they must have tied Cece to a chair to keep her away. Tomah and a few others from the village brought up the rear. He and Joe were carrying coils of rope.

Joe tossed his rope but could not get it to come anywhere near the canoe. The minute it hit the water the current carried it away. Jack knew he had to try to paddle them closer. Soon he was scraping rocks along the side and knew if he tore the bark and took on water it would be a disaster for all of them.

Marisol understood as she could see the rocks underwater and felt it must be getting shallow. Without a thought she suddenly slipped over the side of the canoe and stumbled to find her footing on the irregular and slippery bottom. She held Frankie to her and he instinctively wrapped his arms around her neck.

Jack could not believe what she did. "Hang on to the canoe until you get your balance. If you slip, you could be carried back out towards the middle of the river."

Letting go, Marisol gingerly put one foot in front of the other, nearly slipping as smaller rocks rolled. On the shore, Joe tied one of the ropes around his waist, carried the other, and started the same balancing act into the river. Tomah used a tree as an anchor where he could control the length of Joe's line.

Marisol thought over and over, *you can do it. Don't panic.* It was the first time in her life she was grateful for her height. Even more, she was grateful to feel Joe tying the second rope around her waist. Joe took Frankie as the shore contingency slowly pulled them in. Marisol slipped and was unceremoniously drawn through the water knowing how a fish felt as he was landed.

Jack pushed back and paddled as fast as possible to the wharf. Quickly tying up the canoe, he ran along the shore reaching Marisol just as she put her feet on solid ground. He swept her soggy shivering body into his arms and began the walk to Adele's. No words were needed.

The mystery of Cece became apparent to Jack. She had been left in charge of Holly who was inconsolable until she saw Frankie. Jack wondered who had been so clever to charge her with that responsibility.

Frankie nearly choked his father as he clung around his neck. Hearing him cry was like music to Annie's ears. As they started down the path to their home, Annie turned back to Marisol.

"Put me down, Jack. I'm alright." Marisol stood with a stumble but gathered herself.

Annie put her arms around her son's rescuer. "I shall ever be in your debt. I'll never be able to thank you enough."

Marisol did not know what to say so hugged Annie and held her close. "My, now you are as wet as I." They laughed in friendship and joy. Still thoroughly chilled she looked to the wigwam through the meadow. "I want to see Tim."

Jack scooped her back up and started through the wild flowers. "You are still waterlogged and will surely catch your death of cold."

"I'm too tough."

"I can't disagree."

Kate had run to Adele's as soon as she heard they pulled Marisol out of the river. She wanted to put the kettles on for hot water to prepare a warm bath. Seeing Cece comforting Holly, she wondered at a girl her age having the know-how to take charge.

Jack walked into the wigwam and set Marisol down next to her twin's sick bed. He had a hard time when he saw Tim fighting for his life. Rage always flared in him with the desire to find the two arsonists and tear them apart. "I'll be outside if you need me."

The woman stoking the small fire came over and took Marisol's hand. "Thank you. Thank you Mr. Tim's sister."

Marisol flushed with the attention.

Nana waved her over. "Dear girl. When I told you to find something to do to take your mind off the wait, that was not what I had in mind."

"Nana, I love you." Even though she was still sopping wet, she hugged her great aunt with all the might she had left.

XXIV

MAGICAL ROOM

Saturday

Marisol was back at the wigwam at dawn. Tomah and some other men were going to bath Tim later in the morning and change the layers on his pallet. Soft, fresh branches of evergreens had been gathered and the pile in the corner had a more pleasing scent to Marisol than the ever-present flag root. Next to them was a pile of fresh laundered quilts.

The resident who had been sitting with Tim for the night stretched and picked up the box of glass beads she had been using to decorate small white ash baskets made for the shops in Bangor. She put one of the lovely trinket boxes in Marisol's hand on her way to the door. "For you lady."

Not knowing what to say, Marisol tried to hand it back.

"No Miss. It is for you. Thank you. Thank you." The volunteer quickly left the wigwam leaving her still speechless.

Marisol rearranged the water pitcher and basin and other items on the wooden crate being used as a bedside table to make room for the fresh cup of warm tea made by steeping feverwort. There was some thin gruel left from overnight.

She was surprised when Tim reached for her arm as she was sitting.

"Mar, that you?" His voice was just a whisper.

"Timmy, save your strength."

"Mar. You got dunked?"

"How did you know that?

"Ears still work, my heroine."

"Hush. The doctor will be here in the morning to check your hand." She rung out a fresh cool cloth and placed it on his head.

"Feels good."

"You need to sip some of this tea." She held the porcelain invalid cup to his lips and poured some of the brew into his mouth.

Tim scrunched up his face. "Awful."

"Be good."

Tim swallowed just about as much as he could take and shook his head. "You drink."

Marisol laughed. "I think you are starting to feel better." She took a spoon and tasted a bit of the concoction and immediately spit it out. "Sorry Timmy but you know what father said, 'you have to take the bitter with the sweet'. I'll make sure you get plenty of sweet once you are making my life miserable again."

Tim smiled and fell back into a deep sleep.

Marisol's stomach growled but she saw nothing on the crate she would put in her mouth. Picking up her trinket basket she marveled at the delicate work in the weaving and decoration. *How do they have the sight to do this type of work?* Her thoughts were jarred when Nana and Jack came in the wigwam. "You're not supposed to be here this morning."

"I'm only going to stay until Tomah gets here. Jack has come to get you for breakfast at Joe and Annie's home." Nana was happy to see more than half of the medicinal tea was gone.

"I don't think I should leave."

"You have no choice Miss Hodge. It was not an invitation but a command from Joe." Jack took a moment to check on Tim and felt he had failed since yesterday. "Nana, he's bleeding."

Marisol had not noticed as she kept from looking at the bandage. Nana came around to the wounded arm. "My goodness, over a third of the dressing has been soiled. Dr. Hingham said to leave it unless it was saturated. Looks like the little devils are doing their job."

To that the young lady felt light-headed and walked outside to take in the fresh morning breezes off the river.

Jack gave his Nana a playful hug with a grin then went out and took Marisol by the hand. "Come on, breakfast awaits and my Aunt Annie is a great cook."

The path to Joe's house soon swept the visions of the leeches from her mind. At least the walk buried the thoughts for the time being. She had often seen Joe and family disappear down this trail. Once out of the built-up settlement, the pathway became more rugged with occasional rocks and roots to dodge, and ledge to climb like natural steps. The river flowed with rhythmical sounds of splashes and spray as it washed against the shoreline. Some trees looked like they were dunking their roots in the water to test the temperature. The footpath wove between old growth trees until Marisol saw a fairly large cabin made of logs with barn red blinds and door. Across the front was a deep porch looking over the river with a beautiful stand of birches just beyond. Marisol remembered the birches when they were in the canoe but the cabin blended so well into the natural environment she didn't notice it.

The front door opened, and out ran three children waving wildly. "Jack! Mary!"

"Sorry about Cece's influence with your name. Also you must have figured out the other two are my cousins. Uncle Joe and Annie were married a number of years after Ma and Pa."

"I think it's a good fit. You often act their age."

"One of these days, I'll show you how much a man I am."

Joe called them inside. Marisol's first impression of this Ryan house was one of warmth. The large living room had an oversized divan in front of a lovely fieldstone fireplace. There was a Boston rocker on each side, and a lovely cabinet sat against the wall to the left between two doors. Above the cabinet was a large painting Gert had done of a field of wild-flowers with the river in the background. To the right were floor-to-ceiling bookcases on each side of a bedroom door. The children's rooms were to the left. In the back by a large window was a table set for seven. *Lovely.*

Annie came around the fireplace and gave Marisol a hug. "Thank you for visiting and welcome to our home."

"I'm sorry I didn't get here sooner."

"You've had more to think about than visiting. Come and sit, everything's ready."

Marisol was taken aback when she got to the table. Annie's kitchen was to the right with the same fireplace facing her work area. The kitchen side had a bread oven and wrought iron tools for cooking. A door to the right obviously led to a pantry and storage area. The rest of the kitchen was fitted with a counter, kitchen sink with a pump, and a wood stove. There were two large windows over the sink and two in the dining area.

Joe watched Marisol and then laughed. "Bet you are looking for the back door."

She blushed a bit and nodded.

"It goes out from the pantry which also doubles as a mud room with a stairway to the root cellar. We learned from Sean not to have an outside door directly into the house, especially during mud season."

Jack was certainly right about one thing. His Aunt Annie was a wonderful cook. She even had a pot of coffee for Marisol as they talked at the table after the meal. The children were sent to out to play.

"Have you had any time to find your way around here? I know you've been spending most of the day caring for your brother." Annie filled Marisol's cup again with coffee and poured a round of strong tea for the rest.

"Yesterday Jack took me up the river to see more of the islands of the reservation. It was fascinating and the first time I had ridden in a birch bark canoe."

"She proved that when she nearly tipped us climbing in." For that Jack got a glare.

Joe put his hand on her shoulder. "We are so grateful that you allowed my nephew here to take you out on the river. I'm not sure I would have been that brave, but then you went on to show even more bravery when you saved our son from being carried away to certain death."

"O dear, how could I have been so stupid not to remember that you know all about my ride on the river."

"It's one day I'll never forget. And to help you remember, I have something that I made last winter. I've just been waiting for the right person for them."

Annie handed Marisol a packaged wrapped in a piece of cotton that looked like a remnant of her pale blue tablecloth of delicate white daisies, and tied with a strand of dove soft leather.

"I didn't want you to give me anything. I just happened to be there."

Jack grabbed the end of the tie and gave it a yank. "For Pete's sake, see what it is. You weren't just there, you tossed yourself in the river to help Frankie and could have been carried away with him. That's not just happening to be there. I could have lost you too."

Annie and Joe looked at each other with huge smiles.

"They're so beautiful!" Marisol held up a pair of pale doeskin moccasins detailed with tiny glass beads. On the front was a pink lady slipper wrapped in two long leaves. The same beads decorated the back of the heel.

"No more beautiful than watching our boy reading a favorite book. You kept our family complete."

"Come on Miss Hodge, I want you to see the rest of Uncle Joe's estate." Jack helped her up as she was not about to stop clutching her gift and Joe joined them for the tour.

They went out the back door and passed a small summer kitchen with a wood-cooking stove. Behind that was a large garden cleared to catch the direct sun. The crop was obviously doing well and Marisol was quite proud that she could name the various plants. "How did you manage to find this perfect field?

"It was far from perfect when we started," Joe explained. "The forest was just as thick as the area you walked through on the path. As we cut down the trees we prepared the logs for building rather than having them sawn into boards. As we cleared the fieldstones to prepare the earth for tilling, they were piled to construct the fireplace and the foundation. We managed to get that done in the few years before

Holly came along and then three of us lived in the wigwam while the house was being built. We had just moved in to complete the insides when we realized Frankie was on the way. So what you see gives Annie and me a great sense of accomplishment."

"I can see why." In her mind, Marisol felt inadequate.

On the way back towards the path she noticed two swings hanging from a strong limb of an old oak tree, and on the edge of the garden was a teepee just big enough to be a playhouse. She smiled at the splendor of simplicity. She had a lot to think about.

The Milford ferry was pulling up to the Indian Island wharf as Marisol and Jack came down the path. Just stepping ashore was Sean.

"Does Ma know you're coming? Or are you going to catch her with one of your sneaky surprises."

"Not trying to be sneaky. I just want to fill her in on what is going on at the house. Also I want to check on Tim. The scuttlebutt creeping down the river is dreadful."

When he saw Marisol, Sean picked her up to spin her in circles. As he set her down, Jack steadied her from the vertigo. "Get used to it my dear, Ryan men are known for swinging their ladies at special times."

"The most exciting thing I pulled off the rumor mill was how you saved my nephew Frankie from becoming the latest victim of Penobscot River currents."

Sean reached out to pick Marisol up again but Jack interceded. "If anyone swings this lovely lady, it will be me."

"Papa. Papa. Papa!" Running towards them was Cece on the way to the community house with her cousins. "I'd say your secret is out." Jack took Marisol's hand as Cece jumped into her father's arms, then up on his shoulders.

Nana opened the kitchen door when she heard all the ruckus. "Gert, come see what the cat dragged in." She kissed Sean on the cheek but was wary of any messages he may have.

Kate peeked around the corner then turned back into the sitting room. "We're going to need more chairs. I'll go and get the two in my bedroom."

Gert dropped her knitting needles on the kitchen table being careful not to lose any stitches. "Sean, what in the world are you doing here?"

He turned and pretended to leave. "I'll see if I can catch the ferryman before he starts back."

"No, Papa." Cece tried to turn her father around.

"Come on Sean, no teasing. We want to hear how things are going at home. I was just surprised, that's all. But in a good way."

Sean took Nana's arm thinking she had aged many years over just a few days.

All eyes turned to Sean. Cece was sitting on his lap taking in the conversation as usual. She looked up and in her straight forth way asked what everyone had wanted to ask. "Papa, why are you here? Do you have something to tell us?"

To that the group relaxed and waited for Sean's answer.

"I'll try to make this short so we have time to talk about it. I want time to visit with Tim and then make an afternoon ferry ride to Milford where Patsy and Nana's surrey is waiting."

Jack chuckled out loud. "Patsy? Patsy! You drove the fancy surrey with a mule?"

"I'll have you know she did a great job even with the strange looks we got up the River Road from Bucksport. Argos was already up here at the livery and we needed the stronger mule to move building supplies. We'll be heading back this afternoon. The crew expects me back before sunset.

"Don't forget lunch Papa. You never forget to eat."

"Don't worry little one, I'm sure I can get some lunch." Sean looked around the room and saw every one of the ladies grinning.

"Nana's neighbors and friends have done an astonishing amount of work to get things in order. There have been meetings at the schoolhouse to plan the basic needs. The military captain in charge at the fort has placed the ground crew at my disposal to clean the grounds and help any necessary building."

Gert looked puzzled. "What do you mean build? I don't understand."

Nana also looked perplexed and wondered what they could be constructing.

"Jacob, Dan, Joey and I have made some decisions for the family with which we feel the rest would agree. However, we are not sure about Nana Hodge's reaction to our idea but it has been acted upon and is in progress for completion by the time Tim is well enough to travel."

The room was silent waiting for the next announcement.

Cece stood and stared at her father. "Come on Papa."

"It has been decided that Nana will come live with us."

"No, I can't let you change your family routine by having me bumping around. I've been thinking about looking into a rooming house in Bucksport."

Gert reached out and took Nana's hand. "Don't you realize you have been part of our family ever since the first day you came bouncing across the pumpkin patch wearing that big straw hat covered in bright silk flowers? I had never seen a silk flower before. You came to welcome us with a hello and since then we have never said good-bye. You've been with me at each birth of my babies and immediately became their true Nana. You've introduced me to changes in society that opened my eyes to possibilities for women I never imagined. You became sister/mother/grandmother to me as well as best friend. Do you honestly think I'd let you move to a boarding house? You're living with us."

"There's just not enough room Gert. I was hoping Tim could stay with you while he recovers."

"We have taken all that in consideration." Sean looked into Nana's eyes and saw a bit of fright and insecurity.

"The minute you started across the river to Bucksport, Uncle Jacob started the building project. Gert, we had to disassemble part of your fieldstone wall at the end of the garden so Jacob could use the stones for the foundation."

Gert looked very confused. "I don't care about the stones, I just don't understand what you are building."

"We are adding a bedroom to the house for Nana."

Cece jumped off her papa's lap and ran over in front of Nana. "Wow! Your very own room."

"How Sean and where?" Gert could not picture it in her imagination.

"It will attach to the right parlor wall and run towards the river. The back window of the parlor will be moved to become the back window of the new room so Nana will still have a view of the river. We will knock out a door near the old corner fireplace in the kitchen so Nana will be able to get to the kitchen easily and out the back door to the porch."

Gert still couldn't visualize it.

Cece tapped on her arm. "Mama, if you could fly with the eagles our house would look like a big 'H' from the clouds."

Marisol leaned into Jack on the couch. "That child is a marvel."

"Yah, she takes after me." That brought chuckles all around the room including Nana.

"When can this project start? We pray Tim's treatment will have worked when Dr. Hingham comes in the morning. How long before Nana can move in?"

"Gert, look at me. When I left this morning the foundation was done and the framing was being prepared to be lifted in place tomorrow. Rather than a barn raising, it will be a bedroom raising. Even though it is Sunday, the whole ground crew will be coming up from the fort. They expect to start the floor and roof Monday while a group works on the walls."

"Sean, where could you find that much lumber in so little time?"

"Our son Joey has come up with that solution. He has worked a deal with the same sawmill we used. He will supply dry boards right away and we will cut trees to replace two times the board feet to the sawyer. We were supposed to replace three times the amount but since it is for Mrs. Hodge he will do it for less."

Nana was weeping silently.

"Where will that many trees come from, Sean? With all our room additions and out buildings, most of our timber is gone." Gert still did not understand clearly.

"Joey is donating the trees and it will give him a chance to clear more farm land for him and Peg."

Jack was curious. "Are they cutting the lot towards the river?"

"No, he is saving those trees for the future expansion of their own home. They are cutting the lovely stand of trees behind his house. Peg is excited about having a real back yard."

Almost at the same moment, Kate and Marisol wanted to know if those were the trees around a big boulder.

"How did you know about that? As the trees were felled, Joey was surprised to find that rock. It's much too big for him to break up and remove so Peg wants to plant flowers around it."

Marisol, Kate, and Gert gasped and looked at Cece who was sorting out the news in her mind.

"What's the problem Gert.?" Sean noticed tension among the ladies.

Then Cece sighed one of her biggest sighs ever and got in her mother's lap. "Not to worry, Mama. This would make Nana's new bedroom full of the magic and peace of my secret place."

XXV

THE LIGHT

Sunday

Unable to sleep, Marisol lit a lantern, quietly left the house before dawn and gingerly made her way to the wigwam. The lady sitting with Tim fairly jumped out of her skin when his sister walked out of the dark into the shelter. She held her hand over her heart until there was recognition.

Marisol saw it was same person who gave her the lovely little basket. "I'm sorry." She noticed Tim was perspiring enough to make his hair look like he had been caught in a downpour. "How long has this been going on?"

"For a few hours. I've been constantly changing the cool rag, but it's not helping. He's was mumbling but I couldn't make out what he was saying. Also there is more fresh blood on the bandage."

Gathering her courage, Marisol picked up his light quilt and saw the goodly amount of blood seeping through. "I'll be right back. We need some help." The sun was just peeping over the trees along the river so she was able to dodge obstacles in the path as she ran back to the house and was relieved a see a light through the kitchen window.

This time she put a scare in both Adele and Nana as she burst through the door. "What in the world, Marisol?"

"It's Timmy. He's getting sicker. His fever is hotter and the blood on his bandage is almost leaking."

Adele took the shaking girl and sat her down. "Catch your breath. I'll get Gert."

Nana got herself back up with her root walking stick. "I knew there was some reason I got myself dressed early this morning. When Gert gets here we'll go up and see what we can do before Dr. Hingham arrives."

Adele came back into the kitchen and stoked up the woodstove for the kettle. "Gert will be right here. Where is the walking lantern?"

"I left so fast I forgot it. There was enough light for me to follow the path." Marisol was still catching her breath.

Adele went to the door. "I'm afraid not all of us have your young eyes. I'll run to the shed and get another."

After what seemed like an eternity to Marisol, Gert stumbled into the kitchen still trying to get her bearings. "Come on Nana. Let's go see what is going on." She got Nana to her feet just as Adele ran in with a fresh filled lantern. "Marisol, strike a match for the wick and lead the way through the path. Remember, not too fast."

Nana's view of the Tim's situation bounced between positive and negative. She was excited to see the amount of blood on the dressing and decided not to do anything until the doctor came that morning. Her concern was about the fever and how Tim's breathing was becoming labored. *Dear God, please watch over this boy.*

Gert was going through the same exercise of thoughts that ran from optimistic to pessimistic. His pillow was soaked so she made a new one from folding up a smaller quilt and wrapping it in the same cotton material they were cutting for water cloths for his forehead. At first she thought they should change the badly soiled binding but the thought of uncovering the doctor's little helpers turned her stomach so much she went outside to catch a breeze from the river that now stretched gold from the sunrise. After a few deep breaths she went back in and looked at the young man fighting for his life. *Please watch over this boy and his loved ones.*

Marisol sat on the floor next to her twin. Two of the women she trusted most in her life were not offering any words of encouragement. She did all she could. Cooled his fever, held his hand and whispered loving support. *Where's Kate? I need Kate.*

As if called by Marisol's desperate thoughts, Kate walked into the wigwam. She carried a picnic basket Adele sent to make sure Tim's caregivers received care themselves. The message sent with Kate was to be strong for Tim, they must eat to keep up that strength.

Kate sat on a short stool at the head of the pallet cooling Tim's head so Marisol could hold his hand and talk to him. No one took a second look at the basket. That is until Adele walked in with two kettles and four tin cups. One held extra strong black tea, the other coffee she had boiled in a pan for Marisol.

Adele put together a makeshift table and set out biscuits with apple butter. She looked at the frail young man and two distraught young ladies. Leaving, she turned back once more. *May the ancients ease their pain.*

Nana sat in the wicker chair and Gert carried her breakfast out to the log bench.. Kate took her cup of tea and set it on the floor next to her stool. Even though Marisol refused, Kate set her cup of coffee on the little table used for their supplies. The aroma finally got the best of her and Marisol sipped the wonderful black brew.

She barely heard the whisper from her brother but Kate picked it up right away. She bent closer to his ear. "What did you say Tim?"

That brought Nana to attention and she waved Gert back in.

"Coffee. That you Mar?" It was very soft but heard by all.

"I'm here Timmy." She squeezed his hand. "Kate's with you, too."

"My lovely Kate. No coffee." He slipped back into a deep sleep.

Kate took off the cloth to freshen with cold water. "Dear God, he's so hot."

"May I see him?"

Gert turned to see Uncle Jacob standing just outside the flap. She grabbed both his hands. "Jacob. I was hoping you would come."

"When I talked with Sean last night he was very worried about Timothy."

"Yes, he was shocked at how much Tim had failed. His fever spikes, he starts to sweat badly but then the dry heat comes back. Like now."

"Does he speak?"

"Just a bit ago he whispered to the girls."

"Good."

When Marisol and Kate saw him enter they jumped up and ran into his arms, then stood back so he could get close to Tim. He nodded to Nana who came to stand with Gert. "The blood is a good sign." Jacob closed his eyes and placed his hands on either side of Tim's head, then on his forehead. You could have heard a beading needle drop. Even the insects in the field stopped buzzing and the birds in the trees stopped chirping for just a moment. Jacob opened his eye and looked at Nana. "I'm going to Adele's but will be back shortly."

"What is your plan?"

He opened his medicine pouch and pulled out a small-carved container of some type of bone with a wood stopper. "I have some dried yarrow and will make a tea."

"Is he strong enough?"

"We truly have no choice. Gert, find Jack and have him wait at the Old Town ferry dock to hurry the doctor along." And with that he was gone.

Marisol sat back down with Tim. Her face was drawn with anxiety about the unknown. "Nana, what is yarrow?"

"It's a wild flower with a long stem and many leaves. When in bloom it has clusters of small white or lavender daisy-like flowers at the top of the stalk. The Micmacs chew on pieces of the stalk when they have a fever. It brings on a sweat to drive it out. Jacob has some dried and is going to steep it into a tea. We'll use the feeder to get him to swallow it."

Kate laid her cheek on Tim's forehead then looked at Nana. "He's not strong enough for that."

"No. He's not strong enough. It could kill him." Marisol stood and started pacing. "No!"

Gert caught the end of the conversation and confronted the distraught sister. "Look at me. The fever could take him. We need to break it."

Nana knew she had to get a handle on the situation for Tim was going to have a very rough day and he didn't need to hear any of this. "Gert, Annie is helping the young girls cut out patterns to make moccasins. Please get her." She came face to face with Marisol and Kate. "You both need to get back to Tim. Speak softly to him. Repeat funny stories. Cool his forehead and keep him as positive as possible."

Nana took her firm toughness outside, looked into the sky and melted on the inside holding her tears privately. *Dear Captain, I can hear you saying 'what kind of pickle have you put yourself in now Fiona'? I never could figure out that saying but have come to realize that the chopped vegetables that are pickled are in a mixed up mess. Knowing I have lost all the loving work you put in building our home and collecting my treasures from around the world is devastating, but if I should lose Timothy, who carries the blood of your blood, it will surely break my heart beyond repair. Please help me keep strong beyond my strength as we fight for this boy.* She then giggled at the sight of a cloud floating by that looked just like the Cheshire Cat.

Gert just reached the wigwam. "Nana, did I hear you laughing out loud?"

"Look at the cat in the sky, Gert."

"No wonder Cece has such an awareness of the world around her and the imagination to try to make sense of it. How I love you Mrs. Hodge. Annie will be up soon. She didn't want to leave the children with the cutting tools so one of the other mothers is coming to play games. That is if she can get Cece and her friends to stop practicing the spirit dance."

"You must admit Gert that Cece has been a leader since birth. Remember how she managed her brothers even though they made her life miserable at times?"

Joe came up the path. "Jack has sent the ferryman to pick up the doctor. One of the passengers that just came over said the doctor was talking with a group of people on the other side. Jack practically tossed the confused ferryman back in his boat to go get him as this was an emergency. You don't have long to wait. Jacob has the yarrow tea ready and will be up before the doctor arrives. Annie will be here shortly." He took a peek at Tim, sighed and just shook his head. "By the way, Cece and her loyal friends including Holly and Frankie are getting dressed in ceremonial garb. You have any idea what that is about?"

Both ladies shrugged before Gert answered. "We not know."

A fretful Kate ran out. "Nana, he is having a hard time breathing."

"Go back. Talk with him softly. Tell him everything is going to be alright. Have Marisol talk to him about sailing. Anything he enjoys to keep him calm." *Stay with us Timothy. Help is coming. Keep fighting.* Nana teetered a bit. Gert steadied her.

"Look Nana."

Uncle Jacob was coming through the meadow with Jack and Dr. Hingham not far behind.

The doctor took one look at his patient and saw the struggle. He looked at the blood soaked bandage and went to touch it. Marisol and Kate cringed and turned their heads. "There are too many in here for me to examine Timothy."

Annie walked in and took the friends by the hand. "Come with me. I know a quiet place we can wait. I promise someone will come for us when the doctor is finished."

Joe and Jack slipped out to the log bench overlooking the river leaving Jacob, Nana and Gert to assist the doctor. They replaced the stool by Tim's head with the wicker chair and Nana was relieved to sit.

"He has wasted a lot since Thursday. Has he been aware?" Dr. Hingham was judging the fever.

Gert reported he had talked to his sister, been able to sip herbal tea and took some watery gruel.

"Better than I expected. The soiled dressing gives me promise."

"The blood was light then suddenly flowed heavier. We knew you would be here this morning so did not rebind the wound." Gert was beginning to wonder if she wanted to watch.

"It is going to take me a while to detach each leech. We want to be careful to make sure we leave nothing behind." The doctor lifted the material with caution. "Oh my. This is wonderful."

Nana smiled, Jacob was fascinated but Gert was having a hard time keeping her meager breakfast down.

Meanwhile Annie and her charges walked in the opposite direction to the shore. Marisol could hear the rushing rapids more clearly and realized they were close to where she and Frankie were pulled ashore. *No wonder the current was so strong.*

"Come this way. The door is open." Annie led the way.

Marisol felt the peace. "What is this place?"

"This is Saint Anne's, the catholic church on the island."

The group made their way down the center aisle and sat in the front pew. Annie grinned. "Do you know what you just did?"

Marisol shrugged.

"You walked down the aisle I did to meet my Joe at the altar the day we got married."

"It's lovely. I had no idea there was a church here." Marisol was quite taken by the hand painted Indian motifs around the sanctuary.

"I would wager you thought the natives would not have any religion other than ancient customs."

Kate came to the rescue. "I thought the same the first time I visited the island with Mike." She turned to Marisol. "This church was built in the 1600's when the French missionaries worked with the tribe here and in Canada. Since then, nuns taught most Penobscots and Micmacs in missionary schools. Yet here we are surrounded by symbols of the Penobscot Nation that is one of the oldest governments in the world. We are surrounded by a blend of two societies.

Marisol stood and examined a large carved eagle in a glass case used as the base for a podium on the altar. "This is marvelous. I've never seen such delicate work in wood."

Whenever I find myself in turmoil, I come and sit in the calmness of this serene place. I thought this was the best place to sit and wait for news of Tim."

In the wigwam the news was split. With the unorthodox treatment of his hand, the decaying flesh was at a minimum. As the leeches fed the capillaries began to repair. The doctor from Harvard thought saliva from the leeches provided a secretion preventing blood from clotting and thus opening circulation. Dr. Hingham planned to report to him it seemed to be true. The start of healing could be seen. That means Tim would not need to lose his arm. On the other hand, fever still held his body captive and was draining his life. The fever had to be broken and soon.

Gert went out to send Jack to get Marisol and Kate. She was grateful for the chance to fill her lungs with fresh air.

Joe took one look at his sister-in-law. "You didn't care for the little suckers?" He snickered at her greenish complexion.

"It's not funny Joe." She stamped her foot.

"So that's where Cece gets it from."

She was out of words so Gert just enjoyed a cool breeze while watching a mackerel sky forming in the west. "Looks like we are going to get rain in a bit. As Cece tells me, there is going to be another change."

Joe took a deep breath. "You can smell it in the air. We really need it for the garden and I imagine it's the same down your way."

Gert just nodded as she watched the group walking back from the church. Annie and Kate were chatting away while Jack just kept his arms around Marisol's waist as she rested her head on his shoulder. *Those two don't need words.* She smiled.

Coming from the other direction was Adele carrying a heavy basket with one of the neighbor boys balancing an old oak yoke on his shoulders with a bucket hanging on each side. She was determined everyone be fed. Kate pointed out the boy to Marisol. "Look. My father has one of those yokes hanging on the wall in his living room. He used it as a boy as Uncle Jacob's cookee in the lumber camps. He would carry hole beans on one side and hot tea in the other with a tin pan of hot biscuits on top. Sometimes he'd trudge quite a way through snow and ice to make sure the men were fed."

Jack gave Marisol a squeeze. "That's hard for a city girl to imagine. Ma, may they go back in?"

"Yes, the doctor will explain."

"I'm glad you're here Miss Hodge." The doctor was checking the clean dressing on Tim's burn. "It appears we have a conundrum. I'm pleased to tell you that the experiment on your brother's hand was quite successful. I'm confident his arm is safe and his hand will heal. It will be slow and I'm not sure it will ever regain strength. Our immediate problem is the fever. It could break with continuing to keep him cool but we have little time. Jacob has steeped yarrow to make a tea. I've never used it but have heard stories from those that have faith in natural treatments."

"Molly Molasses?"

"No, my dear. Molly would not be seen anywhere near a white 'medicine man'.

Marisol was reticent. "I don't think my brother is strong enough for the heavy sweating the tea would cause. He could die."

Nana nodded to Jacob. He stood in front of Marisol and took both hands.

He looked her straight in her eyes and was blunt. "If we don't break this fever soon there is no question. He will die."

Her legs began to buckle so needed support. "I'll give him the tea."

When the boy helping Adele heard they were going to use the tea to break the fever, he ran across the field.

Jack looked at Joe. "I bet it has something to do with Cece."

Over the next half hour, Marisol used the invalid feeder to slowly coax Tim to swallow. Kate held his hand and told him about their walk to the church, the beautiful sound of the rapids where you could see salmon fighting their way to spawn, reading stories to the children and planning classes for the school, stitching clothes and blankets for Peg's baby, and anything else that came to mind to keep him calm. She felt joy whenever he squeezed her hand.

While this was going on, the rest of the caregivers tried to encourage each other while eating Adele's lunch set near the wigwam. They stretched and filled their lungs with air not tainted with flag root while their energy was replaced. The next task was to convince Marisol and Kate to do the same.

JJ joined those waiting for the outcome. "Any news?"

Jack waved him over to the wigwam. "I'll fill you in on everything but right now we need to get the girls out for some food."

They refused when the doctor confirmed the tea was beginning to work. Marisol wiped her brother's face and whispered a message in his ear that only he could hear.

Jacob cocked his head. "Did you hear that?" He listened for few more seconds and pointed. Coming up the narrow path through the white daisies and black-eyed-susies was a line of children following the beat of a drum and lead by Cece. "Well, I'll be." He waved for Gert to come look.

The children, dressed in their tunics, formed a circle in front of the wigwam and began a rhythmic dance in their best moccasins while four of the older boys kept the beat with three skin covered drums and a horn rattle. Jacob scratched his head and smiled. "How did she talk those boys into doing this?"

"What are they doing? Won't that drumming irritate Tim?" Gert looked back into the wigwam and saw Nana smiling ear to ear.

"They are doing the spirit dance. I'm assuming it is aimed at Molly." Jacob began to bob his head to the beat.

Marisol didn't hear anything for Tim was sweating profusely and beginning to thrash. Kate held on to his hand and brought it up to her lips. The doctor was keeping an eye on his labored breathing.

The spirit dance did not miss a beat. A group of brown-eyed children with pitch-black braids whirled and tramped the earth while one blue-eyed little girl with golden-red pigtails kept pace. Tucked in the sash around her waist was Lacey, her little head bouncing with the beat. Around her head, a tiny beaded headband.

Jack came up behind his mother. "Do you suppose that the spirit of Molly Molasses now rests with your daughter?"

"Oh my God, don't say that!"

Joe caught Jacob's attention and nodded toward the path where Tomah was coming in full ceremonial garb. He nodded to the men and told them several more were coming. Most men were off to work in the mills on the mainland or foraging in the forest. Those in the village who saw what the children were trying to do felt they should join if it would help Mr. Tim and his sister.

As the adults began to join the circle to dance, two drummers joined the boys. Nana could hear the crescendo and looked up. Gert came in to tell her what was happening. One of the men began to chant a Penobscot medicine song while the beat of the drums and rattle mixed with the stomp of the expanded circle started to increase. Marisol and Kate were alarmed but Nana told them to be calm and think positive. Tim's face was turning red and the perspiration profuse. The doctor showed concern as he continuously checked his pulse.

Tomah handed Jacob a handful of herbs and the two of them came in to stand at the small pit fire with a repetitive singsong. They stopped, tossed the herbs forming a gust of white smoke. Suddenly a blast of cool air came through the wigwam door causing the smoke to swirl and disappear through the draft at the top of the shelter.

Startled, Marisol jumped up and tried to squelch a scream with her hands. "What is going on?"

Tim squeezed Kate's hand. "Stop yelling Mar."

Tomah waved at the dancers. Everything went silent, inside and out.

Marisol sat back down. "What did you say?"

"Why are you shouting? I was dreaming that I was floating in a dark place, drifting towards a bright light ahead of me. There was a gentle white figure standing next to the light. I wondered if I was dead but I heard a steady beat. It got louder and I thought it must be my heart so I must be alive. Suddenly I was here and you were noisy."

The doctor checked the pulse and felt his head. "The fever has broken."

Tim dozed off just as the first of the rain started tapping against the birch walls.

All the dancers but Cece ran for shelter. Knowing she was forbidden in the wigwam, she peeked around the corner.

When Marisol saw her she jumped up and ran outside, picked up the child and danced around. Just then the heavens opened up and they both laughed as Marisol's tears of joy mixed with the downpour.

XXVI

More Decisions

It took a week for the routine on Indian Island to settle into a normal pattern. Kate worked full days with Annie and those planning lessons for the new school year. The children were going to be taught in English for the first time so a curriculum was being formed to ease the transition. Kate had been teaching near her parent's home on the Aroostook River but as in many small towns, a school master was now preferred. She could do substitution when needed and that did not suit her fancy.

The wigwam had been swept clean, flag root pot removed, but Tim still stayed there while regaining his strength. Marisol spent most of the day with him making sure he ate and took short walks outside to sit on the bench. His hand was healing but so were nerve endings that at times were quite painful so he was taking regular doses of a solution of opium. Tim slept a lot and that is when his sister would work on stitching baby clothes or reading while sitting in the wicker chair. In the evening Jack would come for the night to help with the change of clothes. He, JJ and Jacob still slept in the wigwam near Joe's home.

The rain had been wonderful for the gardens. Cece began to tell a story that when the healing spirits came to help Tim, they also brought rain to heal the crops. The peas were going to be plump for the fourth day of July tomorrow.

After supper, JJ and Jacob went to Adele's to visit at the kitchen table. All the houseguests were there. Tomah was out fishing for salmon.

JJ took an envelope out of his pocket and looked at his sister. "I have a letter from Mother."

"When did that come? Why didn't you come get me?" Kate was a bit put out.

"I wanted to share it with all of you as there are decisions to be made."

Now he had everyone's attention. He pulled the note out of the envelope and Kate smiled when she caught the scent of the lavender Nettie stored in her writing desk.

My dears JJ and Kate,

Word came to us that Timothy Hodge survived. All here were praying for him and some went into Nuga's wigwam to intone the ancients.

We are anxiously waiting for the two of you to return so we will have time together before Kate leaves for Indian Island to teach. I hope there were no problems with the stagecoach schedules. Is Jacob staying longer to help with the cleanup?

I am sending an invitation for you to extend to Cara and T. You mentioned they were a bit nervous about the future. Your father and I see their predicament as an opportunity for us. My mother has been having a hard time caring for the farmhouse and cooking so we were hoping Cara would come to Aroostook with you to be live-in help like she did with Mrs. Hodge. It would ease my mind to have someone (other than my brothers) living with her now your grandfather is gone. Also your father has been impressed by T's dedicated work in the fields. He would like to offer him a job at the farm with a room off the barn office. We would fix it up for a personal dwelling.

One more request for Gert and Sean. Hanna asked me to see if you would let Cece come up for a month with JJ and Kate for a visit and then home with Kate before school starts. Ben and I would love to have her spend some time with us and I know her Granma Hanna would be thrilled. Perhaps her Granpa Frank could teach her how to fiddle.

Looking for a speedy reply and I hope for a positive answer from all.

Love you both. See you soon.

With much love, Mom

For a minute or two one could hear the faint dripping from the water pump.

Gert broke the spell. "A month without Comfort?"

"With all she has to face when you go back to your house and the disaster, it might be a good idea. I'm not sure if I am ready to look at what we left behind." Nana rubbed her hand on her forehead trying to soothe a headache.

Adele brought a pitcher of water and some cups to the table. Sitting down, she looked at Gert. "You are going to be doing the finish work on the new addition. It could be good for both of you.

JJ nodded at the ideas. "I think it would be brilliant to have T there to help Pop and me. T has never ducked from hard work and he has a keen mind to organize timetables for crops. Yes he would be an asset."

Nana sighed. "If Cara assists Mrs. Thorpe like she took care of my needs, neither of you would need to worry about your grandmother."

JJ nudged his sister's arm. "You're quiet. Don't you have any ideas about our trip to the Aroostook River?"

Kate mumbled something into her water cup.

"What did you say?" JJ was trying to figure out his sister's mood.

"I'm not going back with you for a month."

"What?"

Marisol reached out to hold her friend's hand while she explained her decision. "I'm staying at Indian Island. We have more to do for the new classes and I want to incorporate tribal traditions so the children will not be stripped of everything Penobscot.

Flabergasted, JJ questioned his sister's decision. "There has to be more to it than that."

Kate slapped her hand on the table causing some of the water from her cup to splash over the tablecloth. "You're not blind. You must see how much I care for Tim. I will not desert him. I'm not leaving."

"Do our parents know?"

"Not yet. I'll write them." Kate tried to keep her voice from trembling.

"Mother won't be happy."

His sister looked down and whispered, "I'm sorry about that."

JJ snapped, "Write her soon. The news won't come from me."

Gert showed her concern. "That would mean Comfort would come back on the coach alone. No. That would not do."

Jacob put in his few words. "Gert. I have a plan. Cece will not be alone. You need to trust me on this."

Obviously upset, JJ stood and pushed in his chair. "Jacob, I'm going to take the Old Town train to Bangor day after tomorrow to pick up some books my father ordered and learn more about the new agriculture college starting this year. Since you are going to take Argos and wagon back to Nana's barn, could I meet you on the Brewer side of the bridge? I'd like to visit Prospect Ferry again before I go back to Aroostook."

"I'm not going to the livery until late that morning so we could make that work."

"JJ, may Comfort and I go with you? I promised her a new pair of shoes for school. We can do some shopping then go home to talk with Sean about the trip to Aroostook. Please don't mention anything to Comfort or she will drive us all into the river with her questions."

With a nod he was gone.

Marisol laid her head on her friend's shoulder. "I'm so glad you're staying. Tim is going up to Joe's home to rest and recuperate"

"Quiet with the cousins?" Nana smiled and had a twinkle in her eye for the first time since the fire.

Standing with a stretch, Marisol took her light sweater off the peg by the kitchen door. "I'm going to spend some time with Tim."

"May I join you? I want to see him with my news about not going north before school." Kate sighed deeply in relief that her decision was made. "In truth, I just want to hold his hand and be close."

Always practical, Adele picked up a walking lantern. "Take this. With the overcast, darkness will fall earlier tonight."

The low slant of the sun was catching the tops of the field flowers. To Marisol this was a romp into one of the impressionist paintings she so enjoyed.

They were both delighted to see Tim propped up on folded quilts talking with Jack.

"Look Jack, you never know what critters are going to straggle in from the woods." Tim laughed at himself for what he thought was witty.

Marisol did not agree. "Timothy Hodge, what a terrible thing to say to such lovely ladies."

Moving a stool over to Tim's "good side", Kate settled down to hold his hand. "I have made plans I want you to hear from me."

Marisol gave her brother a kiss on the forehead, mostly to check for any sign of fever.

Knowing her intentions he laughed. "Cool as can be, wouldn't you say?"

"No pulling the wool over your eyes." She kissed him on his cheek in true affection.

With a tug, Jack led her to the door. "What say we give these two a chance to have some private time. Let's take a walk."

Marisol picked up the lantern. "Just in case the overcast hastens the sunset."

"Does Cece have everyone watching the skies?"

The meadow had already lost brilliance but the soft muted color was still lovely to saunter through.

"Where in the world are you taking me?"

"I thought we might go looking for salmon again."

"Jack, there won't be any sunset on the river tonight. How do you expect us to see reflections?"

"We'll just have to listen and imagine." He squeezed her hand a little harder.

As they went down the slope towards the ferry landing they met Tomah coming up.

"Oh, my goodness, look at the size of those fish." Tomah had one hanging from each hand.

"These are the salmon for our feast tomorrow. It's getting dreary so don't go too close to the river."

As Tomah passed them, Marisol felt bad. She thought those beautiful salmon should be in the river making circles.

They walked a bit up Joe's path then turned through some tall Timothy grass towards the rock steps to the river. Jack pulled a few stems of the Timothy.

Marisol pulled the sweater over her shoulders for it was cool when they settled on the flat rock. The color was not there but the rhythm of the water along the shoreline was soothing. Jack handed her one of the stems.

"Why in the world would I want this?"

"See the bit of white at the root end? Taste it."

"Do I look like Argos? He would like this."

"Be adventurous."

"It's moist and a bit sweet but it's still fodder."

"It may be somewhat sweet but never nearly as sweet as you." Jack gave her a kiss on the cheek.

A haze began to rise from the surface making it hard to see the lights across the river in Milford.

"Adele was certainly right about it getting dark early." Marisol snuggled closer to ward off the chill.

He rocked her gently in his arms. "Did you hear it?"

"What am I listening for? I just heard a splash like some-one tossing a stone in the water." She concentrated harder then heard another and grinned. "It's the salmon. The rings are still there."

"Are you happy Miss Sea and Sun?"

"Happier than I ever dreamed I could be again." She turned and kissed him gently.

"Do you know what would make me happy?" He kissed her but hardly gently.

She giggled from somewhere deep in her throat, put her arms around his neck and teased him with short quick kisses on his face and then neck.

"You little scamp."

"It's very dark in your secret place. Yes indeed, very dark."

"I'd say the only eyes looking at us belong to the owls lin-ing up on the limbs above, but they won't give a hoot."

"She laughed with gusto. Her delight echoed across the water."

He muffled her with a kiss. "That, my dear, could give us away."

She blew a "Shh" his ear. With that he lay beside her on the rock as they explored each other, setting off a flame that consumed their bodies. They didn't notice the rattle of pebbles tumbling into their love nest, yet the noise was enough to frighten the bobcat away from the rocks and back into the fir trees.

Kate was relaxed in the wicker chair reading "Alice in Wonderland" by Lewis Carroll when they walked in. Tim seemed asleep.

"I thought you had deserted me." Kate marked her place with a bookmark Cece made her from a scrap of leather.

"We were walking along the river searching for wildlife." Jack filled a cup of water from the stoneware pitcher. "How did things go here?"

"Tim and I had a lovely talk. I told him about my plans to stay the rest of the summer."

Jack put a small log in the fire pit. "You two better start for home before Adele sends Tomah to find you."

All were surprised to hear Tim speak up. "Mar, you better brush those pebbles and dirt off the back of your sweater."

They barely needed the lantern to light the way home. Marisol's red face would have sufficed.

XXVII

JULY 4TH - 1868

Mid morning, Jacob walked down Joe's river path with his grand niece on his shoulders. Her golden raspberry braids bounced in rhythm with his steps. Around her forehead was a headband designed in Indian motifs with colorful glass beads. Around Jacob's head an identical band. They stopped for a while in front of the central lodge to watch a group of teen age boys building the pile of bonfire logs, then continued behind Adele's house to pick garden peas.

Jacob swung his passenger to the ground. "Mama, look at my new headband. I made it myself." Gert looked a bit skeptical. "Honest Mama, Aunt Annie made the one for Uncle Jacob and I followed her."

Gert looked at Jacob who nodded with a broad smile. "Lovely, now it's our job to get these peas picked and out of the pods. Marisol is going to help."

That brought on a Cece pout. "I don't like pea picking."

"I'll tell you a secret. Neither do I but there are many things you'll need to do in life that you won't like to do. You might as well get used to it at an early age."

With an almost inaudible grunt, the little girl started plucking the pods and chucking them in the basket. Shortly she heard the same unhappy grunts from Marisol.

Adele smiled. "I've put a cooking kettle on the back porch. I think this will do it as long as Cece doesn't eat half of them."

"I don't like them cooked. Sometimes they get soft and yucky." Cece scrunched up her nose. "I like them raw and tasty."

Once the shelling of the peas started, Marisol decided she didn't like that chore any more than picking them. "At least I now understand what Joey meant about him and Jack being called two peas in a pod when they were babies. Gert, just how did you tell them apart?"

"Joey has a tiny birth mark on the back of his neck. When they were changing seats in class to fool the teacher, I told the teacher where to look. Also, when Jack would run into Nana's kitchen and tell Cara that Joey had a cookie and he didn't get one, she would give him a cookie only to find out Jack got both. I showed her where to look too."

As she grabbed another handful of pods, Marisol shook her head and giggled. "I bet Jack was the instigator."

"Ah yes, but one of his devious schemes backfired. When they were in third grade, Jack pretended to be Joey and took a plain, chunky, freckled-face Peggy behind the school house, kissed her and told her he loved her."

"He didn't!" Marisol grabbed her chest and acted surprised.

"Joey found out when love sick little Peggy followed him around like a puppy dog. He and I had a talk and decided maybe this little girl needed a friend not another bully. He became her protector, they grew close and now beautiful Peg and devoted Joey are expecting their first baby in their own home."

With their conversation the chore of shelling peas went faster and soon the kettle filled even with Cece popping a pea in her mouth every few pods.

Jacob and Tomah brought the lovely freshly cleaned salmon to Adele to set in a shallow water bath to be poached. Then she tended to making a butter egg sauce where she added a bit of flour to melted butter then milk.

With the kitchen table set for nine, the three children had a makeshift table and chairs on the kitchen porch. Marisol, Jack and Kate were making up trays for the wigwam to eat with Tim. On her way out, JJ caught his sister's eye with a scowl. "Don't worry big brother. It took most of the morning, but my letter is ready to mail. Our parents will know my thinking so you need not worry about being in the middle."

"It's too bad Sean and the rest of your family could not join us." Tomah carried the large serving platter to the table holding the tender salmon steaks covered with sauce and chopped hard-boiled eggs.

"They felt they needed to supervise the building and clean up. Gert carried a large yellow ware bowl of boiled tiny new potatoes with melting globs of butter on top. "In truth, I think Peg enjoyed having a chance to prepare her own July fourth dinner for Sean, Dan and Joey. I'm sure one of them managed to catch a salmon." Next, Gert brought the bowl of steaming peas and Adele finished cutting the fresh sourdough bread.

No matter if in the kitchen, porch or wigwam, the family and friends feasted. The surprise dessert? Jacob had soaked and plumped up a basket of dried apples and made three wonderful pies.

The glow of the bonfire turned dusk into day. Some of the children started dancing in circles, the drums came out and then the rattles. Everyone clapped and laughed. Kate held Tim's hand and walked him out of the wigwam so he could see the celebration. Sitting on the bench, Tim laughed out loud at the antics of Cece plainly seen dancing in the firelight. Then basking in the warmth from the fire, Kate laid her head on his shoulder and smiled for the joy in her heart.

Soon the fireflies started rising from the grasses punctuating the air with their own little flashes. Standing behind Marisol, Jack wrapped his arms around her waist and whispered in her ear. "What say we find a hidden spot and strike a fire of our own?"

Marisol saw that her brother and Kate were in their own little world, so slipped quietly with Jack behind the wigwam to find a perfect spot to let the sparks fly.

As the bonfire began to settle to embers, families took their tired children home. Before Cece went off with Holly, Gert told her they were going to Bangor in the morning.

"No, mama. I don't want to go. Aunt Annie is starting to teach us how to make bead designs."

"I'm sure your aunt will show you how to bead some other time. But tomorrow you are going to leave the island."

Cece pouted with arms crossed. "Why?"

"You and I are going to buy your new school shoes and a few other things. Then we have some other plans to talk about."

"What plans, mama? What are we doing?"

"First things first, little girl. Now you go with Holly and Frankie and get a good night's sleep and don't bother Uncle Joe with questions because he doesn't know the answers. Come down with Uncle Jacob after breakfast and the adventure will start."

A confab at Adele's confirmed the train trip to Bangor to meet Jacob at the Brewer end of the bridge. Then Argos would take them all to Milford and across the river to Prospect Ferry.

The goodbyes in the morning were early and short. Cece arrived on Jacobs's shoulders, her strawberry blonde hair brushed out and curlier than ever once the braids were released. It was held back with a green ribbon and bow. Tim and Marisol were standing outside of the wigwam and Cece jumped up and down with waves. Riding the train from Old Town was a first for Cece. She waved out the window to any one paying attention. The engine moved its passengers, baggage cars with several freight cars of lumber, laths, and shingles to the docks to travel the world.

In Bangor JJ pointed to where they would meet near the bank.

"Perfect," noted Gert. "Comfort and I will be school shopping, then I need to do some banking for Nana. See you soon."

It didn't take long at the shoe store. Cece spotted a pair of high top black leather shoes with four buttons and would not look at another style. Gert suspected it was because they were similar to Marisol's five-button dress footwear. Next door they bought three pairs of high black cotton lisle stockings to keep her legs warm at school. Since the painting money was more than the pilfered egg money, they found two white cotton blouses for Cece to wear under her jumpers. It was the first time she had store bought clothes.

The trio was quickly on their way as the meeting at the bank was perfectly timed. Gert decided it was time to talk about the next leg of the trip. "Comfort, we are going home to see your papa."

"But what about Nana and Mary and, everyone else?"

"We'll be with them soon. Now, you have always wanted to walk across the river bridge."

Approaching the entrance to the covered bridge, Cece suddenly stopped. "Mama, why do I feel Molly Molasses looking at me?"

Gert was so rattled she nearly tripped over a stone from a scattered pile of curbing. JJ reached out and steadied her while she took a deep breath. With Cece clutching her bundles while peeking into the entrance of the bridge, Gert gathered her thoughts. "Molly would stand here at the entrance trying to sell her Indian trinkets to visitors. She always caught my eye with a look that cut to my soul and I felt she knew me far more than I. The last time Comfort was here, she was a toddler."

"You must remember Gert, that your daughter has a direct blood line to Nuga. She was a powerful woman but her spirituality was positive. She controlled with wisdom and love where Molly, so bitter about the rape of her homelands, controlled with fear and revenge. If Cece gains half the intuitiveness of Nuga, she will be an exceptional woman, one that could very well pick up the essence of the spirits."

"JJ, how did you get so smart!"

"I'm Ben Smythe's son."

This made Gert double up.. "Oh yes, my dear school mate who called me Dirty Gertie in the potato fields."

Cece was getting restless and wanted to enter the covered bridge over the river. "Come on Mama. Uncle Jacob is waiting."

Gert gave JJ a playful punch in the arm. "You young man, have been saved by Comfort."

With Cece peering through every crack she could find between boards, and out every window along the seven-hundred and twenty-nine foot bridge, the walk was slow. "Look, Mama. There is a boat going under us and it's big. Look, Mama. I can see through this hole by the wall. The water is way down and hitting rocks." She covered her ears and hid behind her mama's long skirt when a large wagon, heavy with lumber, rumbled past. "That sounds like rolling thunder and I don't like thunder."

Gert hoped that would get Comfort to rush to the end of the bridge, but no. "Look, Mama. Here comes one of those fancy buggies with glass beads around the sunshade. If they are covered against the sun why do the ladies hold umbrellas with more dangly beads?"

JJ snickered about that one. "Cece, I have wondered that myself."

The clippity-clop of a fine Morgan horse echoed up and down the bridge. "Mama, that horse is singing with his feet."

The light was getting brighter at the other end of the bridge. "Come on Comfort. Let's get out of this dark tunnel." They held hands and skipped towards the exit.

JJ smiled at the sight. *I must find a wife that likes to skip.*

Waiting patiently at the Brewer end of the bridge, Uncle Jacob was leaning against the wagon talking to Argos. Soon he had an armful of Cece as if they had been separated for days. "Let me take your bundles." She shook her head so Jacob lifted her with her attached buys into the back of the wagon with her mother and baskets of supplies for Prospect Ferry.

With JJ settled on the wagon bench, Jacob brought Argos up to speed and away they went towards Bucksport in a cloud of dust.

XXVIII

Surprises

As the ferry approached the landing, Cece spotted her father and Dan waiting. She was poised to jump as soon as they touched the landing but her mother grabbed her by the back of the skirt. "Hold on young lady, you want to end up in the river?"

"If Mary were here, she would jump in and get me."

"Well, she's not. So hold your horses and your bundles."

That did not stop her from waving vigorously with her one free arm so Gert still needed to hold on. "Let Argos off first. I don't want you getting tangled up in those wagon spokes."

"Like Jack did when he got beat up?"

Jacob led the steady steed to the dock then gave the go ahead. "Go get your papa."

Sean let out a loud "oomph" when Cece jumped up in his arms. "What in the world did your Aunt Annie feed you up on the island?"

"O Papa, that's not me, just the bundle with my new school clothes and shoes."

"What did you do? Find the goose that laid the golden egg that Aesop wrote about?"

"No. Mama sold a painting to take the place of the egg money."

Gert picked up a basket of little things for the coming baby. "Sorry. I meant to tell you."

"Always surprises. But this time, I bet I have a bigger one!"

"What is it papa? What? What?" She wiggled down and wrapped herself around Dan's leg. "Tell me big brother. Please. I can see two little eagle heads. Are there three like I thought?"

Sean and Dan only smiled. "JJ, we'll walk up through the orchard and pick up our supplies later. Peg is cooking supper for all of us." Jacob hopped up on the seat hoping to block the view of the black scar where Nana's home once stood from Cece."

Coming nearer the house, Cece ran ahead and jumped on her swing without letting go of her treasures. That was a juggling act that almost failed but Dan grabbed her just before she toppled backwards. "Wow, Papa! Look at the new room. Is that Nana's bedroom? Can I see? Can I see?"

Finally relinquishing her precious school bundle to her mother, Cece held on to Lacey as Dan swung her up to his shoulders. He ducked her through the back door before she squirmed down. Running to the new opening near the corner fireplace, she put one hand on each side of the doorjamb and let out a loud "Wow!" She ran around to inspect all corners causing echoes like the Morgan horse. "The window is big so Nana can watch the river."

Gert wrapped her arms around Sean's waist. "You and Dan have done an amazing job."

"Jacob and the fort crew had the major part of the structure in place before he went to the island. Joey has been helping me in the evening with the plaster."

"I'll be able to paint Nana's favorite flowers on the walls and hang print curtains around lace panels. There is a large braided rug stored in the barn that she made when first starting housekeeping. It will be perfect to keep this floor warm. She's always wanted a new brass bed. Sean, this can be her private oasis."

"Hold on, my little dreamer. It will take a long time and money to be able to fix up this room to the plans dancing in your head."

"Sean, you should know Nana would never put that burden on us. She had me stop in to see her banker in Bangor with a fairly large draft. He was shocked he hadn't heard the news and rushed the withdrawal so I could take the cash with me. We snuck our little pot of gold past the riff-raff wandering in and out of the Devil's Half Acre."

"Do you know how dangerous that was? You had Comfort with you. How did you dare?"

"Sean, my love, how many years will it take for you realize how devious we women can be?"

He threw up his arms in surrender. "Tell me then. How can you find the hours needed to finish this room while the crops are beginning to come in? Things need to be prepared and stored for the winter."

Gert smiled and whispered in Sean's ear. "Comfort is going to visit your mother and Nettie for a month."

"What?"

Gert quickly put her finger over his mouth. "Shh, she doesn't know yet."

"Lady!" Cece sat down in the middle of the floor and the big cuddly coon cat ran to her lap and starting purring loud enough to fill the room with happy cat noises. "Look Mama, Lady isn't fat anymore."

Now it was Sean's turn to whisper in Gert's ear. "Told you I had a big surprise."

As if on cue, Lady jumped up and stood by the door, then ran back in and around Cece and back to the door.

"Looks like Lady wants you to follow her." Sean gave Gert a mischievous wink.

"What's wrong kitty cat?"

Lady turned with a very impatient 'meow' and jumped among the pile of rags in the kitchen.

When Cece finally digested the scene, her piercing scream could have given all six coon kittens a heart attack.

Lady responded with a low rolling purr when Gert softly stroked her ruff. "Sweet baby, no wonder you waddled like a furry duck."

"Look Mama, they're all different, not like Joey and Jack. Look at the little one, the hair is so light and shiny. Do you think she is a little girl? Can I keep her? Lady was your kitten, this one could be my princess."

"Not so fast young lady. These babies need a few weeks to grow strong enough to prevent them from being loved to death."

"I'll be careful, Mama. I promise."

"No. You will be starting your adventure."

"What kind of adventure? Am I going to be an explorer? Or climb mountains. Or ..."

"Comfort, my love, you are going on the stage with JJ to visit your family in Aroostook County."

"Grandma Hanna?" Cece hugged Lacey close to her as she does when nervous or upset.

"And your Grandpa Frank. JJ and Kate's parents also want you to visit. They are Papa and my best friends."

Cece started to fidget with Lacey's little knotted hand and a tiny tear was forming in the corner of her eye. "Will they know who I am?"

Picking up his little girl, Sean gave her a tickling raspberry kiss on her neck and made her laugh out loud. "Comfort, everyone will know who you are the minute they see you. You are the perfect combination of your mother and me. You can't hide the Irish in your looks, the stubbornness of your Papa, the beauty of your mother and the wisdom of your Micmac ancients."

"How will I get back? Do I have to take the coach all by myself?"

Gert started putting together a late lunch realizing just how much she missed her own kitchen. "Uncle Jacob has made plans for your trip home. You will be coming back middle of August, in plenty of time to get ready for school. By then I'll have Nana's bedroom ready and she'll be here."

Cece shuddered. "Can Lacey come?"

"Of course. We will pay her way."

Cece was subdued during supper but no fever was detected when Peg checked her forehead. "It's not like you to be so quiet. What's wrong?"

"Mama and Papa are sending me away." A tear rolled slowly down her cheek. Gert dropped her mug, splashing tea over the table but Sean got to his Comfort first and lifted her into his lap.

"Your Grandma misses you. It's been three years since she last held you. Do you remember Grandpa playing a special Cece song on his fiddle? You danced like you did for Tim in the spirit circle."

Gert took Cece's hands. "We didn't mean to upset you. I thought this would be a great adventure. Would you rather stay home?"

"I not know." She trembled behind a frown, her green eyes dulled behind a sheet of moisture. "Lady needs my help with her babies."

Sean laughed making his daughter pout with her lower lip stuck out. "Little girl, only Lady knows how to take the best care of her kittens. By the time you get back they should be big enough for lots of hugs and nearly ready to go to their new homes. We will need your help to decide what is best for them."

"My Princess?"

"By then we will know if it is a princess or a prince." Sean rolled his eyes. "And there will be a lot of discussion before we have two cats."

Wiping the corn bread in his chicken gravy, JJ spoke up. "I have some news about the stage coach. There will be others you know sharing the ride."

That caught Cece's attention. With a snuff of her nose, she waited for JJ's story.

"T and Cara have accepted an invitation from my Pop. Cara is going to move to my grandmother's farm to be her helper. T is going to work on the potato farm. So there won't be many strangers travelling with us. I'm going to the stage office in the morning to book a trip that will hold all four of us."

"Make that five of us." Uncle Jacob took everyone by surprise. "It's time I get back to Smytheville. Things are coming together here and I want to make sure things have stayed together there."

"Uncle Jacob, will you show me Nuga's wigwam?"

"Of course, and we'll walk the path around the settlement that I walked when your Papa was your age."

"Can I ride on your boot?"

That brought laughs all around. "It's been forty plus years since the last time I did that but we'll give it a try."

Gert fixed the ribbon and bow holding back Cece's ringlets. "Does that mean you are going?"

"Of course. I have a lot of people to meet."

When Dan took his mug of tea outside, Sean nodded at Gert to follow. He usually was Indian quiet but was more so this evening.

"Anything I can do to help?" Gert brushed his stray hair out of his eyes exposing the scar on his forehead. She didn't notice it as much lately but tonight it sent a shiver through her. It had been five years since the battle at Gettysburg where Mike gave his life to save his brother from a sniper. .

"Don't laugh, Ma but I think I'm jealous of my little sister. I sometimes daydream about tracking in the forests along the Aroostook, especially now that the Penobscot is so busy. Jacob has asked me to go so I can bring Cece home."

"When I saw that mop of black hair the day you were born I knew you favored your Pa's Uncle Jacob. You've always carried the Micmac ancestry more than your siblings with their red curly hair and looks of the Irish. Every day when you left for school, I feared you'd get hurt by one of the boys being filled with bigotry at home.

Dan nodded.. "That's when I learned to move around with silent steps and if sounds were made, brother Mike quieted them."

Gert hugged her son. "Are you ready to travel alone with your sister? She can be a handful."

"Cece and I have always had our own special relationship."

"Having your eyes on Comfort would make me less nervous about the whole idea." She pulled Dan back in. "JJ do you think you could find a coach for six? Dan is going to enjoy the Aroostook wilderness for a while and bring his sister home."

Peg saw her husband caught totally by surprise. "Joey, don't you even think of it. The last place you are going is Aroostook County. If I don't get a month off from having your baby, neither do you."

"Can anyone else sit in our coach, Uncle Jacob?" All of a sudden Cece felt very possessive about her horse drawn carriage.

Jacob laughed out loud. "Cece, no one is going to take a seat on a stagecoach with a very active little girl and two Indians.

XXIX

CECE'S ADVENTURE

The next few days spun by like a waterspout on the river. Cece's chatter was incessant making Gert wish she had kept the trip a secret until the stagecoach was in sight. Before Jacob and JJ went back to the island to make arrangements there was quite a to-do over payment for the tickets. Jacob made it known that all plans had been set and he wanted no further discussions. JJ put a bundle together of Tim's clothes from the wigwam at the Ryan's because he would soon go to stay with Joe and Annie for a bit.

Early morning of the start of Cece's journey, she had to unpack and repack her travel bag and make sure Lacey was decked out with a new ribbon and bow around her neck. The doll had been scrubbed as clean as was possible for being loved and dragged around since Dan returned from the grand parade in Washington, DC three years ago. Cece checked the covered basket and counted the ten glass Mason jars Nana wanted her to bring back from the barn. Finally hugs for Lady and her six babies.

Gert decided not to go to Indian Island. She had visions of herself grabbing her baby and running the other way when the stage approached. Dan carried the bags while Cece rode to the ferry on her father's shoulders giving an energetic wave to Thomas in the field as the passed by. T and Cara were waiting at the landing as the ferry from Bucksport approached. In a flash the luggage was loaded, hugs made, and all were on board, waving goodbye.

Uncle Jacob hired a wagon from the Milford Livery to carry the group on the first segment of their trek. He asked Dan to drive so he could take in the scene of the fields and gardens surrounding the Ryan homes on the hill across the water. The crops had filled in enough to hide the hideous scar where the lovely Hodge home once stood. It was though Jacob wanted to permanently etch the scene in his memory.

Watching the wagon go out of sight up the Brewer Road across the Penobscot River, Gert grabbed Sean's hand and leaned on his shoulder. "Couldn't she at least have shed one tear?"

"Once her mind is made up, she doesn't waver. Sort of like her mother, I would say." Sean gave her a wink and walked towards his office at the fort.

Gert walked slowly up the path and saw some of the crabapples had fallen so she could make up a batch of jelly. With a deep sigh she realized more blueberries needed to be picked to add to the ones Cara left for her. She gave the swing a casual push and looked up into the old apple tree. For a brief moment her imagination took her back to when all her boys would have their meetings in those branches. It was obvious the family garden had been somewhat neglected but she just shrugged while casually plucking some weeds between the rows of potatoes. Lady was lying in the sun on the back steps purring loudly as her mistress approached. Gert tugged the hefty longhaired cat onto her lap, burying her face in the soft fine fur. "Lady, I can't remember the last time I have been the only one home. I don't like it." She finally let all the stress of the past weeks escape.

At Indian Island, all her friends treated Cece like a celebrity. Some of them had never been off the island, never mind travel a hundred miles. Some were very happy, some quite jealous and others in awe of her bravery to go so far away. That night the youngsters chased fireflies, put them in Nana's Mason jars then made a large circle of the magical twinkling containers. The children sat in the center while Nana told a story about being at sea. It was a stormy dark night where not a wisp of light could be seen. Captain Hodge was having a hard time navigating their schooner to the safety of a harbor when suddenly a swarm of fireflies swooped around the ship and led them to a safe inlet. She told the children Cece was going off on a trip and we all wanted her to find the way home again. They took the lids off the jars and all the little lights swirled around the circle and then straight up to split off in different directions. "Cece, watch for them in Smytheville and think about us."

That night Cece slept with her Nana Hodge, which gave both a lot of comfort.

The coach was due to arrive mid morning. Since there were no passengers boarding in Brewer, they were going to be picked up in Milford probably at the request of Tomah so the family could see them off.

Before T and Cara boarded the Milford ferryboat with their belongings, Nana gave each an envelope to be opened later. She wasn't going to the stage so she said her goodbyes with gratitude and wished them the very best in their new home.

The next small boat was loaded with JJ and Dan's few pieces of luggage. Dan looked around. "Where's Cece?"

Jacob assured him he would bring her over although he also had no idea where she went. Taking her hand, he looked into Nana's eyes. "I am honored to know you Mrs. Hodge."

"You're not coming back, are you Jacob."

"Whatever days I have left will be spent guiding the growth of our Micmac settlement on the Aroostook despite ever present narrow-mindedness."

Taking his hand, Nana just nodded her head. "Never forget, you have my undying gratitude."

"I'm coming. Don't go without me." Cece was running down the path with her doll flapping in the wind. "Lacey was still in Nana's bed. I guess she overslept." She gave Nana a huge hug and pointed to the sky. "Look, nothing but happy clouds playing in the sky. Where are Holly and Frankie?"

"They have already gone over with Tomah to see you off." Nana blew her another kiss as the ferry pushed away. Suddenly she greatly missed Gert.

There was quite a gaggle at the stage office on Main Street when Cece arrived. Holly and Frankie were hugging her as if she were heading for the moon. Joe and Annie were sending off T and Cara with good wishes for their new future. Joe put a good-sized picnic basket in the corner of the cab. Annie had packed enough eats to feed an army for days. Dan and JJ were having their jollies by ordering Jack to take good care of 'the girls'.

Jacob, Adele and Tomah were quiet for all knew this was the end of an era for them. Jacob put his arm around Adele's shoulders and broke the silence. "You will always live in my heart sweet girl." Then he turned to Tomah and spoke in the language of the Wabanaki tribes as they shook hands in the manner of blood brothers.

After checking the large load of luggage was secure, the driver shouted "all aboard". Cece showed her first bit of apprehension as she was lifted into the cab. Hugging Lacey she nestled between her Uncle Jacob and big brother while her big green eyes took in every inch of the enclosure. Never having been in an enclosed carriage before, she grabbed Dan's hand. Then with a snap of the whip and a jolt they were off.

Downriver, Gert took a look at the pile of work clothes in the corner of her bedroom and thought of the beautiful paddle washer Nana once had in her mudroom. With a sigh she put the water kettles on and pulled the washtub out to the porch. While waiting, she checked the line strung from the corner of the porch to the stately old pine out by the chicken coop, then over to the maple tree. Gert took a good look to the top of the pine to make sure no turkeys were resting up there. She's had to rewash some clothes more than once. But since they usually nest up there at night, all was clear. With a peek in the coop, she saw enough eggs to bake tonight and have some eggs for breakfast. Like her daughter, she had a good conversation with the chickens.

Actually, working with the scrub board and washing stick was good for the mother who was stressed about her baby off for a hundred-mile trip. The breeze picking up from the water lifted Gert's spirits as she hung the wash with the Shaker clothespins Nana had given her for her last birthday. As the lines began to sag, tall clothesline poles made from a limb with a fork propped up the line to keep the clothes from hitting the ground. Satisfied with the job, Gert stood, hands on hips, as someone grabbed her from the back. She came around quickly and elbowed the intruder who fell to the ground.

Sean lay laughing on the ground. "I see age has not dulled your defensive moves."

"Sean Ryan. You about gave me a stroke. In twenty four years, you've never voluntarily come home for lunch."

He jumped and grabbed Gert's hand and ran her into the house. "I'm really hungry." As she turned towards the kitchen, he grabbed her by the back of her apron. "But, not for food." He picked her up in his arms spun around and headed for the bedroom.

Gert feigned panic. "Oh no! Not the wicked feather bed."

"I'm willing to chance it."

"Sure, you don't have to deal with the possible consequences."

Sean teased with a few light kisses across the back of her neck and then whispered in her ear. "How long has it been since we've been in the house all by ourselves?"

"How old is Comfort?" As he began to unbutton her blouse, she began some teasing of her own.

"That does it. No more defense."

Pulling her blouse off, Gert raised her arms as she fell back. "I surrender."

For a sweet moment of time all the trauma of the past several weeks was forgotten in a flurry of feathers.

"Anyone home?" Peg walked in with a loaf of fresh baked sour dough bread and placed it on the sideboard.

Gert came out of her bedroom brushing her long curly hair. "I was freshening up after getting the wash out. The way the wind is whipping it will be ready in no time."

"I thought I got a glimpse of Sean going down the path."

"He knew I was upset this morning so he came for lunch."

Peg smiled without a word as it was quite obvious her mother-in-law looked a bit disheveled.

"My grandbaby is really showing its presence. What is it now Peg, about four-and-a-half months?"

"Around that, give or take, and I think I felt Buddy kicking last night. There was a sense of hiccups in my belly but Joey couldn't feel anything."

"Wait until the baby gives him a good swift kick. The first time it happened with Dan, I thought Sean was going to jump out of bed. And Buddy?"

"Joey thinks the baby is a boy and has all kinds of plans for him working in the fields. He wants his son to be his buddy."

Gert laughed out loud for the first time in a long time. "Good luck with that idea."

"Cece is your little side-kick," Peg pointed out.

"I think that happened because her brothers were so much older and she needed reinforcement from the only other female in the house, Lady not included."

"How do you think she is doing on the road?"

"I've been thinking about Comfort since the ferry pulled away wondering if the rocking of the coach is making her sick. I picture her hugging Lacey and sitting as close to Dan as she can."

Meanwhile in the coach somewhere on the road that followed the old Indian paths to Houlton, Cece was vigorously waving out the window to everyone they passed while her brother hung on to the waist of her skirt. "I'm Cece and I'm on an adventure."

XXX

The Month Begins

A steady rain fell the day after the travelers left Indian Island. The soft gray atmosphere was the break needed from the tension of Tim's battle with his injuries. It gave the village a moment to take a deep breath and slowly let it out as residents spent personal time on their own projects. The crops in the fields stood taller as roots reached for the life-giving moisture. Rivulets of rainwater carried debris from the grounds to the river leaving the village refreshed.

Reviving a sense of normalcy, the Ryan family initiated their plans for the month ahead at Prospect Ferry, the Aroostook River, and Indian Island. It would be a challenge to make all the pieces come together for the reunion at Sean and Gert's remodeled home.

All going well, tomorrow Cece should finally reach Gramma Hanna's house by noon, Gert would start decorating Nana's new room and Tim should be well settled at Joe's house. But as Robert Burns penned in his poem "To the Mouse", "the best laid schemes of mice and men go often awry."

Shortly after dawn Tim was anxious to leave his 'jail' but found it was not as easy as planned to get dressed for the walk to Joe's. His wounded hand was useless when it came to pulling and buttoning so Tim was embarrassed when Jack had to help him finish putting on his clothes.

"Are you sure you're ready for the walk along the river path? It gets uneven and rocky over a steady incline."

"Mar walked me so much around this enclosure I felt like a horse on a carousel. Then Kate took me through the paths in the meadow. I'll make it just fine."

Marisol started up the path as her brother walked out of the wigwam. It took away her breath to see the change in his appearance. The newest shirt he bought in Searsport hung on him. His leather belt had to be cinched tight at the waist to hold up the baggy trousers. She had not realized how bony he had become.

When Kate heard he was coming, she raced out of the schoolroom and stopped dead in her tracks seeing how emaciated he had become. It took her a minute to regain her senses before running to hold his good hand.

—⚹—

In Aroostook County, the stage was a few miles south of the growing township of Presque Isle. It was fortuitous Cece was napping in Uncle Jacob's arms when a pack of wild dogs suddenly ran across the road barking and spooking the horses. The coach lurched ahead at great speed tossing the passengers about. Uncle Jacob instinctively tightened his grip on his grandniece saving her from being thrown across the cab.

Struggling to control the reins, the driver combined all his strength and experience to take charge of the steeds. The passengers made a great effort to get back into their seats and braced themselves. Jacob and Dan worked together to support and protect Cece during the discombobulated situation. With use of brakes and a steady hand, the team began to react, but the coach was still going too fast to negotiate the curve cleanly and hit a projecting rock, splintering a back wheel. With this, the driver was thrown from his seat out into the tall grasses while dragging the coach up the road to a stop slowed the horses. Jacob jumped out, grabbed the tackle and calmed the team. JJ ran back to check on the driver.

In the cab, T and Cara found themselves on the floor amidst the scattered remains of Peg's lunch. They were seemingly unhurt, most likely just bruised from being tossed about like the apples. Cece was clutching Dan around his neck with her eyes closed as tight as possible for fear peeking would bring on more jostling.

Witnessing the mishap, a farmer stopped and helped JJ put the driver in the bed of his wagon between a few barrels of tiny new potatoes. He had a nasty gash on his forehead and an obviously broken arm. The farmer would take him into Presque Isle for help and report the accident at the stagecoach office explaining the plight of the deserted passengers.

Climbing gingerly back into the coach, Jacob just shook his head. "We're very fortunate it didn't roll over. How are you doing Cece?"

She finally opened her eyes and took in the jumble questioning Danny, "What happened?"

"The horses were scared by a pack of barking dogs."

With a deep sigh, Cece hugged Lacey as tight as possible. "That's why I like cats."

At Prospect, Gert was sipping on her tea before working in Nana's room. Up before dawn to work on the family garden, she was hoping for a surge of renewed energy. Standing, she stretched her arms up and with a huge yawn swung back to wake up her tired muscles. As she swerved them towards the side, her hand caught the teacup rim hurling it to the floor. The resounding crash brought such a cry from Gert you would have thought some of the shards of china pierced her heart. In a way they did for that was her favorite cup. It was a birthday gift from Nana's collection, the set that was now buried under ashes and mud. It was not until one of her tears fell into the puddle of tea that she realized most of it splashed all over the pile of clean clothes in the wicker basket. She actually giggled while gathering tiny pieces of hand-painted roses. "My goodness, what next?" Now as the wife of Sean Ryan for the past twenty-four years, mother of four Ryan boys and then Cece, she knew better than say that out loud.

There was just a bit of white washing left to finish in Nana's room before Gert could begin decorating the walls with paintings of wild flowers. As she passed Lady's basket, a chorus of mews grabbed her attention. She sat on the floor and gave each kitten some loving comfort, which in turn comforted her. "Where in the world is your mama? Lady, your babies are hungry. Where are you hiding?"

It didn't take long to uncover the beautiful coon cat trying to conceal herself under the stool used for reaching high on the walls in the new room. Gert laughed out loud seeing half of Lady poking out but believing as long as her head was covered, she was invisible. "What have you been up to?" The puzzle was soon solved for the floor was covered with whitewash paw prints. "No lady." The cat tried to pull herself into a tighter ball.

On examination Gert found the trough holding the whitewash had not been covered the night before. *Sean Ryan, I could strangle you.* The patterns from the lime water went back and forth up to the door and at times back across the paint container again. *She has more sense than her father so did not drag the paint into the rest of the house.* "Come on out big girl. Let's see what kind of problems we're dealing with." It was easy to see the wash had dried on her nose and paws from investigating the trough. The tips of her long hair had dragged through the mess and dried into tangled knots. It took a lot of snipping with Gert's sewing scissors to get the sharp hard pieces off Lady's belly so her kittens could nurse. "Your feet will be fine once you scuff through the dirt and sand in the yard, and your nose will clear in time. Now go take care of your babies."

Suddenly the kitchen door slammed. "Damn it Gert. I've had a lousy day. A new idiot supervisor from Washington walked in and started spouting orders on preparing for closing. He hasn't even toured the fort. Now I walk in and nothing is started for supper."

With her hands on her hips she stared at her husband. "Hold it. My day has not been a bed of roses. I'm just thankful Comfort is away and out of the tumult."

—⁂—

On the carriage road, working gingerly, everyone and everything was removed from the coach that teetered on the edge of toppling. As the sun was getting lower in the sky, a wagon pulled up beside the stranded travelers. "Heard you needed a lift."

Jacob whooped while tossing his arms over his head, "Frank Ryan, I never thought I'd be so happy to see your ugly face."

"That's a great greeting for your brother-in-law who is now your rescuer. I was waiting for you at the stage station when I heard about the driver and the run-away team. I got here as fast as possible. Where's my little granddaughter? I'm sure her Gramma is going frantic waiting for us."

"Hey Gramps. She's right here." Cece was hanging on so tight to Dan he wondered if his face was blue.

"Danny. My God, Hanna will be so glad to see you. What a great surprise."

"Cece, you remember Grampa Ryan?" She lifted her head off her brother's shoulder and gave Frank an uncertain wave.

Jacob lifted the little traveler into the wagon. "She's had an afternoon with more excitement than if she were home. Right Cece?"

—m—

On Indian Island, Tim's walk had taken some nasty turns. By the time he got to the beginning of the path he realized the weakness in his legs. But stubborn, as many men tend to be, he pushed on. Losing balance at one point, he fell into the thistle weed on the edge of the precipice over the river. Jack came along and lifted Tim back to his feet ignoring a tirade at how he could do it himself. Kate finally took his hand and gently talked him back to the trail realizing how fortunate it was that Nana insisted they double bandage his slowly healing wound. Looking over the rock face, Marisol could see just how well the flat rock was hidden from prying eyes. She turned to find Jack grinning. Her face turned bright red, not from embarrassment but from the sudden heat coursing through her body.

It took two grueling hours to move Tim to Joe's house. He rested rock to rock then sat on the steps of ledge and used his trembling legs to push himself up one stair at a time with an occasionally lift from Jack. With the house in sight Marisol lost her patience, grabbed her twin around his waist and half walked, half dragged him to the porch. Tim demanded that she stop being so pushy. She in turn told him she'd stop the minute he ceased being so pig-headed.

Taking on the job of referee, Jack stopped the squabble then gave Tim a hand up to the porch. Once settled in Frankie's room, the weary patient fell into a deep sleep under a quilt decorated with an appliquéd schooner on every other square.

Marisol and Kate caught their breaths sitting on the steps of Joe's porch listening to the soothing sound of water gently lapping against the rocks along the shore of the Penobscot River. Not a word was spoken until Jack wiggled in between them. "I believe you both had quite a day."

"I'm sorry my brother made it so difficult. Our father could be very obstinate and I'm afraid some of that rubbed off on him."

"And I wonder who received the remaining willful attitude. Hmm? I bet you two were bickering before you were born."

Holding back an elbow jab in Jack's side, Marisol just gave him an exhausted grin. "My Mum did tell me she felt we were boxing once in a while."

Jack stood, took their hands and pulled both the girls up. "I'd say both of you need to take yourselves back to Adele's to freshen up and get some rest. I'm going out back to help Joe get some of the early potatoes up."

Kate stretched out the kinks from just sitting, even though briefly. "I'll go tell Annie we're going."

Putting his arm around Marisol's neck, he pulled closer to whisper in her ear. "See that wigwam down the path? Dan, JJ and Uncle Jacob are gone so I'm going to be rattling around in there all alone tonight. You don't want me to be lonely do you?"

Not overcoming the impulse, she gave him a good sharp elbow jab in the ribs. "Are you daft?"

"No, just day dreaming." With a quick kiss on the cheek he set her free and trotted off to the gardens.

With a deep sigh, Marisol released her long dark hair from a black velvet ribbon and shook it free with her fingers.

Kate bounced down the porch steps. "Come on friend, I doubt Tim wakes until morning. We need to have Adele make your favorite coffee and bring Nana up to date. She has been beside herself with worry and it is beginning to drag on her health.

As they walked past the wigwam, Marisol heaved another deep sigh.

"Is there something wrong?"

"It's just been a trying day. Tim is changing. He's bitter. I worry about his future and how he will fight this melancholy frame of mind."

Kate took Marisol's hand. "I won't give up on him, I promise. But I will confess there were moments today when I wished I was with Cece in the peace and quiet of a trip to Aroostook County.

XXXI

Four Weeks

News of the stagecoach accident travelled quickly to the Bangor area nearly tearing Gert's heart in two. "She must have been so frightened. I pray they send me a message soon or I'll go out of my mind."

Peg was holding small pieces of cloth up to the windows to find the perfect material for Nana's curtains. Gert was doing her best to keep her mind on the flowers she was painting randomly on the walls while tears formed at unexpected moments.

"Look, this is absolutely perfect." The pattern of tiny rosebuds and violets picked up the colors in Gert's palette. "Nana will be surrounded by some of her favorite things. Yes, this is perfect."

Both ladies were on pins and needles so jumped when the back door slammed. Sean poked his head in the bedroom door. "We received a telegraph message at the Bangor office and they forwarded it to the fort."

Gert spun around so fast she lost her balance and stumbled into her husband's arms. "Let me see it. Did you read it?"

"Settle down." He pulled her over to a kitchen chair. "Sit. Just take a deep breath."

WESTERN UNION: Everyone fine STOP Hanna and Cece bonded quickly STOP No worries STOP Jacob

Gert buried her head in her arms on the kitchen table and sobbed in relief.

The accident also brought worry to Indian Island until a telegraph was delivered to Kate. "WESTERN UNION: All fine STOP few bumps/bruises STOP Mother still not happy STOP JJ"

Relieved, the residents of both locations were able to get back to the tasks at hand. Hours turned into days, days into a week, with plans to start the move early August. With Cece away, Gert finished decorating the walls and was deciding what to do about the paw print floor. Blueberry picking would have to wait until Jack got home but some new potatoes were packed in the root cellar.

Tim was improving in strength but not in attitude. His sister was nearly drained of her patience. For a couple days Nana made the walk along the river with Kate so she could read to him but nothing could break through his hard protective shell. It was hoped once settled in a steady routine at the Ryan's, he would perk up. Time would tell.

To start the second week, Sean and Joey hung the new bedroom door to keep Lady from making more designs while they put down two coats of popular olive green floor paint.

An apple almost hit Sean on the head as he passed through their little orchard. He knew it would be sour but always liked them that way early in the season so took a big bite. Shocking the taste buds, his eyes squeezed tight and body gave a little shiver. Approaching the chicken coop, a thump-thump caught his attention. Gert had Nana's braided rug over the clothesline and was whacking it with her heart-shaped wire beater.

"Hey, Gertrude, what did that poor rug do to make you so angry?"

"It's not the rug." She wound up and gave the carpet another full force wallop. "But the rage helps in pounding out the dust." Thump! A cloud of powdery dirt flew over Sean making him sneeze and toss away the now soiled apple. "Your mother sent a letter. Go read it and see if you might like to take a whack."

Sean removed his work boots outside the back door. *No sense making her any madder.* The offending note sat on the kitchen table.

July 25, 1868

Dear Sean and Gertrude,

Your Comfort is such a delight. She's determined to be called Cece because the other name belongs to her Mama and Papa. It did not take her long to rid herself of shyness and enjoys every minute of the day. It's too bad her Uncle Peter moved out of the area. Her cousins would have had such fun. It would be wonderful if all three of our sons could come here at the same time. There are still tales floating around of the Ryan boys, Peter, Joe and Sean.

I don't think Frank and I have ever seen such an inquisitive child of her age. Each day it seems she teaches us just as much as she learns from us.

I'm sure she is going to tell you about our incident yesterday so I'll give you my version. Cece loves to sit on the long dock we have built for the village. She can watch the fish dart in and out under the planks. Don't worry, she never goes alone. She and I were watching the clouds in the west. She told me the weather was going to change for a mackerel sky was forming. She loved it best at first when the clouds made lacey patterns like the trim on her doll. While dancing and swinging Lacey in circles, her beautiful curly strawberry red hair came free of the ribbon so was blowing in the breeze. There were two men in a canoe paddling by. They looked like lumbermen scouting the best places to set camp for the winter. Suddenly they swung to the dock. We backed to the shore when one of the men jumped out. He asked Cece what she was doing here? Did someone force her to come here? Why are you with this squaw?"

Now Sean was getting hot under the collar. Pouring himself a glass of water he walked around the table a couple times to settle down. Then read on.

She stomped her foot and told him I was her Gramma Hanna then with all her might kicked him in the shin. You could hear his yelp echoing up the river. He tried to grab Cece calling her nothing I would repeat. Jacob shouted while running down the slope with Frank and Dan. The intruder turned tail to the canoe. Jacob laughed because he didn't know white men could paddle so fast.

Speaking of Dan, you must be so proud of the man he has become. His grandfather and I certainly are.

After all the excitement, that night Cece and I slept in Nuga's wigwam. Even after all these years her home is the center of our town and we do our best to maintain it. Cece listened to all the stories about Nuga's possessions and sat proudly when she wore the pointed Micmac princess hat. She felt her great-great grandmother was giving her a warm hug and I believe it.

Sean smiled. "And so do I."

With love,

Mother

"Let me have the rug beater. I'll work on the other side." Sean began some whacking of his own. "This could become the cleanest rug along the Penobscot River"

"Sean, when will it ever end? When will men accept each other no matter the difference?"

"Perhaps Comfort will see it. But never in our lifetimes."

—w—

At Indian Island, Marisol was getting impatient. The wait for the move to the next phase of her life seemed to be taking forever. She firmly believed Tim would improve surrounded by those close to him, not to say Joe and Annie had not tried. Holly and Frankie loved him, read stories to him and made every effort to include him as their new Uncle Tim. But he rarely saw his Aunt Fiona. He was the only one allowed to call her that.

Kate had meetings with the Bangor and Orono school leaders that morning so Marisol was alone on the path to Joes. At one point she rested on a random log tossed high during a spring drive. It didn't take her long to realize the log was now home to more than one family of ants. They were not the biting red ones or the larger carpenter ants that are dangerous for your home, just plain black ants that make your life miserable when carrying away crumbs from your picnic or getting in your clothing giving you the creeps. The latter is where Marisol found herself. She was flapping her skirt and jumping up and down to try to dislodge some of the trespassers.

"Say there Sunshine, is that the newest dance craze from the seacoast society?"

"Jack, that's not funny. I accidently sat on an ant's nest and they are driving me crazy."

"Come here." He pulled her to him and began to look down the front of her blouse.

"John Ryan, you are incorrigible. People can see you."

"Well, let's take care of that problem." He picked her up and carried her into the forest and leaned her against a large old growth pine tree. "No one will see us here so let's get those unwanted insects out of there." He unbuttoned her blouse. "There's one." The ant was protesting with all six flailing legs.

"You promise not to bother my lady and she'll promise not to sit on your house." He tossed the critter away.

"I can feel at least two on my back."

"Take off your blouse and let me check the back of your chemise. Here's the intruder and his partner is further down." His hand slipped down her back to snatch another. "How about your knickers?"

"They are just fine thank you. The others must have climbed up, then into my blouse."

"What a missed opportunity for me to say what we all know. You tend to have ants in your pants."

She melted in tears against his chest. He tipped her chin up and kissed the tears on each cheek. "What's bothering you?"

"I need to get away. I need a break from all the illness, stress, sudden ups and downs and Tim pushing me away. Kate is able to pick up his spirits more than I can and frankly, that hurts. I need to see my aunt and friends in Searsport, at least just for a while. I feel lost and I want to find myself again."

"You're not lost. You are right here beside me." He pulled her closer and ran his hands up and down her back. "But I can understand your need for some time away. I was planning to go help my mother with the blueberries and this would be a good time. When are you planning to leave?"

Marisol hardly took a minute. "Right now." She took a deep breath. "Yes right away. I'll put a few things together, say goodbye to Nana and Adele, and pick up everything else when Tim is moved to Prospect Ferry."

"I like a woman that can make a decision without studying all the ramifications. But I also worry about one that has no problem quickly jumping into a new situation. Should I worry?"

Marisol just smiled. "Why don't you run into the community house and tell Kate. I have a feeling she'll love the idea of having Tim all to herself and I know he will have no problem doing without my nagging."

—⁓—

At Prospect Ferry, after starting the stew, Gert slipped off her shoes and grabbed a cookie off the sideboard to nibble while rocking off a bit of tension. With a heavy leap, Lady joined her mistress for some loving. "You know Lady, I forget Comfort is away so make too many cookies at a time. She better get home soon or you'll see me rolling down the Ferry Road to the get the mail." Suddenly something ran across her feet. "What was that Lady? You've never let me down when it comes to mice. You know how I hate mice." Just then something scampered across her instep. She picked up her feet and shook them. "Lady, don't just lay here. Do something!" She tried to see past the mass of hair on the bulky body but it wasn't until she stopped yelling and started listening that she heard the soft chorus of mews. "No, not so soon." Sliding her big baby on the floor, she saw four tiny kittens. "How did you get out?"

Gert gathered the very young coon cats and carried them back to the basket just as Comfort's Princess made a nosedive to the floor from the edge. The kitten never had a chance to run before it was unceremoniously scooped up and plunked back with her siblings. The last kitten, the one that looks so much like Lady, was more laid back and just waited for all the others to return. Their mother hopped in and immediately the litter began massaging her belly with their paws as they suckled. "Now I miss Comfort. She would make a perfect kitten wrangler."

When Lady finished her motherly duties, Gert slipped a piece of chicken coop wire over the basket then forced herself to get back to work. The pace set to get ready for the move was taking a toll. Putting her hands on her hips, she stared at the rolled up braided rug on the porch. Then with an 'oomph' began to slowly push the carpet in the kitchen door.

"Hey Lady, could you use a hand?"

Gert snapped up so quickly she nearly toppled over the porch rail. "Jack Ryan. You nearly scared the life out of me." With a moment to regain her senses she hugged her son. "You are a very welcome sight."

"How about me?" Marisol peeked from behind Jack.

"You're travelling with this scalawag?" With a hug, Gert could feel just how difficult Tim's ordeal has been for his sister. "If you lose any more weight my dear, you'll blow away in the wind. Peg and I can do something about that. How did you get away?"

"It was a mutual decision. Tim is getting stronger and we both needed a break from each other. I know he will have all the care he needs from Kate. What are you trying to do Gert?"

"I want to get this on the floor in Nana's room."

"Consider it done." Jack walked to the mid-point of the roll, hauled it up under his arm and carried it in. "Point the way."

It took only minutes for the three to lay the rug. Marisol was amazed at the addition. "This is beautiful. With the paintings and curtains Nana will be surrounded by her favorite things."

Jack kissed his mother on the cheek. "You did good Ma. Oh, I nearly forgot, they gave me a letter for you on the ride over on the ferry." He pointed at Lady's basket. "Are you bringing in the chickens to save your walk for eggs?"

As she began to open her letter she told him to take a look.

Marisol let out an excited squeal as loud as Cece's. "How many?"

"Six."

Jack picked up the black one with a white ruff. "You did well Lady. This one even looks like you." As the kittens began to scramble up the wicker, Jack could see the need of the wire and quickly set it back.

Gert settled at the table. "The tea is hot so please help me get rid of the newest batch of lumberjacks." They were Jack's favorite big molasses cookies.

August 4, 1868

My Dear Gert,

Cece is with Ben and I. JJ brought her up in the canoe and she helped with paddling. She is settled in Kate's room. I was in hopes Kate would be in there with her. I pray she knows what she is doing devoting herself so quickly to this young man. I know, Ben and I were committed to our future in our early teens and married on his eighteenth birthday. How can I judge?

Dan and JJ are off to the potato fields to inspect the crop and check on the hands. T is just what we needed to pull together a harvest plan. Cara and my mother chatter in the kitchen like they have known each other for years. I imagine there was the same bond between Cara and Nana. It is a shame that this help for us was the result of such a tragedy. Cece visited both and was quite happy with their new homes.

I have my writing desk in my lap on the porch so I can keep an eye on Cece. I know you can picture this. She is at the top of the large boulder near the river. I know she feels like the "queen of the world" and spends time telling stories to Lacey. Remember when we used to clamor over that rock and figure out what mischief we could pull on the boys?

I must tell you, yesterday Dan took her down the overgrown path to your father's cabin.

"No. I was hoping Dan would not do that. Why did he have to?"

"What's wrong Ma?"

"Let me finish and we'll talk about it."

He told her the story of you living there and working in the potato fields. She is quite proud of her mother making such a nice house for her family.

Cece will be here for three more days and then back to Smytheville until the trip back to Prospect Ferry. She is a joy and I will surely miss her. She has promised to send me notes.

You are ever in my heart, dear friend ~

Nettie

"Comfort is doing well. Dan walked her to my old family cabin near the Thorpe Farm fields. Nettie said the path is fairly grown in so I can imagine what the cabin looks like. It was falling down around my parent's ears last time I saw them."

"Ma, I remember going to your home. I saw my grandfather on the porch. He smiled at Joey and me and asked how our mother told us apart. He gave us each a penny and I still have mine. We kept it a secret because I don't think Mike and Danny got one."

"I never knew he cared."

"So let Cece have her peek at your past."

Gert jumped up at the sound of a wagon out front. "Wonderful! They are delivering the armoire, brass bed and new mattress. You two arrived in the nick of time."

By the time Sean arrived home, the room had been transformed from a shell of a project to a cozy sanctuary for Nana's soul. They needed to bring a few things out of storage in the barn. There was a crate of books for the shelves Sean built next to the door, a washstand with bowl and pitcher Nana had put away for one of Gert's children, and her original rocking chair from the porch. The precious bundle of Captain Hodge's letters were taken from the parlor mantle and placed on a reading table next to her chair.

Gert held up an unfinished covering that was displayed in the parlor. "The only undertaking not complete is her new quilt. Peg hosted a bee with several ladies who constructed a top of alternating squares of remnants from the new floral curtains and bleached muslin. We found an old wool blanket in the barn that was washed to be used for the lining but no one had enough fabric for the backing."

"Let me take that to Searsport. Aunt Daphne may be able to help."

"When are you leaving?"

"I'm going to catch a river schooner as soon as I catch my breath. Is it possible for someone to pick me up Monday so I can bring back some winter clothes and a few more personal items?"

Jack winked. "Consider it done."

The next morning was glorious. Once Gert finished tending to her kitchen garden and Sean was off to the fort, she set some coffee to boil as a surprise. It didn't take long for Marisol to almost float out to the kitchen with great expectations. After a few sips of her favorite beverage, she went out to bask in the fresh air wafting gently from the river. Her long, freshly brushed, coal-black hair glistened in the morning sun.

Coming out of the wigwam, Jack nearly fell over an errant tree limb that fell in the path overnight. He couldn't see anything but the vision on the porch that set his heart to flutter. Coming up the steps he shouted to his mother. "Did you know there was an angel out here?"

Gert shouted out the kitchen winidow. "Drop the Irish malarkey and bring your angel in for breakfast."

"I didn't realize how hungry I was. Thank you Gert. Now I'm ready for the day."

As Gert rinsed the dishes, Marisol began to wipe and stack them on the open shelves. "Are you leaving us today?"

"No. I need to rest another day and take the early boat in the morning."

"I was hoping you would say that." Gert handed both Marisol and Jack a galvanized bucket with a wooden handle on the carrying wire. "I'd like to save some of the blueberries from the birds."

Jack filled his canteen with water. "We better go before the sun gets high."

Walking up the hill into the woods across the street from Nana's lot, they soon found the blueberry fields. Most were the low-to-the-ground berries but some along the edge of the clearing were knee-high with a bit bigger berries.

Jack pointed towards Waldo Mountain. "Look over there."

Between the trees you could see a covering of the higher slopes that looked like a blue carpet. "I've never seen anything like it."

They separated and picked, berry-by-berry, bush-by-bush. "Have you tasted any?"

Marisol looked a bit dubious but plunked a few berries in her mouth and smiled in appreciation. Soon it became a handful for the pail, then a few for the mouth.

As the sun began to beat on their backs and Jack called for a break. Sitting under a canopy of leaves, they shared the cool water. "I'd say just another half hour we should have enough between us to make a full pail. That's what she needs for now. I'll come picking after you leave."

On their way back through the woods, Jack stopped and pointed to a tall boulder. He lifted her to the top and scrambled up next. "Look over there."

Focusing through a gap in the leaves she saw the magnificent river view from the hill.

"Someday I'm going to build a home right here. The timber will come from the stand of trees around us and then that view will be from the front porch and the large window I'll put in the parlor."

"That's quite a dream, Jack."

"Don't you have dreams Marisol? That's what keeps me going."

"Dreams are just that and they disappear in the same thin air in which they come. You can't live your life daydreaming. To survive you must deal with reality."

"I have a plan with Nana. Once I have saved enough for a fair down payment, she is going to let me buy this lot. That's why I odd job as much as I can, sometimes at the brick factory, at times logging for the sawmill, and working the fields at the Hodge Farm. Most goes straight to the bank. Will you share this dream with me Marisol? It may take a while but this could be our future."

Marisol took a moment to look around. "We would call our home Blueberry Hill."

He jumped down. Marisol slid down landing in his arms. "Let me give you a tour. Right where these twin pine trees entwine their branches is where I will place our bedroom. I think we should try it out for size, just don't tip the blueberry bucket."

He picked up a giggling Marisol and settled her in the softness of the pine needles.

XXXII

Rags to Riches

Since she was unexpected, Marisol walked from the landing in Searsport Harbor to her aunt's shop. The hill was long and the quilt heavy along with her travel bag, so she was breathless by the time she turned the corner to the fabric shop. The "closed" sign was posted in the inside of the door window. She knocked but there was no reply. *She never closes mid-week.* Worried, she went into the shop next door. "Has anyone seen my aunt?"

"Marisol we haven't seen you since you left with that Indian fellow. Is it true you have been staying at Indian Island? Did your brother die in the fire at the Hodge Farm?"

"My brother is alive and well, thank you. Where I have been is none of your business. Have you seen my aunt?"

"Wow you sure haven't changed your uppity ways. If you kept in touch, you would know that Daphne is closed Wednesday mornings as it is the slowest time of the week. She is most likely at home if not at the market."

Out on the street she had a talk with herself. *For heaven's sake, it's just a few blocks. You've lived through Tim's near death, worked as a hand in the fields, picked blueberries in the hot sun and even jumped in the river to save a boy. Get yourself together and walk.*

Two friends from the Methodist Church walked by and smiled. She heard them giggling behind her back as she caught her reflection in a storefront. *Good grief. Why didn't you change your walking shoes and do something with your hair? You're a mess. So what. Who do they think they are? They certainly are no better than I and their lazy asses can't compare to anyone at Prospect Ferry and the island. Come on, you're half way there. Pick up your head and let them giggle. They don't have a Blueberry Hill to daydream about.*

Turning the corner to Mount Ephraim Road, Marisol was about to drop the quilt when she reached the front steps to Aunt Daphne's house. *Please be home.* Between knocking and peeking through the window on the small entry porch, it was soon evident she was not around. This was not the reunion she wanted. *Where are you?* Marisol tipped the terra cotta plant pot very carefully so as not to upset the large Boston fern that was summering near the front door. *Yes, thank you.* She finally dislodged the spare door key from a combination of sticky mud and cobwebs. She was amazed the slightly bent, long brass opener still worked. Once inside she dropped her bundles and ran out the kitchen door to the privy. Second on her mind was to put on the teakettle and then check the ice-box for any leftovers.

After a hot cup of black tea, a chunk of cheese and a cream of tartar biscuit, Marisol left her boots in the kitchen and curled up on the overstuffed sofa in the sitting room. Deep asleep for an hour, she never heard her aunt come through the door and drop several packages on the kitchen floor.

After the groceries were put away, Daphne couldn't wait any longer and nudged her niece on her shoulder which startled Marisol so, she sat straight up with a half-swallowed scream.

"I didn't mean to scare you, dear but I was quite afraid to poke my head in the house when I found the door unlocked. So let's say we're even. Give me a hug."

So thus her five-day sojourn to Searsport began where she could laugh with old stories, walk the harbor side, enjoy rough seas against the rocky Maine coast, and sit in the healing sunshine without worrying about her next step with Tim. She could not bring herself to go near the ship-building docks but enjoyed sitting on the hill above them thoroughly amazed at the size of the newest schooner under construction. There were now eighteen builders along the harbor. With a deep sigh she re-ran memories of her beloved father and his tales of the sea. She wondered if Tim would ever have the strength in his hand to follow his dream of being captain of his own ship.

In the evening, she and Daphne reminisced about London, art galleries and concerts. Daphne solved the backing problem on Nana's quilt by stitching together three long cuts of a soft green cotton fabric. When Marisol was ready, she told her aunt of Tim's ordeal and how the care of the Penobscot Indians carried him through. They laughed at how Cece organized the spirit dance. During these lovely girl talk evenings they tied the layers of the quilt together with tight little knots. Daphne was going to take it to the shop to work on the binding on the edges between customers.

With a couple nice soaking baths and extra sleep, Marisol was finally relaxing. She promised Daphne she'd come out of hiding and face the residents by going to the pastry shop for a treat Saturday morning. She went through her clothes and laughed at the fancy outfits she would never use on the river. A small pile of sweaters, two skirts, four blouses, a dress, a heavy wool coat, hat and gloves and shawl would go back with her. Aunt Daphne gave her material for aprons and work skirts. She also was sending material for baby clothes. Everything else would be given to the charity at the church for the poor.

"Are you sure you are not jumping too fast?"

"Aunt Daphne, my heart now belongs at Prospect Ferry. If my wish should not come true, I could never come back to the mind set among many here especially when it comes to the Penobscot people. I won't be that far away."

"What about your brother?"

"He is very sweet on Kate. She will be living and teaching on Indian Island so I'm not sure about his plans. He could be on the sea with just visits to the area."

Saturday turned lovely after just a bit of fog that burned off quickly. Marisol brushed her hair to a sheen, pulling the sides to the top of her head and held with an azure blue ribbon that made her eyes look even bigger. She chose a plain navy blue skirt and smocked white blouse. Gathering her courage, she walked down Main Street with Aunt Daphne, head held high. The fresh-baked currant scone with lemon curd and cup of fragrant coffee brought a smile. If she had seen the man at the corner table, it would not have lasted.

The bell on the fancy glass door jingled as they left. The man followed, stopping at the counter to pay his bill. He had some difficulty getting the coins out of the bottom of his leather purse since he was missing a finger.

At Prospect Ferry, Sean and Gert worked the morning in their family garden. Crops were beginning to come in and they wanted none to go to waste. Sean filled the barrel in the cellar with fresh sand so they could begin storing the carrots. Gert started making blueberry jam, boiling the berries with sugar until the mixture thickened. She had to keep her eye for the setting point when a skin formed. Jack brought over an unopened box of Mason jars from the barn. Nana had ordered the improved design for preserving this season. There was no sense in not using them. In the meantime she put together a blueberry cake with the leftover berries from the first pail. Once the thick hot mixture was poured into the jars, she stored them upside down until they cooled.

"Do I smell blueberry cake? Please say yes." Jack popped into the kitchen like a primitive jack-in-the-box. "I'll swap you a letter from Aroostook County for a chunk of it."

Gert grabbed it out of his hand and went to the kitchen table. "Help yourself." Sean read over her shoulder.

August 9, 1868

Dear Sean and Gert,

It is going to be hard to send Cece off on the coach. She is getting anxious to see how the kittens are growing, especially her Princess. It's hard for me to imagine Sean having two cats in the house since he never liked them. She's also excited about starting school. Frankly, I feel the schoolmaster is going to have his hands full keeping her interest.

Dan has spent much of his time with Jacob. They walk the boundary of Smytheville every morning making sure every bit of the fieldstone wall is in place. Of course they are only doing their favorite thing–joining with the forest and all the creatures therein. They hardly ever speak but communicate more than those who rattle on. I can see Jacob in Dan in looks, mannerisms and love of our village.

Gert's heart sank a bit.

After much pleading, Cece made the morning boundry trip with them yesterday, proudly going off on Dan's shoulders. They make short walks each day and she comes home with another tale about her father and his brothers. Sean, you better be prepared for questions. She has me saying 'I not know' many times. Believe it or not, the beaver dam is still active after all these years and she has become fascinated by the creatures. (Don't worry, she is well watched.) They found a good-sized beehive the other day. She wanted to hang around to see if a bear came. We got a good amount of honey from that one.

All in all we have had a marvelous time. Don't be surprised if she wants a fiddle like her Grampa Frank plays.

I trust you have been able to get the addition to the house ready for Nana during this Cece break. We are quite proud of the way you are caring for the Hodge family.

We send our love from Aroostook County.

With love,

Mother

Sean didn't like what he read. "Why did he have to take her to the beaver pond?"

"That's was a big part of your background, Sean."

"I bet he let her swim."

Gert stood up for her son. "Don't be foolish, she doesn't know how to swim and Dan wouldn't be so careless.

In Searsport Marisol was rushing to make the bank as they closed early on Saturday. She planned to make a withdrawal to open an account in Bangor. Then Daphne and her niece browsed the Searsport stores hunting for just the right thing, at times giggling like schoolgirls. Window-shopping along the brick sidewalk, Marisol stopped with a shiver. "I keep feeling someone watching me."

"It's most likely because you are carrying an envelope of currency and are afraid someone saw you make the transaction. We're not anywhere near the docks but from the look of your foot-wear, I would suggest the shoe store."

Marisol bought herself a pair of work boots that fit and some practical winter galoshes. At the lady's store she purchased three new pair of knickers, two plain chemises and one with lace and tiny bows. When she held this one up a smile crossed her face and her cheeks turned rosy. She finished at that department with two new flannel nightgowns, one with tiny daisies. The other embellished with delicate embroidery around the collar with a matching bathrobe. "I don't think my silk nighties and dressing gowns would do me well along the river this winter. But please save them in my wardrobe as I bought them in London and may have a want for them some day." As she passed through the children's section, she bought a flannel nightgown set for Cece much like her own.

Back at Daphne's house, Marisol felt much more like herself. "Auntie, I want to take you to the Inn at the Harbor for dinner. I think we deserve it." Marisol rescued one of her discarded silk dresses and gussied up a bit. She pushed her hair back in a chignon and pinned a large silk rose to the side of it. She slipped on a pair of high-buttoned shoes, pinched her cheeks pink and added a bit of bees wax gloss to her lips.

At the inn, they were warmly welcomed and given her favorite table by the large window overlooking the harbor. Dinner was a savory soup, thin sliced roast pork, potatoes whipped with cream and butter, tiny carrots glazed with honey, and fresh-baked, small, clover dinner rolls. With a demitasse of rich black coffee, Daphne enjoyed a lemon tartlet topped high with meringue and Marisol practically hummed her way through an éclair, which matched those at the cafes in Paris.

Daphne gently felt the soft petals of the pink rose in the cut glass bud vase placed between them on the linen covered table. "Tell me dear niece, when are you going to tell your Jack that you and Tim inherited your father's share of the shipping company and you are quite wealthy?"

"In time Auntie, in time."

XXXIII

REUNIONS

By camping over night, Jack was in Daphne's cheery kitchen for breakfast with Marisol Monday morning. He was giddy to see her and could not believe how much he could miss someone. "I like your new work shoes."

Marisol grinned and handed him his old pair. "Do you want these back?"

"Afraid they passed fitting several years ago. I suggest a proper burial."

"Consider it done." Daphne laughed out loud as she gingerly picked up the boots with her thumb and middle finger.

Once the wagon was loaded, Marisol hugged her aunt. "I'll be back to visit, don't worry. And I promise to send lots of notes about Tim's progress."

Jack shouted from the wagon seat. "I nearly forgot. My mother said to tell you she has been sketching for your paintings."

With one last hug, Daphne whispered a warning. "He adores you. Secrets have a way of getting out. Don't let him hear your situation from anyone but you."

In Prospect Ferry, Sean passed Gert sitting on the back steps as he left for work. She was chewing her nails. "I haven't seen you bite your fingernails in years. What's the problem? Did I do something wrong again?"

"Cece will be boarding the coach just about now. She's leaving her Uncle Jacob behind. She's probably afraid of another crash and he won't be there."

"She's in good hands with her big brother. He'll keep her feeling safe."

"I don't like thinking she is going to be scared for a couple days. I won't be happy until she's in my arms."

"Keep yourself busy, Gert. Go find another rug to beat. Your reunion is coming."

On the Aroostook River, Cece had been up at dawn to be ready for one of Uncle Jacob's special breakfasts. He was known for his fabulous flapjacks with axmen trying to get jobs wherever he was working. But this morning all his skills were for his grandniece and he did not disappoint. The butter-topped pancakes were fluffy and drowned in maple syrup boiled down that spring. Jacob browned the thick-cut slab bacon to perfection.

Once her sticky fingers were washed, Cece and Hanna checked her packed bags one more time. They almost couldn't close it with the addition of her new sweater and jumper her grandmother made, and the hat with matching mittens Nettie knitted. She ran around and hugged everyone not out hunting for game or fishing. She promised her young playmates she would write as soon as she learned to.

As the canoe with JJ and his parents came into sight at the bend in the river, Cece ran back up the slope. "I have to go talk with Nuga."

No one said a word. "I'll keep an eye on her." Jacob followed her to the wigwam.

While everyone else was loading Frank's wagon, Jacob pushed the skin flap back just a bit to peek inside. Cece was sitting cross legged beneath the pole that held Nuga's hat with an old hand woven blanket wrapped around her. She was hugging a small piece of pottery decorated with Micmac symbols that Nuga crafted as a young girl in New Brunswick. In the eathernware was an eagle feather Jacob had never seen before, Her face was tilted up with eyes shut. *I honor you with a gift from the great eagle that lives near my house on the Penobscot River. May his spirit soar with yours.*

Outside a strong Indian leader who led his family through years of adversity watched with a tear slowly sliding down his weathered cheek. He thought of his grandmother, her strength and wise leadership. *I have no doubt this child can hear Nuga in her heart.*

After another round of goodbyes, and a minute where Cece did not want to unwrap from around Jacob's neck, the wagon was off with her waving until out of sight.

At the stage office, the scene repeated with Frank and Hanna who had some of the same concerns as Gert. As Dan lifted her into the stage, she wondered if the dogs would scare the horses again so they would run away. If they did, she wanted to be awake for the excitement. Her grandparents just tossed up their arms with laughter. Cece was off on the last leg on her adventure.

At Indian Island, things were buzzing with preparations for Nana and Tim's move to the Ryan home the next day. Tomah and Kate would take them down in the wagon. There really wasn't a lot to pack beside a good-sized basket of things for Peg's baby, a few clothes for Tim, and what clothes Nana was given after the fire. Adele knitted her an Irish pattern cardigan and crocheted a soft shawl to keep her warm from chilly drafts. Tim was improving daily from his injuries but still not in his attitude. It was said by many, Kate had the patience of Job when it came to his outbursts of self-pity and anger over the loss of use in his right hand. He obviously cared deeply for Kate but the only one who soothed his soul was Nana. He started using a tall sturdy stick to aid his walk on the river path to visit his newfound aunt whenever the weather permitted. Kate walked back with him to share the evening meal at Joe's home. Tonight would be their last time.

A great deal of the ride up from Searsport was spent in quiet. It turned out that Jack and Marisol didn't need a lot of conversation to communicate which was surprising from a couple who spent most of their time bickering when they first met. After enjoying a basket lunch provided by Daphne during a break in Stockton, Marisol tried to engage Jack in casual chat about his background.

"What you see is pretty much what it has always been. I've lived in our house over many transformations, which included the death of our oldest brother Mike. The war ended at the age where Joey and I wanted to join, much to my mother's relief. And as for you, you were obviously privileged as a child in London, I assume because your father was a ship's captain. It's a shame both your parents are deceased and you needed to relocate but I am happy you chose Searsport. If a relationship is real, it should make no difference whether haves or have-nots. Do I have it right?"

"Close, but there are always other situations."

"I like our situation just the way it is."

With a snap of the reins, they were off. Barely in sight, a buggy followed carrying two figures shadowed by the dust.

Jack dropped off Marisol and her packages in the front yard so he could take the wagon and Argos back to the barn. Walking in the house, there seemed no one home. "Hello. Hello." She went to the back bedroom with some bundles. "Wow, how did she do all this in a few days?" She hung her shawl on one of the new pegs on the wall and tossed the shopping bags on her bed. It was easy to tell for the other bed was covered with Cece's favorite quilt with birds in every other square. Under the river window was a chest big enough for a good amount of clothes. "She thinks of everything."

Marisol was completely captivated by Nana's bedroom as she arranged the new coverlet. "My goodness, everything is ready for the move. You'd never know hidden under the paint and braided rug, the floor was covered with Lady's footprint artwork." The new brass Oxford bed completed the simple room especially when made up with the matching quilt. Leaving, she turned, looked once again and smiled. "She'll love it."

Lady rubbed against Marisol's leg as she filled the kettle for afternoon tea. "My goodness Lady, you've made me feel at home." She was surprised to get a glimpse of Gert sitting quite still in Cece's swing. "What's wrong with your mother Lady? She's usually bouncing around in perpetual motion."

Gert's mind was so occupied, she never noticed Marisol until startled by a touch on the shoulder. "Penny for your thoughts?"

"They are so rattled right now, they would not even be worth a half penny. I'm so happy to see you home. I'm worrying myself silly thinking about Cece on the stage. What if something happens. Why did I let her go?"

"I have the kettle on. Let's go and pass the time catching up."

Moving day started at dawn. Gert was back to non-stop running around. Joey came by with a wheelbarrow holding a large kettle of baked beans, a big basket of biscuits and dozens of cookies. Jack laughed saying the Ryans never go hungry as he stirred his mother's turkey stew thick with a plethora of fresh root vegetables.

The quilt took Peg's breath away. It was far beyond the ideas at the quilting parties.

Marisol gave the front bedroom the once over and unpacked the few clothes Tim had with him before the fire. She organized a shelf with a few books brought back from Searsport and placed a gilt framed tintype of their father on the bedside table shared by the two beds. *Please give these good people a chance to help you recover.*

Breathless, Jack ran in to grab his sweetheart by the hand. "Let's go little lady, Ma's spotted Tomah's wagon coming down the Brewer Road. She's already gone to the fort to get Pa."

It was obvious that the horse was not used to being on a cross-river ferry and was making his dislike known. Once at the landing, he was more than anxious to get off and needed Tomah to help quiet him. Nana was on the bench seat hanging on for dear life. Kate was trying to calm Tim who was complaining he was probably going to end up in the Penobscot, but Jack led the steed safely to the Ferry Road. so Tomah could drive the wagon up to the front of the Ryan house.

Nana didn't feel ready to look at the scar that was once her home so kept her eye on the small Ryan orchard. "I've never seen the fruit so plentiful. I'm going to have to get busy with the preserves."

Once Sean and Jack steadied Tim off the back of the wagon, Marisol was finally able to embrace her brother. The tears she had held in check for all these weeks broke through the dam that held in her emotions. "Knock it off Mar. You're getting my shirt wet."

Kate and Gert eased Nana off her seat and held on until she got her bearings.

"I bet both of you would like to freshen up and have a snack before Joey and Peg come for supper. We have enough food in here for an army. Marisol, put the kettle on while Kate and I help Nana up the steps."

Once inside, Nana stood straight with her new root cane Joe fashioned from the big oak tree in front of his house. As a parting gift the village children decorated it with carvings and paintings. At the doorway, Gert took her dear friend's hand and led her into her room. "Welcome home."

The new quilt was a sight to behold as rays of sun made patterns over the delicate flowers then bounced off the rounded corners of the brass headboard. Nana gasped. "It's beautiful Gert, so very beautiful." She sat in the familiar rocking chair and let her eyes digest the rest of her room.

"This is lovely." Kate walked in and gave Nana a kiss on the cheek. "Tomah and I have to head right back as dusk comes sooner now. Tim is already asleep." She turned and hugged Gert. "I don't know how to thank you for opening your home for him."

"My house was starting to get too quiet."

"With Cece coming home and the harvest starting to come in, this place will be hopping before you know it so if you need some peace and quiet, come spend a couple days with me at Indian Island.

Marisol placed a cup of tea and a sugar cookie on Nana's lamp table. "You need to rest."

With no warning Lady hauled her bulky body up on Nana's lap with fine hairs flying in every direction. Blowing the ruff away from her face, Nana laughed. "Why sweet Lady, you've made me feel most very welcome."

Gert opened the lid on a small basket to find the carved river boat with oars. "Shall I put this on the book shelf with Captain Hodge's letters and pipe?

Nana nodded. "I guess not all is lost."

"You have memories of places and adventures we will never have. You have us and we're not going anywhere." Gert helped her to the bed where she barely had the crocheted afghan over her before Nana was sound asleep.

Suddenly all was quiet. Marisol stretched with a yawn. . "Gert, do you mind if I boil up some coffee?"

"Go right ahead. I might even try some of your brew myself."

Sean put a small log in the warming stove should the night take on a chill from the river. "Relax ladies. Cece will be here in the morning so peace and quiet will disappear like leaves in the wind."

Joey and Peg peeked in the backdoor. "Sorry we didn't get over here sooner. Thomas needed help getting some hay bales into the barn."

"Leave the back door open." Gert started setting the table. "It's getting a bit stuffy in here from keeping all this food warm. We'll eat soon and set some aside in case Nana or Tim wake up."

It was still enough in the house to hear the chorus of kittens purring when Peg sat on the floor to pet them.

Suddenly there was a ruckus on the back porch. "Anything to eat in there? There're some hungry travelers out here."

Startled, Gert nearly jumped out of her skin. "What in the world?"

In came Dan with Cece on his shoulders. "We made such good time coming back, the driver decided to go through without another stop for the night. Jack, come help me get the wagon for the luggage at the landing."

Dan turned his little sister over to her Mama who near squeezed her to death.

"Guess what Papa, I went swimming with the beavers where you almost got drownded."

XXXIV

Angry Mackerel Sky

Next morning, Gert was nearly dancing around the house. She had hummed her way through gathering the eggs and feeding the hens. She danced around the kitchen getting Sean off to work and Dan to Joey's house to work the fields, then cooked for her enlarged family still sleeping from travel and excitement. The only other sounds in the kitchen were the kittens doing their best to push away the wire and escape.

"I know babies. I'm not sure where I can keep you so you can eat, run and play without risking Nana or Tim falling over you. It won't be long before you'll be going to your new homes once you can leave Lady."

The little traveler ran out of her bedroom. "I need to play with them and give them Cece-love."

"You do know they can't stay here?" Gert laughed at how such an angel in her pink nightdress could manage such a pout.

"What about my Princess? She's not going anywhere."

"Comfort, you were not told you could keep her."

"So, it is a girl! I knew it. I knew it."

"Your father does not want another cat in the house. He doesn't like cats so for him to first give me Captain and then many years later Lady, was a big surprise to his mother. He has never told me why."

"Cuz, when he was a little boy he was scared by a cat, that's why."

"Who in the world told you that?"

"Gramma Hanna. She said a cat jumped on Papa's back when he was little and he screamed all the way home while the cat hung on by the claws. After that his brothers teased him with cats when they could and made him hate cats."

"Well I'll be. Looks like he truly loves me."

"You think if I promised not to scare him, he'll let me keep Princess?"

"I think it would be best if you never tell him what Hanna said."

"Just what did my grandmother say?" Jack strolled in from the wigwam finger combing his hair.

"It's just girl talk Jack." Gert gave Cece a wink.

"Girl talk you say?" Marisol stretched high as she walked from the back bedroom. You could nearly hear Jack sigh watching her hair fall loosely around her shoulders.

"Good morning Miss Sunshine."

"Good morning Mr. Ryan. If you stand between me and my coffee, I will not be responsible for your safety."

Putting the cups on the table Gert watched Cece take Princess out of the basket leaving five very agitated kittens behind. "Comfort, go put some clothes on for breakfast. Nana should be waking soon and she'll want to see you."

Little green yellow eyes looked up at Cece who in turn gave her Mama a pleading look.

"Go ahead, take Princess but if there are any messes on the floor, you clean up, understand?"

Hugging the strawberry-blonde, tiger-marked coon cat, Cece skipped to her room. "Look Mama, her hair is the same color as mine."

"Do you mind Marisol?"

"Not if she cleans up. I'm going to look in on my brother. He must be starved."

"I left some biscuits and fresh blueberry jam out with a pitcher of water. I suspect he came out for a snack during the night. I'll check on Nana.".

Cece came paddling out barefoot, kitten cuddled in one arm and hairbrush and ribbon in the other hand. "Mama. Mama?"

"In here little girl. I'm in the new room."

Cece peeked around the doorframe and let out with a squeal of delight. "Nana!" She ran and jumped in the lap of the lady more like a grandmother to her and squeezed her tight around the neck much to the displeasure of the kitten.

Nana laughed out loud as the frightened animal escaped and clawed her way up to the back of the wicker rocker still complaining heartedly while trying to balance by leaning against Nana's neck.

Gert had to work hard to get the tiny claws dislodged from the woven reed and calm her pathetic little mews. "You two visit while I take the kitten to her mother for breakfast."

Cece wrestled free from the hugs and jumped up on the new bed. "Nana this is a princess bed. Look, I can see myself in the balls on the spindles. They look like small gold fortune-teller balls. Is this a magic bed that can fly? Look at your new room. It's so pretty. Do you like it?"

"Come on chatter-box. Let Nana catch her breath while I finish brushing your hair so we can tie that bow. Breakfast is on the table for both of you."

"There's Tim. Mama, Tim's here too." Cece ran out to the kitchen and hugged her new friend around his leg. She was careful not to grab his right hand.

"Thanks for leaving the snack out. I couldn't believe how hungry I felt when I woke during the night. That had to be the best biscuits and jam I've ever tasted."

"You're welcome Tim. I'd say you're feeling better this morning."

"I'd say so too."

Nana waved the Hodge twins to the breakfast table, I haven't seen you together for over a week. Marisol, tell me about Daphne?"

Gert snatched Jack by the back of his collar. "Come on. Help me check out the gardens.. Comfort, finish your meal and then give each of those kittens some loving, one at a time."

"Yah!"

On the way out the door, Gert took a moment to look back and smiled deeply.

Jack teased, "Ma, you look like the cat that swallowed the canary."

"It's so satisfying to see my new household members finally together after all the planning and work."

"Well, don't look too smug. In this family, peace of mind does not always last very long."

"That's my Jack, always the wet blanket." She picked up a large handled basket. "Grab the garden fork. I want to take up a row of our potatoes."

And so the day went. The first hours of the new Ryan family circle slipped into a sense of normalcy. Marisol unpacked and was very grateful for the good-sized chest. She walked Tim to the ruins of the Hodge home where he finally released pent up emotions that had kept him from thinking rationally.

"Look at this Mar. This beautiful dream of Captain Hodge destroyed by man's insane loathing of others. I'm even more disturbed by my own closed mind to those I believed were less than I."

Cece played with all of Lady's children each in their own turn. They in turn left her a few messes to clean up.

Mid afternoon, Gert set a small fire in the kitchen corner fireplace. She was building a bank of coals and hot ashes to bake the newly dug potatoes. Jacket potatoes with lots of fresh butter were a favorite for her boys. Joey brought down a young buck that was perfectly aged and she was going to grill steaks in her cast iron spider fry pan over the coals for a welcome home supper.

And what a jovial meal it was. Nana beamed when she saw how far along Peg's baby was coming. Catch-up stories were shared, especially by Cece, about her great adventure and the pretty jumper she was wearing made by her Gramma Hanna. Hardly a bit of crispy potato skin and bite of steak was left when the basket of baby items from Indian Island were displayed as a surprise for Peg.

An out of breath Cece ran in from the back porch. "Mama, the sky is bleeding. It's a mackerel sky and it is all red. Is a bad change coming?"

Even Nana rushed to the porch where the glow from the cloud reflected on the family.

"Wow!" Jack held Marisol's hand as everyone stood in silence watching the brilliant display.

Nana put her hand on Cece's shoulder. "Don't worry your pretty little head. I've seen this before. The sun is getting lower in the western sky and the reflecting light is hitting the rows of clouds at just the right angle to make them turn red and orange. It won't last long."

Cece looked doubtful. "I still think it looks angry."

As the clouds moved on, the color faded to pink and light mauve and the sun poked through ahead of another bank of gray. Peg and Nana sat at the kitchen table watching Gert finish up the dishes. The men relaxed on the porch.

"Jack, come in and help me a minute," said Gert.

"What you need Ma?"

"Put the heavy spider on the bottom shelf under the work counter. My back doesn't like when I do it."

"Well, don't tell me you are getting old." To that he got the elbow in the ribs. Looking through the kitchen window, Jack could see Marisol sitting on the swing with Cece in her lap. They were watching three young eagles taking turns flapping around the nest to strengthen their wings. He let his thoughts slip out loud. "How I love those two girls."

All the ladies looked at each other and smiled broadly.

"Sit down Ma. I'll put the rest of the dishes away and tend to the ashes."

Joining the men on the porch Jack noticed the empty swing swaying in the breeze. "Where did they go?"

"They've gone to the ferry landing to see if the sun will make gold ripples on the water before it goes behind the clouds." Sean noticed his son's frown. "They'll be back soon."

"I might have wanted to see the gold ripples." His twin got a big chuckle out of that one.

Dan pointed to the orchard. "Look at the size of that tom." The turkey was nonchalantly pecking his way past the wigwam, then suddenly ran a few feet and lifted his bulky body to a high branch in the pine. "Guess he's settling in for the night."

Sean laughed whole-heartedly. "He better find a better place to visit when we get closer to Thanksgiving." He turned quickly and asked, "Did you hear something from the woods?"

"Probably it's your laugh still bouncing around the trees." Then Joey stood and listened. "I hear someone yelling for help."

"I hear it." Sean shouted to Gert to get his rifle.

"What's wrong?" Gert ran out with the gun and box of bullets. "Dear God, that's Cece."

"Papa, help. Papa, help!"

As the group ran towards the cries, Joey shouted to Peg to stay with Nana.

Running through the orchard they turned into the woods that ran up to the fort, Gert was frantic. "Cece, where are you?"

"Mama. Help Mama!"

They started to make their way down to the side of Fort Knox and suddenly saw the little girl struggling to get through the brush. Her new jumper was torn and forehead bleeding. Reaching her first, Dan lifted his sister high above the brambles and ran back to Gert.

"Mama. The mean man grabbed my arm but I bit his hand and he pushed me down against a rock. He swung his arm at me but I ducked and started running as hard as I could." Cece was sobbing when her mother took her.

Jack was frantic. Joey and Dan held him back while Sean asked his daughter what happened to Marisol.

"The other bad man grabbed Mary from the back. She yelled for me to run so he put his hand over her mouth and lifted her up and she kicked and kicked." The child sobbed. "Mary! Mary!"

Jack was beside himself. "Where Cece? Point where." She pointed to the front of the fort.

Sean loaded his rifle and put the extra bullets in his pocket. "Gert, take her home. We'll take care of this." Sean and his sons went with such stealth that even the creatures of the forest did not scatter as they moved towards the fort. Sean had closed and locked the main gate and the workers only knew the ways into the tunnels. So if they tried to take her inside the fort, they had to be hiding in the open entrance. Dan signaled for Joey to watch the fort landing in case they had another partner with a boat. The three men crept close to the granite wall towards the gate not disturbing a single pebble on the walk.

As Gert came out of the orchard Peg could see Cece's condition and ran to her mother-in-law. "Where's Marisol?"

"They're looking for her."

Peg started towards the woods. "Joey."

"They're all together. They'll take care of each other. Get the kettle on so I can clean up Cece."

At the top of the stairs to the porch, Nana was clutching her heart while tears dripped off her chin.

A muffled scream could be heard from the darkness of the entrance. Sean raised his hand and raised his fingers, one–two–three. The men were in quicker than an eagle can snatch his prey. Marisol had a gag in her mouth, her blouse was torn off. She was kicking fiercely as Matthew was on his knees trying to pull off her knickers while the second man held her arms to the ground.

"I'll show you what a real man can do, you little whore."

In a flash Dan yanked him up and had the blade of his knife so tight against his throat that it showed blood. Sean pointed his rifle at the accomplice who quickly stood with his hands over his head. It was easy to see his missing finger.

Jack took off his shirt and covered his love's nakedness and removed her gag. Next he pushed the cohort against the bars of the gate and began to pound his face with his fist.

Marisol quickly put on the shirt and grabbed him by the leg and pleaded that he stop.

Sean bellowed sharply. "Jack, stop! Take Marisol home. Cece will be out of her mind with worry."

As Jack carried Marisol out into the fading sunlight, Sean made a promise to her. "Don't worry. This piece of trash will never bother you again."

Matthew screamed at her. "You ruined my life. You're nothing but a spoiled rich bitch. Between your wealth and my connections, we could have ruled Boston society." Dan pressed the blade tighter against the windpipe.

Marisol wept uncontrollably against Jack's neck.

Jack looked like he'd been in a close encounter with a bolt of lightning when he heard of Marisol's wealthy status but comforted her close in his arms as he carried her home.

In the fort entrance both intruders were backed up against the granite wall.

Matt puffed his ego up and spouted disdain at the half-breeds. "Just what do you think you can do about us?"

Sean smiled broadly. "See that hapless black beetle crawling close to your right ear?"

Startled by the creepy-crawly on the wall, Matt jumped to the side just as a shot rang out ending the short life of the creature. The wide-eyed trespasser stared at the barrel of the rifle as the retort of the first shot still bounced from wall to wall in the entrance.

Hearing the shot, Joey ran up from the landing. "What's going on?"

"I was just showing Mr. Roberts what is going to happened when the next bullet goes between his eyes. It might not be as messy as he has no brain."

"You wouldn't dare."

"No? I am the foreman here at the fort and one of my duties is to protect the property. I'd say you and your buddy were caught on fort grounds without my permission and you were up to no good."

"You wouldn't shoot us."

"I bet that beetle felt the same way."

Joey played right along with his father. "Pa, you hate to use bullets. You always tell us they are too expensive."

"I'd take a loan if that's what it took to buy the bullets to make sure this worthless piece of dung stays away from my family." He raised the rifle and aimed at each man. "My, it seems the last time one of your gang messed with my family he wet his pants. Looks like history is repeating."

"You have any other ideas, Pa?"

"We could turn the two over to the fort commander in the morning. Yes, that's what I should do. I'll report they attempted rape on federal property."

The two men paled.

"You didn't know this fort is the property of the United States?"

"What would the commander do Pa?"

"He'd hang them of course."

Unable to control his serious face, Dan quietly turned his face to the wall.

"What to do? What to do?"

"Please Mr. Ryan. I'll never come back this way." Matt's partner in crime stretched his nine fingers high over his head. "Please."

Sean looked at his sons and they nodded.

"Get the hell out of here. Show your ugly face again and charges will be at the fort."

The Ryans controlled their anger as the miserable man tip-toed past Joey on the walk and stumbled away at great speed.

Sean pointed his rifle back at Matt's head. "Now what about you?"

Dan finally spoke. "After what he was trying to do with Mrs. Hodge's niece, let me finish him with my knife and toss him in the river."

"I'd rather not pollute the water." Sean aimed one more time. "You get your sorry ass out of here before Jack returns for I'm sure he'll tear you apart with his bare hands. I don't care where you go but never come back or I'll prove my marksmanship. And this will be reported to Mr. Merithew who in turn will write your uncle. Good luck. You're going to need it."

Dan jumped at him. Out he ran towards the safety of the woods. Sean took aim and took down a few pinecones in his path. One bopped him on the top of his head.

"Let's get out of here. He won't be back but to make sure I don't want any of the girls in the fields without one of you having the gun."

At the house, Jack sat quietly on the back steps with his head in his hands. Inside Peg and Gert were helping Marisol clean up and get her nightclothes on. Cece was curled up in her blanket on Nana's lap.

"I told you it was an angry sky."

XXXV

Thinking Things Out

Dawn rose on the lovely late summer morning. There was not a cloud in the sky so the river looked like a blue gray ribbon before boat traffic began to stir up the surface. Tim wandered out of his room to find Dan and Jack quietly eating breakfast while Gert stood in the doorway enjoying the fresh brisk air.

"Is Marisol awake?"

Jack pointed towards the new bedroom. "Take a look. You'll find your sister in there."

The door was just open a crack but what Tim saw caused his heart to sink. Nana was asleep with Cece cuddled next to her and Marisol on her other side. He turned to Gert with a 'what can I do' look.

"Try to be quiet. They need to get as much rest as possible." She filled his teacup and put out some more scones.

Jack was staring at the random tealeaves floating in his cup. "I don't need Nana to read these to tell me I am confused and unsure about the future. See how they are scattered."

"Mother would read our tea leaves. I had almost forgotten." Tim smiled at the memory. "Mar would give the last of her tea a swirl to see what kind of interpretation she could get about the leaves stuck to the side of the cup. I think Mother would make up some fanciful stories but many times she was amazingly correct. Perhaps Nana will give me a reading on my future with this useless hand."

Suddenly Jack shot a very blunt question at Tim. "Are you rich?"

"Jack! That's rude." Gert was embarrassed.

"No problem Gert. Our parents did their best to provide a normal upbringing so we never thought much about it. Marisol did pick up an air in appearances in her teens but I could bring her back to earth. She has really grown since meeting our Aunt Fiona and being surrounded by so many caring people."

"You mean common folk. I thought her bigotry was due to lack of knowledge, not superiority." Jack banged the table in frustration.

"It is all in the eye of the beholder. Being wealthy can be tenuous. My father's family built a large shipping fleet during the peak of the great schooners. He taught me that nothing is forever especially in business. He could foresee ships run by steam engines and once he read of iron clad war ships in your civil war, he was unsure if our shipyards could survive the transition. His wish was for us to handle our money carefully and use it for good, not for prestige as was the plan of Matthew Roberts."

Thoroughly intrigued, Gert refilled the teacups and sat herself down.

Jack was obviously still bitter about the sudden revelation. "Well, I've never rubbed elbows with the well to do."

Tim smiled. "You were raised in part by my aunt Fiona Hodge. Your Nana is a prime example of the way to live a wealthy life. Do you believe she and Captain Hodge built their dream on the Penobscot River with the income of a farmer? They took pride in sustaining their farm with their own labor but that would never cover their beautiful possessions and her extensive library. I imagine she has been quite active in charities and a leader in social causes."

Gert popped a piece of a broken scone in her mouth before answering. "The women's league in Bangor is going to honor her for years of support at a dinner this fall."

Tim nodded. "I imagine there will be many women of prestige present."

"Well I'll be." Gert stared at the new bedroom door. "I knew the captain had a good amount of savings but nothing like this. The wives of Vice President Hannibal Hamlin and Governor Joshua Chamberlain will be there. I was planning on taking Comfort."

"True wealth is never rubbed in the face of others."

Jack turned to Dan who as usual had not uttered a word. "Are you leaving right now for Joe's?"

"Yes, I told him I'd be there this morning to help with the gardens on the island before we start the final harvest here and in Nana's fields."

Jack jumped up and looked at his mother. "I'm going too. I have things to think out."

It was nearly an hour before Cece paddled out in her bare feet rubbing the rest of the sleepiness out of her eyes. She was carrying Lacey by her little knotted hand. Gert picked her up and sat on the rocking chair to check out the scratches from the brambles.

"Ouch. That hurts Mama. So does my arm where the bad man grabbed me."

"I'd like to grab that man where it would really hurt him," added Nana. She was feisty and obviously no less angry than she was last night. Wrapped up in a new flannel robe, she was also barefoot. "Did your posse of Ryan men leave any crumbs of what I could smell baking earlier?"

"I tucked a few out of sight. We certainly know them, don't we? Cece, go get moccasins for Nana and yourself. We have enough scratches on your skin without adding splinters in your feet."

"I'll get Mary's moccasins too and I have a surprise for her."

"Did someone mention my name?" A very bedraggled Marisol wandered from Nana's bedroom, her hair sticking out in every direction and obviously flattened on the sides by tears. And what seemed the style of the day, barefoot. "I need to run through so none of your sons see me."

Cece skipped into the room with her feet safely protected carrying Nana and Marisol's moccasins and a mysterious package wrapped in a remnant of fabric. "Not to worry Mary. Dan and Jack have already left for Indian Island."

Marisol was stunned as though she had suddenly been struck across the face.

"Sit down next to me sweetheart and we'll have a chance for girl time." Nana patted the space next to at the kitchen table.

"Yah, no big brothers. Tim has gone for a walk." Cece handed the package to Marisol. "Gramma Hanna helped me make this for you."

Untying the knot of fabric, Marisol smiled in delight. "Thank you." It was a change purse of dark blue wool, decorated with a stylized flower on the flap.

"Gramma Hanna helped me cut it out and then I did the decorating all by myself. She helped me stitch it together."

"I see glass beads but what are the long pieces?"

"Those are cut up porcupine needles."

"Like the porcupine animal?"

"Of course, silly. My papa used to pull needles off porcupines with a blanket. Right Mama?"

Gert looked rightly proud of her Comfort's accomplishment. "You must have Sean tell you the story."

With Gert's strong coffee and perfect scones, Marisol was ready to talk.

"Comfort, I want you to take Princess and little Lady into your room and give them some love."

"Come on kitties, Mama wants to get rid of us so they can have some big girl talk."

Nana shook her head and smiled, then turned to her niece. "Tell us, what set Jack off?"

"Aunt Daphne warned me to tell Jack about the family money. She told me not to let him hear of it from anyone else."

Gert took her hand. "She is a wise lady."

"I tried to talk to him on the way home from Searsport. We were having lunch and I told him he didn't know my whole story. He jumped in and told me he could tell I had a privileged childhood but what did it matter whether we were haves or have-nots. And he didn't need to hear any more."

"That's my son Jack. He has all the answers. How did he find out?"

Marisol stiffened and squeezed Gert's hand tight. "Matt was on top of me trying to ..." She sobbed. "Sean pulled him off while Jack covered me. In the melee, Matt shouted I was nothing but a spoiled rich bitch. 'With his brains and my wealth we could have become high in Boston Society.' Jack looked shocked but quickly carried me to safety never speaking."

Nothing was said for a minute or so.

Marisol stood with her arms folded as if to hug herself. "It's just as well he's gone. I have things to think out."

Cece's bedroom door opened. "Can I come out? I need a rag. Princess made a mess."

Marisol tossed up her hands and laughed. "If only my mess with Jack could be wiped up with a rag."

XXXVI

New Beginnings

Over the next week, the turmoil since June began to wane. Each day Tim read letters Captain Hodge wrote his mother. Nana never tired of hearing them and added stories of her own to add the color to their sailing adventures.

Cece came bouncing into Nana's room with another of her new school outfits on. "Little girl, if you keep trying on the new clothes you'll have them worn out before you go off to school next week."

"But Mama, I've never had store bought jumpers and blouses before."

"Why do you keep trying on your new socks?"

"Lisle stockings are tricky and I want to make sure I can get them on quickly when it gets colder out."

"Well, I'd like it better if all the schoolhouse clothes were put away and you get your work clothes on to pull our carrots after lunch. Papa is filling the sand barrel."

Nana looked up from her book and feigned annoyance with Cece. "You know that if you keep pouting like that it will stay on your face forever."

"No stomping out." Gert was taking a short break to finish a blanket stitch edging on a piece of pale yellow and green plaid flannel for Peg's cradle.

"You-hoo, is any one home?"

"Kate! Yippee! Look Mama it's Kate."

"I can't remember getting that kind of enthusiastic greeting before."

"Kate, want to see all my new school clothes?"

"Nice try Comfort. Go change." Gert shooed her towards the bedroom.

Tossing her book on the brass bed, Nana walked over to Kate with a hug. "I'm surprised to see you with school starting up."

"I have a few days so I travelled down river with Dan and Jack to work on your harvest and of course, visit Tim."

Gert shouted from the kitchen. "Tim and Marisol are up in the blueberry fields trying to glean enough berries for a couple pies."

Looking surprised, she checked out the woods across the street. "Is Tim ready for that?"

"His walking is getting stronger but Marisol wants to see if he can pick the small berries left handed. His right one is simply worthless right now and he is getting very discouraged. I think you would be the perfect medicine."

"Go ahead, honey. You know the way." Nana gave Kate a peck on the cheek. "I agree, you would be a sight for sore eyes for him."

What Kate found was not calming to her own eyes. Tim was sprawled on the ground while laying Marisol out in lavender. He had been picking berries into a tin cup that his sister would pour into the bucket. His berries were scattered.

"Why the hell did you take me into this woodland field? How am I supposed to keep my balance while stooping over with one useless hand?"

"For heaven's sake, don't scold me for your clumsiness. Watch where you are walking and stop blaming everything on your injury. Sean told you with exercise and with patience it should get stronger."

"Maybe it would not be as bad if you didn't carry me off to Indian Island."

"Well, let me see. Perhaps I should have gone with my other option and let the surgeon hack off your arm then you would not have a crippled hand to blame for being incapable to accept your present disability." Her hands snapped to hips as punctuation.

Tree limbs became spectator stands for small creatures and birds from chick-a-dee to turkey watching the human squabble. Tim sat up and tried to reach his walking stick as if he wanted to throw it at his sister.

"Now children, behave." Kate finally made her presence known. Marisol ran to give her a hug while Tim hung his head to hide his embarrassment. "Jack is waiting to talk with you. Why don't you take the berries back so I can share one of Gert's pies. I'll make sure Tim gets home."

"Jack came back with you?" Marisol made figure eights in the pine needles with the toe of her work boot. "Is he still mad at me?"

"He's not mad, just confused and is tired of folks trying to tell him they know how he feels. Let him start the conversation.

As his sister disappeared into the woods, Tim reached up and pulled Kate down to sit. He looked deep into her eyes. "How did you become so wise?"

"Living with a brother like JJ teaches one to let him lead the conversation so you can finish it."

"Okay, I'll start the conversation and let you end it." He kissed her gently, she finished with passion.

Marisol tried to tiptoe into Gert's kitchen so she could leave the blueberries then disappear into the bedroom. Jack suddenly blew in her ear and she nearly dropped the pail. "Ma would not be happy if you dumped those berries but not as unhappy as I would be if she couldn't make a pie. Let's go for a walk."

"I don't want to go near the fort and the blueberry field is occupied." She blushed thinking she actually said that.

"How about the apple tree?"

"Perfect."

Nana left her reading chair to get a glass of water and stopped short as Gert was coming in from gathering the eggs.

"Am I turning into a hallucinating old lady or are Jack and Marisol sitting in the apple tree?"

"That's where Jack and his brothers always went to work out family issues. When Mike died they spent days up there, sometimes never saying a word. Those limbs know more about my family than I do.

"Where's Dan? I thought he came back with Jack. Is he hiding from his Nana?"

"I get more of a feeling that he is hiding from me." A poof of powder flew in Gert's face when she tossed a chunk of lard into the bowl of flour.

"My, what did that hunk of fat ever do to you?"

"I'm taking out a bit of nervous energy." She set to work cutting the ingredients to pieces the size of a small pea to make the crust as flaky as possible with just as bit of cold water. Just the way her family liked it.

Nana looked into her water glass like it were a fortune teller's globe. "You think our Daniel is going to leave us?"

Gert pitched one of four balls of dough on the counter and went at it with her wooden rolling pin. With just a few quick strokes she formed a perfect circle being careful not to over-work and toughen the shell. "You can feel it too? He has always been quiet but more so since returning from Aroostook. And just think, I'm the one that pushed him into taking the trip."

"Gert, my dear friend, he has been churning on this since Jacob arrived to help with the planting. They took many quiet sunrise walks that I bet did not include a lot of conversation. He is your child with the most Micmac tendencies. I remember you saw that from the day he was born and was afraid his life would not be easy in Prospect Ferry. It was his big brother Mike who was a buffer in school. His experiences made him strong and more serious than others his age. I suspect he and Jack talked things out this past week and right now he's getting Joey's views."

"That means Sean and I won't have a say in it."

"If I remember correctly, you and Sean were younger than Dan when you left home on the Aroostook River to start your life as a new bride. I can see the look on your face when you arrived as if it were yesterday."

Gert made a very good impersonation of Cece's pout as she tossed the dough for the top crusts on the work counter. Berries, sugar and a good chunk of butter filled two pies that Gert tossed in the oven. "Nana, would you keep an eye on those? I'm going to dig potatoes and gather some squash."

"Keeping yourself busy won't keep him from making a decision."

"Are you talking about me Mama? I'm making decisions." Cece dragged her carrot basket up to the open porch doorway, limp greens hanging over the edges.

"Leave them there, Comfort. Papa will cut the tops off tonight for the root cellar. Don't come in until I bring you a washbowl so you won't deposit all that sticky sand and dirt in the kitchen."

Nana leaned against the doorjamb getting some sun on her face. "Tell me, little girl, what big decision are you pondering?"

"I simply can't make up my mind what to wear for the first day of school."

Gert's mouth tightened as she snapped. "Comfort, do you have any idea how many children don't have a choice? You are a very lucky girl and it's about time you knew it. Now hurry up and wash off the dirt so you can change clothes for supper."

Cece was surprised by her mother's displeasure so washed and ran by her quickly.

"It's not like you to be so sharp Gert." Nana stuck out her foot to stop one of the growing kittens from getting outside. "I'm going to step on you one day or you're going to send me flying."

"I guess no matter your age, there are some things that stick with you." Gert grabbed two roaming little coon cats and plopped them back into the basket knowing they would soon wiggle their way out again. "I never once had a new outfit when I was in the early grades of school. Nettie was a year ahead of me so Mrs. Thorpe gave my mother her outgrown clothes. They were nice but never just mine. Yep, it's funny how something like that sticks with you."

"Did your mother not teach you to sew?"

"My mother's life was totally wrapped around tending to my father. It took me many years to realize she was looking for approval and a sign of love from him." Gert gave her friend a hug. "Nana, without you in my young life, I may have been just like her."

"Never. You had to tend to yourself and whether you knew it or not, developed an independent streak that blossomed as a young bride. You reminded me of myself, determined not to follow in the footsteps of a mother who accepted her place as the wife of a domineering Irishman. Who taught you your sewing skills?"

"Mrs. Thorpe. When she realized my state, she took me under her wing and that is when Nettie and I became like sisters. I've never told a soul but I was actually jealous of her time with Ben but when Sean realized there was more to me than some farming brat, we all became close friends."

After some time of reminiscing that afternoon, Gert realized at the supper table how much of Nettie was in Kate and what a lucky young man Timothy Hodge would be if they built a life together. When Peg, Joey and Dan joined them, she looked at her complete family as if trying to etch them in her mind much like an itinerant photographer would capture their images on a tintype. "Yes, that's what I want."

Nana saw the distress in the eyes of her friend. "What is it Gert? What do you want?"

"I said that out loud? I'm sorry. I'll clear the supper dishes and bring over the pies."

"Wait just a minute." Sean was not about to take the unusual mood hanging over the meal any longer. "Just what is going on here?"

Cece blurted out that Mama had yelled at her. Then Dan managed to catch his mother's eye. "I'm moving to Smytheville."

Jack jumped up and whacked his brother on the back. "It's about time you made a decision."

Dan looked at Jack with a grin. "You're the last one who should say that."

Tim took a look at his sister who was turning bright red.

"Wow." Cece ran to her big brother and jumped up in his lap. "Does that mean I can visit you and see Gramma Hanna and my friends anytime I want?"

With a deep sigh and tears trying to escape, Gert turned and grabbed the pies off the sideboard. "We'll talk that all out in the days to come. Right now let's enjoy Tim's efforts in the blueberry fields today." Kate's face flushed while Marisol stifled a giggle.

"Here we go again, more new beginnings in our mackerel sky family. And the biggest of all - I am going to start school!"

And the Ryan household filled with laughter.

XXXVII

1868 Wanes

SEPTEMBER

During the next couple of days, Kate spent most of her time with Nana getting as much advice as possible from her experience with the children on Indian Island. Each day she'd walk with Tim to the Prospect Ferry landing or around the fields of the Hodge Farm. They would stand where Nana's home once stood and wondered what it must have been like for the Captain to build his dream.

One afternoon they picked up the largest kitten, the big charcoal colored fluffy boy. Kate carried him to his new home with Peg who was taking a break in the kitchen rocker with her feet up on a box. Tim kept Joey company in the yard while he split wood for the pile.

Peg stroked the kitten in her lap as he tried to climb up to her shoulder. She brought him down and restrained him in her apron. "Take it easy Champ, you are going to be well loved." It was hard to see his big green eyes in all that fluff but he could see hers and felt safe enough to curl in a ball.

"Why did you favor this one, and why the name Champ?"

"The minute Joey saw him he knew this was the cat for Buddy. They would grow up together and could play rough-house with each other. He'd be Buddy's champion."

Kate put her hand on Peg's expanding belly. "Buddy, I will see you in person on my next trip. Be a good boy for your Mama."

Next day she had a hard time saying goodbye at the ferry. She left Tim with a ball of yarn and made him promise to squeeze it daily to exercise. He whispered he'd make believe he was squeezing her. What she took with her was one of the ginger coon kittens for the Joe Ryan family.

The following Monday Cece started school. She literally skipped to the schoolhouse. Gert told Nana her boys never were that excited to learn.

That afternoon Dan shared afternoon tea with his mother. He stayed strong to his convictions he belonged on the Aroostook River and knew he would find happiness among the people of his heritage. He told his mother he would share Jacob's cabin at the edge of the river during the summer and work as a scout plotting timber to be harvested during the winter, and guide the spring run to the sawmills on the Saint John River.

"Daniel, that is very dangerous work." Gert still could not allow herself the thought of him leaving.

"Ma, if it was not for that work, Smytheville would not exist and there is a good chance Jacob and our people would be living on a reservation over the New Brunswick border. Ben and Nettie would not be part of the young town of Washburn with a thriving potato farm. I know I was born here but my heart has belonged to that bend in the river since we visited as children. And by the way, Jack and Joey think they were the only ones to get a penny from your father. He also pressed a coin in my hand

and ruffled my hair. Mine is a nickel and it's still in my medicine pouch. I've known since that time, I would go back."

Nana came out of her room, "I heard you say you were making plans. Have you set a date? I have a few things I need to take care of before you go."

"I'm making travel plans for the day after Thanksgiving."

Nana clapped her hands, at least the most her arthritic fingers would allow. "Perfect. When I get to Bangor next I'll take care of things."

Gert looked puzzled but knew enough not to question. "Nana, you are being honored at the women's luncheon two weeks hence. Would that be a good day for you to take care of things?

"I had let myself forget about all that folderol but it would be a good time to complete my plans. Will you be with me Gert?"

"I wouldn't miss it and I plan to take Marisol and keep Comfort out of school. I don't think she's too young to think about her place in the world as a woman."

Dan just shook his head. "Bet Pa doesn't know about that. He'd say you were putting daydreams in her head like being able to vote or having property rights."

"Dan, she has been raised where she can see Nana as a property owner."

"Ma, you know that's not the usual. When men die the wife has no rights, most being left with nothing. It goes to a male family member or business partner."

"I believe Cece's generation will have a lot to say about that." Nana was a bit put out that Dan could still feel women's rights of today would stay the norm. "There will come a day when someone like Cara and her son T will not be shoved aside by town fathers."

"Maybe more men like your Captain will legally plan that property go to their spouse, but a Micmac chief will get the vote before women and you know the chances of an Indian getting into a voting booth."

"Dan, I've never seen you as a cynic."

"I'm sorry Ma. You've never seen some of the malarkey I've been through even when working at the brickyard. When you all lost Mike, I lost my guide through this white world."

"Dan, even the Irish immigrants fight for their place in society," added Nana. "But, I must admit Captain Hodge was my path to a life I cherished and I can see now where the forests of the Aroostook could be where you'll find your happiness."

Dan hugged his Nana. "I somehow knew you would come around to my decision."

Gert sighed and picked up her tea, only to have it splash over the clean tablecloth when Cece rushed in from school, slamming the door behind her. "I'm just plain mad!"

Gert grabbed her as she rushed by. "What's the problem Comfort?"

"That's the problem. Comfort–Comfort–Comfort! Cece is my name except for you and Pa and the schoolmaster. You're the only ones I let call me by my given name. My name is Cece to everyone else. That's the name my brothers gave me, right Dan?"

"I told you Ma. We knew Comfort Claire would be a problem when she got to school."

Nana helped Cece out of her school shoes then pulled the sulking little girl on her lap. "You know, I had a friend in Boston with the name Comfort and everyone thought it was beautiful."

"Well, everyone at school think it's silly, especially Zeke."

"Aha and who would that be? Is some boy sweet on my sister? I may have to have a talk with him."

She was off Nana's lap and in her brother's face in a flash. "Sweet on me? Huh! He said I'm not Comfort. I'm more like Dumbfort."

"What did you do?"

"I kicked him in the leg with the pointy toe of my shoe. Sure made him squeal in front of his friends but he still calls me Comfort. And then Mr. Wilson took his side and made me sit in the corner. It was only one kick. I should have given him two."

Gert just put her head in her hands on the table with a groan.

Cece couldn't help but giggle when Dan picked her up and spun in circles. When he stopped, they both fell to the floor dizzy as can be. "I have an idea, my dear."

"What is it Dan? Tell me. Tell me."

"What does Mr. Wilson call Zeke?"

"His given name of course."

"And that is?"

"Ezekiel."

"Then every time he calls you Comfort, you call him Ezekiel."

"He'll hate that. I love it. I love you Dan. You can't go away and leave me."

"How I wish it were so," mumbled Gert.

"Did you say something Ma?"

"I said we better go. I want to pick the apples to dry."

"Did you say apple pie?"

Gert whacked Dan on the backside with a wet dishrag and chased him out the door. "Comfort, get changed and out with you too."

What remained of September 1868 was beautiful. There were bright blue skies, sunny warm days and brisk nights while the color of fall foliage turned the Penobscot Valley into a canvas worthy of the finest painter. This was Marisol's first harvest and she marveled at the process of drying, preserving and storing. She helped shell the dry yellow eye beans and now appreciated the baked sweet molasses staple.

The morning of the Charity Association luncheon Cece was all agog. Gert and Nana had made her a real dress with puff sleeves and lace collar. Her high button shoes were buffed to a high shine and one of her mother's smaller shawls was taken out of the cedar chest, aired on the clothesline to top the outfit. She couldn't believe her mother changed Mr. Wilson's mind when he hesitated to excuse her for the day. It seems he felt it was not proper to fill a little girl's head full of imaginings. Marisol was also quite excited for it had been quite a while since she went to a special charity luncheon with her mother in London.

The reception at Bangor's Norumbega Hall took Cece's breath away with all the flowers, fancy foods and white tablecloths. Her heart swelled with pride when the president of the auxiliary praised Nana's accomplishments over the years and showed the plaque to honor her that was to be placed in the library at the Bangor Seminary. Her attention never waned when the speaker reported on the latest Women's Rights meeting held in Boston and announced a special day of discussion on the subject in February. She clapped as loud as anyone when the treasurer gave a positive account of the monies raised for the orphanage. She held her skipping in place when Nana sent her to the podium to receive a gift from the women to their dear friend Fiona Hodge.

Nana's favorite part of the day was watching Cece.

That afternoon Gert drove the surrey to the attorney's office for Nana's meeting while Marisol and Cece took a tour of Bangor to the river walk and back to the striking Greek Revival style building. The pigeons soon found her location on the bench in the park when she retrieved a dinner roll that somehow made its way into her small tapestry handbag and teased them one little piece at a time.

"Mary, is it true a lady can't vote for the president?"

"The men feel that decision belongs with them."

"Why?"

"Well, they believe woman do not have the education needed to make such a vote."

"Why?"

"They believe a woman's place is in the home, devoted to the house while raising their children."

Before the next 'why', Gert pulled up to the curb. "Thank goodness. Nana, your turn to try to answer questions." Marisol helped the inquisitor into the surrey.

As they neared the covered bridge, Cece came up with her next inquiry. "Nana, do boys really think girls have smaller brains then they do?" Laughs from the surrey, mixing with the clip-clop of the horse, echoed through the long covered overpass.

OCTOBER

Soon the patch was covered with pumpkins of all sizes sitting atop the brown foliage remains. Cece stood in the middle of the field, arms folded in front and slowly turned in a circle. "Found it, my perfect pumpkin for my perfect jack-o-lantern."

Gert looked up from the warming stove after lighting a good-sized chunk of wood to take the chill off. She was surprised to see her daughter hugging a fairly small pumpkin. "Cece, you had the choice of any in the field. I've seen some much, much bigger than that one."

"This one is perfect. It's not the biggest but the most beautiful. Sort of like my kitty Princess."

As Halloween rolled around, Jack wielded the knife as they designed Marisol's first jack-o-lantern. He thought it more prudent to hold the blade while Cece and Mary told him where to cut and what pattern they wanted. Everyone had to come out of the house for the lighting of the candles. With clapping hands, the ladies showed approval of the artwork.

Marisol wrapped her shawl tightly to protect her body against the frosty October night. Jack crossed his arms in front of him and stared at the carved round orange fruits. You would think he was comparing the smile of the whittled pumpkin to the smile of Mona Lisa at The Louvre. "What are you staring at Mr. Ryan? I think the jack-o-lanterns are superb."

"It's nice to see you can still get excited about something, Miss Hodge."

Cece skipped over the lawn, dressed all in black with whiskers drawn across her cheeks with stove ashes, triangle rawhide cat ears sewn on a band of cloth tied around her head and a long black tail made from a single lisle stocking stuffed with scraps hanging in the back. "Come on Mary."

Jack ran after them. "Where are you going with the black cat?"

"I'm a scary All Hallow's Eve black cat and can give you all kinds of bad luck if you are not careful. Mary's going to the party at the school house with me."

"We never had Halloween parties when Joey and I were at the school."

"It's on Saturday this year so Mr. Wilson thought it would be fun. We're going to have a parade and bob for apples and I'm going to win the costume prize," announced Cece.

Jack reached out and took the "girls" by the hands, making sure the black cat did not cross his path. "I'm going too."

NOVEMBER

November arrived with a frigid blast from the north and an unexpected light blanket of snow. Now Cece appreciated the warmth of lisle stockings when she walked off to school and her daily confrontation with Zeke. She learned very quickly to get her point across without raising problems with Mr. Wilson. Zeke changed her name to Sneaky.

Marisol went with Tim for his walk for things were a bit slippery underfoot. "It's a wonderland, Timmy. Who would believe just under this fresh white blanket is a black scar of treachery that caused you so much pain?"

"Take a look at the field. The white goes on forever only broken by what is left of the short corn stocks." Tim shaded his eyes against the glare. "It looks like there is a army of little soldiers marching to the ferry landing in perfect formation."

"Ah, I see a glimmer of the wonderful imagination my brother had hidden under a veneer of self-pity all these months. Keep working on it. I like this version of you."

"If I had two working hands, I'd make a snowball and let you have it."

"I say, go ahead. See what kind of weapon you can make." Marisol scraped enough wet snow from the side of the road to form an icy missal that she tossed directly at Tim's head, missing but hitting his shoulder causing the snow to fly up in his face.

"Why you little devil." Tim dropped his walking stick, gathered some snow with his good hand and packed it with his "crippled" one. Then without thinking he threw it with great accuracy at his sister's head with his right arm.

"You did it!" Wiping the snow out of her eyes, Marisol laughed, jumped up and down and threw her arms around her twin.

Watching the scene from the side window of her bedroom, Nana smiled broadly. "Good girl. Smart girl."

Gert called in from the pantry. "Did you say something?"

"I said I think Timothy Hodge is going to be fine. He just needs to find a bit more patience."

"I agree. But you know he is a man and many don't come with much staying power."

Next day, things turned warm again changing the beautiful landscape into a muddy countryside. Dan swung his faithful lumbering jacket on. "Come on brother Jack. Get on your high boots, we need to scrub out the barn before a big freeze sets in and we can't scrape the stuff off the floor."

"I may as well get into the routine with you heading for the wilderness and T already there."

"I don't know if all the livestock will stay. Nana has to make that decision."

When Tim went off for a nap and her chores in the kitchen were done, Marisol decided to take another walk and see what the Ryan boys were up to. "Hello. Hello." The barn was so neat her voice bounced around the stalls and into the loft.

"Quiet down there." Jack stood on the upper level with a pitchfork.

"What are you doing?"

"I'm trying to pack in as much hay as I can. Come on up and help."

"I didn't sign up to work one of those weird long forks."

"Then just keep me company while Dan is down helping Joey build a shelter and pen for the goat."

"They have a goat?"

"Peg thought the milk would be rich and good for her while she builds herself up after the birth."

Marisol climbed the rough hewn ladder to the loft. With the second floor doors open, quite a brisk breeze was roaring through storage area. She pulled her shawl tightly around shoulders but was so enthralled about the view, she didn't mind the cold. "How I wish I were talented enough to paint like your mother. This scene looking down to the river with Joey's small home as a focal point would make a wonderful canvas. I must tell Gert to bring her easel up here."

"Sit over in that corner so you get some protection from the chill. Or sit in this corner and let me protect you from the frost."

"I'll take my chances over here, thank you. Isn't that manure pile down there a bit close to the barn?"

"No problem this time of year. The air and sun never get hot enough to cause any combustion. It will be spread in the spring." Jack coaxed another few clumps of straw from the center pile to the corner.

"Well, I better go see if your mother needs any help getting things ready for supper."

"Well, you sure are getting domesticated for a well-to-do young lady."

"Good grief! Let go of it." She stood and went towards the ladder.

"I don't want to let go of it. I want to take hold of you and never let go." He reached out and pulled Marisol to him, kissing her with a passion that had been building like a piece of kindling slowly building to a flame. "Have you ever had a roll in some sweet smelling hay?"

She put her arms around his neck, kissed him teasingly then whispered in his ear. "I'm not planning to do any rolling of any kind until you find some way to get yourself down from that high horse." She gave him a shove backwards.

Before he regained his balance, his toe got caught under the hayfork sending him toppling out of the open loft door.

"Jack! Jack! I'm sorry." Marisol practically slid down the ladder and ran through the office to the back of the barn. There was no Jack to be seen.

Walking up the path, Dan and Joey saw Marisol spinning like a top. "What's going on?"

"Jack fell out the loft door and just plain disappeared. Dan, where did he go?"

Joey took one look at the pile by the wall and started belly laughing. "Could my dear twin be where we all hope he isn't?"

Looking at the mound of manure, Marisol held her nose while Dan grabbed a shovel that was leaning against the wall.

"Don't bother." A very embarrassed Jack popped up like a disheveled jack-in-a-box, rolled out of the pile, brushed himself off, put his head up high and walked home.

With Thanksgiving approaching, the Ryan house was bustling. Finished at the fort until spring, Sean was loading the wood box in the pantry and filling any spare inch available in the root cellar with more. Two of the cats ran between his legs nearly tipping him over with an armful of hardwood. "Gert, we have five cats in the house! Do something before I throw them all in the river."

"Don't you dare let Comfort hear you. We are working on that. Be patient."

"It better be soon. Either they go or I go."

Marisol, Nana and Gert looked at each other with a grin.

As for Cece, she was still talking about the apple bobbing a month ago and how Jack couldn't do it but Mary did because she wasn't afraid of getting her hair wet. And she still wore her wooden medal on a blue ribbon for winning best costume. Mr. Wilson called it a tie between her and Zeke. Cece called his costume a stupid pirate ghost outfit. But she got hers first and that was all she needed.

Snow blew in during the night letting the family know in no uncertain terms that winter was on the way. Next morning, Dan and Jack were already in the kitchen at dawn, which surprised Marisol, no end. She came out for a glass of water and nearly bumped straight into them. "I like the pretty flowers on that nightdress." Jack winked and turned her around sending her pinky faced back to the bedroom.

A loud screech filled the kitchen. "What in the world was that?" Marisol grabbed her robe and went back in as the sound pierced through the kitchen again.

Next Tim came out. "What's that noise?"

"That's the sound of a turkey looking to find a friend. Never heard that before?" Dan took his small piece of slate, held it in the curve of his hand and scraped it with a wood friction stick.

Both twins covered their ears as the sounds changed while Dan manipulated the call.

Jack picked up his father's hunting rifle and a small box of bullets. "Go back to sleep and if luck holds, we'll be back later with Thanksgiving dinner."

Dan took his bow off the rack over the back door and the quiver of arrows from the peg next to the window. Surprised, Marisol said, "I thought those were kitchen decorations."

Jack smiled as he pushed Marisol's un-brushed hair behind her ear. "You have a lot to learn about the ways of the forest, fancy lady. Tracking will be a lot easier in the new snow and if Danny boy has not lost his touch, we'll bring back all Pa's bullets."

The back door shut with a click just as Cece ran across the kitchen in a panic. The blast of cold and huge snowflakes predicting the end of the storm did not stop her from running barefoot onto the porch. "Don't you hurt Big Tom. You promised."

"Not to worry. He'd be too tough"

Thanksgiving morning Nana stood mesmerized by the scene across the fields to the river. "Gert, come take a look at this. It looks like a lithograph from Currier and Ives. It just needs a horse and sleigh."

"I need to get some sketches of the shadows on the snow as the sun moves from morning to night. Marisol told me the view from your hayloft looking over Joey's house to the river is something she thinks I should paint."

"Was that observation from the day Jack ended up in the dung?"

"I guess it was."

Nana nudged Gert in the ribs. "I wonder why they were in the hay loft?"

The final preparations for dinner took up every minute left in the morning. Not happy, Marisol questioned why Dan killed two large hens. "We respect how the animals nourish us and give thanks for their sacrifice. We would never hunt the hens in the spring when they are nesting and raising chicks but it would be a good time for young toms to hide."

With a bit of ingenuity with boxes, crates and the like, Sean managed a table with seats for ten. Gert did her magic with cotton sheeting to cover the eating surface and set it with Staffordshire stoneware plates, hand me downs from Nana.

Jack came in with the egg basket. "Ma, did you forget to visit the hen house this morning?"

"I've never done that before. Guess I have a lot on my mind along with all this cooking."

"Lady and her brood did not seem happy in the chicken wire pen you built against the side of the coop. Leave it to you to pen the cats in the chicken yard," joked Jack.

"They'll live but I'm not sure they would have if under your father's feet today."

"I've hardly ever seen these dishes. And cloth napkins? Are ye putting on the dog Ma?"

Both Gert and Marisol snapped around and gave him a look that could pierce the walls of the fort.

"John Ryan, you get your skinny ass out of here and don't come to the table until you have dressed for the occasion. This is an important meal for me."

Marisol peeked as Jack went into Timothy's room where he kept his company clothes. She couldn't help but check out his backside on the way by.

Gert took a few deep breaths as she put the sourdough rolls in her porcupine quill basket. She had watched Sean's aunt weave the white ash reed into the intricate twisted design for their wedding gift. Now there was a stack of her son's possessions on the pantry floor, ready for Dan's move to where she grew up and left for a new beginning. "Guess it's tit for tat." She took another look at Dan's bags, sighed deeply and took the rolls to the table.

"How are we doing, Gert?" Nana crossed over to the table from her bedroom and picked up one of the pale copper colored napkins. "Isn't this the material you bought to make yourself a new summer frock?"

"I'll get more sometime."

"Have you told anyone about my plans this afternoon?"

"Nana, I don't know what your plans are but I have made sure the whole family will be here, we will all be in the parlor at two and dressed for a special day."

And it was a special day. Looking around the table, Gert focused on the joking and laughter during the meal and felt proud. Comfort sat straight in her puffy armed dress, Marisol wore one of her fancy silk blouses with a slim black skirt. She had pulled her hair to the top of her head with a lovely mother-of-pearl comb. Gert was sure Jack saw none but her. Nana hired a seamstress to make a lovely pearl gray dress that nearly matched her hair. Poor Peg, radiant in a loose green gingham smock, was getting so big that Sean remarked he should have added another seat for Buddy. All the men were so handsome in their Sunday best. Looking at her sons, two red heads with blue eyes and Dan with his pitch black braids and black-brown eyes, she felt a calmness fill her. "Dan, I know going north is the right move for you but you better write or I'll haunt you."

"Ma, trust me. Besides, between my grandmother and your best friend, you'll probably know more about me than I will." He went around the table and hugged his mother to the applause of the rest of the family.

It was a unanimous decision to keep dessert to late afternoon. As usual, two pies were piled high with apples while the other two were something new Nana wanted to try. There had been an article in one of her newspapers about Charles Dickens visiting poet Henry Longfellow at his home in Portland last Thanksgiving. For dessert they had Longfellow's favorite, pumpkin molasses pie. For many years, *A Christmas Carol* had been read at the Ryan household during the holiday season so it seemed perfect they should try the pie.

Jack stood and patted his belly. "Ma that was the best ever. I'm going to get out of these duds and take a walk."

Nana panicked and shot a look at Gert.

"Hold on there, mister. Who told you the afternoon was over? Take a walk if need be or visit on the porch but I want you and everyone else in the parlor by two this afternoon. And if any of you men would like to help clean up all these dishes, you would be most welcome."

Jack looked at his father who just shrugged.

Many hands make light work is what Jacob would tell the Ryan boys. When Dan grabbed a dish towel, the rest did the same. So the dishes were done and piled on the table to be stored later. Pans were scrubbed and back under the sideboard. Food was placed on the back shelf in the root cellar furthest from the stairs where it was the coolest. Then everyone freshened up and joined Cece in the parlor where she was keeping Peg and Nana amused with some of the rhymes from class.

It was so quiet in the room, the pendulum in the mantle clock could be heard swinging the seconds away. Everyone was waiting for Nana to say something. A few minutes after two, Cece ran to the window. "There's a surrey pulling up front. It has fancy sides to keep out the cold."

Sean met the visitor at the front door. He nodded to the group and Gert recognized him right away as Nana's attorney from Bangor. He was clutching a leather portfolio and went into the parlor to greet his client. "I see you have the folks gathered, Fiona." Noting there was not enough comfortable seating for everyone he turned to Gert. "Mrs. Ryan, would it be an inconvenience for us to sit around your holiday table where I could easily talk to all?"

"Of course not." Gert and her sons quickly took all the extraneous dishes and serving pieces off the table while Tim walked Nana into the kitchen.

Once everyone was in place, Attorney Bigelow stood at the head of the table. Nana spoke first. "Arthur, I can't thank you enough for coming down river on the holiday."

"My family is scheduled for Thanksgiving dinner at eight this evening. I will be finished with our business quickly." He opened his case and placed five sets of documents on the table and two envelopes. Clearing his throat, he began his tasks. "This is the first time I have lead a meeting of this sort. Mrs. Hodge has asked that I divide her goods and property as set out in the final plans as written in her will."

"What?" Gert reach over and took Nana's hand. "All anyone wants is for you to be here and safe with us. Nothing else."

"When Mrs. Hodge asked me to work this out for her, I told her I have never seen worldly possessions disbursed this way but she convinced me it would give her joy to do it now so she could be part of the changes for each of you."

"And with Daniel moving I wasn't sure when I would have another chance to have my whole family together. Continue, Arthur," Nana requested.

"I am going to read the wishes of Mrs. Hodge and then papers will need to be signed so I can file them with the court tomorrow." Within an hour, all signatures were done and Attorney Bigelow was heading home to his holiday feast.

In the Ryan house a stunned silence still filled the rooms. Sean and Joey's property was doubled to the river, Tim owned the Hodge fields, barn and home plot, Dan was deeded Nana's last three acres of pristine forest butting the river, but the most explosive reaction was from Jack who was now the owner of Nana's four acres on Blueberry Hill. Gert and Marisol were given envelopes to be opened privately. Tim would divide the livestock with the cow definitely going to Joey for his Buddy.

Not long after the surrey left for Bangor there was a loud knock on the front door. Everyone turned and looked at Nana who was smiling broadly. The stranger was carrying an armload of equipment. He looked in the parlor door. "We need to tend to this quickly while I still have afternoon sun. Did Mrs. Hodge not tell you I was coming to take your photograph?"

Cece was jumping up and down and clapping her hands. She had always wanted to be in a picture like the one on the mantel of her brothers before Mike and Dan left for war.

He quickly set up and placed the family on and behind the sofa. You'll need to hold tight for the longer exposure needed this time of day. Peg pleaded that she be in the back as she felt like Bessie wearing a tent and Buddy would never stay still. Her wish was granted.

And so, Thanksgiving for the Ryan family concluded with a bright flash.

DECEMBER

Once Dan was off, Sean, Joey and Jack dismantled the wigwam. The poles were cut for fire kindling, canvas rolled back under the porch and the heavy hide was folded and put back in Gert's painting workshop. Jack moved into his old bedroom with Tim.

Dan sent his mother a note after an uneventful trip to Smytheville. Even the two young cats made the trip well. He had taken the black with white ruff like Lady and the last ginger tiger like Princess for his grandmother. He liked the idea of the two growing up together and reminded him of the pair back in Prospect Ferry.

Tim and Marisol took the Boston Steamer to Searsport for a visit with Aunt Daphne. The week on the docks relit a fire of wanting to go to sea that Tim did not think would ever return. He took several schooner runs along the coast under the bright sun and brilliant blue winter sky. At one point he thought of Cece when a mackerel sky appeared and then he missed her. He was able to handle a rope but his hand was far too weak to do the work needed on deck. It would take time and a lot of exercise and he set his mind to the task.

Marisol on the other hand was ready to return to the farm after one shopping trip and a couple lunches out. She saw her contemporaries as lazy and wasteful. They had no goals other than snatching a wealthy son of a shipbuilder or captain. She and Aunt Daphne spent hours in her pleasant kitchen drinking tea and sharing stories.

As a batch of scones in the oven filled the Searsport kitchen with warm sweetness, Marisol finally relaxed. Perhaps for the first time since last June. "Gert wants me to stay with them as she enjoys the company and I am learning to be a fairly good housekeeper and cook."

Daphne looked her niece in the eyes. "And what do you want?"

"I'll stay until things work out for Tim. He is really anxious to get back to a ship but I also see him looking over his new land and thinking about rebuilding the house. Not grand, but a place to call home. Perhaps a place for Kate and he to begin a life together."

"What about Jack?"

"He is still a little boy in many ways but I truly love him. I'm not sure if he will ever want to settle down. Anyway, no matter, I will be busy following Nana's charge to me to oversee her charitable work in Bangor and Indian Island. I was shocked when I opened the envelope and saw the money in trust for her charity work with an annual stipend for me to manage her wishes."

"Your heart will show you the way."

That week the Ryans also did a lot of planning for the future. Many suppers ended with one idea or another tossed into the mixture. Gert held her instructions from Nana close to her vest for she didn't want Comfort to get caught up in future plans. Nana had set up a trust to make sure her education did not stop at the fifth grade as was the norm. She was to go to a private school to continue her studies and then attend college. Nana knew this child would not be happy without a challenge.

Cece was very happy when her Mary and Tim walked up from the landing. "Just in time Mary."

"In time for what?"

"Look at the mackerel sky coming. Things are going to change and I just know there is snow coming. I think it will be lots and lots. Papa is putting up the ropes."

"What are the ropes for?"

"To help Mama find the chicken coop if the snow lasts a long time."

Jack ran over to the Ferry Road and grabbed her travel bag and some packages. "Don't look so puzzled. If we get a blizzard it is easy to get turned around and believe me you don't want to get lost in a storm."

"Why not just stay inside?"

Cece tugged on Marisol's cape. "That's silly. Someone has to feed the animals."

On the porch, Jack pointed across the field where Joey was stringing rope from his house up to the barn. We're going to run one from the front over to the post at the Ferry Road. Then another to pick up and tie if a storm starts as no one will be using the road. There used to be just one needed from the Hodge house over for T to use to the barn."

Tim and Marisol looked at each other with looks of disbelief"

But kidding, they were not. That evening while Tim and Nana shared tales of the sea, Marisol was reading in the rocker in the parlor. Sudden there was a roar of wind that rattled the windows. "What was that?"

Cece came skipping in with her numbers book. "Hear that, Mary? That's old man winter flying through the river valley."

The next morning the snow had not slowed and was drifting to where it came to the top of the back steps. Sean and Jack did their best to keep ahead with the shovels along the coop rope line. Late morning they worked on trying to clear a bit along the barn path. It was nearly hopeless as the snow filled in behind them. At the barn they met Joey coming the other way to pump fresh water for the animals and put a blanket over Argos and old Hector for they were obviously uncomfortable. Sean milked Bessie and divided the milk between two tins. Corn was scattered for the chickens, grain scooped in the feeders. Joey gave each mule a small apple and treated the horses to a carrot. Jack pitched some hay from the loft and did not feel the cold as he thought of Marisol.

Exasperated, Marisol nearly tossed the ball of worsted wool across the room. "I'll never learn how to do this."

Gert laughed as she mended a hole in Sean's stockings. "I felt the same way when she tried to teach me to knit. You'll learn."

"Mary, would you like to play tic-tat-toe with me on my slate?"

"Anything to escape knit and purls."

Cece drew the game on her board.

"That's what I call naughts and crosses. Be careful, I'm good at this."

In the kitchen, Sean and Jack were very seriously into a game of checkers when Tim took a break from his book. "I love playing draughts. May I play the winner?"

"I guess there is the English language and an English language." Nana winked. "You'll soon learn how these colonists have ruined the mother tongue."

"Mary look. We can play our own game on the windows." There was enough frost on the inside of the panes to scratch the tic-tat-toe game on the glass.

"You two won't want to stay near that glass long." Gert placed another log on the fire.

Suddenly there was a loud banging on the front door.

Sean pulled the latch to find a panicked Joey on the steps. "Ma, I think Buddy is coming. Hurry Ma, hurry!"

Gert ran to the kitchen and pulled on her working boots. "Come on Marisol, don't just sit there."

"Me? Me! You want me to help birth a baby?"

"Nana always helped me and I've helped her with others. Now you need to help me."

Cece ran in with her boots. "I want to help."

"I need you stay with Nana. Sleep with her tonight so you will both be warmer. Make sure she gets her breakfast. Jack will keep the fires going and Papa will be back later with any news."

"You can do it Marisol." Tim was almost enjoying the scrambling.

The ladies bundled in sweaters and capes with wool scarves around the head. Joey ran ahead and Sean followed with the shovel should drifts get deep. "Hang on tight and follow the rope." Sean's shouts were barely heard above the wind.

With great effort they pushed through. With one gust, Marisol was literally lifted off her feet. Gert grabbed her and got her back to the rope. Once in the front door of the barn, the ladies took a minute to catch their breath. Joey ran right through and out the back door. He disappeared in the swirling snow in seconds.

"Ready?" With a nod Marisol and Gert followed Sean into the tempest.

The winds closer to the river were more violent so the group was most happy to be in Joey's kitchen. They all looked like the kind of snowmen Cece would build.

Tossing her outer garments on the floor near the wood stove, Gert went to check on Peg who she found to be quite far along in her labor. "Marisol, I need you in here. Sean you know what to do. Get the water boiling and keep your son amused."

Sean literally pushed reticent Marisol into the bedroom, put the kettle on, hung some sheets on the chair to warm near the stove and took Joey's chess set off the shelf. He had planned to take Joey for a long walk along the river and perhaps take him through all the tunnels at the fort but there was no escaping the little house.

Gert looked around to see Marisol standing in the corner. "Get over here. Peg needs your help and Buddy is not going to bite, he has no teeth."

Peg moaned but giggled. "Are you sure? I swear he has been teething on my insides. Oh, dear. Here we go again."

"Marisol, hold Peg's hand. Try to keep her mind on the baby and not on the birth."

That was the first labor pain Joey heard through the door and tipped his chair over as he jumped. Sean took him by the shoulder and put him in his place. "Boy, you stay in your place or I'll have to take you up to the barn. We can start sorting through all the boxes stored overhead."

"Sean, put the kitchen shears in a pan of boiling water and keep the kettle going." Gert closed the door tightly then went through the materials she and Peg had gathered. "Marisol, dampen this flannel for her forehead."

Marisol was puzzled. "Why do the men have to keep the water boiling?"

"Well it gives them something to do and besides we're going to want many cups of tea before this is over."

Once again Peg's giggle was cut short by her labor.

Marisol soon found her place and began to tell Peg stories about her life in England and jaunts to Scotland. But mostly her travels across the channel to France and visits to Paris.

Many cups of tea later, it was obvious the birth was near. Peg, exhausted, declared that this was the last baby for her and how Joey could build himself a year-round wigwam.

Marisol finally took a look and saw the head crowning. Instinctively she got on the bed in back of Peg, cradled her during the intense pain and helped position her for the final push.

"My, oh my." Marisol get the scissors.

She was in and out of the kitchen so fast, the men just saw a blur as they looked up from a game of hearts. Coming through the door, she saw the baby make its final slide into the world. Gert turned the infant over, thumped its back until there was a wail in protest.

Sean nearly tackled Joey as he sprang towards the bedroom. "They still have chores to do. I want to see my grandson just as badly as you want to hold your son."

Peg was anxious. "Is everything alright?"

"We're nearly there sweetheart. Marisol is going to cut the cord."

Suddenly pale, Marisol's complexion turned white. "I am?"

Gert quickly tied the birth cord in two places. "I will hold this steady and you clip between the knots."

"There you go honey. You are free to be." Gert wrapped her grandchild in a warm piece of flannel. "Peg, your baby Buddy is more of a rose bud. Meet your beautiful daughter."

Holding her little girl, Peg's heart swelled with love. "Dear Rose, my beautiful Rose."

—∭—

Christmas was nearly anticlimactic after the excitement of Thanksgiving and the birth of Rose. In the past week, Joey fell head over heels for his little girl and decided that Champ was perfect for her kitten as he was soft and cuddly. He and Peg had decided that she would be named Gertrude Rose for his mother who had been like a mother to Peg. Cece nearly had a tantrum when she heard.

"Mama. The teacher will call her Gertrude and the children will make fun of her. I thought they made fun of you in school."

Joey remembered the story his mother told him of being called Dirty Gertie as a poor farm girl. It was then decided that Cece's niece would be named Rose Gertrude Ryan.

At Christmas, they brought in a small spruce tree and decorated it with Nana's collection of ornaments rescued from the cabinet before the wall came down. Lady liked to lie under the tree while Princess and Tim's cat, now named Matey, found it more fun to try and climb it. Nana ordered a roast of beef from the butcher and supervised Gert as she made a Yorkshire pudding. Dessert was venison minced pie. Joey stayed home with his family but did make a visit with gifts of mittens Peg knitted for everyone. Among the gifts Marisol and Tim gave, Sean received a new set of chisels for his granite work, Gert got three pieces of fabric for dresses and two new storybooks for Cece. Everyone's breath was taken away when Nana revealed the gifts that Jack had picked up for her in Bangor. There was a large sepia photograph of the entire family taken at Thanksgiving in a lovely gold gilt frame for hanging on the wall. The other photo was of the Ryan children in a horizontal oval frame on a stand for the mantel.

Cece was overjoyed, "Look at me. I'm in a picture. Look at it. Now there will always be a Cece."

"My goodness, Comfort, I nearly forgot." Gert went into her bedroom and came back with a bundle in a soft white doeskin pouch gathered at the top with a rawhide drawstring. "Uncle Jacob sent this back with Dan when he brought you home from Smytheville. I was to handle it with care and give it to you at Christmas.

That got the family's attention. Cece opened the draw and took a peek. "Oh my. Oh my."

Gert shook her head. *She sounds just like me.*

When Cece removed her gift, she hugged it close.

Sean looked at Gert and Jack. "I don't believe it."

Nana was puzzled. "What is it?"

Cece answered in a whisper. "It's my favorite piece of pottery from Nuga's wigwam. She looked at the small pot that Nuga threw as a young girl and decorated with Micmac symbols. "She is right here with me. Thank you. Thank you. Thank you."

XXXVIII

1869 Cabin Fever

With the new year, the Ryan family slipped into routines of the season. Most steamers went as far as Bucksport where the tidal river began to lose its salinity. All river traffic stopped three miles further at Winterport when the river becomes ice blocked and all traffic to Bangor has to go overland. This kept the family close to home catching up on projects.

Gert found the large window in the new bedroom had perfect lighting for her easel and Nana had no problem moving her reading chair to the other corner. She took great joy in seeing Gert's technique of pulling her paintings out of the blank canvas one layer at a time. She looked through the sketches in the notebook and chose which she liked the best. "Those are the ones I plan to work on this winter. You have a good eye, Nana."

Marisol spent most mornings with Peg as they became close friends when Rose was born. She helped Peg with the baby and housework while Peg tutored her on the ways with the stove. Jack would meet his brother every morning at the barn to take care of the animals and then warm up with tea at

Joey's house. He couldn't get enough of holding his niece and watching "his girl".

"Guess what?" Marisol straightened her apron and put her hands on her hips. "I milked the goat this morning."

That brought a laugh from Jack. "I don't believe it."

Peg smiled. "Yes she did. She also baked those molasses cookies you're enjoying. Come on sweet Rose. Mama's going to feed you then you are going to sleep. Right? Come on Papa. Keep us company."

Jack took Marisol's hand and pulled her to his lap.

"You have a nerve," Marisol smirked.

"I just wanted you to know that I'm doing my best to get down from my high horse and I think I need a taste of my reward."

"You had a taste of my molasses cookies, that's enough."

"You must have something else you can give me to make me keep trying."

Marisol reached up, pulled his head down to the kind of kiss he had been dreaming about. "Now, let me know when you are ready to grow up."

Sean and Tim spent a lot of daylight in his workshop where the small woodstove kept things warmer than any spot in the house. He was working on a secret project while helping Tim strengthen his hand. Knowing that Sean worked back to nearly normal after losing the use of his arm inspired Tim. Having Tim in the shop helped Sean fill a bit of the hole caused by Dan moving on.

Nana looked forward every afternoon to helping Cece with her numbers and letters. After, they would share a page of reading in one of the story books to help the committed student work out new words.

The days passed with each tick of the mantel clock, taking them closer to spring.

Early February the kitchen table was covered with bits and pieces of fabric, ribbon, lace, tiny buttons and whatever magazine ephemera they had squirreled away for this special day. Cece loved this activity and this year it would be even more fun with Nana and her Mary working with her. The flour and water paste was ready and Nana was going to let her use the stork embroidery scissors to cut the tiny decorations. Best of all, Marisol picked up some paper lace doilies when last in Searsport.

Cece found a small picture of a schooner and knew what she wanted to do. "Nana, this valentine is for you."

"That's funny. This one is for you." They both giggled.

"Mary, I bet your valentine is for Jack."

"Why in the world would you think that, Cece?"

"Because you're always sneaking peeks at him and he sneaks looks at you. I'd say you are sweet on each other. And isn't your sweetheart the person you would give a valentine to?"

Marisol's cheeks pinked up.

The back door opened. "Looks like I'm here just in time."

"Kate!" squealed Cece. "We're making valentines. You can make one for Tim. I think you are sweethearts too."

Marisol jumped up and gave her friend a bear hug. She whispered in her ear that there was no fooling that little one.

Kate gave Nana a kiss on the cheek and then hugged Gert who was already putting the kettle on the stove. "I was hoping to get here in January but the usual thaw never happened. Tomah thinks the next couple days will make up for it so I managed a sleigh ride down the River Road. I'll be heading back in two days."

Nana shifted in her seat and rewrapped her shawl. "The top of the cut corn stalks are peeking up through the snow so I'd say he was right, but I hope it doesn't last long enough to bring on an early mud season. How I hate mud. That's one thing I never had to deal with at sea."

Everyone was so caught up in their artistic creations they never saw Jack slip in with an armful of small wood for the cook stove. That was until he dropped the whole pile in the wood box startling all at the table.

Gert grabbed her chest and confronted her son. "John Ryan, you about caused my real heart to fall into the paper ones."

"Guess growing up is still on hold!" Marisol was not pleased for he made her cut a tiny bouquet in half. She had patiently cut the tiny flowers from the Godey Women's Magazine.

"Well, look who's here." Jack picked up Kate and twirled her around until dizzy. "I think Tim has a nice surprise for you. He's right behind me."

Coming through the door, Tim's tongue was wedged in the corner of his mouth as he concentrated on getting through the door with a bundle of small, split hardwood. When he caught a glimpse of Kate he nearly stumbled but managed to regain control.

"Show her Tim." Jack egged his friend on.

The bundle of wood was balanced in the crook of his left arm. He clasped his right hand around a piece, picked it up and placed it in the wood box. Astonished, both Marisol and Kate stood speechless with eyes wide open. Tim took another piece and did the same then dropped all the rest in the container with a clatter, ran over and gave Kate a twirl of his own.

Marisol nearly tipped over the pot of glue running around the table to her brother to join in a hug for three.

"Me too! Me too!" Cece crawled on her hands and knees under the table to get into the act. Tim picked her up to form a four-way hug while the room filled with joy.

Later in the afternoon, all the card-making decorations were stored. Nana stood at her side bedroom window. She could see Tim and Kate walking hand in hand on the road towards her old house lot. Looking over the snow-covered scar, Tim pointed to the fields, barn and back to the house lot. Nana could see Kate's astonished reaction to his news. She stared at the property and wrapped her arms around Tim's neck. Marisol and Jack strolled over and pointed to the woods across the street they called Blueberry Hill to add to the excitement. Then the couples stood holding hands without a word.

A fair-weather cloud floated out of the way of the sun so rays could warm Nana's face through the window pane. "I can feel your presence dear. Is this your way of telling me I did the right thing? I thought you'd be happy to know your work would be continued by another of your blood."

"Did you say something Nana?"

"No Gert. Having a conversation with one's self comes with age."

Valentine's Day was truly a breath of fresh air with a tease of temperatures to match spring where you could watch the snow pack receding. Cece wanted a party for exchanging cards so spent the morning making heart-shaped cookies with Gert's new tin cutter. Marisol got very good at rolling the butter and sugar dough.

Mid afternoon, the aroma of fresh-baked cookies, steeping tea and boiling coffee was all that was needed to gather the Ryan household around the kitchen table. Cece overlapped three paper doilies on a large tin charger and carefully arranged the delicate hearts. This was just as lovely as the platter of sweets she saw at the ladies luncheon. Then the handmade love notes were passed out. Cece had fashioned small paper hearts decorated personally to each. Kate's had images of school books, Tim and Nana's with a schooner, Marisol's with lupine, and so forth. Each with "I Love You'" meticulously printed on them. Nana made one for Cece edged by clouds. Her words were inked in fancy script, "Keep your dreams safely in your heart and never let them go."

Gert took Nana by the hand and settled her in the rocker by the fireplace. We have a special valentine for you.

Joey and Peg came through the back door making sure not to make too much noise while cleaning their boots of mud. "Happy Valentine's Day, Nana." It was the first time in this brutal winter they felt Rose could go out in the elements. They placed their flannel-wrapped bundle on Nana's lap.

Nana's introduction to Rose was joyous. She pulled aside the blanket to see a cherub face with startling bright blue eyes, tiny nose and rosebud lips. Nana felt her heart melt when the baby girl grabbed her finger.

Joey knelt beside the rocker, placing his hand on Nana's shoulder. "Is anything wrong? You've gone silent."

She looked at everyone forming a circle of love around the room. "I could never have imagined as a young girl reading on the sweltering docks of Boston, that I would see as much, do as much, become as much, but most of all, be part of a family such as this. I am truly, truly blessed."

Just then little Rose raised her tiny arms with a cry that sounded a lot like "Amen".

The next morning Tim saw Kate off and promised to meet her in Bangor when the ice went out. He was anxious to see the schooners back at the docks and was going to keep working on his hand so he could soon handle the ropes again. She smiled with encouragement but her heart was full of dread at the thought of him sailing off.

Within twenty-four hours, any signs of spring disappeared as a strong Yankee Clipper northeaster roared in from the coast and forced everyone back into human hibernation.

Gert finished three paintings. Two for Daphne and a large Bucksport waterfront landscape for the bank in Searsport. Sean and Joey were working on carved frames in the super secret man shack. They missed their Dan, their carving artist.

By the first of March the nights were still freezing but days started warming. That's all Joey needed to get his sugar shack stacked with wood and sap pan scrubbed. One morning he ran in while everyone was having breakfast. "Let's go gang! It's running."

Marisol looked from one to the other. "Who's running?"

Cece laughed. "No one is running Mary. The sap is running. Mama can I go?"

"Nice try little girl but you need to head out to school. Perhaps this weekend."

Jack smacked Marisol on the back. "How about it lady, how are you with a hammer and carrying buckets?"

Marisol bristled. "If you can do it, so can I."

It didn't take her long to realize she may have bitten off more then she could chew. The snow was still quite deep between the maple trees and it soon went up over her work boots. Pounding the tap into the tree was harder than she expected. It took a few tries before she could get the right angle to hang the pail. But she didn't give up until she picked off one of the buckets Joey had set the day before, and was so surprised by it's weight, she slid off balance and landed flat on her seat still protecting every bit of sap.

"Nice save." Jack lifted the pail off her lap. "Tim, take this to the sugar house and I'll bring your sister so she can warm up."

Joey was adding hardwood to the fire under the sap pan when Jack carried Marisol into the warmth of the shack.

Marisol stood with a grunt and grabbed her back. "Is that how you make the syrup?"

"Here, try this." Joey scooped a small ladle of raw sap.

"It's tastes like water with just a tiny bit of sweetness."

"What I am doing is boiling away the water to condense the sugar solution into syrup. The longer it boils, the darker it gets."

"How did Peg make the maple sugar squares?"

"She continues to boil down the syrup in a smaller pan and beats it until it thickens."

"I can't wait to taste it."

"Jack, go fill up a tin cup with snow." Joey checked the sap pan where the first batch of sap was taking on an amber glow. He took the cup from Jack, ladled a bit of hot syrup on the icy surface where it solidified into a gooey glob. "Try this Marisol."

"That's divine." With a shiver she once again twisted the wrong way and her back did not like it. "Let's go home."

March lived up to its reputation with winds that whipped through the valley piercing all in its path with bone-chilling cold. As they walked Marisol pulled her wrap tightly around her. "When will this wind cease? In London, spring flowers would be nearly in bloom."

"What we need to do is make some kites." Jack kicked a few rocks off the carriage road.

"Are you daft?"

"Trust me. Or is that asking too much?"

When Cece came home from school, they gathered the material and made simple diamond kites and before long, were running towards the barn getting them in the air. You could hear the squeals of merriment across the field which brought Nana to the window. "Gert, take a look. That's one thing the Captain and I didn't try. Now I feel I really missed something."

As if the kites were magic, spring suddenly swept into the valley bringing mud season in full force as the snow dissolved in plain sight. Joey worked as long and hard as possible to get trees tapped and syrup boiled before the night temps went above freezing and the sap stopped flowing. This year he invested in the new tin cans available with pure maple syrup printed on the side. Even Kate wrote she would come down and help the family with packing the final product.

That gave Tim the idea to meet her in Bangor now that the river was open above Winterport. The lumber schooners had started up river and he wanted to walk the docks with her. He was in hopes she would understand his yearning to go back to sea once she saw the ships and perhaps even meet some of his old mates. Plans were made for the next weekend including breakfast in the tea room on the river front before their walk.

Marisol now understood what Nana dreaded, a season she had never experienced before. Mud. Worst of all, making the mistake of trying to take a shortcut to Peg's kitchen one morning by walking through the pumpkin patch, she found herself mired in the goo and as she went on, her boots remained behind.

The barn doors were swung open wide to air out the odor of winter. Argos was hitched to the wagon to exercise the beast and get the grease turning the squeaks out of wagon wheels that dried out over the past months. If one used their imagination, even the mules and Bessie were smiling. There was nothing like the first breath of clean spring air to lift the spirit with the promise of newness.

The doors of the Ryan house were also swung wide with Gert vigorously sweeping the remnants of winter work out front and back. Windows were opened to air the staleness of many cooped up weeks. Sean was raking the straw insulation away from the foundation of the house. One could almost feel the earth itself taking a deep breath and slowly blowing it out again.

XXXIX

The Bitter with the Sweet

Dawn on Saturday showed promise that the day would be lovely. Tim was up and out to catch the earliest water craft he could find to take him to the waterfront in Bangor. When he stepped out onto the public wharf there stood Kate. She was dressed in a long blue dress that matched her beautiful blue eyes. Over her shoulders was a spring-weight white shawl with a long fringe. He couldn't believe how lucky he was to have met her. How his move to Searsport in America had put him in the company of Aunt Fiona who so loved this sweet young lady.

When Kate saw Tim step up to meet her, she felt giddy like she had never seen him before and the sight of him swept her off her feet. He took her to the Tea Room where they sat in a lovely room with large windows that overlooked the vista of the waterfront that was already bustling with schooners and steam ships of all sizes. Some were loading passengers for a trip to Boston or beyond, others were loaded with lumber harvested from the forests and arriving at the saw mills daily from the spring run. Kate could not keep her eyes off Tim who couldn't keep his eyes off the schooners. His mind was filled with excitement, hers with dread.

They topped off a lovely meal of poached eggs and scones with clotted cream by trying a new Irish breakfast tea.

"Are you ready to get into the sticky work of ladling syrup?" Tim picked up her tapestry-print travel bag.

"I've done it before. My father always taps a few trees to get us a store of sugar and several small crocks of syrup for our flapjacks. It sounds like Joey had a good harvest. I know he wants to sell it at market to pick up money to hold them until the field crops are harvested, but I didn't realize he had so many trees."

"We all told him to tap any trees of the right size in our lots. I'm sure he'll share. Ready? I think I see one of my mates from Searsport."

Shading his eyes against the morning sun rising higher over the eastern forests, Tim scanned the myriad of schooners docked side by side. "There he is on the Susan Duncan." Two sharp whistles caught the ear of his former deck mate, Skip, who waved him over to the vessel that was sitting low in the water.

Kate hesitated at the bottom of the gangplank.

"It's fine sweetheart. Come and visit my world."

Skip grabbed his buddy with a huge bear hug. "I heard dire stories about you. Captain Ross, come see who showed up."

"Well, I'll be. Timothy Hodge, we could use a hand like you. Are you ready?"

"I'm working on that, sir. I would say sooner rather than later."

"Make sure you touch base with me first. This is a regular route for us now."

Kate forced her smile while her heart was pounding in dismay.

"Now where are you and this pretty lady going?"

"We're looking for a ride to Prospect Ferry."

"Welcome aboard. It would be my pleasure. Just be prepared for a quick departure at the ferry landing as we slip by. Skip, prepare the Susan Duncan to leave. I want to get ahead of the bulk of our lumber caravan to snatch a good slot in Boston Harbor."

Skip gave Tim a playful slap on the back. "Wait for me by the rail so we can have a quick visit once we leave Bangor."

Kate was mesmerized by the activity on deck. She could see the excitement in Tim's face as they sailed by the rugged shore on both sides. The gentle wind was blowing through his shoulder length black hair and she imagined hugging him close and running her fingers through the curls.

Approaching Winterport, the sailing mates had a few minutes to visit. Skip was about to be a father for the first time and took this run to Boston and New York in hopes to be home when the baby arrived. Tim explained his injuries and how he was working on strength. Skip nodded towards Kate and wished his friend a happy future.

They sailed by Waldo Mountain and saw the landing coming up. The fort looked so grand from this vantage point.

Joey couldn't believe his eyes as the schooner slipped closer to the ferry landing. He was tapping a few final trees on his father's newest land near the river. When he saw what was happening he ran over to grab Kate as she leapt quickly to the dock. "Well, I'll be. You never know what you two will be up to." They all waved to the Captain and Skip as the schooner sailed on to carry Maine lumber to the world.

The next two days everyone hustled as the sap began to slow. It was Ryan family teamwork at its best.

The third day Joey declared the season over. Taps were removed from the trees while he processed the final sap in the boiler pan. The ladies covered Peg's kitchen table with a piece of linseed oiled sailcloth and filled the remaining tins while Peg boiled down a soup kettle of syrup to the sugar stage.

Tim pointed as the darkening skies. "I suggest you ladies head for home. There are some nasty storm clouds piling up with the winds turning from the northeast."

By the time Gert, Marisol and Kate ran in the back door, they were already being hit with large drops of rain. Cece was home showing Nana her letters and numbers for the day. By the time Sean, Jack and Tim came in from the woods, they looked like drowned rats.

Nana glanced out the kitchen window. "This is turning into a true tempest. With the winds there are white caps on the river."

Cece loved it when Kate came to visit for she got to sleep in the princess bed with Nana. And this particular night snuggled as close as she could not only to keep warm, but because she felt safer as the rain and hail pounded the windows, the wind howled down the chimneys, and trees screamed as limbs were torn away. By dawn the sun rose on such a sight. Part of the roof was torn from the chicken coop, hardly any snow remained and mud was now the rule. When Lady, Princess and Matey came in from their morning romp, Gert had to wipe each paw and belly before they could roam the house.

School was still open the next morning so Jack gave his sister a piggyback ride on his way to the barn. Gert could only imagine what she would look like after the walk. Sean went down to check out the fort and see if repairs or flood cleanup were needed. At Nana's request, Tim re-read two of her favorite letters from Captain Hodge and then talked about his offer to join a crew. The ladies, sat around the kitchen table where Gert was teaching them how to smock for Kate wanted to make Rose a dress.

They barely noticed Sean come silently back from the fort. "Kate."

All of them were startled.

"Kate, where's Tim?"

"I'll get him." She went into Nana's room wondering why he was so grim.

Sean poured himself a hot cup of tea.

The couple came into the kitchen. Tim took Kate's hand. "What's wrong Sean?"

"The Bangor lumber caravan had a hard time with the storm. Two ships were lost." He took a deep breath. "One wreck off Cape Cod was the Susan Duncan."

Kate looked wide-eyed and squeezed his hand so tight it hurt. Tim asked the question she didn't want to hear. "Captain and Skip?"

"There were no survivors."

Kate screamed and collapsed.

Tim carried her into the bedroom and sat holding her hand while Marisol hovered with a cup of water. "That could have been you." She was mad, pounding her fists against his chest. "That could have been you!"

Marisol got on the bed, cradled her friend and talked softly. "He is fine, Kate. He's fine."

Nana was sitting in the parlor rocker watching the flames dance in the fireplace. That was one way she could always carry herself from her worries but since flames destroyed her home, they were not as soothing as they once were.

Tim joined her, sitting on the floor next to the rocker. "What do I do Aunt Fiona? I love that girl with all my heart but feel I'll let Captain Hodge and my father down by giving up the goal of being the skipper of my own ship."

"Is that your father's dream or yours? My Captain would never press his desires on you. He would want you to follow your own heart. Where is your heart? On the sea or with Kate? You must remember that she lost her first love to the war. I'm not sure she could stand to lose another love tragically."

"I love you." He stood, cupped her face in his hands and kissed his aunt with a smack.

She ran her fingers through his hair and smiled. "Ah, yes Timothy Hodge."

Tim peeked into the girl's bedroom. Kate was asleep so he motioned to Marisol to come out and he took her into his room. "Do you still have mother's engagement ring?"

"Why Timmy, are you going to make my wish come true?"

"And what is that?"

"I've been fighting with you since before we were born and I always wanted a sister to take my side on occasion. Are you going to give me a sister? I'll let you have our mother's ring if you do that for me."

"It's not up to me. It's up to her."

"She loves you to pieces, Timmy. Don't mess this up." Marisol tiptoed back to her room and covered Kate with Cece's bird quilt. She opened the satin covered box on the shelf over her bed and took out a small silk pouch. She took another look at Kate and nearly jumped up and down in anticipation.

Jack rushed through the back door as she came out. "I just heard. How's Kate?"

"She's sleeping but I think she'll work through this just fine. Right Timmy?" She pressed the pouch in his hand. "Do this right, hear me?"

Jack looked totally confused when Marisol grabbed his hand and pulled him out the door. "It's been a long time since I've seen you so wound up. What did I miss?"

"Just be happy that I am so happy and so excited."

Jack stopped short and looked her in the eyes. "And just how excited are you?"

"Heart thumping excited."

"Hayloft excited?"

"Would there be any dry hay left in the loft after the winter?"

"I'm sure there will be a nice spot in a corner."

"I may be too hot to roll in dry hay."

Gert poked her head in Nana's room where she was looking out over the field. "Where are Jack and Marisol off to? They went out of here like they were going to put out a fire."

Smiling broadly, Nana looked at the couple practically skipping towards the barn. *I'd say that is just what they are going to do.*

XL

PROMISES MADE

Supper was quiet. Kate came out as everyone was settling down. She was embarrassed by her outburst earlier and found it hard to make eye contact with anyone, especially Tim.

He on the other hand could not keep his eyes off her. Her beautiful hair had been brushed to a sheen, cheeks had been pinched rosy, but the circles under her eyes still showed the remnants of crying in despair.

Neither Jack nor Marisol were up to their usual bickering. They just quietly ate their supper and Gert swore she could hear Jack humming.

Even Cece was not babbling about her problems with Zeke. As a matter of fact, not a bit about her day was mentioned.

Sean looked at Gert with a questioning stare. She just shrugged. Not even her special sugar cookies got much attention. She had sprinkled the tops with a bit of maple sugar when they first came out of the oven. All she got was an occasional quiet "yum".

Nana took her cup of tea and went into the parlor near the fire as she felt a chill.

Tim opened the back door. "What a wonderful evening. It's still quite warm and it looks like the sunset is going to be wonderful. Kate, let's take a walk."

"I don't think I'd be good company Timothy."

Jack gave his buddy a warning. "Watch out Tim, it's Timothy tonight."

Marisol tossed her napkin at him then turned to Kate. "It's been a hard day for both of you. I really think you should get out of the house and take a moment to talk things out."

"I'll get a walking lantern." Gert started for the pantry.

"There is supposed to be full moon tonight. Thanks anyway." Tim walked over and took Kate's hand. "Go and get your wrap. I'm sure it is cooler by the river."

As they left, Sean gave them a lantern anyway. "Take it just in case some of Cece's clouds come floating by. And stay on the road. Some of the mud out there is deep enough to act like quicksand."

"Don't worry. I promise to take good care of her."

"I'm going to hold you to that Timmy." Marisol smiled at her brother with a slight giggle as he closed the door.

"All right. Just what is going on here?" Gert really wanted an explanation of the strange meal.

Sean filled his cup again. "As for me, I ran into a problem with one of my workshop projects and was thinking out solutions."

She looked at Marisol. "My brother and Kate had quite a shock earlier. I can't help but wonder how they will work things out."

She looked at Jack. "Guess I'm just tired Ma. I worked especially hard in the barn today but it feels great to accomplish a personal project."

Marisol gave him a kick in the shin under the table.

She looked at Cece. "What's your excuse for being so quiet tonight?"

"I gave stupid Ezekiel a black eye."

"Comfort!"

"See. I knew I would get yelled at but he deserved it and I'll do it again if he tries to kiss me another time." She stomped into the parlor. "I'll be working on my numbers."

Gert just stared with her mouth wide open. Sean plunked his head into his arms on the table. Jack and Marisol were laughing so hard on the inside they had to fold their arms around their bellies.

Not a word was spoken on the walk down the hill to the ferry landing. Tim pointed at the bench on the edge of the water and they sat and listened to the natural sounds around them. The water lapped gently against the granite wall, a horned owl was warming up his hoot, and somewhere in the branches a creature was either trying to escape a predator or a predator was scrambling to catch his prey. As the sun hung lower on the horizon, the sky took on the hue of mauve with tinges of orange accenting some lazy puffs of clouds. Tim could feel Kate starting to relax next to him.

"It's marvelous." Kate whispered into the gentle breeze. "So beautiful."

Tim pointed to the center of the river where a fairly large fish broke water to catch an early spring water bug. The ever lower sun caught the splash turning the ripples to gold. "Are you feeling more relaxed honey?"

"I'm so sorry Tim. I tried not to react but I couldn't control it. Skip will never see his baby and the child will never know its father. I just couldn't control it. I would never survive if that happened to you. I can't commit my heart to where it could be broken again." The tear slipping down her cheeks also took on a glint from the sun.

"I understand sweetheart but please listen. I've decided to stay in Prospect Ferry to restore Captain Hodge's dream."

"You can't do that. That means you would have to give up on your own dreams of going to sea."

Tim wiped away the tears now ready to fall from Kate's chin. "Nana asked me a question I had never thought of. Was it my dream to go to sea or was it my father's? And my thinking that I should follow in Captain Hodge's footsteps never took in to consideration the fact that his dream was to leave the schooner and settle this piece of land."

Kate was speechless. She looked out over the water that was turning hues of gold to brass with touches of amethyst. Then another river inhabitant jumped with a loud splash creating a perfect ring. "Stunning."

"Are you admiring the rings spreading across the surface?"

"I guess I am."

"Do you think you could like this ring as much."

"What in the world do mean. What ring?"

"This one." Tim held up a delicate white gold band set with three small rubies. The sun falling beneath the horizon, caught the precious metal making it glow and the rubies sparkle. "Miss Kate Smythe, would you do me the honor of becoming my wife?"

"Oh, dear God!" Kate started to shake. "I don't know what to do. It's so sudden." It was like she was thinking out loud. "But I love you Timothy Hodge."

"I love you with my whole heart. I never thought I would meet someone who made me feel so complete."

"But Tim. I saw the look in your eyes while we on the schooner."

"I imagine I'm going to get that same look when we start framing the new house. It will start much smaller but just as grand to me. Perhaps the same look when my first crop of potatoes is dug. And I'm positive I'll have that same look when our first child is born."

Kate put her hand on his cheek and stared into his eyes. "O Tim, dear Tim."

He slipped to one knee and took her left hand. "Please make me the happiest man in the state of Maine."

"Yes Timothy Hodge. I will be your wife. Forever and ever."

He slipped his mother's ring on her finger and the whole world changed. As they sealed their love with a kiss, the sun fell below the horizon. The clouds in the sky filled with a celebratory brilliance.

Gert kept looking out the window while doing dishes. I wish they'd get back. It is getting darker by the minute and clouds are starting to cover the moon.

"They'll be fine." Marisol finished putting the dishes on the shelf over the side board. "Yes, indeed. Everything will be more than fine."

Bursting with curiosity, Gert was about to come right out and ask what was going on when the back door open and in floated Tim and Kate.

"Well?" Marisol ran to the couple.

Kate just smiled and flashed her ring.

Jumping up and down, Marisol let out a squeal that brought the Ryans from every direction.

The couple held hands. "Where's Aunt Fiona? We need to see her."

Cece stood like her mama with her hands on her hips. "She's in the parlor listening to me read. That is until Mary yelled."

The Ryans just hovered around the couple. "Come on. You should hear what we tell her." They walked through the family circle. Sitting on the floor, one on each side of the rocker, Tim took Nana's hand.

"Aunt Fiona, you figuratively hammered some sense into this Hodge hard head."

"I've done that more than once." Thinking of her captain, she smiled.

"I have decided to stay in Prospect Ferry, build a home and do my best to maintain the Hodge Farm."

Nana smiled broadly and looked at Gert.

"I know I could never face this responsibility alone so have asked Miss Kate Smythe to share the journey with me as my wife."

Kate held up her hand, displayed the lovely ring with a wiggle of her fingers. "I said yes."

Now the loudest squeal in the room came from Cece, followed closely by her mother and her Mary.

Nana clapped her hands in glee while the ladies hugged Kate and the men shared handshakes and slaps on the back. Sean stamped his feet on the floor in a quasi Irish jig. "If this were a drinking house, I'd pull out the jug." Then he feigned being hit by a bolt of lightning through the look from Gert. "But I'd settle for a bunch of those fabulous maple cookies in the pantry."

Marisol ran to the kitchen to set things up and Jack followed to help. They held their own mini celebration in the pantry.

After an hour of excited talk over talk, that must have sounded like a close encounter with the Tower of Babel, Nana stood to go to bed. She stumbled just a bit but Gert steadied her. "Are you not feeling well Nana? You seem a bit feverish."

"I think it is just my long stay near the fire. I'll be fine in the morning.

But she wasn't. The fever had not gone but increased alarmingly.

Gert helped her change into a fresh nightgown as the other was drenched in sweat. She kept a cool flannel on her head and encouraged drinking water and broth from the invalid feeder.

Kate did not want to leave for Indian Island but Nana insisted.

"The children at the school need you more than an old lady who is already well hovered over." Nana punctuated the sentence with a hacking fit of coughing.

Gert helped her repack the travel bag and promised to keep her informed of Nana's health. "Now you go and spread your good news."

On the way to catch the ferry to Bucksport, Tim walked her over to see Peg and hold Rose. Gert swore she could hear the cry of joy all the way across the field.

Nana did not bounce back as quickly as hoped. Gert could hardly remember her friend bedridden due to her health. Next morning she sent Sean to Bucksport to fetch the new doctor but he was in Winterport treating several with influenza. Gert's fear was dreaded pneumonia so Sean took the wagon to Stockton even though they did not really care for that physician.

She was never left alone. Gert and Marisol took turns sitting in her bedroom night and day. Peg wanted to help but everyone wanted her to stay away to protect Rose. Cece could only go as far as the doorway, not necessarily to shield her, but to keep any other illness from Nana as the school was reporting many maladies. She demanded Lacey stay in the princess bed in her place.

When the senior doctor knocked on the door, Tim let him in. The shock on the face of the surgeon was palpable.

"Yes. I still have my arm with a functioning hand. May I take your coat?"

After examination, the doctor did not hear definitive sounds of pneumonia but declared they must drive out the fever and keep her from getting more congested by alternating hot and cold flannel pads on her chest. Since there was not much relief from the cough, he left a codeine solution to settle it.

Gert let him out. "You know Mrs. Ryan that Mrs. Hodge is of an advanced age. This could be very serious for her. You should be prepared." He looked at Tim. "If I were you I'd tend to her the way you tended to him." With another look of disbelief, he was gone.

Gert's eyes open wide. "Of course." She climbed up to the top shelf of the pantry and pulled down a carved wooden box and slid open the top. She put a small open pot of hot water on the warming stove, shook the spruce gum box that Uncle Jacob had given her and out dropped a piece of flag root. She shaved off a bit and dropped it in the water to steep.

With the first spoonful of cough solution Nana got some relief but it was hard to keep her awake so they needed to work on fluids whenever she came out of the stupor.

Tim came in from the wood pile. "Don't tell me. I thought I had inhaled the last of that vapor in the wigwam."

"Let's hope it won't be for long. I can't seem to be able to rouse her right now. Marisol is sitting with her but would you read some of the letters to her? You know which ones mean the most."

Jack came in from the barn grumbling at the scent. "I think I did better with the animals."

"Go take care of your own aroma." Marisol held her nose as she walked by him.

Tim worked with Cece after school. He told her stories about how numbers were very important when you are on the sea. Now he was going to learn the how to use them as a farmer to plan for seeds and crops. "I can help you with those numbers Tim."

Marisol shook her head. "It seems as though she's got your number."

That night Gert decided to sleep with Nana as she was restless and sometimes mumbled nonsense. Gert closed all the other bedroom doors so most of the moist flag root was sent into the new room. She changed the hot and cold flannels twice and left on the hot. Nana was shivering so Gert got under the covers with her and held her tight. She softly sang her favorite lullaby: "*Toora, loora, loora. Toora, loora, li. Toora, loora, loora. Hush, now, don't you cry. Ah, Toora, loora, loora. Toora, loora, li. Toora, loora, loora. It's an Irish lullaby.*" Gert found herself falling off.

Just as the first glimmer of sunrise broke through the window, Gert woke with a start. The room was silent. She jumped out of bed and lit a candle. "Nana!"

"What is it dear?" She was sitting up just a bit hugging Lacey.

Gert could not help bursting into tears.

"I bet you thought I had gone to be with dear Captain Hodge." Her voice was weak but it was there. I decided to stay right here." She laughed just a little but that brought on a cough.

"You gave me such a scare." Gert leaned over and kissed her friend's cool forehead.

"You do know Gertrude Ryan that I am not going to live forever. I will be leaving sooner or later."

"I prefer later."

The next few days were delightfully warm. The grasses were showing some green and the buds on the trees were trying hard to burst open. Each day Nana sat on the porch in the late morning sun.

Gert brought her a fresh cup of tea. "You seem deep in thought."

"I've made a decision Gert. It's time to let go of my grief and get myself up off my widening back side. There is a lot for me to do and I'm not going to sit here and waste what time I have left. I want to get my legs strong enough to walk to see Rose in her home without getting weary."

"Sounds like a plan to me. Just promise not to be too stubborn and let us help. Anything I can get you?"

"After this hard winter, I yearn for a plate of fresh greens."

Jack came around the corner. "You mean like these little critters I picked along the river in Dan's woods. There will be more ready next trip."

Nana clapped her hands. "Fresh fiddleheads, Jack you have become my favorite Ryan man for this day."

Greens cleaned and Nana down for a nap, Gert ambled down among the apple trees to see how much pruning would be needed.

"I thought I saw you down here." Cece came skipping through the tall grass.

"You've still got your school clothes on. Better skedaddle back to the house and change."

"I'll be careful not to tear my stockings" Cece spun around in the wonderfully fresh air. "Look Mama. The eagles are cleaning up their nest. I bet they are going to lay eggs. Where are last year's babies. Won't they come back?"

"They are off finding their own territory where they will meet a mate and build a nest for their own families."

"Is that like my brothers? Dan left to make his new home on the Aroostook. Joey has a new home across the fields. I bet Jack's going to leave too? Is that like the eagles leaving the nest?"

"I guess it is. Everyone leaves one day to start his or her own life."

"Well, I'm making a promise, I'm not leaving your nest. I am going to stay here forever."

If only that could be.

XLI

THE CIRCLE REALIZED

April showers proved victorious over the bleakness of winter by helping produce an amazing display of May wild flowers. No matter which window, Marisol found delight in the view. The sweetness in the air and warmth of the longer days beckoned renewed life not only in the earth and the animals, but also in the caregivers. Marisol had never before understood the joy of seeing new shoots of living green pushing up through the earth. Now she even understood the delight of eating baby fiddle head ferns.

Jack crept in the back door to grab a cup of tea and leftover biscuit while everyone was busy.

"I know you're out there." Marisol called as she came out of the bedroom with a load of clothes to soak out on the porch. "How'd you work up an appetite so fast?"

"We had to fix a good length of fence that lost the battle with snow banks. Now all of our four-legged family is happily stretching their legs." He took an appreciated swig of the hot strong black tea. "Joey and Tim went to snitch one of Peg's sour dough rolls with molasses. How'd you know I was here?"

"Well, you happen to have brought a bit of all the grazers with you."

"You couldn't even get by me with my old nose." Nana laughed from her reading chair in the bedroom.

"Miss Hodge, let's take some time for a walk. There are spring plants that may not be as bright but are still something to see."

"Going to hike up Blueberry Hill?"

"Nana. I can never put anything over on you."

"And don't you forget that. Be careful, there may be icy spots still left in the gullies shaded by the pines."

Marisol dropped the clothes in the washtub of hot water and soap shavings, then started agitating with the washing stick.

Jack, not known for his patience, started pacing. "Aren't you washing too late to hang?"

"Gert wants them to soak overnight. Most are work clothes from the barn so I can understand why."

They had not been up on the hill since Nana deeded it to Jack. "Wow. Walking through the trees seems a lot different knowing they are your trees."

Marisol had never seen Jack so emotional. He was near tears. But even she saw the beauty of this rugged piece of land leading to the blueberry fields. "Jack what are these darling little white flowers in the clearing."

"Mayflowers."

"Seems a proper name."

"And what would you call this little fellow?" Marisol wondered "It may sound silly, but it looks like a pipe with its stem stuck in the ground. But it is somehow unworldly."

"Very good little white girl. Those are Indian pipes. They can be used to make a sedative and Uncle Jacob says it has many healing properties. You'll find many medicinal plants this time of year."

"Oh, look. What is this? It has a long leaf folded over like a roof protecting the green rod inside."

"Nice find. It's a jack-in-the-pulpit."

That tickled Marisol. "Funny, but I can see why."

"We always stayed away from them because Uncle Jacob told stories of the berries formed under the hood being poisonous."

"Look. There's your bedroom."

"Too bad there's ice in the bed." Jack leaned into a kiss. "I bet there's no ice in the hayloft."

Marisol whispered in his ear. "You are a naughty, naughty boy." She grabbed his hand and led the way.

By the time they got to the barn they were practically dancing. "It's nice of the animal residents to leave us all this space to play."

Marisol giggled. "I rather like the coziness of the loft." They scrambled up the ladder only to nearly bump into Gert.

"Hi, Ma. What are you doing up here?"

"Well, I'm standing at a canvas on an easel with many colors on a palette and a brush in my hand. I must be baking a cake. Just what are you two doing here?"

"Jack told me how beautiful the field flowers look from up here. I wanted to see."

Gert looked at the two until they both turned a slight pink. "The light is perfect to catch the patches of purple wild pansies between the dandelions. Those two colors make each other more intense. The sparkle of the river in the distance runs like a ribbon tying everything together."

"You have a wonderful eye Gert. We call the tiny wild pansies johnny-jump-ups."

"I like that." She added more dabs of purple between the gold, which made the flowers appear to jump off the canvas.

Marisol tugged at Jack's shirtsleeve. "Come on Johnny. Let's jump down and finish our chores."

Tim was sitting at the kitchen table reading a note from Kate. He looked a bit perplexed. "Mar, she wants to be married on the Aroostook River at the Thorpe farm. Isn't that near the Indian village where Jacob and the rest of the Ryans live?"

"And what's the problem with that? Do you still have trouble being around natives, especially after all they have done for you?"

"Is it terrible of me?"

"You better set your thinking straight or you and Kate will never have a happy life. Her heart is tied to the Micmacs and Penobscots. Making her choose would be cruel and the last thing I want for Kate is another broken heart."

"What should I do? I don't want to lose Kate but I still have this nagging dread I may not be able to handle my ingrained feelings."

"Idiot! Sean and his sons and even little Rose have Indian blood. Are you going to be no more than one of the bigots this family has had to endure for generations?"

Tim looked at his sister with anguish.

"Pack your bag and go to Kate. Stay on Indian Island and work with the children, and help Tomah with the winter cleanup. Don't come back until your mind is settled one way or the other."

"I have the sawyer coming."

"You've marked the trees for him to take. By the time you come back he'll have them down and your share in dry lumber will be here to start framing."

Matey jumped up in his master's lap and soothed his soul with a gentle purr. "You're right as usual Mar, I'll leave in the morning."

When Tim arrived, he saw a different side of Indian Island he never appreciated being cooped up in the wigwam while recuperating. He had never enjoyed a wonderful dinner prepared by Adele in her cozy kitchen. He found Tomah a wise man devoting his life to the good of the village. Most of all, he assisted Kate in the school and finally understood her need to be part of the transitional lesson planning for the eager students. He thought, *you fool; you damn fool,* and wished sometimes that he could manage giving himself a good kick in the ass. He would let Marisol have that privilege.

Tim stayed with Joe and Annie. Where Holly and Frankie were always on his nerves before, they were playmates at the end of the day. Every night he read their bedtime stories and started thinking about his own family. In the evening Kate would come up and they would spread paper on the kitchen table to sketch ideas for their home. Joe was a great help for he had been through the decisions, some good, some not so good.

"I want a mud room like Annie." Kate pointed to the back corner of the floor plan where the steps went down to the root cellar. "I want a door right there off the back porch for boots and outside clothes and then a door to the right that goes into a pantry."

Annie nodded in approval. "Wish I had thought of the extra door so I would not have to climb over shoes and boots to get to some shelves."

"And I want a real back door so I can go in and out from the kitchen and leave it open in good weather for fresh breezes."

Annie laughed. "My sister-in-law Gert is going to be so jealous if you have two extra doors. I love it."

"We will keep things simple to start. This will be our shelter while we make plans to rebuild on the foundation of

Nana's home." Tim wrapped his arm around Kate. "Then we have rooms to fill with little Kates and Tims."

The usually quiet Annie giggled. "Be careful Kate. There's something about the water in that part of the river. Look how quickly Gert filled up her bedrooms."

A red-faced Kate took a letter from her skirt pocket. "There is going to be a slight change in my plans on the Aroostook River. I wanted to stand where my parents stood when they married but JJ says the clearing in front of the Dan Thorpe farm has grown in during the past several years. It was my grandfather that kept the clearing but when his health began to wane, it turned wild again."

"I'm sorry sweetheart. I know you had your heart set on it."

"I was disappointed at first but Uncle Jacob has a solution. We will have the ceremony on the front grounds of Smytheville where Gert and Sean were married. I will still be surrounded by my family and friends."

Joe grinned as Annie gave him a nod. "We're going to be there. It's about time Holly and Frankie spent some time with their Gramma Hanna and Grampa Frank."

That sealed the deal for Tim. He looked around at the joy and any remnants of learned bias slipped away.

Gert missed having Dan home May fifth for his birthday, but Cece turning six years old the next day made up for it. The little lady had a grand party surrounded by her family and friends. Even Zeke was invited.

The fields were prepared for planting. Tim had his first experience with the mules and plow in Joey's fields. The famed manure was carted off to be spread where needed. Gert was preparing the Hodge pumpkin patch to generate some income in the fall, and worked each day on her own kitchen garden and root vegetables. Everyone worked on early seeding and prepared for the major plantings after Decoration Day. To Jack's delight, Marisol was now quite adept at cutting seed potatoes.

One pleasant spring evening, Sean, Gert and family walked their new acres to find a young tree to plant in the front yard in memory of Mike. It seems it should have been easy but everyone had a different idea. Would it be oak, pine or maple? Cece insisted it be a balsam so each Christmas it could be decorated with food for the birds. Balsam it would be.

Decoration Day, Nana did not fuss at all when helped to the small cemetery to lay newly blossomed lilacs on Captain Hodge's grave. This area now belonged to Joey and he pledged his family would always take care of it. Kate was there to place wild flowers on Mike's marker with Tim's support. On the way back the ladies stopped by to visit Rose who at five and a half months was a delight. Mysteriously, the men went ahead.

Next came the planting of the tree on the front lawn inspired by the Abraham Lincoln memorial white cedar in Searsport. Mike's tree was a beautifully shaped balsam gradually narrowing to a peak.

Marisol whispered to Jack reminding him it was just a year since they met. He in turn, felt queasy at the memory. "How could I ever forget?"

Gert held Kate's hand as they shared their sorrow. "It's perfect. I don't know what to say."

"I do. I wrote a poem." Cece walked to the tree as if speaking just to it. She took off the ribbon around her neck that held one of Mike's uniform buttons.

"For my brother Mike.
I wish I could have met you but I know you in my heart.

You knew when I was born and loved me from the start.
I played with your brass buttons you sent home to me
Now I tie one on a branch in your spirit tree."

Then the little girl skipped over to her stunned family. No one spoke.

"Can we show Mama her surprise now?" Cece asked, breaking the silence..

Sean picked up his Comfort and walked over to the Gert's rose garden. The secret was in the center covered with a blanket.

"Can I Papa. Can I?"

Cece tiptoed through the budding bushes. She took hold of the blanket and grinned ear to ear. "Papa made this for you."

She carefully picked off the blanket to reveal a granite bird bath chiseled with flowers around the edge. The center of the bowl was meticulously chipped to form a chick-a-dee in relief. The bowl sat on a granite pedestal with a wide bottom with carved vine roses creeping upward.

Left speechless, Gert could do nothing but cry.

"Did I do something wrong Papa?"

"No Honey, I think that is your mother's way of saying thank you to both of us."

Two weeks later, Cece finished her first year of school. Gert looked up from the carrot seedlings and saw her sitting quietly on the swing. "I didn't hear you walk by. You look unhappy. Are you sad school is done until fall?"

"I don't want to go back to school. I don't like Mr. Wilson."

"He thinks you are a special student. He helped you with your poem."

"He's stupid and boring. I learn more from Nana and reading books. And Tim teaches me about numbers. More than Mr. Wilson knows. Why can't I just study at home?" She leaned back and pushed herself forward and back in the swing then slowly came to rest. "There are two eagle babies this year."

Gert looked to the top of the tall pine. "How do you know that? All I can see is one of the parents perched on the side of the nest."

"The mother and father are taking turns bringing food but not as much as when there were three, so two babies have hatched."

Gert just shook her head. "Let's get back to school. What is the real reason you don't want to go back?"

"Ezekiel."

"What has he done now?"

"Papa said when the work stops at the fort Zeke's father would be leaving to find a job near Boston. Now his father is going to work for the saw mill and they are going to stay in town."

"That's wonderful his father found another job so quickly."

"But that means Zeke will stay and the teacher says we have to share a desk when school opens again. It would help Mr. Wilson teach us if we were together.. I don't want to sit with him. It's bad enough to be in the same room."

"Come on. Change your clothes and help me weed carrots. That job makes you pay attention so the carrots won't be pulled. You'll soon forget about Zeke and Mr. Wilson."

Sean was distressed at supper. This had been the last day of building at the fort. "Twenty-five years of my life and they would not even let us finish the officer's quarters. Had to just store away our tools and leave." He ranted on. "Took this long for federal autocrats to figure out the British were no longer a threat to Bangor and the furnaces we built to send hot cannon balls would do no harm anyhow, now that their warships are iron clad." He took a deep breath and rattled on. "Such a magnificent granite fort will probably go to seed."

Jack felt his father's anguish. "Won't they use it for troops Pa?"

"Maybe some training or occasional bivouacs but military presence will be minimal." He banged his fist on the table. Marisol grabbed her coffee so it wouldn't land in her lap.

Cece steadied her tin of milk. "Mama, maybe you should have Papa weed the carrots."

The next very busy, six weeks flew by in a blur. Joey's fields, Gert's gardens and the expanding apple orchard were done and thriving. Tim hired a crew of men that lost their jobs at the fort and put them to work framing his starter home with a floor and roof. He kept a close watch to check the studs and joints with his mathematical mind. Sean managed the building of the fireplace from the fieldstone pile. The building team boarded and the little house took shape. Gert was jealous of the mud room door as predicted. Tim had a cooking stove delivered and few pieces of furniture. His sister told him the rest of the house would be ready by the time he and his bride got there. She was anxious to paint walls, make curtains and arrange the small kitchen. Gert had painted a landscape of Kate's childhood home on the bend in the river with her climbing boulder surrounded by flowers. They would have that in their living area as a surprise. They were also surprising the newlyweds by hanging Nana's door on the front, the one with the cobalt blue border around the window.

Kate left for Aroostook County the first of August to spend time with her parents and brother before the wedding mid August. Tim would not see her again until the ceremony. Joey, Peg and little Rose were staying with Nana while he kept an eye on the crops and animals.

The morning the wedding party was leaving for Smytheville, looked like a circus act. The men juggled with all the baskets and luggage. They would use Argos and the big wagon to get everything to the ferry.

Tim had a travelling trunk for he was taking Kate on a honeymoon to Boston to see all the places he and Nana talked about on the waterfront and in the city. He wanted a trip along the Aroostook River to the St John in New Brunswick where they would cruise the coast to Boston. She was still too shaken by the loss of the Susan Duncan so they would take a coach to Houlton then south to Portland to take the train to Boston.

Saying their goodbyes, Nana hugged Gert with a message of well wishes for Jacob.

Gert whispered some advice to Peg. "Be careful of that feather bed." To which they both giggled.

Cece hugged Princess and told her to be good and stay near her mama. Then she waved to the pair of eagles watching two babies bouncing up and down for attention.. She looked at the blue sky and the fluffy clouds that changed with her imagination. They would join Uncle Joe and his family in Milford. "It's going to be a great day to start a wedding adventure."

The welcome in Smytheville was festive when Frank's wagon pulled in from Presque Isle. It had been a long time since Sean and Joe saw their mother. Tears of joy ran uncontrollably. And Gert finally got her arms back around Dan.

Cece grabbed her cousins Holly and Frankie by the hand. "Come on. I'll show you the beaver pond where my Papa almost drownded."

A resounding "no" came from all directions.

Tim stood on the grounds and watched the gentle flow of the river as it ran along the banks of the wilderness. He could see how Kate loved the peacefulness of the scene in contrast to the hustle and bustle of the Penobscot River. Tomorrow he would pledge his love to start their life together. He smiled and said, "Cece would call it another change."

Marisol, Gert, Cece, and Holly with her brother, were settled at Hanna's house while the men bedded down in Nuga's wigwam. Tim was intrigued by the obvious history surrounding them and asked about the eagle feather hanging next to Nuga's ceremonial hat. Jacob smiled and told of Cece's tribute to Nuga with respect to the eagle. Tim listened intently half the night to stories from Jacob and Frank of Kate's grandfather Jed Smythe and how big a part he took in saving the family from being sent to a reservation in New Brunswick. Thus the town was named in his honor.

Very little sleep was had as the owls hooted and night creatures hunted their prey.

As dawn peeked through the tips of the grand old growth pines, someone burst into the wigwam and jumped on Sean. "Get up you lazy bum. Someone would think you were an old grandfather. Wait a minute, you are!"

"Ben Smythe, get the hell off of me! I'll take care of you." Next thing the two were wrestling and Joe told them if they broke any of Nuga's items, Jacob would ban them from the village. So they tumbled through the flap together.

"That has to be Joe, the sensible brother." Ben grabbed Joe by the ankle and all three were laughing as they rolled on the ground.

Frank and Jacob stood with arms folded in front of them while Tim was puzzled by the ruckus.

"Ben and the Ryan boys were very close at a young age. That was when Sean would ride around on my boot," explained Jacob.

"I heard about that."

Frank just shook his head as he did forty years ago. "The only one missing is my oldest son Peter. He couldn't get away from the potato farm or he would be in the middle of that pile."

Jacob gave them a whistle and the tangle of arms and legs came to attention. Dan laughed. "You have not lost your authority Uncle."

"Take everyone to our cabin. I'll be there in a minute to fix flapjacks. It's going to be a long day."

They could see JJ coming across the path from the Frank Ryan home. It suddenly dawned on Tim if her brother and father were here, she must be. "Is Kate with Gert and the girls?"

JJ laughed. "Yes she is but if you try to get anywhere near the house, Cece and Holly will make sure you don't get in. Go and get breakfast. You'll need it."

Suddenly Ben stopped and nearly caused Tim to tumble. "I'm sorry, in the happiness of seeing Sean and Joe, I did not take time to meet you. I understand you are going to be my son-in-law."

"Yes, sir. I am very glad to meet you."

"Well you are a quite handsome young man with manners. And in talks, it is evident that our Kate thinks the world of you. I've heard you have overcome major complications, so you are a fighter."

"Sir, it was Kate that carried me through much of that trauma. She and my sister Marisol held the load of my recovery and I was not an easy patient. I want to use my second chance for life to make Kate happy and provide a good home."

"As my father-in-law once whispered to me, 'you'll do young man'. I know I have not seen my Kate this happy in years."

"Since Mike died at Gettysburg?"

"I'm happy to hear you understand. Welcome to our family Timothy Hodge. Now it's time for Uncle Jacob's flapjacks."

At the Ryan home the ladies were also having a joyous reunion. Nettie Thorpe and Gertie were close as children working in the fields and as schoolmates. Once married, they became even closer as their children were born. This was such a special night for them. While preparing the bride they regaled her with many stories. For Cece it was a reunion with Princess's sister. They looked just alike and Gramma Hanna had named her Honey.

There was a tap on the door when Cece peeked in Jacob's cabin. "Mama wants to know if you all have your clothes for the wedding or do we have to find things for you."

Sean came over and gave his daughter a peck on the cheek. "You tell your Mama, we have things in hand."

Cece turned. "Can I see Little Lady?"

Dan clucked his tongue and the cat came out from under the bunks.

"She's grown so big like Princess. The cat sensed the familiarity of Cece and let the girl stroke her soft, long shiny hair."

Sean gave her a stern look. "Now skedaddle!"

She turned back. "You all be on top of the slope at high noon." Then she ran before her Papa could yell again.

As the sun inched closer to being overhead, village residents began to gather on blankets on the grounds. Flowers were placed on both sides of the path for the bride and around the circle where the couple would take their vows from the pastor of the small new church in Presque Isle with a blessing by Jacob. There were two long benches for the family. The men were in place on time with Tim looking nervous in his outfit of black trousers, white shirt with white waistcoat and black tailcoat topped off by a dark gray cravat. Jack wore a traditionally decorated Micmac tunic over slacks. Along the path came the two best friends. Nettie in pale yellow tiny check gingham with square neck edged with hand crocheted white lace. She had a yellow bonnet to match. Gert's dress was made from the light copper colored material Marisol had given her for Christmas. Her neckline was smocked and waist pulled tight by a rust sash. Her golden red hair was pulled high and held in place in the back by a large bow of the same material as the dress. Sean could not help but think of when she was the bride coming up that path to him. "She is just as beautiful now as then."

Joe leaned in from the second bench. "Did you say something?"

"Just thinking out loud."

Gert sat down beside him with Nettie next to her. Then Dan approached looking quite handsome in a fine tunic and beaded sash. Holding his hand was a tiny Micmac maiden with startling black/brown eyes and a sweet young face. "Ma and Pa, I'd like you to meet Abby." She nodded her head and barely whispered. "Very nice to meet you." Tongue tied, his parents smiled and nodded back. Gert grabbed Sean's hand as the couple took a seat behind them.

Frank picked up his fiddle and began to play. Up the path came Cece and Holly holding small wildflower bouquets. The cousins were dressed in identical soft doeskin tunics with beautiful embroidery around the neckline. Holly's black hair was in braids hanging with feathers to the front of her shoulders, her brown eyes fairly smiling. Cece's strawberry blonde hair was also in braids with feathers. Her blue/green eyes shimmered with excitement. They both had headbands with patterns of colorful glass beads. They took their place in the circle.

Next came Frankie carrying a small porcupine weave basket holding a wedding ring for Kate. Then JJ appeared wearing a gentleman's suit of white with a dark blue cravat but most eyes were on Marisol. Her black wavy hair falling over her shoulders glimmered in the sun. She was wearing one of the silk flowered dresses rescued from her closet at Daphne's. It clung to her body in all the right places. Jack just about fell off the bench.

Now Frank's tune changed to a lovely ballad. Coming up the path was a very proud Ben dressed like JJ in a white gentlemen's suit but with a black cravat. On his arm was his Kate wearing the lace wedding dress her Grandmother wore when marrying Dan Thorpe in Ireland. Then her mother wore the same dress when she married Ben.

When Ben turned his daughter over to Tim, he sat next to Nettie. Sean reached over and pointed to the birch tree. There were more chickadees than he had ever seen on the limbs. The bird was Jed Smythe's favorite. Ben looked at Sean with a nod. Perhaps his father's spirit was among them.

The love between the young couple was obvious. There was not a dry eye among the women on the benches when they took their vows. Cece was mesmerized when Uncle Jacob finished the ceremony in his headdress and long, chief's red-wool coat. His stole was of the finest embroidery she had ever seen. He reached his hands to the sky and spoke in the ancient tongue. Then he held the couple's hands together and smiled to announce them married.

Everyone stood and cheered as the couple kissed. Kate blushed as she acknowledged her guests.

The bonfire was lit. Food was carried to load the tables and the party began.

Jack took Marisol by the hand and walked her into a small grove of birches next to the water. "What say we make an honest woman out of you."

"Why John Ryan, that had to be the most romantic proposal any woman could have."

"Did it work?"

"Indeed it did, with one condition."

"He looked at her with trepidation."

"I want to design the bedroom on blueberry hill near those two birches."

He picked her up and swung her around while shouting yes, yes, yes!

While everyone was talking, Cece walked up beside Uncle Jacob and pulled on his hand. He picked her up. "What do you need Cece?"

She whispered in his ear. "Thank you for sharing the pottery from the wigwam. I'll keep it forever."

"My grandmother would have wanted you to have it. She would have known the special girl you are."

The little, golden-red-haired, Indian maiden wrapped her arms around the neck of the aging Micmac sagamore and snuggled closer.

"Where are your clouds Cece? There are none to be seen."

She kissed her Uncle Jacob on the cheek. "Don't be silly. If there were clouds, how could Nuga watch us?"

Looking to the brilliant blue sky they were enveloped in an unexpected breeze.